Summoning of the Siren

Vinamre
Elrin
Skohyn
Astilar
Homera
Claroin
Denimoore
Noorde Point
Bellham
Celinde
Carion
Wahstane
Bascala
Shores
Siren's Cove
Grimslar
New Moreel

Skohyn
Lychnals
Scattered Islands
Shores of Helreene
W
E
S

K. GODIN

SUMMONING OF THE SIREN

K. GODIN

Print edition ISBN: 9781777880538
E-book edition ISBN: 9781777880552
Hardback edition ISBN: 9781777880545

First edition: August 2023
10 9 8 7 6 5 4 3 2 1

WWW.AUTHORKGODIN.COM

This is a work of fiction. Names, characters, places, and incidents either are the product of the author's imagination or are used fictitiously, and any resemblance to actual persons, living or dead, business establishments, events or locales is entirely coincidental.

Cover Design and Interior Layouts by Miss Nat Mack
Map by Amy Elizabeth Sayers
Editor Beth Attwood

For those who always find the strength to
shoulder the burdens of others,
Know that your value goes beyond what
you can do for the people around you.

THE EVENTS OF *Legend of the Huntress*

The Crimson and their Goddess, the Seductress, had ruled Elrin for centuries. Their reign was full of desolation and death as their hunt for the halflings wreaked havoc over the lands, and there was no end in sight. However, after a fever hit the small village of Noorde Point, Skylahr Reed was thrust out into the world and had no choice but to step into her fated role as the Huntress's Chosen.

During her journey, Skylahr comes across the legendary Lupines, the God of Protection's people, and his Chosen, Kalian. She is unable to keep herself or her heart from him, and so the two follow the footsteps of their Gods, and the Huntress and Protector are together once more.

That is until Skylahr learns of the deal the Alpha of the Lupines made with the Crimson Goddess long ago, the bargain being her life in exchange for his people's safety. Knowing she cannot trust him with her heart any longer, Skylahr continues her crusade on her own, her anger only driving her need to end the Seductress's rule.

Travelling across Elrin, Skylahr meets Ella, a fellow halfling turned immortal, and is introduced to Gaelon, the Healer's Chosen. Together the three gather an army, ready to take down the Crimson once and for all, and Skylahr is reunited with her childhood friend who she thought had succumbed to the fire that had taken her parents after the Crimson had begun their hunt for her.

Knowing this will be the battle of their lives, Skylahr prepares to face the Seductress's Chosen and his army only to be reconnected with the man she had left behind. She knows she will need all the help she can find, so Skylahr has no choice but to accept his aid. Though even with the Lupines' assistance the losses of the war are still great and will continue to plague the Huntress for the rest of her days.

But that isn't the only thing that will haunt her—her broken heart and the memories she shares with Kalian will be impossible to forget.

Chapter 1

Blood.

The warmth of it soaked through my shift as the weapon was pulled from my shoulder. My hands searched frantically for my assailant while my eyes adjusted to the darkness. My chambers were nearly black, the fire obviously long forgotten, but the shining silver of the blade gleamed in the soft glow of moonlight that filtered past the curtains, and I watched as the tip was aimed at my face. Rolling from my back just in time, I narrowly missed the lethal point, though it tangled in my bronze waves as it sank into the feather mattress. I slid from my bed and tugged at my hair forcefully until I was free.

Snarling what sounded to be a curse in the tongue of old, my attacker dislodged the dagger from the mattress and rounded the bed. I staggered to my feet and backed away from them. My arms flailed through the space around me, my fingers searching for a weapon of some sort, and it was then that I noticed our height difference. They came just past my shoulder, and they moved with a quiet speed that only someone so petite could manage. Their face was covered with a hood, and I could scarcely make out the black material over their jaw. Even their hands were concealed, the entirety of their body shielded in dark fabric, and I wondered who had sent them and how they made it through the halls without raising suspicion.

Glancing at the door, I noticed the heavy wood was still shut tightly, and I tried to plan my escape now that I realized my lady's maids had most definitely moved my sword and daggers from their place next to it. My attacker followed my eyes, also examining the exit, and then seemingly decided to take their chance. Lunging forward with their weapon in hand, they swung at me, nicking the flesh of my right arm as I dove to the floor and out of their reach.

Rolling across the cold stone, I scrambled once more to my feet and moved to the other side of the room, never once turning my back to my assailant as they followed. Knowing that my best chance of getting out of this without further injury would be to charge at them, I readied myself. However, just as I had moved to take a step forward, I heard a deep, vicious growl echoing from the hallway. Startled by the noise, the stranger paused in their pursuit, and then we both turned to the door when the sound of splintering wood filled my chambers.

A massive black snout crashed through the middle of the broken door, enormous white teeth gleaming as the rest of the head fought its way through the cracked wood, all while the growls grew in volume. And then with one last push, a golden furred body broke through the barrier, sending pieces of the door flying across the room.

"Reif." His name was a sob of relief. One ear flickered as he lowered his body, his hackles rising while his ruby-red eyes focused on the intruder.

Slinking across the space, the failinis moved with lethal grace as he circled the stranger. His eyes watched their every move while he stalked his prey, searching for their weakest point. Sensing just how dangerous this had become for them, the attacker bolted, narrowly missing the snapping jaws as they dodged the beast and then ran from the room, their feet stumbling over the broken wood.

Shouts came from the hall followed by thundering footsteps, and a group of guards passed the destroyed doorway as they chased after the stranger. I, however, remained rooted in my spot, too unnerved and exhausted from the adrenaline to do much else, and Reif pressed against my hip as he nuzzled into my belly. I lifted a shaking hand and stroked his fur while I tried to catch my breath.

"Huntress!" a booming voice called from the door. I glanced at Barrick's massive form as he searched my room with frantic eyes before he saw my bloodstained shift. Anger darkened his face, replacing the concern that had been painted there, before he closed the distance between us with two long strides.

Anyone else probably would have recoiled from him, fearful of his size and the deep, dark eyes that burned with fury, but I knew that my head guard was angry at only himself. One side of my mouth lifted in a half-hearted smile as I stared up into the scarred face before me. His own lips pulled down in a frown beneath his black beard, and he raised one enormous hand to wipe at the right side of his face—the ruined side—before he gripped my arm carefully.

"This one has healed." He paused, his eyes moving to my shoulder before he lifted the bronze waves that had clung to the drying blood. "And this is nearly closed."

Stepping away from him, I nodded and gathered his huge hands in my own before giving them a reassuring squeeze. "I'm fine, truly. Just a little shaken is all."

"I should have been here sooner." He sighed angrily while glancing at the failinis, who now sat at my feet. "I suppose I should be grateful for your beast."

As if Reif understood the guard, he turned his head to face him, blinking his ruby eyes before tilting his head and letting his tongue loll from his mouth all while his massive tail thumped against the floor. Smiling at the dog, I stroked his fur once more and then sighed heavily.

"I'm not sure what would have happened if he hadn't been here," I admitted as I scanned my room. "My weapons are not where I had put them tonight, and whoever it was had been able to sneak in here without drawing any attention."

"That's because there was a disturbance in the west wing." My guard moved to the window, checking the area below before facing me once more. "Obviously a diversion, I see that now. But it worked, we had all moved to that area, allowing a perfect opening for them to come here."

The manor of Noordeign was enormous, its stone walls and halls impressive and mighty. It had taken me months to finally feel confident in finding my way around. It had been gifted to me after my coronation nearly a year ago, and though I now knew my way, I wondered how a stranger had managed to find me so easily.

"Sky!" Elizabeth called, her voice high and shrill with worry. Barrick and I turned as she skidded to a stop at the sight of the broken door. Ella was right behind her, and they both looked panicked as they took in the scene before launching themselves at me.

"I'm okay, I'm fine," I gasped as they both squeezed me tightly. I looked at Barrick, silently begging for help as my friends nearly suffocated me with their worry.

"I'm not sure how choking the Huntress will help her," he snorted as he watched me struggle in their hold.

Ella pulled from me, her dark eyes narrowing at the guard's teasing, and then her hands pried Elizabeth's from around my neck. Backing a step away from them, I smiled down at the pair reassuringly before patting their shoulders. "I'm fine, I promise."

"What happened?" Ella demanded as she crossed her arms over her chest and tilted her pretty face to search my own.

"I woke up to someone in my room. I didn't even notice them until they had lodged their dagger into my shoulder."

Her dark eyes widened worriedly, and Elizabeth crowded in behind her. "Who were they? Did you recognize them?"

Shaking my head, I frowned. "They were completely covered; obviously they had thought this plan through." The very idea made me shiver, and Elizabeth reached around the immortal to grab my arm.

"Did they say anything?" she whispered, her pale face still ashen from the shock of seeing the state of my room, and I shook my head again.

"Nothing loud enough that I could decipher."

"How did you fight them off?" Her gaze moved from me to the pieces of wood strewn across the floor, and then to the tangled sheets and furs that hung off the side of the mattress.

"To be honest, it was more a game of cat and mouse, at least until Reif came to the rescue."

Perking up at his name, the failinis pushed between the group of us, leaning his entire weight on my friends, his tail swinging back and forth happily. A gentle laugh bubbled from Elizabeth as she bent to hug him, and then her light brown eyes lifted to my stained shift.

"It's already healed." She nodded, her gaze moving higher. Her attention focused on my hair for a pause, and I touched the bronze waves. The front strands that should have hung past my chest now ended at my shoulder, and I lifted the jagged ends with a frown. "Well, it could have been my face, I suppose."

"Never mind that, Sky, we can fix it in the morning," Ella reassured me. "For tonight let's just get you settled and wait to see if the guards have captured the intruder."

Nodding, I turned to glance at my chambers with a grimace, and Elizabeth wrapped a careful arm around my waist. "Why don't you grab a new shift and then come stay with us?" Elizabeth offered. "I'll feel better having us all together in one place for the night."

Barrick hummed under his breath, nodding his head in agreement. "I will grab more men to station at both ends of the hall, and I will personally take watch outside of the door," he promised my friends, and they smiled gratefully at the guard, completely ignoring my frown.

"That seems like a bit much. Surely we should be using every spare guard to find the person who did this?"

"The search can spare a few men. If there is something to find, they will find it, but knowing you are guarded is just as important at this point. I don't want to risk the chance that whoever it was will come back to try to finish what they started." His voice lowered, his tone changing to the one he used any time he tried to appease me when we were in a disagreement. "While you are out of this room, we will figure out how your attacker managed to get in. For the night you will stay with these two, and tomorrow I will gather the rest of the guards and see what they have found."

Sighing, I nodded my head. "Let me grab a change of clothes."

I walked to the wardrobe, flung open the doors, and began rifling my way through the items. However, remembering the last time I reorganized the space, I shot my friends a quick smile from over my shoulder and then pushed the gowns to the side before grabbing the dagger I had hidden there. "Best not to go empty-handed this time."

"Really, Sky? A dagger tucked away with all those dresses?"

I shrugged at Elizabeth, my grin growing.

"Doesn't it seem like a good idea now?" I asked. "And tomorrow I am putting one under my pillow."

A strong knock sounded from the door, the echo interrupting what little sleep I had been chasing, and I rubbed at my eyes before glancing at the bed. Ella's dark gaze met my own over Elizabeth's head, and she gave me a soft smile before peeking down at the human curled in her arms. Her fingers stroked the deep chestnut hair away from Elizabeth's face, and my heart warmed at the sight of them.

"Huntress?" Barrick's deep voice called as he knocked again, the sound interrupting my musings, and I pulled myself from my cot before padding to the door.

Opening it, I glanced up at my guard tiredly. "Did you find them?"

Barrick's face hardened with a frown before he shook his head. "There is no sign of the intruder, but we will keep looking. I will post more guards around the grounds and halls just to be sure there isn't another issue."

Rubbing at my face in worry, I took in a deep breath, and it was then I heard the quiet whispers echoing from behind him. I turned towards the end of the hall, stepped around my guard, and watched as my lady's maids carefully approached.

"Hello, you two," I greeted them with a cautious smile, hoping that my face had rid itself of the worry I had been feeling just a moment ago. "What is it you need?"

Mary, the shorter of the pair, glanced at Barrick quickly before offering a curtsey and ducking her chin. "You have court this morning, my lady. We didn't want to intrude, but it's nearly time, and we thought perhaps after all the whispers about last night it may be best that you be there early."

Barrick's brows rose at the young girl. "What whispers?"

"Just that there was an intruder, sir…" Mary stumbled over her words while her face flushed and her attention flickered to the other maid, Claire.

"And who told you that?" Barrick snapped, and I could see his mind spinning. He was concerned as to how word had already gotten out, but I rolled my eyes and lifted my hand to pat his metal-clad shoulder. He had no true reason to worry, at least not about this. Mary had most definitely heard the news from a soldier, the two of whom often spent their fair share of time in her bed, and I doubted she had told anyone else of consequence.

"Thank you, Mary." I nodded at her while grabbing the dresses in her arms. "And we would greatly appreciate it if you both spoke nothing else about last night—as a personal favour to me. No need to cause any worry amongst the lords of the court."

Her pretty brown eyes widened a fraction before she frantically nodded her head.

Glancing down at the light pink fabric, I lifted the pile and pushed them into Barrick's arms, ignoring his dirty look and the grumbling under his breath. "I was sure I had given you the day off today, Mary?"

Bowing her head once more, she smiled brightly at me. "You did, my lady, but Terian was not feeling well, so I offered to take her place."

"That was kind of you. Why don't the two of you take the rest of the morning for yourselves. There should be fresh bread and jams in the kitchen. Help yourself and be sure to bring some to Terian." Curtseying once more, the girls smiled and then scampered off down the hall.

"You're getting good at this," Barrick offered as he nudged me gently with an elbow.

"At what?"

"Being the Lady of Noordeign, being the Huntress's Chosen." Rolling my eyes, I ignored the heat filling my cheeks and glared at the fabric in his armoured arms.

"Go hide those." I tipped my chin at the gowns. "The lords will just have to settle for my breeches and tunic today."

Barrick's lips lifted on one side, and his dark eyes warmed. "Perhaps I spoke too soon."

Dodging my swat, he ducked out of my reach and turned to the hall, only pausing to glance over his shoulder with a furrowed brow. "Should they hear these apparent whispers, be sure to show them there is nothing to be concerned about, and I will see to it that the grounds are searched once more before meeting you in the hall."

Dipping my head in agreement, I inhaled swiftly and squared my shoulders only to face Barrick once more as he called out to me.

"Oh, and Huntress? Don't offend anyone too badly until I'm there," he said sarcastically with a wink, and had it not been for the guards stationed at either end of the hall, I was sure I would have stuck my tongue out at him.

Chapter 2

"Well, the breeches are one thing, but this hair is another. For now, I can try to pin it, but what about the celebration tonight?" Elizabeth's voice grumbled from behind me as her hands cupped my shoulders. Glancing at her in the mirror, I watched as she struggled to tuck the shorter section amongst the rest, and then she exhaled roughly in irritation.

"Why not just cut it?" I asked, already moving to the dagger that had been placed on the tabletop, just reaching the hilt when Ella's dark hand swatted mine.

"Good Gods, Sky." She gently ushered Elizabeth away, lifting the dagger and handing it to her with a knowing look, one I had learned was obviously about me. "We can cut it, but at least let us do so carefully. No one wants to see the monstrosity you'll create hacking away at it impatiently with a dagger. Especially not before your assembly with the lords and on Bloomingdae of all days!"

She opened the drawer to my left, and her nimble fingers pulled out the pair of delicate shears Elizabeth often used when sewing. I leaned back against my chair as the immortal assessed my long bronze waves. Ella brushed the strands back and paused, her eyes finding my own in our reflection, and I lifted a brow in question.

"Are you sure?" she asked softly. "If we cut it, your scar will be out in the open. You'll have a harder time using your hair to shield it from others." The tone was meant to ease any upset the words may cause, and I took a deep breath before nodding my head. I had spent many hours studying the ruined flesh of my cheek, agonizing over the scar that sat so prominently on my pale face. I had thought I had grown used to it after the battle at the shores, but the lingering stares and quiet whispers at court had always managed to push through the cracks of my façade, and behind closed doors I willed myself to find a way to hide it. But that was no longer an option now.

"I'm sure."

Ella handed the shears to Elizabeth, and the immortal gave my shoulder one last lingering squeeze before they began.

Piece after piece of hair fell to the floor, and I lowered my eyes to my lap as the soft sound of clipping surrounded me. It was a quiet, methodical experience, and when the final strand was cut, I glanced at the mirror. My face was the same, unappealing and round, and my eyes moved across my mismatched features before drifting to the raised flesh of the burn. The skin's colour had faded over time, but the burning heart still sat proudly against my cheekbone, and I exhaled roughly as I eyed it.

"Okay," I sighed, but Ella lifted from her seat next to me and bent so that her face was beside mine in our reflection.

"*Are* you okay?" It was such a silly thing. Truly it was just hair, and I felt foolish for being so vain, especially considering I had never been a true beauty to begin with. I tipped my head as I studied myself once more.

"Yes," I reassured her. "But I'm sure the lords have begun to gather, and they will not be pleased if they are stuck waiting on me. I better be off."

Elizabeth worried her lower lip, seeing right through my tactic, but knowing I liked to be left alone while I dealt with my feelings, she grasped Ella's hand and nodded her head.

"We will see you after? Maybe we can take tea in the gardens?" she offered with a soft smile.

"That sounds perfect," I agreed. "Though I may need something stronger." Snorting, Ella shot me a wink, and with a nod of my head, I moved to the door, all while pulling at the hem of my tunic nervously. And then with a small wave at my friends, I ducked out of the room.

"It is the biggest celebration of the year and should certainly be taken more seriously than this!" Lord Samius exclaimed as he paced across the floor of the room. I watched him carefully while sagging against the hard back of my throne, wallowing in the sudden wave of frustration that coursed through me.

None of them would act this way with Gaelon. They wouldn't dare move from their place at the long tables that sat in the centre of the room. They wouldn't question his every move, every decision, just waiting for him to make a mistake that they could judge him for. Glancing at the rest of the court, I watched as they observed the highborn lord while he crossed the room once more.

"Bloomingdae is a sacred tradition. One that is meant to honour the Huntress." He spun on his heel and pointed one long finger at me. "The Huntress, who is said to be *your* Goddess!"

"I understand that, my lord." I winced at the crack in my voice and tried again. "This was all an oversight on my part. Had I known your expectations—"

A wave of whispers began amongst the rest of the men, and my eyes scanned the crowd, only moving back to Samius when a deep conceding laugh burst from his lips. "Had you known? The people have gathered on this day for centuries, as far back as to when it was only the Divine Triad we worshiped, not that you would have any idea about that history."

My shoulders slumped in defeat. His assumption was correct, and the handsome immortal shook his head in disbelief. "This day is our true beginning. It is our chance to gather our strength once more and receive the blessings of the Goddess. We pay homage to the Huntress and her power, and *you* should have known. The Healer would have if he was here!"

It took everything in me not to roll my eyes at Samius, and I inhaled sharply, forcing myself to calm, knowing there was no rebuttal to his argument.

Over the last year, the Healer had left me stranded here alone for long periods at a time while he took on the role of overseeing the rebuilding of Elrin and the removal of the Crimson army. His last voyage had begun over a month ago, and he was not due back for weeks still. Which meant I was not only forced to navigate these dreary meetings at court while facing these men on my own, but apparently, I was also required to sit silently while the ancient immortal lords scolded me for my lack of knowledge of our history and customs.

"I understand your frustrations, Lord Samius, but planning elaborate celebrations is not something I am familiar with." It was immediately clear that had been the wrong thing to say, and the quiet whispers grew in volume while my face heated.

"Trust me, we are well aware of that, *Huntress*," he hissed out the title viciously. "But perhaps if you spent more time learning your place as the *lady* of this court and what that all that entails, you would be." The sound of Barrick's heavy footfalls was the only indication that he had moved, and I glanced at him as he strode down the stairs towards Samius.

"Barrick," I warned, but he paid me no mind and closed the space between them before curling a fist in the lord's tunic. Tugging at the material, my guard lifted the immortal onto his toes and then bent until his face was just mere inches away from Samius's.

"You are one of the last remaining lords of the old court, you prick," Barrick snarled. "And *she* has willingly allowed you to keep your position though you've never done anything to deserve it. You have not once earned your place or the respect you so often demand, and *this* is how you treat her? This is how you repay her graciousness?"

"Earned? What would you know of that, Sir Barrick?" Samius's mouth twisted in a grin. "You have yet to reach your fiftieth birthday and I have had my title for centuries. I have watched rulers rise and fall. I have seen humans and halflings tear themselves apart, over and over again as they grew hungry with greed only to succumb to the power of us immortals. I have been alive for all of this. I have been here for longer than any of your poor, unbecoming ancestors. I can trace my lineage to Aglrid the Clever himself. As for your Huntress, well, she is just a child compared to all of that, isn't she?" His eyes slowly slid to my own. "So tell me, what gallantry do I owe *her*?"

His fist tightened in the elaborate embroidered tunic, and Barrick lifted his free hand, curling his long fingers in an obvious threat. Sensing that this quarrel would come back to haunt me should I let it go much further, I decided to put an end to it.

"Barrick." My voice was stern as I stood from my seat, and all eyes moved from the pair, turning to me once more as I stepped down from my throne. "Enough now."

For a pause, no one moved, and I approached the pair slowly before resting a hand on Barrick's arm. Sighing, my guard slowly loosened his hold before spinning to face me, and I tilted my head, directing him to his place once more. Barrick hesitated, his dark eyes searching mine carefully, and I gestured again, waiting until my guard moved back beside the heavy stone throne before clearing my throat and addressing the court.

"I know the importance of tradition to the people of Noordeign and Elrin." I paused before taking a deep breath. "I also know that I have not come to you with the experience you had been hoping your Chosen would have. I am not what you pictured; I understand that. But I hope you will give me the chance to prove to you I can be the Huntress you have wished for. That I can lead with honour and strength and show you why the Goddess has given me this fate." With that I ducked my chin and lowered my eyes to the floor and then moved swiftly for the exit. Keeping my gaze on my boots, I fled from the men and their whispers, only to hear one that cut me to the very core.

"What a disappointment she is."

The grand hallways of the manor were empty, though they were immaculately decorated with fresh-cut flowers and twists of vines and fine greenery that hung from the ceiling. However, I barely took in the colours as my heavy footfalls echoed across the space as I searched for the nearest escape.

Bursting through the back door, I was immediately met with the warm, dewy air, and I inhaled deeply before striding across the damp grass to the training yards. Everything seemed to glow in the warmth of the spring sun, and I gazed across the magnificent grounds, eyeing the stone archways of the stables before taking in the surrounding forest.

Turning towards the armoury, I noticed a few stares from the staff who had been in the middle of their morning chores, and I quickened my pace as my cheeks heated from their scrutiny. Once in the shelter of the walls, I leaned against the doorway and sighed before reaching for a dull training sword.

"Are you okay?" Barrick asked as he followed me through the door. I turned to him with a weak smile before tossing one of the other sparring blades at him.

"I'm fine," I lied.

Seeing right through my fib, my guard frowned. "Samius had no right to say any—"

"But it was true," I interrupted. "Every word he said was true. I have no idea what I'm doing. I have no knowledge of our history, no real understanding of the past, and what do you think that says about me? What do you imagine those immortal lords think of me?"

Barrick sighed, his frown deepening. "You're being too hard on yourself; their expectations are not fair."

"Maybe, but perhaps I don't help myself either. I just…" I rubbed my eyes tiredly. "This is not how I thought it would be."

"Things rarely are what we imagined," my guard agreed.

"After last night and now that meeting, it seems that everything is escaping my control all at once, and yet, it's almost as if I can sense something more is coming, and I know I am not prepared for the outcome." Barrick's brow furrowed, and I sighed before squaring my shoulders. "This is not why I came out here. I meant to clear my mind, so let's change the subject."

His dark eyes narrowed under his heavy black brows, and my gaze traced the jagged scar that ran from hairline to neck on the right side of his face before I noticed his mouth twitch and he stroked his beard in thought.

"You look different, I forgot to mention it before court. Did you change something?" My cheeks heated at his teasing, and I rolled my eyes before shoving past him towards the yard.

"You best shut up before I knock that grin off of your face," I called from over my shoulder as I found my place in the training ring, pleased that he followed my request.

"Who are you kidding, Huntress? You are going to knock it off whether I keep my mouth shut or not. I might as well get a few laughs in beforehand." Gripping the hilt of his weapon, Barrick held it in front of him before bracing his knees, and I smirked as I waited.

"Are you ready yet, old man?" I called as he made a show of stretching his neck and rolling his shoulders.

"Now you're just being unpleasant," he grumbled, and I laughed under my breath before finally charging at him. Barrick was skilled with a blade and an excellent sport, and I truly did try my best to keep the strength of my ignite at bay while we sparred. However, the longer we went on, the stronger my instincts became, and our matches would always result in the man flat on his back.

"You shouldn't have brought up my hair," I growled as our blades clashed. I pressed against him with my weight before springing back, causing him to lose his balance for a quick second. Finding his footing, he pursued me with calculating eyes as he followed my movements.

"It is not my fault you showed up with a haystack for a head. I had no warning; I was taken by surprise." His tone was teasing, but I could see the tension in his face as his frustration grew.

"Insults are a cheap shot for the head guard, I expected more from you." Dodging his swing, I spun on my heel, and in four swift moves, I had not only unarmed him, but had kicked his feet out from under him as well. I smiled down at his shocked face as his mind processed the turn of events.

"Why in the heavens do I guard you when I am the one at risk?" he muttered as he slapped my offered hand away. Laughing, I waited for him to pull himself to his feet so we could start again, but just as he righted himself, I heard the frantic calls of my name and glanced behind me to see Ella waving her hands above her head as she ran to us.

"Sky!" she called again, and I strode across the yard while concern filled my chest. My hands stretched to reach for her shoulders as I closed the distance, but her dainty fingers wrapped around one of my wrists before she turned on her heel and pulled me in tow.

Stumbling after her, I looked back over my shoulder, searching for Barrick. All humour had been wiped from his face and was now replaced with the stern mask he wore while acting as my guard. He stiffened his spine, matching our hurried strides while leaving his palm on the hilt of his real weapon, and I realized he must have strapped it to his hip when he had noticed Ella's alarm.

"What is it, Miss Ella?" His deep voice pulled her attention to his massive form, and she spared him a glance before hurrying her strides.

"It's Gaelon."

Chapter 3

I was ushered into my room by a swarm of servants, each one grasping and tugging at my clothes before I was shoved towards the bath that had been filled with warm, sweet-smelling water. Forced through the doorway by their pushing hands, I stumbled to the tub and then glanced back at Ella as she spoke with the lady's maids who were pulling gown after gown from my wardrobe before laying them across the bed.

"The water is ready for you, my lady," Terian whispered to me gently as her hand pressed against my shoulders, her gaze focusing on the flesh of the left for a pause before I stepped into the warmth. Kneeling next to the tub, she grasped the cloth and began scrubbing at my back until one of my hands circled her wrist gently.

"I can do it, Terian." Light blue eyes blinked at me, and I made sure to smile reassuringly as I took in her appearance. Her skin was unusually pale, and her fingers shook as I took the cloth from her. "Mary mentioned you've been unwell; you should go rest," I whispered as I patted her hand before dismissing her.

She was a kind and sensitive lady's maid, and I had made the mistake of being too harsh with her in the past, and with her being ill, I made certain she knew that I wasn't ungrateful but rather concerned for her. That and, well, I truly hated being waited on and longed for some privacy.

As if she could hear my thoughts, Ella clapped her hands together, startling Terian and the crowd of women before herding them out of the room and shutting the door with a resounding slam.

"Good Gods. I swear, where there is one there's twenty," she grumbled loudly as she crossed the room and perched on the soft corner of my bed.

"Remind me why I had to bathe and change before greeting Gaelon? Surely his reasons for his early arrival are more important, couldn't this all wait?" I called from the tub and then dunked my head under the water quickly.

"Because that's how things are done now," Ella reminded me once I rose, and I wiped the water from my eyes. "You are the crowned Huntress; you cannot greet your fellow Chosen in breeches and filth. Or so everyone says, and maybe this once we should abide by their rules given that the meeting did not run as smoothly as one would hope."

"I see you've heard about that already," I muttered with a roll of my eyes.

"Word travels fast in these stone walls, and many of the lords were whispering about it once they were dismissed," Ella admitted with a grimace.

"Be that as it may, shouldn't I be the one to make the rules about how things are done considering it's my head that the crown sits on?" I asked with a frown, though I knew she had a point, and Ella smiled gently before swatting at me impatiently.

"Come now, you need to get dressed so you can welcome your Healer like a proper Huntress should, and then you can focus on getting ready for tonight."

I pulled myself from the tub, dried my skin roughly before wrapping the towel around my body, and walked quickly to the bed. Ignoring the pile of dresses that had been left, I instead opted for a pair of loose breeches and a black wool tunic and then tugged my short, damp hair back with a piece of ribbon. Without a glance at a mirror, I grabbed my boots and grinned at Ella.

"I've already disappointed them once today, I can't see the point of trying to win them over after that. Besides, the members of the court seemed bored of their usual gossip this morning anyway." Her dark eyes brightened with humour, and she smiled before linking her arm with mine. Pulling the heavy door open, we greeted Elizabeth as she waited for us, her brown eyes roaming over my attire before she glanced at her partner.

"Breeches *again.*" She sighed in displeasure. "Did you even try to reason with her?" Elizabeth asked before pressing a kiss to Ella's cheek.

"Why waste the effort when I know I won't win? Besides, we still need to wrangle her into a gown for the celebration. We have to pick our battles carefully, sweeting." Unlinking our arms, Ella turned to Elizabeth, and I sighed while they stood wrapped around each other, ignoring the way they whispered and giggled quietly. Even after a year together they acted lovesick, and I rolled my eyes.

"Come on, you two," I called to them from over my shoulder before striding down the hallway. I nodded my head at the few guards I passed and then turned my attention to the great hall where I knew Gaelon would be waiting, and I felt anxiety creep its way into my gut. He had planned to be away for some time still, and I knew the only reason he would have shortened his trip is if something had happened. Hurrying my feet, I jogged through the corridors until I reached the heavy wood doors of the hall, and with one last deep breath, I pushed them open.

"Gaelon," I called when my eyes found his back, and I gasped as he turned to face me. His usual welcoming handsome face was pulled tight with a frown and his skin was dull. Under his normally warm eyes sat heavy purple shadows, and I reached for him as I closed the distance between us.

"Skylahr." My name was a whisper, and his shoulders sagged when my fingers skimmed across his forearm. If I didn't know he was immortal, I would have thought he was ill, and I stepped closer in concern.

"What is it? What's wrong?" My voice was rough with nervousness, and I pulled at his arm until he was seated in the massive throne at the end of the decorated hall. It seemed as if his body buckled all at once under the exhaustion, and he folded himself in half, cradling his head in his hands while his long fingers grasped at his dark curls, and I grew more and more worried while I waited. After a long moment of silence, I knelt beside him and untangled his hands before sliding my index finger under his strong jaw, lifting his chin.

"Gaelon?" I whispered in concern, and his eyes searched mine. "What happened?"

Shaking his head, he took in a deep breath and wiped his palms across his thighs before standing from the heavy stone chair. "I'm fine, truly. I'm just happy to be home. There's nothing for you to worry about right now."

Scrambling from my place on the floor, I too stood and crossed my arms as I waited for him to elaborate, but instead his mouth quirked at the corners, and he lifted a hand to twirl a damp bronze strand that had escaped the ribbon. "What did you do to your hair?"

"Gaelon," I sighed in frustration only to see that the tension had flooded his face once again. Whatever had happened on his travels had been cause enough to shake the Healer, and in all the time we had spent together I had never seen this kind of reaction from him. Stepping closely once more, I placed a gentle hand in his and tightened my fingers in reassurance. But those dark eyes would not meet mine and had instead focused over my shoulder.

"Your hair, it suits you," was his only reply before he turned to Ella and Elizabeth, who had managed to sneak into the room without my knowledge. Nodding at them, he smiled weakly and then excused himself before striding out of the room.

"What is wrong with him?" Elizabeth whispered, her eyes on his retreating form.

"I have no idea."

"He didn't say anything?" Ella's brows were pulled together tightly as she searched my face, and I shook my head. Gaelon had never returned from a trip in this way. He had never been distant and hesitant like this around me before, and his dismissal was not only confusing, it was hurtful.

"No," I answered, praying that the worry sitting in my gut would eventually fade.

Elizabeth growled in frustration for a third time as she tried to wrangle the bronze waves back into the delicate comb before setting it back onto the vanity in defeat.

"I give up, it's impossible," she grumbled as she instead lifted the tin of black that was used to paint my lashes and line my eyes. Both she and Ella had been fussing over me for hours while ignoring the tension that had draped across the room. The halls had been filled with chatter about the Healer's unusual mood, and I could feel the accusing stares as I had passed through the corridors before hiding in my chambers. But even in the shelter of privacy, the three of us could not help but feel uneasy with Gaelon's demeanour.

"Here, let me try." Ella smiled at her lover softly before lifting the comb and effortlessly pinning the hair in place, leaving the unmarked side of my face more exposed. Smoothing the strands, she then opened a delicate wooden box that had been perched on the edge of the vanity, and I watched in fascination as her nimble fingers lifted the protective piece of cloth from the cushion.

"Mary said Gaelon left it here for you." Raising my chin, I peeked over her hands and gasped at the treasure that was nestled in the velvet padding. Brilliant deep blue stones gathered together in a crescent shape that was no longer than my index finger, their tips pointed along the outside, almost creating a feather-like image, and I marvelled at just how exquisite the piece was.

"What is it?" Ella wondered while she gently lifted it from the pillow and cradled it in her palm.

"It looks like an ear cuff. One of the ladies in Noorde Point used to wear one to the festivals we had, but it was never as magnificent as this. You said Gaelon brought this for her?" Elizabeth asked as she took the jewellery from the immortal before lining it up with my ear and carefully attaching the cuff around the curve of cartilage.

I turned my chin towards my shoulder while eyeing my reflection in the mirror. The stones covered the entire ridge of my ear, and I shifted my head back and forth, watching the deep blue jewels glisten in the light.

"That would have cost a near fortune. What an incredible gift," Elizabeth sighed, palming my shoulders before ducking her chin so her face was next to mine in the mirror. "It looks magnificent on you."

"Do we have anything to match?" Ella called from the wardrobe as she pulled gown after gown from their place before tossing them away. Almost all of my gowns were in varying shades of greens, as was customary for the nobles of the north. However, much to my dismay, there were also a number of dresses dyed in light pinks that had been gifted to me by the court. I had been pressured to wear one for my twenty-third birthday in the fall, but that had been a disaster. The colour only highlighted the redness in my face, and the bust barely maintained its stitching as it stretched across my torso. The disapproving looks from the members of court had been humiliating, and I avoided all gatherings for a week afterwards.

"I saw the maids bring in a gown of some sort, they hung it near the tub. Said the steam would do something for it." Elizabeth waved her hand towards the room before lifting the tin of black and moving the small brush towards my eyes.

"Good Gods that man has taste," Ella sighed wistfully, and I pulled my face free from Elizabeth's strong fingers that had grabbed at my jaw to hold me still. The immortal was holding a metal hook high above her head while her other hand uncloaked the deep navy gown. Its bodice was simple and modest; the neckline would sit just below my collarbones, while the waist was cinched higher than normal, which would allow the full skirt to hide the wideness of my hips. But as Ella pulled the gown from the wool that had been wrapped around it, I noticed a gleam of gold and stood from the chair.

"Is that armour?" I asked as I grabbed the plated gold from Ella's grasp and turned it over so I could see the front. The breastplate was smooth with curves for my bust, and the arms were made of thousands of gold feathers stacked on top of each other, overlapping until they created a solid metal sleeve. The details were tiny and precise, and it reminded me of another set of armour that had been given to me last year.

"She wears that over the dress?" Elizabeth's brow lifted as she studied the gold, and I patted her gently on the back.

"I would rather be in armour anyway. Why not combine the two?" Without any further discussion, I stepped into the gown before turning my back to Elizabeth, allowing her to lace the back. "There is no need for corsets when you have armour. We should have thought of this ages ago."

The gown fit my height and body perfectly, the full skirt swirling around my feet in such a way that had my heart lodged in my throat as memories flooded back. Isla would have loved the colour of this dress, though my own mother would have been shocked at my willingness to wear such a gown. I grinned, imagining what she would have to say about the armour that was now being placed on my torso.

"What is the smile for?" Elizabeth asked as she smoothed the skirts around my knees.

"I was just picturing my mother's reaction to the armour. I bet she would have been less than impressed with that choice."

Elizabeth took me in for a long moment before tipping her head to the side.

"No, I don't think so. I think she would have been so proud of you, and she would be pleased to see that even after everything, her Skylahr managed to be the same girl she raised." My throat felt tight, and I smiled down at my friend before pulling her to me.

"Thank you." Those words seemed to soothe the ache that had been festering since this morning.

"Oh, Sky, you never have to thank me. But I would appreciate a looser hold, you're going to bruise me with this armour if you clutch me any tighter." Laughing, I stepped away and turned to Ella as she observed us with a fond grin on her face.

"Alright, you two, are you ready?" Normally I would feel that nervous flutter in my belly at her question, but right now I had my friends next to me, and I knew they would not let me fail. I reached for their hands, gave them each a tight squeeze, and nodded softly.

"As ready as I ever will be."

Chapter 4

The halls were bustling with activity, and I could hear the happy chatter of the court as they socialized while waiting for our presence to be announced. But I had not seen Gaelon since the morning, and I longed to find him before our summons.

"What is it, Huntress?" Barrick whispered with a steady hand on my golden-clad shoulder.

"Have you seen Gaelon since his arrival? We were supposed to enter together."

Barrick frowned at the worry in my voice and shook his head.

"As far as I know the Healer has been sealed away in his room for the day. I haven't even had a chance to inform him of the incident in your room; he has refused to see anyone."

Gaelon had never isolated himself like this before, and I felt my stomach drop in concern.

"What could have happened to make him like this, Barrick?"

The head guard had no words and exhaled roughly before placing his hand on the pommel of his blade.

"I can't say for certain, and there's no time now to worry about it, Huntress. They're ready for you." He nodded towards the now-open doors, and I straightened my spine before lifting my head. "That's right, head high and eyes forward."

I grabbed his hand in thanks and gave it a long squeeze before smoothing my skirts and carefully striding to the entrance. The chandeliers had been replaced with hundreds of individual candles that sat in glass jars hanging from the ceiling. Their golden glow bounced off the greenery and flowers that covered every inch of stone, and I was awestruck by the splendour. It was as if the room had been transformed into an enchanted forest. I gazed up at the blooms and flickering lights for a long, silent moment, only breaking from my trance when I felt a presence step into the space beside me.

"They're waiting on us," Gaelon whispered and directed me to the petal-covered aisle that led to the two massive thrones that remained empty for us. Staring straight ahead, I ignored the heated whispers that echoed across the room and instead focused on the coloured blooms that covered the wall until I reached the stone. Carefully tucking my skirt underneath me, I sat down with as much grace as I could muster and folded my hands in my lap while Gaelon addressed the court.

"Ladies and lords, friends and comrades, we welcome you with open arms. Let the celebration commence." With that, the crowd merged, and music began to play.

"You look radiant, Huntress." The words were whispered as Gaelon leaned onto the armrest of my throne, and I took a long moment to study his face. Sincerity shone in his eyes, but they still appeared dull, and his skin still had the same lifeless quality from the morning.

"I truly do not know how to say thank you for the dress and the jewellery." My tone was careful, and I kept my focus on his face, even when he avoided my gaze. Something was wrong, and I hated that he wouldn't confide in me.

"Yes, well, no need to thank me. It is an honour to have you wear my gifts so proudly. I had the designs sent to the clothier and jeweller before I left, and I am pleased to see they were ready in time for the celebrations."

His wary politeness made my stomach drop and my nervousness worsen.

This man who sat next to me was a shell of himself, and I so desperately wanted to grab him by the shoulders and shake him. I wanted to demand what was wrong and force the answers. But that was not the way to approach Gaelon. He had never responded well to heated conflict; we were similar in that way. So instead, I forced myself to give him the space he so obviously longed for.

"Well, thank you again. If you would excuse me, I think I will see how Ella and Elizabeth are getting on." I could see the Healer stand and reach for me out of the corner of my eye, but I swiftly made my escape and lowered my chin as I weaved through the crowd.

"What fine pieces she is wearing. Thank the Gods she had the sense to allow others to dress her tonight. At least she finally looks as if she is attempting to fill her role properly for the feast."

"She truly does take the battle hero part rather seriously though, doesn't she? She's out in the training yards day in and day out while the Healer repairs the wreckage. She could barely stumble her way through court this morning and then fled to spar with her guard, who, I might mention, was bold enough to approach me during the assembly. I would say he is out of control, but I fear they both are. The two of them are like a pair of rabid dogs," Lord Samius grumbled. "But what she lacks in wit and looks, she makes up for in size, I suppose."

The snickering that followed the whispers had my jaw clenching, and I narrowed my eyes at Samius and his friend, who had huddled together while they insulted me.

In the past, I would have bowed my head and hid from the taunts. But as their laughter rose in volume, so did my anger. I knew the lords of court had been less than accepting of me over the past year, that could not be any clearer after today, but I had been on the receiving end of their disdain for far too long. I had done just as much for the people of Elrin as Gaelon had, and yet, only his praises were sung. The novelty of our combined efforts had worn off, I supposed, and I gathered my skirts in my fists as I turned towards them.

"Not here, Skylahr." Barrick's voice was kind but firm from behind me, and his fingers pulled at my wrist until I turned to him. His jaw was tense, and his eyes peered over my shoulder at the two men. Both of whom were now silent as they met the glare of my guard. "Do not give them even a second of your time."

"Why won't they accept me? What more do I have to do?" The words poured out before I could stop them, and Barrick's eyes softened while he gasped quietly. He moved to block me from onlookers, my guard's eyes darting around, and then a hush fell over the room and he was ushering me forward.

"I will deal with *them*. You, however…" One of his large hands suddenly clasped my shoulder and spun me, turning me to face the Healer as he approached, and then I was pushed onwards.

"Huntress," Gaelon whispered while lifting an open palm towards me. "Please do me the honour and allow me to have a dance with you?"

Swallowing nervously, I slid my hand into his own and glanced at the space that had been cleared while flushing hotly.

"I'm really not suited for it, I'm afraid." The only men I had ever danced with at Noorde Point were my father and on a very rare occasion Liam, and that was only after being persuaded by my mother.

"Dancing is no different than sparring, and you are exceptional at that. I dare say you will outshine us all." His hand was warm and rough as it grabbed my fingers gently, and I tried to push my uneasiness away while the curious eyes of the crowd had settled on us.

Shifting under their scrutiny, I reluctantly agreed and followed him to the centre of the floor. The first notes of music began, Gaelon folded himself gracefully into a bow, and my face heated again as I scrambled to curtsey clumsily in return. And then all at once, I was surrounded by him. His hand pressed into my back, strong and sure as his other gently cupped my own fingers, and then he led me through the steps with ease. Twisting and turning with grace I would have never imagined possessing, we travelled across the floor as if we had done this hundreds of times.

Under the warm glow of the candles and the sweet scent of the flowers, I lost myself. The world all but disappeared as I let the Healer lead me across the stone, and in his embrace, the uneasiness that had weighed on my shoulders lessened just a little and the ghosts seemed to fade. Pressing myself closer, I chased the feeling of peace that had been absent for months and blinked through the mist that had filled my eyes.

"I know, Skylahr." His deep voice whispered into my hair as if he could feel my emotions through my skin, and I wondered what spirits had been haunting him. What *or* who had followed the Healer home?

After a few more trips across the space, our dance finally came to an end, and I felt breathless as I gazed at Gaelon. But his face was not lifted with that soft smile as I had expected it to be, and with a curt nod, he turned on his heel and left for the entrance, leaving me standing all alone amongst the parted crowd. Sensing my need for a saviour now that I had been abandoned by the Healer once more, my friends approached, and Elizabeth lifted a hand.

"Come now, Sky, let's go grab some wine." Elizabeth's fingers tangled with my own and she pulled me gently towards the table littered with refreshments, but my eyes had remained locked on the hallway where the Healer had disappeared to.

"I'm worried, Elizabeth." Suddenly a silver cup was pressed into my grasp, and she guided it closer to my face, encouraging me to drink.

"I know, but you have an audience. Do not let them see your concern. Find your answers when the feast is over." After taking a long sip, I finally met her eyes and nodded my head silently.

She was right. Today had been enough of a disaster as it was; I couldn't allow my worry to create any more concern within the court. And although Gaelon's behaviour was peculiar, he had not given me any reason to cause a scene. Upon finishing my wine, I linked my arm with Elizabeth's, and she smiled at me softly.

"Come on, Ella grabbed the good pastries and she's waiting for us on the terrace." With one last glance at the hall, I allowed Elizabeth to tow me away, though a pang of worry still skittered through my chest.

It was after midnight by the time the celebrations were over, and I had finished more than my share of wine in order to find the courage to seek out the Healer. But now standing in front of his door, I felt a wave of apprehension, and I worried I had made a mistake.

Pulling my robe around my chest tightly, I took in a deep breath before lifting my hand and rapping my knuckles across the rough surface. The noise echoed in the empty hallway, and I held my breath and lowered my eyes to the floor as I waited.

"Skylahr?" Gaelon's voice was rough with sleep, and my eyes rose only to widen when they took in his dishevelled state. The Healer had always been handsome and impressive, although I stood a few inches taller than him. But now as my gaze traced his bare chest and loose breeches, I realized I hadn't noticed just how powerfully built he was.

"Sorry." The word was a croak, and I blushed hotly before clearing my throat while averting my eyes from his pale skin that covered the defined muscles of his torso.

"Did you need something?" A brow lifted in question, and when I hesitated to answer, he pressed the door open and held his arm out in invitation. Stepping through the threshold, I tried to take in his room as subtlety as possible. It was neat and organized, his bed draped with dark linens while the nightstand had a pile of books strewn across it. Tucking a piece of hair behind my ear, I turned to face him and swallowed roughly.

"Wine?" he asked as he held a silver cup, and I shook my head silently while crossing my arms and then moved through the room until I was perched on the edge of the cushioned chair next to the window. Curling my fingers in my lap, I gazed at him from the corner of my eye and waited for him to finish his drink before clearing my throat.

"Gaelon, why won't you tell me what is wrong?" I had meant for my words to come out with confidence, but they were barely a whisper, and I bit my lower lip in frustration before straightening my shoulders. "What I mean to say is that something is obviously troubling you, and I would like to know if there is anything I can do to ease the burden."

"You are always taking on everyone's burdens, Skylahr. I won't ask that of you too." His eyes were warm as they traced my face, and I blushed hotly under his gaze.

"I can take it, I'm strong enough. Why does everyone always question that?"

"No one questions your ability, Skylahr. But just because you have the strength does not mean you should carry the weight." Moving to sit beside me, he reached for my hand and cradled it carefully. Focusing my gaze on his long fingers, I watched as his thumb drummed across my skin soothingly. "Besides, I'm not sure what you or anyone else could do."

My brows furrowed, and I waited a breath for him to continue, but when the air left his lungs in a harsh exhale, I shimmied closer to him before pulling my hand away. "What does that mean, Gaelon? Speak plainly."

"Always so stubborn." He sighed softly with a shake of his head and then lifted himself from his seat before striding across the space in front of me. I followed the subtle wave of agitation that draped across his body. His jaw had tightened, his fists clenching and then unclenching rhythmically again and again while he paced.

When the silence became too much for me, I stood and intercepted his movements, my hands reaching to brace his shoulders. The contact almost seemed to break whatever state he was in, and suddenly his weight sagged against my palms, his body crowding my own until his forehead was resting in the crook of my neck.

Frozen, I held my breath as he appeared to fall into himself, and I swallowed nervously, unsure of what to do. This wasn't the reaction I had been expecting. Gaelon was the one who comforted people, he was who eased someone's pain and hurt away. He had that uncanny ability, though it was far more likely to be the gift from his God. I chewed at my lower lip anxiously as he took in a ragged breath.

"I don't know where to start." I could just barely make out the words, and I wrapped my arm around his waist as I guided him to sit back down. Pulling away from him, I searched his face.

"The beginning is usually the best place." The side of my mouth lifted, and the Healer snorted quietly before sighing.

"That might be so, but I'm not convinced you'll believe me when I tell you." Perching beside him, I reached for his hand once more before offering a gentle squeeze.

"Give me more credit than that. Whatever happened, whatever it is you are worried about, I promise to listen." Dipping my head, I raised a brow and then waited for him to begin.

"Reports started arriving from small villages along the coast. It started with just a handful of odd occurrences: ships would set sail and never make their destinations, or the vessels would be found but without a crew. But we thought nothing of it, the western seas have always been unpredictable."

"Why didn't I know about this?" I demanded. "Why didn't you tell me?"

Running a hand through his dark curls, Gaelon studied me with a soft expression. "I didn't feel there was a need to worry you. As I said I thought it was perhaps a tough winter on the seas or maybe more unskilled sailors had ventured out now that the villages had the freedom to expand without the threat of the Crimson."

I frowned in frustration and narrowed my eyes at the Healer.

"But we are both a Chosen, we are supposed to lead together. Should I not be aware of the happenings of Elrin?" I reminded him sternly, though I couldn't help but notice that the words did not find their mark as his face remained impassive, and it hurt knowing that Gaelon had not only kept this from me, but he didn't seem to understand how it was unfair of him to do so.

As if he could sense my anger and pain, the Healer bowed his head in shame. "I know, Skylahr. But I didn't think there was anything to be concerned about, I promise."

Unwilling to have this fight tonight, I bit my tongue and sighed. "Just tell me the rest. What happened next?" Taking a deep breath, Gaelon closed his eyes almost as if he was picturing the scenes in his mind, and I could feel my heartbeat pound in my ears.

"When I reached the coastline, more people came forward with similar tales, and so I met with a captain who assured me there was nothing peculiar happening but agreed to travel along the coast in the case that there was something there. I had thought perhaps a small group of Crimsons had gathered and were sitting in wait on the sea. That was something we predicted could happen after the battle at the shores, but when he assembled a crew to investigate, we could not find a sign of the Seductress's army anywhere. We searched half a dozen times for anything that might explain what was causing so many losses. But each time we returned empty-handed even though more and more reports of wrecks and lost vessels came in."

The air around us stilled, and I shivered as my skin prickled. Gaelon's own face paled, and his eyes fogged over. Watching him closely, I waited as he gazed at the space in front of him, and it was almost as if he was caught in a daze.

"I had decided to join him on his final trek out to sea, and at first nothing was amiss." Gaelon swallowed noisily as his body shuddered in what seemed to be fear. "But then it came, and it was nothing like I've seen before. It just rose from the waves as if we were in the shallow water of the shore and not in the middle of the ocean."

"Came? What came?" But he didn't hear me; he was too consumed with whatever it was he was reliving.

"At first, we thought it was just a storm rolling in, but then the current grew so strong and so rapidly, I knew something was wrong." His voice shook, while his brows furrowed. "The waves became bigger, and the force of them nearly tipped the ship over a handful of times. And then, suddenly, there was a wall of rock in front of us." He paused and took in a deep, ragged breath. "It just emerged through the surface. But it wasn't an island or a cliff, it was something more. I swear to you now, I saw a face carved into the jagged rock."

My heart thundered in my chest, and I felt my mouth dry as I waited on the edge of my seat for him to continue.

"I stood frozen as I watched it while the storm circled above, and then the air was filled with this horrendous screeching noise, almost a war call of sorts." His body trembled again, and I edged closer in concern. "I can still hear that noise at night when I close my eyes."

He lifted his hands, pressed his palms against his eyes, and took in another shuddering breath. "Most of the crew abandoned ship, launching themselves overboard in hopes of somehow saving themselves. But I couldn't move, I just stood there. And then the next thing I knew, the ship was swallowed by water."

"Gaelon." His name was a gasp, and I reached for him, my hand stroking his jaw tenderly before I turned him to face me, pulling him from his reminiscing.

"I can still see the black nothingness that surrounded me, I can feel the freezing current as it tugged me farther and farther down into the sea's abyss." His dark eyes held mine, and I brushed my thumb across his cheek in comfort. "I have no idea how I survived or who pulled me to land. When I was found on the shore, there were no witnesses. I was the only one who survived."

"Oh, Gaelon," I whispered, my voice trembling. "I am so sorry."

I knew what it was to carry the blame for the deaths of others, and watching the Healer now, I could see that this loss sat heavily on his shoulders and my heart ached for him. The hurt of Suideign Shores was still an open wound for both of us, and I worried what this added guilt would do to him.

As if he couldn't sit still under the pressure, he stood swiftly once again and strode to the table before pouring another glass of wine. Avoiding my eyes, Gaelon lifted the silver to his lips and tipped his head back while swallowing noisily. Upon finishing the cup, he tossed it roughly onto the table and turned to me with a haunted look painted across his face.

"I don't know what it was or where it came from, Skylahr. But whatever it was, it meant to destroy anyone in its path. That, I know for certain."

Chapter 5

Gaelon said nothing else as he poured himself another glass, and I watched with unease as he tipped his head back to finish it with one swallow. The Healer had never been a drinker; he never partook in the evening activities with the men of court or guards. He rarely finished a cup of ale, and I had never seen him the least bit drunk in all our days together. But now a pink rose under the skin of his cheeks and a glossy sheen had coated his dark eyes.

"They were good men, Skylahr. They were great men. And they followed my every order, even when they wanted us to return to shore. The captain himself wanted to turn back and I disagreed. I fought him on it, refusing to listen to any of his reasoning." His long fingers reached for the bottle again, and I stood from my seat before grasping his fingers.

"It wasn't your fault, Gaelon. How could you have known something would happen?"

"They had been on those waters for years. Those men had more experience than I could have ever hoped for, and yet I went against their advice. I argued and demanded we continue. If I'm not to blame then tell me, who is?" His eyes burned with anger as he held my stare for a long moment before striding to his bed and sinking onto the edge of it. "I should have listened, Skylahr. Everything in my gut told me to listen, but my pride blinded me. I didn't want to come back to shore empty-handed. I wanted to find the answers the people of the coast had been searching for and be the Chosen they deserve."

"Gaelon," I sighed as I lowered my gaze to the fur rug under our feet. "You are the Healer. You are a hero. You have rebuilt this land and have taken everything in stride—"

"You're wrong. I am not a hero," he interrupted. His voice was tight with emotion, and I inhaled sharply when I noticed a shining tear rolling down his flushed cheek. "You forget that I spent centuries hiding at those shores, evading the Seductress and her Crimsons even though I knew what they had been doing to the halflings. I hid away like a coward and waited until word of *you* reached me. Don't you see? I am nothing more than a coward."

He lifted an arm and wiped clumsily at his face before turning his dazed stare towards me. "I didn't have the courage to do anything until I knew that you were out there. I allowed so many people to suffer because I could not be brave enough to try to stop her. I was not willing to try to do it myself. This time I wanted to do better. I wanted to find the answers, I wanted to help our people. I wanted to be courageous like *you*."

I knew I should have rushed to reassure and comfort him, but there was a part of me buried far beneath my own guilt and grieving that twisted and burned at his words. Gaelon had been immortal for centuries. He had known who and what he was for years, and yet, he waited for others to step up before he did anything to aid the innocent. He was right. He had turned a blind eye to the atrocities happening around him only to bask in the glory that was being given to him now. I knew if I thought about that for too long, the tiny seed of resentment hidden deep inside of me would grow into something far darker than I ever wanted it to.

Ignoring the sudden sharp chill that echoed through my body, I pressed my palm against Gaelon's shoulder, coaxing him to lie down.

"You need sleep, Gaelon." When he flopped back, I grabbed a corner of the blankets before covering him awkwardly.

"Forgive me for not being better?" he whispered as one of his hands shot out and curled around my wrist, and I blinked down at him for a long pause. "Say you forgive me."

I couldn't, not at this moment. "You don't need my forgiveness, Gaelon."

"I do. I was weak and cowardly, and I don't want you to think of me like you do—" His voice broke off, but the unspoken name still had the power to jab at my heart. Blinking through the sudden dizziness that clouded my brain, I tugged the blankets until they covered Gaelon to his chin.

"Sleep, Healer," I begged while I tried to push away the heaviness that sat on my chest, telling myself that Gaelon may have made a horrible mistake, but he had also been isolated and alone with his fear for years. I was sure it would have been a terrifying life, and now he had to live with the shame of his choices, and I wondered if in all the years he had lived, if he had found anyone to confide in like this.

"I don't need sleep; I'll be fine by morning," he slurred weakly.

"Lucky you, sleep anyway." I gently pried open his hand that was still wrapped around my wrist and moved across the room, gathering the bottles before making my escape. I slipped through the doorway, turned on my heel, and tiptoed down the hall only to be spooked by the deep voice echoing around me.

"Huntress!" Barrick called out, and the bottles I had been cradling tumbled from my arms and crashed across the stone floor.

Turning in annoyance, I glared at the massive man and watched as he approached swiftly. His scarred face looked even more fearsome in the moonlight that shone through the glass windows of the hall, and my eyes traced the deep lines that crossed from brow to jaw. He never told me what had left such a mark, but I could only imagine the pain it caused. My own fingers lifted to trace my cheek carefully before I could stop them, and I averted my eyes when his step faltered at the action.

Dropping my hand, I crossed my arms tightly and moved to meet him. "What is it?"

"Miss Ella has been looking for you. What are you doing wandering the halls at this hour unaccompanied? Need I remind you of what happened just last night?" Although he had a point, I did not feel the need for a guard when I was conscious and aware of my surroundings. But Barrick took his job very seriously, and his posture shifted with relief now that he had found me.

"I'm safe, I was just with Gaelon," I offered, hoping that that explanation would ease whatever worry I had caused him.

"I see that." Barrick's voice was curt, and one of his brows rose in question while he scanned my attire before glancing down the hall to the door I had just exited.

I could feel his unspoken assumption and I scowled at him. "Piss off, Barrick."

"Such a foul mouth on you, Huntress, most people would be absolutely appalled." Rolling my eyes, I turned back to the glass that was scattered across the stone. I loathed the idea of waking anyone to help me clean the sharp shards, especially given what I was wearing, so I moved to gather the larger pieces.

"Leave it, I will clean it." Barrick's voice was quiet but stern, and I glanced over my shoulder at him in question. "I will handle this mess, but if I may speak frankly, you need to watch yourself, Huntress."

"It's fine, I can deal with a bit of glass." Although I found his concern exasperating, I appreciated it, and I lifted my lips in a soft smile before I realized his gaze had narrowed at me.

"I wasn't talking about the wine bottles. I mean you need to watch yourself with that boy." He glowered before shifting his eyes to the closed door once more. If his face hadn't been so stern, I would have laughed at Barrick calling an immortal, who was centuries older than him, a boy.

"You do not need to worry, I'll be okay. My heart is safe from him," I promised, and one of his hands gently pushed against my shoulder until I was on the other side of the hall, away from the mess, and I grinned again in thanks while I waited for him to acknowledge my reassurance. But his eyes never met mine, and instead he crouched down to the floor and began picking up the glass piece by piece before exhaling roughly.

"It is not *your* heart I worry for."

Barrick's warning echoed in my mind the following morning, his words haunting me with every step I took through the halls until I reached the library. But he had been wrong of course, the only thing between the Healer and me these days was distance. And given the previous evening, I wasn't certain that would change.

Pushing the library doors open, I basked in the warm glow filtering through the massive windows before my eyes caught the two bodies curled up on the rug in the middle of the room. Ella was on her side, her legs tucked in tightly with her head resting on Elizabeth's lap, and a pale hand stroked the black curls fondly.

I shut the doors behind me quietly, tiptoed to the rug, and sat beside my childhood friend while I waited for her eyes to turn from the page of her book she was cradling in her free hand and meet mine.

"Been here long?" I whispered before glancing down at the sleeping immortal.

"Ella had a tough night; her nightmares are back, and I don't think the crowded halls and noise helped." I frowned at my friend before lifting an arm and wrapping it around her shoulders. "The most peculiar thing though, we went to check on you and yet, we found your bed empty. Any reason why that might have been?"

Although I had no cause to blush, my face still heated, and I dropped my eyes to the now-discarded book that was tossed onto the floor next to me. "What are you reading?"

"Good try, Sky, answer her question," Ella grumbled from her place on the floor, and one dark eye squinted up at me before she lifted herself from Elizabeth's lap. Even after a mere few hours' sleep, Ella remained perfectly gorgeous, and I rolled my eyes as she fluffed her curls.

"I went to check on Gaelon."

“In the middle of the night?” One of Elizabeth’s brows rose, and I narrowed my eyes at her before picking up the book.

“You were the one who told me to wait until the festival was finished.”

“I meant wait for another day, not sneak through the halls and confront him. What if someone had found you? That gossip would spread like wildfire.”

“Who cares? The members of the court are all stuck-up pricks. Besides, wouldn’t that shut those smug lords up? Imagine their faces when they find out the Healer invited our Huntress into *his* chamber.” Ella laughed before winking at me.

“You two have too much time on your hands if you are this invested in my whereabouts at night. Nothing unbecoming happened between the Healer and me. I just wanted to know what has made him so disengaged from the rest of us, I wanted to hear it from his mouth.”

“And what did you learn?” Any humour disappeared from the room immediately, and I shuffled in closer before motioning for my friends to lean in.

“To be honest, I’m not sure.” My voice was filled with doubt, and I waited with bated breath as my friends looked at each other in question.

“What do you mean?” Ella had crawled closer, and I glanced over my shoulder at the closed doors before continuing.

“I don’t know what to think.” I shrugged helplessly. “Gaelon said there have been issues along the coast. At first it had been assumed that it was a crew of Crimsons, but when they went out onto the waters, they came across some sort of beast. He said it came out of nowhere and capsized the boat. Or at least that might have been what happened. There were no other survivors, and I think his memories of that night are hazy.”

“And he’s sure it wasn’t a whale or maybe they had sailed off course and collided with a sea stack? The western shores are littered with them.”

Ella nodded her head in agreement, but I felt a sharp twinge of guilt pull at my chest.

“I have my doubts as well, but Gaelon has never been one to

embellish anything ever. He's always been rational, and I have never had a reason to doubt him before. He swears it was a creature of some sort, nothing like he had ever seen."

A pounding on the wooden doors echoed around us, and the noisy interruption had my heart leaping from my chest as both Elizabeth and I jumped at the sound.

"Dear Gods!" I cursed while pressing a hand to my chest. "Ella, what is the point of that immortal hearing of yours if you aren't going to warn us when we are about to have a visitor?" I glared at her as Elizabeth caught her breath and then unfolded myself from my place and strode to the door. But just as my hand reached for the metal knob, the wood swung open and a mass of dark gold and black came barrelling through until it crashed into the two women on the floor.

"Next time you go hiding away in the library take your damn beast with ya!" Barrick's deep voice was a growl of frustration that was just loud enough to hear over the squeals of laughter that carried across the room.

"What did he do now?" I asked. Reif circled my friends with excitement as his massive tail collided with anything in its path, sending the books and trinkets that sat on the nearby table scattering across the floor.

"He snuck into the kitchens again, stole an entire roast before they caught him, and then pissed all over my damn boots!" I lifted a hand to hide my smile before patting my guard on the back.

"I'll have the boots replaced." My assurance did little to calm the enormous man, and I grinned as he narrowed his eyes at the failinis.

"What are you doing hiding in here so early in the morning, and what is the reason for all the whispering I interrupted?" Grabbing on to his armoured arm, I pulled him into the room hastily before peering down the hallway. Certain he had come alone, I slammed the doors shut once more.

My guard was not immortal, but he seemed to have a vast amount of knowledge of the land. Surely if there was any truth to Gaelon's version of events, Barrick may know something.

"Barrick, what do you know about sea monsters?" His dark eyes searched my face for a long moment before he stroked his beard.

"Sea monsters? What kind of sea monsters?"

"Is there more than one kind?" My voice was coloured with surprise, and he pressed his lips together firmly before giving me a pointed look.

"I suppose it depends on what you would classify as a monster. There are tales of the sea-maidens in the east of course, and whales and sea serpents that are of unimaginable size." He paused while his dark eyes scanned my own. "But I get the feeling those are not what you are asking about."

"What about a monster that is the size of a mountain? One that would appear out of nowhere just to attack a ship?" I had expected the stern-faced guard to laugh at my question before his teasing started, but when he remained silent, my gaze lingered, and I was shocked to see fear brewing in his dark irises.

"Why are you asking about something like that, Huntress?"

"So it's possible then?" Barrick glanced over my shoulder, and I too turned towards the now-silent couple, my eyes catching Elizabeth's as she lifted her brows in question.

"Legend has it a creature like that can only be summoned with magic as old as the Gods themselves."

Chapter 6

My heart thundered in my chest as the air around us grew tense. But just as I was about to continue my line of questioning, a frantic voice called from the hall, and I turned to the doors as the young soldier plowed through them. Moving from my side, Barrick approached the man, his shoulders tight and expression fierce as he closed the distance.

"What is it?" Barrick demanded, and the man's brown eyes darted to me before he ducked his chin.

"We found something, sir." The words were weak, and he stumbled over them nervously as he glanced at me once more.

"Found what?" Barrick's tone hardened, his patience growing thin, and I winced as the young man grew more flustered.

"A dagger, sir." The man lifted his chin and took in a shaky breath.

Ella and Elizabeth stood from their place, both moving to my side, but I strode to Barrick's side and tipped my head in question. "Where did you find it?"

His brown eyes flickered from me back to Barrick, and then he cleared his throat before bending in a bow. "On the south side of the lake, my lady."

"And what is so concerning about this particular item?" A quiet voice sounded from the door, and my heart stuttered beneath my ribs as Gaelon's questioning dark eyes sought mine.

Everything had happened so quickly since his return; I hadn't even thought to inform him of my attack two nights ago and I glanced at my guard before answering, "It's nothing, truly."

But he didn't believe my lie for a second, and instead raised a single brow at Barrick.

"There was an incident the night before your return. Our Huntress was attacked by an intruder who was armed and cloaked." Clenching my jaw, I narrowed my eyes at my guard for his betrayal, ignoring the swift inhale that came from the Healer.

"And you didn't think to tell me this earlier?" Gaelon's tone was gentle, and my shoulders sagged at the sound. Wiping at my face, I gathered my courage and turned to the Healer, ready to face the look of disappointment I was sure to be met with.

"When was there time?" I knew it was a pitiful excuse, and yet I still bristled when he rolled his eyes and scoffed. "Gaelon, when should I have told you? You avoided all of us for the entirety of the morning yesterday and then last night—"

But Gaelon lifted a hand, silencing me, and I glanced over my shoulder at the others before clearing my throat and lowering my voice. "There wasn't anything I thought you needed to know. I'm fine, there was nothing to tell."

"Someone attacked you," he protested.

Flushing under his watchful gaze, I dropped my eyes and nodded my head. "Yes, but I'm fine, and we doubled the guards outside my room once my door was repaired."

"*Your room?*" It was a rough whisper, the words barely audible, and he glared at Barrick. "They were in her *room*?!"

"Yes, Your Grace." Barrick's chin had dropped, his eyes lowered as he readied himself for the Healer's frustration, but it never came. Instead Gaelon took in a deep breath and lifted a hand to cup my shoulder. Glancing at his handsome face, I offered a small smile in reassurance.

"I wish you would have told me sooner, but you are right, I didn't allow you the opportunity. I am sorry for that." His dark eyes held my own for a pause and then moved to my guard. "I would like you to show me where you found these things, and then I would appreciate it if you could relay exactly what happened that night."

"Of course, Healer, we will be in the hall." Barrick dismissed the soldier and moved to the entrance, patting my back gently as he passed. The door shut behind the men with a soft click, and I glanced at my friends for a heartbeat before focusing on Gaelon once more.

"Are you truly alright?" Rolling my eyes at his concern, I huffed impatiently.

"I am shocked by your lack of faith in me. Of course I'm alright." Tilting my head to the side, I studied his tired, pale face closely. "Are *you*?"

His smile was weak, sad even, and my chest tightened painfully at the expression. "As I've said, I'm happy to be home."

"And what about what we discussed last night?" Gaelon's attention flickered to Ella and Elizabeth before moving back to my face.

"That is not my concern at this moment." My mouth opened, my argument ready to roll off my tongue, but he lifted a hand once more and shook his head. "Skylahr, there is nothing more to it so there is nothing to be done."

His eyes held nothing but sincerity, and I swallowed roughly as he lowered his voice. "For now, let me worry about you."

Without another word, the Healer excused himself, and as I watched him leave once again, I wondered why I was always the one to be left behind.

"Was I imagining things, or did Barrick seem worried when you asked him about what Gaelon had seen?" Elizabeth chewed at her lower lip as she curled her hands around her delicate teacup, her brows pulling together in concern. I wished I had some words of comfort, something I could offer to ease her worry, but my own mind was spinning.

The men had been gone since midmorning, their whereabouts unknown, though my lady's maids had informed me that they had seen them mounting their horses before heading off into the forest. Moving my chin to my shoulder, I glanced at the thick cover of green that surrounded the yards before swallowing the lukewarm tea in my cup.

"Are *you* worried?" Ella whispered as she sank into the chair next to Elizabeth, her dark eyes searching as she studied me.

"I'm always worried." I shrugged, dropping my eyes to the delicate pattern embroidered across the tablecloth. "I never seem to *stop* worrying."

"Maybe we should have opted for wine rather than tea." Ella snorted, and a grin pulled at my lips as she shoved one of the pastries into her mouth. "Get enough wine into you and your worries will disappear."

"I'm not sure that's how it works, El." Elizabeth swatted at the immortal's shoulder, only for the dark-skinned beauty to catch her fingers and then lift them to her lips with a gentle kiss. For a long while I felt envious of my two friends, envious of the affection they had for each other. But now as I watched them lock eyes, I knew that I was lucky just to witness such love.

"Is there any tea left?" I jolted at the sound of Gaelon's voice, my knees hitting the table from below.

I glanced at him from over my shoulder as he lifted a sleeve to wipe at his brow, and then he folded himself into the chair next to my own. His mouth was drawn tight with a frown, his entire face sullen, and I looked at my friends. Both women were also watching the Healer with interest, and the air around the table grew tense as we waited for him to say something, anything.

"Is there any milk?" Gaelon's dark eyes roamed across the table, and I shot Ella a bewildered look before grabbing the hand that had reached for the tin of sugar.

"Gaelon." My voice was sharp in warning, and he pulled his fingers from my own before settling against his chair.

"There was nothing else of interest at the lake, no indication that the assailant had waited around. Whoever it was has long since fled and won't be returning, at least not if they want to keep their life." Lifting the tea, he took in a long sip, though his eyes flickered to my own, and I slumped in my seat as I waited impatiently for him to finish.

"That is not what I wanted to discuss," I grumbled. "Can we talk about what happened on the coast now that you are sober and clear-headed?"

"Sky," he began, but I shook my head, adamant that he would not change the subject this time.

"Gaelon, we are meant to do this together, and we are your friends, talk to us."

The Healer exhaled heavily, and then he nodded while leaning towards the table. Ella and Elizabeth also inched closer, closing the distance between us, and then we waited. Gaelon shifted uneasily in his chair, casting a glance around the yards before lowering his voice.

"My concern is that we don't know what it was, and therefore I'm not sure what can be done. The people of the coast were growing more worried after each wreck or missing ship, and rightfully so. However, I have no answers for them."

"But what do you think it was?" Ella asked, her eyes swiftly moving from the Healer to me and then back again.

Gaelon's face lowered, his gaze dropping as he paused in thought, trying to put what he saw into words without the courage the wine had given him last night. His jaw clenched and his hands fisted on the tabletop before he cleared his throat.

"There are always legends, things from the old world, tall tales and myths. I have heard my share of them at the shores and through the years, of course, but to actually see something—" He stopped, his eyes moving across the manicured lawn of the grounds, searching the treeline, and I moved to pat his back gently in comfort.

"Barrick said that a creature like that could have been summoned?" I offered, my voice quiet and questioning. "If that's true, who would be able to do that? Who would know how to?"

The Healer just shook his head, and I moved my attention to my friends. Elizabeth looked panicked, her face drawn and skin white, while Ella's dark eyes locked on the Healer, her expression serious as she studied Gaelon closely.

"Well, we certainly can't just shrug our shoulders and do nothing." Her voice was stern and then she turned to me.

"Ella is right," I agreed. "If what you saw was real and is responsible for the destruction on the western waters, then we have to do something."

Ella nodded. "Perhaps we can start here, the library is full of scriptures. We can go over every book in that Godsdamn room until we find something useful."

"And if we don't? What do we do if none of these books holds the answers we are looking for?" Elizabeth whispered doubtfully, and I moved my eyes across the group before straightening my spine and clearing my throat.

"Then we find someone who does."

Chapter 7

Ella sat cross-legged on the floor with a dozen piles of books surrounding her while Elizabeth stood on the ladder that rested on the shelves in the far corner, her fingers tracing the spines until she found one of interest. Neither of them acknowledged my presence until the mass of golden fur uncurled himself and bounded over. I smiled at the enormous beast fondly and stroked his ears.

"Have you been watching over them while I was gone?" I whispered to Reif before kissing his head gently.

"More like stealing our food and snoring the day away. To think some of the staff are still terrified of this pitiful furball." Ella laughed without lifting her eyes from the page she was scanning.

"Find anything?" I asked, throwing myself onto the floor next to her. The books all looked the same with their leather covers and worn edges, and I picked up the closest one before flipping through the pages. It was in the tongue of old but the pictures were easily recognizable. Portraits of the Gods and ancient creatures littered the pages, each picture more terrifying than the last, but nothing that matched Gaelon's description could be found.

"What do they say?" I whispered to Ella, tossing the chilling illustrations away from me.

"They're mostly filled with the tales I already know. There are also the stories of the Gods of old, but mostly they all centre around your

Goddess, which isn't a surprise considering where we are." Frowning, I plucked the book from her hands and lifted it, studying the strange, faded words. "That one is the only one with information on the ancient beasts of the north, but there is nothing about a great creature from the seas. However, there is a word I can't quite understand, and it's not something I have heard before, but it is repeated a few times. I think it means *initial* or *earliest*."

My frown deepened, and I handed her the book back carefully. "And what about the western shores? Is there any hint of what could be happening there?"

"No." Ella sighed with a shake of her head. "If it was anyone other than Gaelon who had seen it, I would think they were just spouting sailors' tales."

"I can't find anything either," Elizabeth called from the ladder before returning the book in her hands, and I glanced around the scattered pages desperately for some sort of clue.

"There must be something here," I growled in frustration, moving my hands across the books as if I could conjure the answers with my touch, but they all looked alike, and I grabbed one from another pile.

"I've checked those already," Ella sighed tiredly before flopping onto her back with a huff. "Every book in this room just repeats the same stories over and over. One doesn't have much that really differs from the next."

"What about the new ones? The books not in the tongue of old?" I asked Elizabeth as she crumpled onto the rug next to the immortal, yawning. She shook her head.

"Nothing unusual?" I questioned again as my brows furrowed. "There have to be hundreds of scriptures in here and they all say the same thing?"

"That's the problem with scriptures, Sky." Ella rolled to her side, her dark eyes peering up at me. "They just find prettier ways of retelling the same story."

"Well, maybe this is all for nothing. Maybe it wasn't a creature and Gaelon was mistaken," I whispered, ignoring how my gut churned at the words, as if my body knew that was a lie.

"I am due in the throne room any minute now, but I will come find you after?" Pulling myself from the floor, I wiped my hands across my thighs nervously and then moved to the door.

"Sky?" Elizabeth called softly. "We will keep looking, just to be sure."

With a nod in thanks, I grabbed for the door, my damp palms sliding across the cool metal handle clumsily, and I swore under my breath before trying again. When I had a good grasp, I heaved the door open, ignoring the sudden unease that had flooded my veins before fleeing from the room.

"It's good to have you back, Your Grace," Lord Markees called from his seat as Gaelon entered the room, and I sank lower into my throne while the Healer waved him off with a frown. The men of the court were far more warm and welcoming than normal, and I rolled my eyes as the rest of the assembly cheered in agreement. Gaelon also seemed irritated by the attention, and his eyes narrowed at the group before he folded himself into his place next to mine.

"They very much adore you," I whispered casually while eyeing the crowd.

"I think *adore* is too strong of a word," Gaelon argued back, his mouth lifting in a soft smile before he leaned against the tall back of his chair.

"Well, they certainly prefer you." I should have been grateful to have him back by my side for this meeting; it would alleviate the pressure I had been put under during his absence, and yet there was a bitterness that sank into my bones.

It came so easily to Gaelon. No one questioned him, berated him, judged him—he was their Chosen, and I watched as he began to address the court. His audience was completely enamored by what he had to say, and I knew none of these men would ever show me an ounce of that same respect.

"Our trades with the southern cities have nearly become nonexistent at this point. The vessels have been few and far between. The last shipment of goods was nearly two months ago, and our correspondences have gone unanswered this past fortnight while you've been away." Markees stood from his seat, and Gaelon's brows furrowed as he turned to me.

"It's the first I'm hearing of this," I whispered before narrowing my eyes at the members of the court in accusation.

Shifting uncomfortably under my glare, the lord glanced at his friends behind him before clearing his throat nervously. "I thought it would be best not to worry you, Huntress. You seemed so *overwhelmed* as it was."

My teeth clenched, and I inhaled swiftly at the blatant criticism that he attempted to disguise with care. "Thank you so very much for your concern, Markees."

My voice trembled, and I blinked through the tears of frustration that had gathered before turning to Gaelon. But the Healer was focused on the lords, and I nearly flinched from the anger that was painted across his face.

"Has your Huntress not met your expectations?" The words were cold with fury, and I watched as Gaelon stood, his movements fluid and graceful, the likes of a predator.

Stalking forward, he herded Markees away and waited until the man slowly slid back into his chair before casting a long glance at the others. "Have we all been so bold as to second-guess the Huntress's Chosen? Have we forgotten her sacrifices, her blood right, and our place? Is that it, Lord Markees?"

The room was silent, and I moved my attention to my left, casting a glance at Barrick in concern. But my guard paid me no mind, and he lifted his lips in a smug grin, obviously rejoicing in the Healer's disdain for the members of the court.

"I've heard that there are similar concerns from you, Lord Samius." Gaelon had turned, and all eyes drifted to the handsome lord who had seated himself farthest away from me. I held my breath as Samius's mouth dropped open.

"I—" But Gaelon had no patience for his stammering and lifted one hand, motioning the lord to stand.

"I heard you at Bloomingdae, and rumour has it that it was not the first time you felt so inclined to insult our Huntress. My guards tell me you have had quite a lot to say in my absence these past few weeks."

Anxiety curled in my belly as the Healer approached the lord, his steps even and quiet. I had never seen Gaelon this way. Angry, yes, but not emotionless and calculated. I longed to get between the two men, to keep the Healer from escalating the situation, but my body was unwilling to move, leaving me stuck in my place.

"Your Grace, things have been concerning." Samius looked around the room wildly, waiting for one of his peers to leap to his defence, but no one spoke. "And then there was the attack in *her* room of all places! In all my days, no one has been able to breach Noordeign's walls! That is until now, when she was left here alone. Surely that shows you just how little power she holds over the people!"

"And what would *you* know about the attack on me?" The words had poured out of my mouth before I could stop them, and then I lifted myself from my chair. Realizing his blunder, the lord looked from me to the Healer before glancing over his shoulder at Markees, and I moved towards the men.

"What do *you* know?" I asked again, narrowing my eyes at the man.

"The whispers were hard to ignore!" Samius's gaze was wide as he peered up at me, and he glanced at his friend once more before he lowered his head. "We had been told by a guard that there had been an attack, and surely you see our concern, my lady—"

"*Your Grace*," Gaelon hissed, his voice low and dangerous. "You address her as Your Grace. She is not your lady, she is a Chosen, and you are not familiar enough to address her as anything but."

The lord hastily nodded, stepping away from us before lowering his chin. But the Healer had not finished, and he tipped his head as he regarded the man with cool eyes.

"You are an immortal of the Healer, and one may say we might as well be kin." I glanced at Gaelon in question, but he ignored me. "There are not many of us; we are more uncommon than the immortals of the Huntress, which is why I believe you have held your position of power for so long."

Gaelon paused, his eyes drifting to my face for a quick moment before he continued. "And just like me, you sat by and did nothing to aid those around you. You watched suffering in comfort for *years*."

Samius looked sick, as if he was ready to fall over at any moment, and I stood there, stunned, and not at all anticipating Gaelon's next words.

"And yet, you have been offered a second chance to remain here in Noordeign. You should be grateful, but instead, you have spent your time undermining the very person you should be worshipping."

Heat filled my face at his implication, and I shifted under the questioning glowers of the court. They watched me carefully only to direct their attention back to their Chosen as his voice echoed around us once more.

"So, in light of your constant insolence, I hereby strip you of your titles and lands, Lord Samius. Leave this place, collect your things from your estate, and go to the shores, go to Wahstand. Be anywhere but here."

No one moved, no one spoke, and my eyes widened as Gaelon's order finally registered in my mind. The members of the court also seemed to be at a loss for words as their jaws slackened in the silence.

"Your Grace…" But Gaelon paid him no mind and spun on his heel, turning to face me once again before moving to his throne. As he passed, my fingers stretched, grasping at the sleeve of his tunic before I gave it a gentle tug, urging him closer.

"Gaelon," I whispered in warning, or maybe it was a plea, I couldn't be sure. But I knew that this decision would have consequences. And those consequences wouldn't impact Gaelon, they would be directed at me. These men would blame me for this ruling, and it would only add to their dislike for their Huntress's disappointing Chosen. "Don't you think this may be too harsh?"

But the Healer paid me no mind and pulled his arm from my

touch before sinking back into his throne as he waved his hand in dismissal. "Barrick, you can escort Samius out."

My guard folded himself into a graceful bow, though his dark eyes held my own, and I swallowed down my concern before dipping my head. Arguing now would do us no favours. I needed to show my support of the Healer, and I had just openly questioned him in front of the court, which would no doubt spread like wildfire as it was. Bending my unsteady legs, I rested on the edge of my seat, my hands clasped tightly in my lap while I watched my guard follow the shaken lord to the door.

But just as Barrick's massive hand reached for the brass handle, Samius turned to us. "I truly hope you both know what you are doing. Say what you will about the Crimson army and their Seductress, but they were powerful and they brought an order to Elrin that you will continue to struggle to maintain."

"Powerful they may have been but invincible they were not," Gaelon snapped. "We have saved thousands and we will rebuild Elrin to its former glory. It will be how it was before that wretched Goddess came to this land and betrayed the world."

"Perhaps you are right, Healer, maybe no one is unbeatable, not even the two of *you*." Samius's face was no longer white with shock, and a grin pulled at his lips. The expression forced a trickle of fear down my spine. "So, with one last act as a lord of the north, let me warn you: the stories from the western coast aren't ones to be ignored. You both should be prepared for what and *who* is to come."

Chapter 8

All eyes had turned to Gaelon in question, but I focused on Samius. He was smug, revelling in the Healer's shock, and his grin grew under the quiet of the room. Solely fixated on the lord, I had missed the silent order given to Barrick and was stunned when he dragged a dagger from his belt before pressing it carefully into Samius's side in warning. Understanding just how poorly this meeting had turned for him, the lord made no attempt to struggle in my guard's hold. Barrick ushered his captive to the hall while I remained frozen in place, unmoving until the sound of the heavy wood of the door slamming shut startled me from my daze and I hurried to the Healer's side.

"Gaelon," I whispered anxiously while doing my best to ignore the hardening stares of the other members of the court. But he disregarded my concern, and I swallowed at the painful churn of my stomach before exiting the room in pursuit of my guard and his men. Hoping I could deescalate this quietly, away from the other lords of the north, I scoured the halls, searching for Barrick's tall form, but when I had no luck, I turned back to where I had left the Healer.

"Gaelon!" I called when I spotted him outside the now-empty throne room, his head ducked as he conversed quietly with a group of guards. Ushering the men away, he glanced at me with a frown, and I nearly stopped in my path at his expression.

"Ella and Elizabeth are waiting for you on the terrace with tea."

His voice was soft and placating, but I narrowed my eyes at the obvious dismissal.

"And where are Barrick and Samius?" Gaelon's attention roamed the space around us, his gaze never meeting my own as he searched for an escape from my question. But his sudden unease made me suspicious, and I closed the distance between us, lifting my chin as I peered down at his handsome face. "*Where are they?*"

The Healer sighed, his shoulders sagging in defeat, and he lowered his voice to a whisper. "Barrick and his second-in-command escorted Lord Samius to the same place we would take any other prisoner of the north."

My brows rose in surprise. "Prisoner? Is that what he is now?"

"You heard his threats, Skylahr." Scowling, I shook my head.

"What I heard were words from an immortal who had just had his titles stripped over a minor incident, something I think you were wrong for doing."

Pinching the bridge of his nose, Gaelon exhaled in frustration. "You don't see it for what it was, so of course you don't understand the necessity of why I did what I did."

Crossing my arms over my chest, I inhaled deeply before pressing the Healer once more. "Where are they?"

"Barrick took him to the dungeons." His hand slid from his face, and he assessed me with careful dark eyes.

"Dungeons? We have no dungeons here," I argued. Gaelon peered at me steadily and then his shoulders slumped with a rough exhale. "Gaelon?"

"They are in the south side of the estate, away from the manor," he offered softly, and my heart began to pound in my chest.

"What will they do to him? What orders did you give?" The Healer's eyes hardened with a pointed look and that beating beneath my ribs quickened in pace.

"Skylahr," he whispered as he lifted his hand to cup my shoulder in what he must have thought was comfort.

"What will they *do*, Gaelon?"

His dark eyes lowered to the floor as his jaw clenched, and then he finally told me.

"They will get the answers we need, any way possible."

My pounding footsteps echoed around me as I ran across the estate, searching for any sign of the guards and their captive, but they were nowhere to be seen. Moving my attention under the blinding sun, I growled in frustration and lifted a hand to shield my eyes from the light while I searched the grounds for the dungeons I had no idea existed until now.

Scanning across the lake that sat along the south wall of the manor, I narrowed my eyes at the dense forest and waited. I couldn't see anyone, but the water carried the quiet chatter of a few men, and I bounded around the lake's edge until I reached the treeline. I ducked into the shadows of the massive cedars and waited while I listened. The men were standing off to the side of a building I had never noticed before. Their helmets had been removed, and they leaned against the moss-covered stone wall as they talked.

"How much longer until he breaks, do you think?"

"Who knows? He's a smug bastard that one, and Barrick is not nearly as inclined to use the type of torture it would take to make this go faster."

"I'd be taking fingers off by now if it was me. Samius knows Barrick is too soft to stomach the real ghastly stuff."

Peering through the branches, I paled as the two men chuckled under their breath at the idea of such cruelty, and I gathered my courage before moving from my hiding spot.

"And just where is Barrick?" The two men unsheathed their weapons at my voice only to drop them immediately when they realized who had spooked them. Narrowing my eyes, I waited for the pair to fall to their knees, heads bowed, before asking once more. "Where is your captain?"

"In there, Huntress." The younger of the two pointed to the worn-down stone building, and I motioned for them to stand.

"You would do well to be more aware of your surroundings. You may think Barrick is merciful, but I doubt he'd let your failure at keeping watch go unpunished." With one last glare at the pair, I moved around the corner of the small structure and ducked through the entranceway.

I had expected cells of some sort, or chains attached to the stone structure, but instead I found a dark, narrow stairwell, and I shivered when the light from the outside vanished as the door shut behind me. The air was cool and wet, and I ran my hands along the uneven walls, searching for something to hold on to while I slowly descended down the steps.

I had nearly made it to the bottom when I heard the groans of pain, and then Barrick's harsh voice as he demanded information from Samius. Keeping myself hidden behind the corner, I held my breath as I waited.

"I don't know anything else"—Samius coughed—"I didn't ask any more questions."

"And what of the attack on our Huntress?" Barrick snapped, and I peeked around the corner. The room was dimly lit with two torches on opposite sides of the space, and I watched as my guard paced back and forth in front of the man who sat sprawled across the chair, his arms bound to the wood at his sides.

"What about it?" Samius laughed wetly, his mouth bloody as he grinned up at my guard.

"Who was it?" Barrick demanded, turning on his heel before towering over his hostage. "What did they want?"

"Well, I think the last part is obvious, Barrick. They wanted her dead." Samius's laugh was interrupted by my guard when he slammed his fist into the lord's jaw, and I winced as the spatter of blood hit the ground.

Recovering from the blow, Samius's head lolled, and then he groaned before squinting up at his captor once more. "I have no idea who it was, I just heard the whispers like everyone else in this Godsforsaken place. You really should try to do a better job of keeping your men's mouths shut. That, or get rid of the maids. None of them can help themselves from spreading the Chosen's precious secrets."

"I would think the lot of you would have more respect for them. Your prayers have been answered, you've been given your Chosen."

Samius scoffed as he rolled his eyes. "Whose prayers were those? I was doing just fine for myself before the battle at the shores. I had spent centuries living the life I have wanted."

The lord peered up at my guard through one squinted eye before lifting his lips in a blood-soaked smile. "And let me be honest, Barrick. The Healer, haughty as he may be, is fine. He's a decent leader, he has the knowledge needed to rule, and he is what I expected of a Chosen. But that girl—"

Barrick grabbed the front of Samius's bloody tunic, pulling it as he bent over the man, his body rigid with fury. "Choose your next words very, *very* carefully."

"Oh, come now, surely you're not blind to what we all see? She is not what we wanted; she is not her Goddess. You can put her in the finest gowns, you can try to teach her everything she should know, and she still will never be a true lady of the north, let alone the Huntress we desired. And if it weren't for the Healer's odd interest in her, he would see it too."

Barrick's fist lifted, ready to strike again when I finally stepped around the corner, my voice far more confident than I felt. "Enough, Barrick."

Lifting his swollen face, Samius peered at me. "I wondered when you would come out from your hiding place. Though I hadn't expected it to be to defend me from your great brute of a guard."

Ignoring him, I moved to Barrick's side, grabbing his wrist before lowering his hand. "I don't think striking him is going to make him any more inclined to share what he knows."

"Are you always so weak, girl?" the battered man asked from his chair. "Surely a little blood and brutality doesn't offend you?"

"She intervenes for your sake, and you are so ungrateful that you spit her kindness back in her face?" Barrick asked, his words low and deadly, and I moved, putting myself between them before my guard could deliver another blow.

Certain Barrick wouldn't push past me, I directed my attention to Samius. "So you have no more information on the attack. Fine. But what do you know of the coast, Lord Samius? What did you tell my guard?" I asked, peering down at him.

"It's not lord anymore, girl. Your Healer made sure of that," he spat.

"What do you know? I won't ask again. Refuse to answer and I'll leave you to Barrick once more." Moving his attention to my guard, Samius grinned for a moment only to reel back as Barrick drew his dagger.

"Easy now, no need for all that." For the first time, I saw fear flicker in the lord's eyes, and I shifted uneasily while he cleared his throat. "I know that there have been gatherings of immortals along the western shores, and word is that many ships are leaving their docks but never seem to return. And there are the other whispers of course."

"Whispers of what?" My eyes shot to Barrick in worry as he moved forward.

"Whispers of what spooked the Healer and sent him running back to the north. Tales of what is out in those waters and what is to come."

"What is to come? What does that mean?" I snapped, growing impatient.

"That is all you'll get from me, girl," Samius growled, lifting his chin in defiance. "My loyalties do not lie with *you*."

"This is your last chance, Samius," Barrick barked. "Tell us everything we want to know, or let the Gods see you home."

"Then let them be waiting with open arms," the lord sneered, and then all at once it happened. Barrick moved around me, one strong hand pressing me back as he used the other to run his blade across the lord's throat. My eyes widened in shock as Samius's own gaze locked on to my face, his mouth gaping open while the life left him, and as he took in his last gurgled breath, I grabbed on to Barrick.

“Barrick!?” My mind was scrambling to form words as I watched my guard while he cleaned his blade carefully.

“It needed to be done.” His voice was clipped, and he grabbed at my arm, pulling me to the stairs without any further explanation.

“You could have let him go!” I glanced over my shoulder to look at the body that had slumped in the chair.

“He was a liability, Huntress. He knew more than what he was letting on, and I’m not entirely convinced that it wasn’t him who orchestrated the attack on you before Bloomingdae.” Pushing me forward, he herded me up the stairs and then pressed me back against the closed door once we reached the top. “Letting him go was never an option, especially after what he announced in court. Surely you see that?”

“But—” Barrick reached past me, his hand grabbing for the door before swinging it open, and then he shoved me through the entrance.

“Escort your Huntress back to the manor and tell the Healer it is done.” He paid me no mind while he barked the order at the two guards, and my jaw tightened in annoyance. Shrugging out of the gentle hands of the guards, I stepped forward.

“Barrick!” I protested, but my guard gave me one last long look, his dark eyes scanning my face before he took a step back into the building, and then the door slammed, and I was left staring at the moss-covered wood in silence.

Chapter 9

My body shook with rage as I stormed through the halls, narrowing my eyes at any poor soul who crossed my path. Seeming to feel the fury that coursed through my veins, the giggling group of maids who were admiring the guards stationed outside the Healer's chambers turned towards me before scurrying away. I set my sights on the pair of armed men who had been preening under the ladies' attention and now struggled to right themselves while blushing hotly at my silent judgement.

"Where is your Healer?" The words crawled their way out of my throat in a low growl, and I could feel the power of my Goddess bubble beneath my skin.

Though it was harnessed, my ignite clawed at the chains that had been so carefully crafted. Those very bonds I had reinforced over and over in hopes of smothering the fire that had once consumed me. After all, it had been said that an emotional woman was a dangerous woman. She could not both feel things and be sound. And whispers of my passionate reactions had often been exaggerated, used against me to win the fight that a man would never make the choices or mistakes that I had.

I had been taught that a rageful man could conquer, but an emotional woman would break.

A madwoman could never lead, so therefore, I must be sane.

And so, I had pushed every ounce of control at my ignite, forcing myself into a state of numbness when I could manage it. Surely feeling nothing was better than feeling their disappointment. But now, in this moment, that control was gone, and I was left with only seething fury, so wild it felt as if it would burst from my skin.

And if that made me mad, then so be it.

"Where is your Healer?" I asked again.

Shuddering away from my piercing gaze, the men tipped their heads to the closed door before backing away a few paces, their eyes downcast as they put more space between us. Their nervousness filled me with a confidence that had been long since lost, and for a split second I wondered if my Goddess had basked in others' fear too. Perhaps that was why seeing these two guards shrink away from me brought an unexplainable warmth to my chest.

I moved to the door and curled my long fingers around the handle, ignoring the way the cold metal bit at my overheated skin, and then I heaved the wood open.

"Barrick, I—" Gaelon's voice was tired as he rubbed at his eyes, but then his face lifted, the skin paling when his dark gaze met my own.

"Skylahr." He sighed my name, as if he was exasperated with me, as if he had a reason to be. But I knew what came next. "Have a seat."

There it was. I was about to be placated, shushed, and coddled as if I were a babe throwing a tantrum and not a woman grown who had legitimate thoughts and beliefs. Ignoring his gesture to the empty chair, I crossed my arms and tipped my chin.

"What were your exact orders, Gaelon?" My voice was foreign even to my own ears, and the Healer's eyes widened in surprise.

"Skylahr." Folding himself onto the edge of the bed, Gaelon ran his long fingers through his dark curls. "I only did what needed to be done."

"He's dead now. Was that your order? Is that what *needed* to be done?"

"Yes," he said simply with a shrug of his shoulders. "Samius posed a risk to not only you, but to the harmony we are trying to build once more. We are at a very delicate time, and that kind of threat is far more dangerous than you think."

"There was no threat. He was just one man," I snapped as I took a step forward. "He was a prick, a gossip even, but he was just one immortal man."

"Samius wasn't just one man though, he has been part of this court for a long time and has a vast list of contacts, some of them being those who are not pleased with our victories and have made that known. But even if he had just been one man, sometimes that's all it takes. It only takes one charismatic, radical man who preys on the fear and doubt of others to overthrow any sense of peace."

"If that's true, then the world is far too fragile," I argued.

"The world isn't fragile, Skylahr, people are." Gaelon's voice had gentled, almost as if he was trying to soothe the burning fury that had been bubbling under my flesh, and I begrudgingly moved to the empty plush chair and sank onto the edge, though I refused to soften my face.

"To be honest, Skylahr, I didn't think you had any fondness for Samius."

Leaning back against the cushion, I frowned at the Healer.

"I don't need to feel fondness for someone in order to not want to see their blood spilled. I thought we had finished with that," I scoffed, my tone filled with unspoken accusations.

"Oh, Skylahr." Gaelon shook his head before pinching the bridge of his nose, and I narrowed my eyes.

"What?"

"I don't think there will ever be a way to rule without *some* bloodshed. You can try to live amicably and pray that those who wish to destroy you will have a change of heart. But that just isn't the way the world works."

"So, I am to be lectured about the world by you as well then? How I don't know the politics or ways of the Chosen? I want to rule with peace and mercy, Gaelon!" I snarled, angry that I was once again being treated as if *I* was the only one who didn't understand.

"I'm not trying to lecture you; I am trying to help you see reason and your own self-righteousness keeps that from happening! You are naive and inexperienced, and it shows!" My eyes widened in shock as the air was squeezed from my lungs. I sat there, unable to move while the Healer blinked at me, seemingly surprised that those words had come from him.

For a heartbeat we sat in silence, and then I could hear whispers sounding from the other side of the door.

"You knock, I'm not doing it." Ella's sweet, melodic voice echoed in the space between us, and we both turned to the entrance as Elizabeth argued.

"You're the immortal."

"What does that have to do with anything?"

Sighing, Gaelon moved to the door all while avoiding any eye contact, and then he carefully opened it and stepped to the side. Both women offered me a sheepish smile before eyeing the Healer carefully.

"We heard you from down the hall," Elizabeth offered awkwardly only to flinch at the sharp nudge to her ribs from Ella's elbow.

Standing from my place, I wiped my hands across my breeches before exhaling roughly. The anger had cooled, and I was left reeling and exhausted, as if Gaelon's words had doused the flames that had been burning within me.

"I was just going to come find you two actually." I shot my friends a weak smile as I struggled to find an escape from the Healer's chambers. "Maybe we could go for a ride or perhaps a visit to the lake?"

Elizabeth's front teeth sank into her lower lip as she glanced at her immortal with concern, and I moved my gaze to the beauty as well. Stepping forward, Ella reached towards the Healer, her dark hand clenched tightly around a piece of parchment. My gut churned, almost as if I was remembering the last time her dark fingers had clutched a piece of paper in such a way.

"Barrick found us just now and asked me to deliver this to you. He seemed to think it may be urgent." Gaelon frowned before carefully snatching the letter from her, and then he tore it open without another word. Holding my breath, I waited all while studying his face as his brow furrowed and his frown deepened.

"What is it?" Rather than answering, Gaelon held out the slip of paper, and I hesitantly plucked it from his steady fingers.

> *Healer,*
>
> *The seas are more unforgiving than ever, and more and more ships continue to disappear beneath the waves.*
>
> *I believe this is just the beginning.*
>
> *I worry for our people, Healer. What will become of us if there is no end to our losses? What will we do?*
>
> *We are in dire need of the Chosen's help.*
>
> *Lord Deavion*

"I had written to him during my journey home in hopes of good news, but it appears that nothing has changed since I have left the coast." Gaelon sighed as he took the parchment back and scanned the words once more.

"Everyone continues to talk about rumours, what is being said?" My words were hushed in a worried whisper, and I watched as Gaelon turned to the unlit fireplace. Taking the parchment between his hands, he tore the letter easily and then used his leather-clad toe to bury the pieces under the cool ashes.

"Apparently the maids believe that we are cursed, carrying the wrath of the fallen Crimson Goddess." Gaelon said softly.

Ella scoffed from the doorway, her eyes narrowed as she scanned the Healer's face.

"What silly, superstitious girls. That wouldn't even make sense, the Seductress had no power over the seas," Ella muttered with a roll of her eyes, but Elizabeth glanced at her immortal nervously before moving her attention to the Healer.

Sensing the human's unease, the Healer offered her a gentle smile. "No, she does not."

"Alright, so what of this creature then? Have there been any other witnesses or any other sightings?" I asked, and Gaelon turned once more to the pit before bracing himself on the mantel. His knuckles tightened over the wood, the skin over the joints white, and then he took in a long, deep inhale.

"None that I know of, but that is why I had Samius questioned. He seemed to know something about it."

"What do you mean?" Crossing the space, I crowded in behind Gaelon.

"There are reports that he had been receiving word from the coast on a consistent basis." Guilt filled me as I realized that I had not been paying close enough attention to the happenings of court to even inquire about any unusual correspondence, and I ducked my head in shame.

"I'm sorry. I had no idea." But the Healer waved away the words with a passing flick of his fingers.

"It's no matter. There is nothing we can do about it now, and he has been dealt with." Spinning on his heel, the Healer faced me, and I gnawed at my lower lip as I shifted under his careful stare.

"So, what is our plan? What should we do next?" Elizabeth asked, and I glanced at her from over my shoulder.

"Well, it seems that we have now been called upon by Lord Deavion, and it is our duty to see to the people of Elrin," Gaelon answered, and I lifted a brow.

"*We?*" I repeated, certain that I had misheard him.

"I think my time travelling alone is finished. I have been arrogant to think I may not need my Huntress's aid."

Elizabeth's eyes slid to my face, but Ella remained unmoved, her expression tight with an emotion I couldn't name, and then she spoke. "Or perhaps you've been a bit *self-righteous?*"

Gaelon held her stare for a long pause, his eyes kind even under the heat of the beauty's gaze, and then he dipped his chin, and a soft laugh broke from his lips. "You truly are a fearsome little thing."

Flicking her curls over her shoulder, Ella wrinkled her nose as she scanned him from head to toe. "And you would do best not to forget it."

"You know you both do not have to come." I sighed as Elizabeth chewed anxiously at her thumbnail.

"What should we bring? What do we wear?" Ella called from across the hall, ignoring both my protests and my friend's obvious nervousness.

"You could stay here, Elizabeth," I promised. "You could stay home."

"Ella is my home," Elizabeth assured me. "And I want to be where she is, where you both are."

I was not entirely convinced but exhaled roughly before offering a small nod of understanding as the immortal called for us once more.

"How many gowns do you two think I should bring? Maybe just the light summer ones?"

"Ella," Elizabeth called with a roll of her eyes. "Perhaps now is not the time to be worried about your clothing choices. Just bring what you need." I smiled fondly at my childhood friend before poking my head into the room where the immortal was stuffing her pack.

"The last time Sky and I travelled, I was forced to wear the same two tunics for weeks. I swear it took a month for me to get the stale smell off my skin. So, excuse me if I prefer to have options." She fastened the leather closed with quick, nimble fingers and then turned to me with an expectant glare.

"Is that all you're taking?" Her eyes landed on the gold sword and dark wool cloak before she raised a brow.

"Gaelon has gathered a group of soldiers and will be readying carts filled with the essentials for us, Ella. I doubt you'll need every tunic you own." Ignoring me, the immortal heaved the massive leather sack over her shoulder before brushing past.

"I suppose we will just have to see who packed accordingly, won't we?" Without another word, she strode down the hall, and Elizabeth lifted a pale hand to pinch the bridge of her nose.

"If she's right and you and I end up needing more clothes, we will never hear the end of it." Linking my arm through her own, I pulled us towards the stables and smiled affectionately at the bouncing black curls in front of us.

"I know."

We continued to follow quietly behind the immortal as she crossed the yards to the stables, and I watched Gaelon's face as Ella threw her pack down to the ground roughly. "Sky already tried to scold me, so don't bother, Healer."

Gaelon pressed his lips together tightly and raised a brow as she grabbed the strap before tossing the leather onto the empty cart. I turned to Elizabeth, grabbed her own pack, and placed it next to Ella's before wrapping my cloak around the gold sword. Strapping it to my hip seemed too gaudy, and I had no need for it at this time. Instead, I checked that my dagger was still fastened to the muscle of my thigh and loaded the rest of my things.

Turning from the cart, I gazed across the green and gold banners that had begun to fill the yard with a frown. We would not be discreet travelling with an entire party of soldiers, and the thought of the prying eyes of the guards always watching me, judging my every move, made my stomach drop. My gaze moved over the men quickly until I caught the eyes of a stranger. He was tall, nearly my height, and handsome, but when his dark eyes filled with amusement and his lips lifted, I felt heat fill my cheeks. In response the man turned to his friends and ducked his head to whisper something to them before a burst of laughter came from the group.

"Pay them no mind, Huntress," Barrick called from his horse before glaring at the guards until they scattered from their circle and busied themselves with their own mounts. "They are well trained and will protect you if the time comes, but they are worse than women when it comes to gossip."

"I take that slight on my sex personally, Barrick," I grumbled with a glare. "I may not be as old as you, but I have learned that men can be worse than women in most ways and are far more tactless about it."

A deep barking laugh came from the man, and a tiny tug lifted the corner of my lips as I watched him catch his breath with a smile. "That I won't argue, Huntress."

"Why are you here, Barrick? Surely this journey south does not require an escort of soldiers and the head guard? Wouldn't you rather spend your time bonding with Reif?" I teased, smiling as his eyes narrowed in annoyance.

"Your blasted beast is curled up on my bed currently and I can't say I will miss him. Besides, where you go, I go, Huntress," Barrick answered, and I growled under my breath as I grabbed the reins of my horse and hoisted myself into the saddle.

"I don't need supervision," I argued while I waited for the others to be settled and ready.

"Maybe not, but I think you need someone who will not only fight on your behalf, but who will fight you when you are making a poor decision. I have not known any of you for long, but I do know that those three are not strong enough to say no to you when they know they should." His chin jutted out towards our companions, and I sat with his words for a long moment.

"Barrick, my decisions are my own. No one is responsible for them or me." His black brows furrowed, and I frowned under his scrutiny, uncomfortable with the intensity of his stare.

"We finally found our Huntress and I refuse to allow her to take unnecessary risks."

"You think you could stop me from doing something I put my mind to?" I asked with a small grin, trying to lighten the mood.

"I don't think, I know, and to be honest, you may be a halfling, but I am not above using whatever tactics it takes to stop you from doing something foolish. I'll sit on you if it comes to it."

Chapter 10

Travelling with the five of us would have made for a quick journey, but the two dozen soldiers slowed our pace significantly. I glanced back behind me before wincing at the banners that blew in the wind. We had stopped to rest after only half a day, and I frowned while the party organized themselves under the setting sun.

"It is most certainly crowded," Ella grumbled beside me as she leaned her head on Elizabeth's shoulder, her dark eyes looking towards the tents the soldiers were currently building. "But at least we will be comfortable."

The massive white shelters would offer a much more restful sleep, but I couldn't help but wish it was just my friends and me sleeping under the stars tonight.

"What are you three gossiping about?" Gaelon sank to the ground beside me and tugged the stick I had been using to poke at the fire out of my hands.

"Just because we are women does not mean we are gossiping, Healer. All you men think the same." Elizabeth rolled her eyes before shuffling closer to Ella for warmth, and I smiled at her snark. Elizabeth was generally the most level-headed out of the three of us, but when exhaustion set in, her patience grew weary, as did her normal cheerful demeanour.

Barrick snorted from his post a few feet away, obviously recalling our previous conversation, and I ducked my chin with a grin while Gaelon's eyes widened at my friend for a moment and then he focused on the fire. Things became quiet again while the soldiers organized themselves for watch, and I scanned across the campsite, taking in the row of tents.

"You have admirers," Ella whispered lowly, and I glanced across to a circle of men who were watching us with interest. "A few are rather handsome."

My nose scrunched at her assessment, and I averted my eyes when the same man from before caught my gaze again. "He seems interested."

"Doubt it," I answered while ignoring the sharp nudge of her elbow in my ribs.

"I am sure he is. Why not enjoy yourself on the road?" I felt all eyes turn to me, and I exhaled noisily before glaring at Ella, a silent warning for her to quit talking. "I'm just saying, by the looks of it, he wants you."

"Leave the poor girl alone." Elizabeth tsked, her tone motherly as she swatted at the immortal, and I smiled at her in thanks. Responding in kind, Elizabeth curled her hand around Ella's wrist and tugged. "Come now, we might as well get some rest."

A sly smile pulled at the immortal's lips, and she tossed a wink at me saucily before lowering her voice. "Oh *rest*, is that what we are calling it now, my sweeting?"

Blushing, Elizabeth ducked her head and stomped away, ignoring Ella's husky laughter as she chased after her. The two disappeared behind the white material that flapped in the evening breeze, and I sank back, stretching my legs out in front of me while I braced myself on my palms.

"They are quite the pair, aren't they?" Gaelon whispered from a few feet away, and I glanced at him from the corner of my eye cautiously. Things had been awkward between us since our disagreement in his chambers, but thankfully, with the added bodies, we had been able to occupy ourselves, and I felt no need to approach him. Now, however, we were left alone with only my guard, who still sat a few yards away, and the air was heavy with tension.

Gaelon and I got along naturally, or so it had seemed. But something loomed in the back of my mind. The only word for it would be *resentment*, though I hated to label it as such. We were allies, the Chosen of the Gods, bonded in a way no one else would understand. And if I didn't have him, what would I be left with?

I didn't want to be alone. Not again. The darkness of isolation was daunting, fearsome, and cold, and I had spent my fair share of time there. I wasn't ready to face it again.

So, I swallowed the words I longed to say, and pushed that nagging feeling back into its cell in the far corner of my mind. I could forget my bitterness, my anger at him, and the things I felt like he had done or not done. I could fight my *self-righteousness* if it meant I had my friend.

"Skylahr," his voice called, breaking me from my thoughts, and I blinked up at him in surprise. "Are you alright?"

Lifting the corner of my mouth, I hummed under my breath and nodded, though I could tell he wasn't sure if I was being honest. With more grace than was natural, the Healer shuffled from his place, sliding until he was next to me, and then he leaned over, bumping his shoulder against mine.

"I'm sorry for how I spoke to you earlier. I was out of line," he murmured, his tone gentle. The warmth of his words wrapped around the frost, thawing that fear I had been running from.

"You were right to be upset with me though, I don't know enough and that has made me careless." The admission was far easier to voice than I had thought, and I took in a deep breath in relief as the weight lifted from my shoulders.

"You may not know enough, but our expectations of you have been unfair. You're just a girl." Bristling at the word, I clenched my jaw and turned just as the Healer lifted his hands in surrender. "I'm sorry, a woman. I just mean that you are young and haven't had long enough to learn the things you need to. I have not done my duty by you, and for that I must ask forgiveness."

"There is no forgiveness needed. I can't imagine living in Noordeign as the Healer's Chosen is as easy as existing in your little cottage at the shores," I admitted. The Healer chuckled under his breath while nudging me again and then flopped back, sprawling across the cool grass as he stared up at the darkening sky.

"This is not the existence I ever pictured for myself, that is for certain." I peered down at him as he searched the dimly lit stars in wonder, and then he lifted his arm, pointing one long finger at the space above. "It looks like the Gods will be putting on a show for us tonight."

Falling back, I lay beside him and watched as more tiny glimmering lights appeared before us. "Do you think the Gods are truly watching us? The Huntress and Protector, I mean. They are the fallen Gods after all, and yet we worship them. Do you think it's possible that they are still here somehow?"

He didn't say anything for a long moment, and I felt foolish for even speaking the words. But then just as I was about to try to change the subject, he grabbed my fingers and gave them a long squeeze.

"Power that immense could not just simply disappear. I think that they are out there, somewhere, or maybe they are scattered, bits of them covering the earth the same way the sky is covered in stars. Either way, I know that our righteous Gods are watching over us. They see the good that we have done, and they are proud. She is proud, proud of you, Skylahr."

"And the Healer? What of him?" I asked while my eyes moved from one star to another and then to the Healer's face.

"I have yet to determine what his end was. Perhaps he is out there somewhere hiding away."

"Are there no scriptures or prophecies of him?" Gaelon shook his head, his brows furrowing though he never moved his eyes from the sky above.

"I must say he is awfully inconspicuous for a God; I have only ever been able to locate one true scripture of his. It was crafted by Synrick the Worthy well before the War of the Gods. Though if I am being honest, it held very little interest to me at the time of its discovery. It was mostly focused on the Forefolk and their beginnings and did not hold nearly enough tales of Elrin's *interesting* history."

"The Forefolk? Who are they?" I asked.

"The first men our Gods created from the earth of Vinmare. Are you not familiar with that story?" Gaelon asked, finally turning from the stars to stare at my face.

"No, I've never heard the tale of our supposed origin before." I shrugged while my face flushed in embarrassment when I realized my knowledge was far more lacking than I had thought.

"I suppose I cannot fault you for that," Gaelon admitted. "It has since been overshadowed by the songs of mighty warriors and the ballads of the war. Though it was said that long ago, during the large feasts of Bloomingdae, the poets and troubadours would command the room with their magical versions and re-enactments of the event as they celebrated the Huntress and our creation."

"We never had such entertainment during our celebrations in Noorde Point. I had always assumed Bloomingdae had been in celebration for the first day of spring," I murmured quietly with a frown.

Gaelon's lips lifted into a soft smile. "No, the mortal villages wouldn't, I suppose. None of you would have been around long enough to know the stories, and the immortals would not be the ones to share such traditions with those they see being below them. But I'm certain you can now see why the lords of Noordeign were so alarmed by what they thought was a lack of celebration. It is the day of the Forefolk's first bloom—or so they say."

"What of the other stories? What else do the immortals say happened long ago?" I wondered, my interest now piqued.

"I'm not sure I have enough time or the knowledge to recite all of Elrin's history tonight, dear Skylahr."

Rolling my eyes, I turned onto my side and then tucked my arm under my head. "Then just tell me the important bits, the things I should really know."

Copying me, Gaelon rolled to his side and then lifted a brow.

"I'm not sure how to decide which *bits* are important," he laughed softly. "But I'll try."

Shuffling forward, I tucked my knees in close to my body, ignoring the way my breeches rubbed against Gaelon's thighs, and then moved both of my hands under my scarred cheek.

"In the beginning there were the three Gods of old, otherwise known as the Divine Triad, which consisted of the Huntress, the Healer, and the Protector. They forged the lands and the sea, the beasts and the birds, before gathering to create the Forefolk. It is said they each used a touch of their magic to form the first mortals from the earth. The Lupines of the north were the first, then a while later came the Huntress's people, and finally the Healer's." His dark eyes met my own, and I watched him closely, fully captivated by the way his warm, gentle voice echoed around us in the quiet of the night.

"For centuries there was peace in the lands, and the Forefolk expanded across Elrin, which pleased the Gods. They were so pleased in fact, they appointed four mortals to be the leaders of the Forefolk, and those four beings became the heads of their houses and thus the rulers of the provinces."

"Like the Chosen?" I wondered out loud.

"I suppose so, but they were mortal and without the magic of their Gods. Their duties were to oversee the growing communities and to keep the harmony amongst the land."

"Who were these men?"

"There was Synrick the Worthy of House Moreel, who belonged to the Healer, and he ruled the southern province. Then there was Caedell the Undying of House Reide, and Skileer the Marked of House Baxteel. Both of whom oversaw the heartland of Elrin and the largest province in the name of the Huntress."

"Skileer?" I whispered, focusing on the way the familiar name rolled off of my tongue so effortlessly.

"I often wondered if you had been named after the ancient lord of the Huntress. It is an old name and one not usually used these days."

"I had no idea it was of importance," I admitted quietly, and the Healer lifted a hand to my shoulder and gave it a gentle squeeze.

"I'm sure there are many tales of the great Lord Skileer in Noordeign. When we return, I will help you find them," he promised before continuing. "And the last appointed leader was Krayern of House Demys, who was otherwise known as Swiftsword. He earned that title for being the fiercest warrior and the Protector's appointed ruler of the north."

My mind spun with all of this new information, and then something came to me.

"But what about the other three Gods? Where were they?" I frowned.

Inhaling sharply, Gaelon then turned to face the sky once more. "Now that is something that has been disputed over the years."

"What do you mean?"

"If you were to ask the immortals of the other three, or rather the Second Gods, they would argue that our tales and scriptures are wrong, and their Gods had just been overlooked. However, what I know to be true is that some of the Forefolk grew unhappy under the reign of the old once the houses were selected. They were not satisfied with what they were given and wanted more. Some scriptures, later written by a man named Algrid, mentioned a group of men who had once travelled to Vinmare, and those men are said to be the ones responsible for conjuring the Second Gods."

"How would they do such a thing? Surely the Gods of old would not have allowed that to happen. What magic could a group of men even possess?"

"None of their own, but it is said that when they travelled to Vinmare, they did not find the magic that had been used to create the Forefolk. They had discovered something much darker."

"So what then, these men used that power to create the Second Gods? Is there no other explanation?" It just didn't make sense to me, and it certainly did not seem possible. Creating Gods should not have been so easy.

"That is the explanation we have, and once they were conjured, they ruled alongside our Gods until the Seductress grew tired of the peace. That was when she turned her sights on the Protector and tried to tempt him to turn on the rest, thus starting the War of the Gods, which lasted for years."

"But if this is all true, why is it never spoken about? How are these things not common knowledge?"

Gaelon sighed and then rubbed at his face tiredly. "Time has a way of erasing memories and changing certainties. Soon truths become half-truths and then less and less as people and their memories fade. It is the way things happen."

"But Gaelon," I whispered. "What of the immortals, those who are centuries old, even older than you?"

"I have yet to come across someone who is old enough to know the actuality of the scriptures. Immortals were not created until the war, which was hundreds of years after the conception of the Second Gods."

"And this dark magic that brought them to the world? What of that?"

Gaelon's eyes lifted to the sky once more, though his face looked far more troubled than it had before.

"Perhaps it too is scattered across the world."

Chapter 11

"My backside has gone numb," Elizabeth complained while shifting against the leather of her saddle, and I reached out my wineskin for her to take. Our travels had been quiet thus far, though slow, and I rolled my neck, loosening the tension before scanning the horizon. The thick curtain of evergreens and cedars had thinned, and the breeze had warmed as we moved our way down south although we had been on the road for only a fortnight.

"Healer!" a soldier called from ahead, and I watched as he pushed his horse into a canter while he circled back to us. "There is a group of men just beyond the hill. They are not armed but there are at least a dozen of them."

Frowning, I turned to Gaelon, but he did not seem worried. Instead, a warm smile pulled at his lips, and then he dug his heels into his mount's barrel and took off. Barrick appeared to be just as perplexed as I was, and he moved in next to me, pressing close enough that our stirrups clanged together before leaning over.

"Does the Healer know anyone in Beilham?" I blinked at my guard in surprise and then swung my head back around, watching as Gaelon dismounted before wrapping his arms around the tall, lean man. "Well, that's answer enough, I suppose."

Closing the distance, I watched as the two men whispered amongst each other, their familiarity still shocking to me although I had seen it once before. Gaelon seemed so relaxed and open with the man, and I once again found myself wondering what their past was and how they had grown to know each other.

"Hello, Huntress!" Hectoar called with a large smile as we closed the distance, and I couldn't help but offer a soft smile in return. Gaelon had turned to the guards, ordering them about, and I slid from my mount only to be swept away by the slender hand on my back.

"Let the Healer and your guard sort those boys out. You ladies can come with me." Any protests I had died on my lips when I turned to my friends and watched as Elizabeth sagged in relief before rushing to us.

"It is so nice to see you again, Hectoar," Ella offered softly with a dip of her chin. "How have things been for all of you here?"

"Things have been mostly quiet, though I'm afraid I may be the only familiar face you see during your stay tonight." Ushering to the main road, Hectoar motioned to his newly built home, though I moved my gaze around the quiet little village.

"Where have your comrades gone?" I wondered out loud as he opened his door and invited us in.

"They've all moved on, Huntress." He moved through the wide opening at the far side of the room and disappeared around a corner only to reappear with two loaves of bread and a pitcher a moment later. I strode to his side, took the pitcher from his grasp, and helped set the table before settling in a seat across from him. Ella and Elizabeth paid us no mind as they helped themselves to the warm loaf and jam.

"They've all left? Selbie too?" Nodding his head, Hectoar moved for the pitcher and poured himself a glass of wine before leaning back in his chair.

"Selbie was the first to go. She stayed for a few months' time, but then one morning she was gone, leaving only a note behind. The rest of the halflings slowly ventured out one by one, and then new ones came to replace them, though most of the people here now are humans. There are very few halflings that remain this far north."

Ella turned her attention to the handsome man with a furrowed brow. "Why is that?"

Sighing, the immortal leaned back into his chair, his hand pulling his cup to his chest as he swirled the wine around. "The winters are harsh, the possibilities are limited, and now that the south has been rid of the threat, there is no reason why the halflings shouldn't find peace in the larger cities. They hold far more opportunities than our villages. The newcomers who are here currently will most likely depart in the upcoming months now that spring has come and the weather is decent enough to make the journey."

"Are they all northerners?" I asked.

"Most are from villages that simply couldn't recover from the Crimsons. Some are from other continents. They fled over the years, fearful of their fates if they stayed in Elrin, but have since returned."

Elizabeth cupped her chin in her hands as she leaned across the table, her eyes wide.

"The other continents?" Her voice was full of wonder, and I grinned at her expression. My friend had always had far bigger dreams than me, though she rarely spoke of them. She longed for adventure in far-off lands and had wanted to see the world and everything it had to offer, even if she refused to say as much.

Smiling knowingly at her, Hectoar nodded. "Staflarke mostly, though some ventured all the way from the eastern continent of Osallow."

"Osallow? Really?!" Ella snorted in amusement at her lover's enthusiasm and wrapped an arm around Elizabeth's shoulders. Ignoring our looks of amusement, the human shuffled closer, her wine and bread long forgotten, and then peered up at the immortal man. "Is it true the ruins of Natylity are still there? What about the shores of Helreene? Does the sand truly sparkle like diamonds?"

"You have a taste for adventure." Hectoar smiled, his eyes scanning across the petite brunette's face. "Where did you learn about all those things?"

Tilting my head, I too studied my friend and wondered where she had heard such stories. I knew Elizabeth was far more interested in the world, but I wasn't aware just how vast her knowledge was. Ella, however, grinned softly at her human, lifting a hand to tuck some of the dark hair behind Elizabeth's ear before shuffling closer.

"She found an atlas in the library at the manor during our search for scriptures and hasn't put it down since." Glancing at the far wall, the immortal beauty paused, watching through the window as the men unloaded the wagons. "In fact, she brought it with her. She even managed to find a way to keep a torch nearby so she could study the thing at night."

"Search for what scriptures?" Hectoar asked, his brows furrowing while his eyes moved back and forth between the three of us.

Nervousness bubbled in my gut as my friends glanced at me anxiously. Gaelon and Hectoar appeared close; after all the Healer was far more familiar with him than anyone else. But I still wasn't sure where to even start, and I didn't know Hectoar well enough to divulge any secrets.

"It seems our library is lacking, Hectoar," Gaelon called as he swung open the door. "Our Huntress had been hoping to find more tales about her Goddess and the history of Elrin is all."

I watched the Healer with interest, wondering if he had a reason not to tell his friend about the rumours and his experience on the sea, but Gaelon remained as stoic as ever. He slid the chair next to mine, sat, and then reached for my cup of wine.

"Well, perhaps you will find some on your travels?" Hectoar offered, never taking his eyes off the Healer. "Where is it you are headed? You didn't say in the letter I received."

"Lord Deavion has called on us." Gaelon shrugged before popping a piece of bread into his mouth nonchalantly.

"Deavion, he's an immortal of the Jester, is he not?" The God's name piqued my interest, and I moved my attention to Gaelon. I had met my share of immortals now, many being Lupines—the Protector's people, some in the name of the Healer, though they were uncommon in the north. Many at court were of the Huntress, several of whom fought with us at the shores. But I couldn't recall meeting any belonging to the God of luck and trickery.

“He is.” Gaelon nodded. “He sailed from Astilar many years ago before finding a home on the western coast.”

“Ritari, wasn’t it? That’s where he ended up?” Hectoar’s emerald eyes gazed at the Healer, their depths unreadable.

“Yes, what of it, Hectoar?”

“I just always thought it strange that an immortal of the Jester would choose that village rather than Carlon. After all, it is the only city of his God in Elrin.” Nothing seemed concerning with his tone or expression; it was as if he was simply curious. And yet I knew something was left unspoken.

“The Healer’s sanctuary is in Lythnals, but I have never been. Is that strange as well given that I am his Chosen?” Gaelon raised a single brow before taking a long swig of wine, and I glanced at my friends.

Sighing, Hectoar pressed back in his chair. “We both know Lythnals was desolated in the war; there’s nothing there for you.”

“Then why are you concerned about Deavion?” I felt lost in this conversation and too self-conscious to ask my questions. Not that it mattered, the two immortal men were locked in a silent conversation of sorts, and my friends and I sat quietly while we waited for one of them to say something.

Hectoar was the first to break and pinched the bridge of his nose in frustration before replying. “I’m just cautioning you to be careful with him.”

“You are still so prejudiced against the Jester’s immortals after all this time? I expected better of you, Hectoar.”

“You may be our God’s Chosen, but I was there when the Huntress fell.” It took me a moment to register his words, and then I stared wide-eyed at the Healer’s friend. “I know what the Jester and *some* of his immortals are capable of, Gaelon, and I would be lying if I said Deavion hadn’t always worried me. Do not let your new role fool you into thinking you can outsmart him; you may be crowned but you are not nearly as wise as you think you are.”

It was the first time the Healer’s friend had been anything but pleasant, and I recoiled at the firmness in his voice only to notice

Gaelon do the same while he paled. Narrowing his eyes, the Healer searched his friend's face for a pause and then turned on his heel before fleeing the room.

Crawling onto my friends' bed, I pressed in tightly and glanced at the page over Elizabeth's shoulder with searching eyes. Gaelon had not returned after Hectoar's warning, and I had not seen him since. The other immortal man had all but ignored us after the conversation, obviously irritated that his cautioning seemed to fall on deaf ears. Only it hadn't. I continued to repeat his words over and over in my mind.

"Where is Lythnals?" I asked, my eyes roaming across the tattered page. Elrin I recognized immediately, and I traced the shape of our home before marveling at the other smaller continents that surrounded it. I had never thought that the world could be so vast.

"Here." Ella pointed to a land mass on the right of the map, though it was only half the size of Elrin. "However, I don't know the whereabouts of the sanctuary Hectoar mentioned."

"And the other place he spoke of, where the lord is from?" Elizabeth wondered out loud.

"Gaelon said Astilar?" Smoothing the page, Ella slid a long, elegant finger until she reached the continent to the west. "Here it is."

Lifting the atlas closer to our faces, I tried to read the faded words only to realize they were in the tongue of old, and then I huffed with frustration. Snorting, Ella pulled the book from me and placed it in her lap once more. "No point in hogging it if you can't read it."

"Why do you think Hectoar is so concerned about the immortal?" Elizabeth had leaned forward, glancing at me from across her immortal, and I could see the worry on her face.

"I—" I began only for my words to be cut short as Gaelon's rising voice echoed from the floor below.

"He called on us! What would you have me do?!" I uncrossed my legs and moved to stand only to be stopped by Ella's firm grip. Turning to her, I watched as she indicated to her ear before pointing to the floor, warning me that they would hear me.

But Gaelon was an immortal; surely he had heard us talking, though perhaps he had been too distracted to notice. Holding my breath, I waited and listened, only managing to pick up on Hectoar's hushed whisper, though I couldn't make out what was said. Ella, however, must have been able to decipher the quiet tone, and she had narrowed her eyes at the wooden floor in concentration.

"I won't abandon the people of Elrin to fend for themselves based on your superstitions alone, Hectoar!" The immortal answered the Chosen quietly once more, and then there was nothing but silence.

Nudging Ella, I raised a brow in question, and her face tightened in a frown. Her eyes scanned the floor for another pause, and then she lifted her hands, interlocking her fingers before mouthing the words: *I think they are embracing.*

I remained rooted in my place, waiting for her to motion again, but she did not. Instead, she flopped back, pulling Elizabeth and me with her before lifting the atlas to cover our faces. Her eyes shot to mine before peeking over the edge of the pages, and it was then that I could hear the footsteps approaching from the hall.

"Skylahr," Gaelon called as his knuckles tapped against the door. A beat passed, and then another, and the Healer sighed before calling for me once more. "Skylahr, if you three are going to eavesdrop so blatantly, you could at least have the courage to face me."

My face flushed hotly, and I moved from the bed to the door, taking in a deep breath before opening it. Gaelon leaned against the frame, his curls mussed and face ashen, and I wondered what else was said that I was unable to hear.

"May I come in?" Moving aside, I lifted a hand in invitation and waited for the Healer to pass me before I shut the door once more. "I wanted to speak to you about earlier. I figured you may be concerned about Deavion and what Hectoar had mentioned."

"I'm worried there is more to it, and you know how much I hate to be left out." His lips quirked in a half smile, and he tipped his head to the side.

"Yes, of that I am aware." Sighing, he moved across the room, gesturing to the end of the bed where Ella's and Elizabeth's feet lay, and waited for them to shift them out of the way before sitting. "Who wants to ask their questions first?"

"Gaelon," Elizabeth began before I could even manage to open my mouth, and I eyed her carefully while she crossed her legs and leaned forward. "How do you know Hectoar? What is your history with him? How old is he? Was he really present for the War of the Gods?"

Gaelon reeled back from her and her onslaught of questions only to turn to me. Lifting his hand, he waved me over, though remained silent until I complied and perched next to him. The Healer then turned to my friend with a sigh.

"I have known Hectoar for many years, though last year was the first time I had seen him since my ceremony." My eyes widened in surprise. Gaelon had been immortal for over two hundred years, and from what he told me he had never ventured far past the shores after losing his mortality, so I wondered why they had remained separated for so long.

"Why? What happened for him to leave you isolated for all those years?" Elizabeth asked, voicing my very own thought. Gaelon's dark gaze slowly drifted up until he met my own, and I waited while he seemed to gather his courage.

"I met him when I was five and twenty, a young halfling on the cusp of my ignite." He paused before taking a shallow breath. "You see, Healers don't burn with the kind of power that you do, Skylahr. It's quieter, a soft glow almost like warm embers. Or that's how it should be. Mine, however, was consuming. I felt everything so deeply, so entirely that it would keep me awake for days, and word of my strange behaviour began to spread. That was when Hectoar learned of my existence and travelled to my village, New Moreel."

Grabbing the atlas, Ella searched the map for a moment before Gaelon carefully plucked it from her hands and turned it to face us.

"It's here or rather, it was." He pointed to one of the southernmost points on the east side of Elrin. "Hectoar found me there, just before the Crimson Goddess sent her troops. We escaped just days before my village would be burned to the ground."

Bile bubbled in the back of my throat as the memories of my own village slammed into me, and I felt Elizabeth move before coming closer and then her small hand grabbed my own. Offering me a sad smile, Gaelon cleared his throat.

"We were on the run for nearly a year before we decided to set sail and leave Elrin, like so many others had, but before we could reach the docks we were ambushed and separated. A group of low-ranking officers had found us and took me captive. I was held prisoner for a few days before they disposed of me, or at least they thought they had."

"Disposed of you?" Elizabeth questioned with wide eyes.

"Yes, they had grown bored of the torture and finally decided to end me, or rather tried to. Had they been wiser they would have at least made sure that I was truly dead before leaving the prison."

"So someone found you and was able to perform the ceremony—that's how you became immortal?" Ella clarified. "Who was it?"

"I don't know. That question has haunted me for all these years. Whoever it was had pulled me from my cell and dragged me into the cover of the forest. That is where I woke, my clothes were still soaked in my blood, and I was left with just a note. A piece of parchment telling me to go to the shores and hide there."

"And Hectoar? What happened to him?" Gaelon's head turned, moving to the door for a pause before he faced us once more.

"He had managed to find the Crimsons' hideout and searched for me. But when he saw my cell, and the obvious signs of what had happened, he assumed I had been killed."

"He never looked for you after that?" I had meant for it to sound like an honest question, but I could hear the disbelief and accusation in my tone. Gaelon smiled at me softly while patting my thigh.

"He had no reason to. There was not a single scenario where a

Crimson immortal would perform the ceremony, and there had been no sign that I had made it out of that cell alive. And once I had settled at the shores, I had been too afraid to search for him again."

Silence filled the room, all of us lost in thought as we gazed at the Healer's Chosen. Gaelon, however, had focused on the forgotten book that lay on the bed, and he stroked his fingers across the image, smiling softly at the southern point of Elrin. He was obviously reminiscing, and I felt my heart lurch at the thought, knowing exactly how he felt. After all, my own village no longer existed even though I could just make out the shape of it on the page. Map or not, Noorde Point was now just a memory.

"And Hectoar? How did he become an immortal?" Elizabeth's voice drew my attention, offering me an escape from the grief and pain that had begun to push at my chest, and my shoulders sagged at the relief.

"Hectoar was one of the first to receive the Healer's gift of immortality just as the war began, and that was six hundred years ago." Elizabeth's mouth went slack with awe, and the Healer's Chosen chuckled under his breath while raising a finger to close her jaw.

The contact seemed to rouse the human from her shock, and she pulled away from his touch with a furrowed brow. "But the war was between the Seductress and the Protector, why did the other Gods offer such a gift to their followers?"

Folding one leg over the other, Gaelon shifted until he was more comfortable and then smiled at my friend. "When the other Gods learned of the Seductress's plans, they took whatever measures they could to stop the Crimson army and its destruction. First, the Protector offered his people eternal life, creating the Lupines and their ability to transform into the animal of his sigil. The other Gods, though powerful in their own ways, did not have the magic to change forms, and so they gave their followers immortality and their own gifts. The Huntress's immortals, for example, are excellent warriors and share a closeness to the earth that none of the others have. The Healer's people are just that, healers. They bring a balance to life and have skills in restoring the body and mind to those who need it."

"And the Jester?" Ella asked. Gaelon turned to her and scanned across her face for a long moment before answering.

"He also gave his people eternal life, though they refused to pick a side during the war. Unsurprising given that he is the God of trickery and luck. His followers are skilled in many ways, fortunate fates always seem to follow them, and they are far more cunning than most."

"Is this why Hectoar is worried? Does he think that Deavion is being insincere?" My voice was laced with apprehension, and the Healer swallowed roughly.

"Hectoar has never trusted the Jester's people after the war. The Jester had led our Gods to believe that he would aid them in their time of need, but when that moment came, he and his followers fled. This is what caused the Huntress to further split her magic and create her Chosen." Dark eyes shot me a pointed look, and I blushed under Gaelon's obvious pride. "She taught the others how to do the same before she and her Protector fell. And the Healer, my God, was never to be seen or heard from again."

For a heartbeat no one said anything, and it was then that it occurred to me that something was missing from the story. "What of the Siren?"

Gaelon's brows furrowed, and he ran a hand through his curls with a frown. "There is little knowledge of the sea Goddess, though she too refused to pick a side in the war. Her temper and loyalties were as changing as the very tides she controlled."

"And Hectoar told you all of this?" I asked.

"He did," Gaelon assured me.

"And he's telling the truth?" I asked doubtfully. "How can you be certain?"

"He is a Healer; deception is not his way, and he has nothing to gain in lying. He has never been dishonest before." My friends both studied Gaelon carefully.

Ella's dark eyes roamed his face once more before they darted to my own and then her voice broke the quiet. "Then should we be worried about his concerns of the Jester's immortal?"

"Concerned or not, our duty is to aid those who call upon us. Something has been happening on the coast, that is not a lie, I have seen it."

A shiver crawled down my spine at the Healer's words while a tension blanketed the room.

Huddling closer to my friends, I grabbed their hands before casting a glance at the Healer. "Then we will go to the shores, we will aid the people there, and no matter what waits for us, we face it together."

Chapter 12

Hectoar hummed under his breath as he moved back and forth across the kitchen, and I watched from the door in interest. Our host had been quiet all night, so much so that I wondered if he had slept outside with the men rather than in his bed.

"Did you need something, Huntress?" he called, though remained turned away from me. I pushed from the wall before closing the distance and sitting at the table.

"Can I help with anything?" My offer hadn't been genuine; I was counting on the immortal to wave it away, but instead he turned and handed me a long knife before placing two loaves of bread in front of me.

"You can cut the bread, and then when you're done, slice the cheese. After that you can set the table and help me clean the rabbit." Without further instruction Hectoar turned away once more and I regretted asking.

"I'm afraid we won't have time to eat all that," Gaelon called from the hallway before sauntering into the small room. He looked better, brighter, and well rested, and Hectoar's eyes scanned him from head to toe before a pink tinged his cheeks.

"You need to eat, and your men have been up for hours, I doubt they left you anything." Gaelon looked to me. My nervousness had kept me awake most of the night, and though I would usually be in a hurry to start our journey once more, I couldn't help but notice just how tempting the bread smelled. Turning my pleading eyes to the Healer, I tipped my head to the table in hopes he would agree.

"Did someone say something about food?" Ella asked as she pulled Elizabeth along. Sighing in defeat, the Healer moved and allowed the two to pass. After settling at the table, Ella picked up the knife and began to slice the bread while Elizabeth approached Hectoar, her smile warm as she took the rabbit from him and began to clean it.

"Fine, eat, but then we really should be on our way." Gaelon ran a hand through his curls, and Hectoar frowned as he studied the Healer closely.

"So you still plan on going to Ritari?" Gaelon sighed once more before approaching the immortal man.

"I appreciate your hospitality and your concern, my friend, and if I thought that this would be a waste of time, we would not be going. I told you about the missing ships and what I myself have experienced. There is something happening on those waters, and the last account of an incident occurred on the coast near Ritari."

"Very well, I know better than to try to convince you. I've said my piece." Grabbing Elizabeth's hands, Hectoar stopped her from continuing with a gentle smile. "Sit and eat, I can roast this while you organize yourselves and pack it for your journey."

Leaving us to the food that had been set out, the immortal breezed by the Healer, though said nothing. I waited, watching as Gaelon stood frozen for a moment, as if deciding what he should do. Surprisingly he did not go after his friend and instead tugged on the chair next to mine before slumping into it.

"Bread?" Ella offered, lifting a slice, and the Healer smiled softly before dipping his head in thanks. For a pause, no one said anything, as if we were all unsure of which topic to broach. But just as I began to shift in my chair at the uncomfortable feeling, Elizabeth huffed and sagged in her seat.

"I can't believe you would rush us before we could have a taste of that rabbit. I hope you realize just how miserable I'll be for the rest of the morning." Elizabeth pouted while crossing her arms, and Gaelon lifted a brow at her.

"Is that any different from any other morning so far?" the Healer drawled before Ella snorted into her cup in laughter. But the noise sounded wet, and I glanced up to see her covering her face in horror while tea dribbled down her chin.

"Did that just come out of your nose?!" Elizabeth exclaimed while sliding away from the immortal, and a burst of amusement bubbled in my chest, rising until I could no longer contain it. And for a moment the tension disappeared while the room filled with my laughter.

Packing the wagon, I glanced once more at the Healer as he said goodbye to his friend. Hectoar had not returned to the kitchen to break his fast with us, and instead opted to help the men take down the tents. Turning to the wagon, I made certain that the golden blade was still safely tucked away and traced the cool metal with my fingers.

"It's remarkable." Startling at the voice, I spun on my heel to face our host. "I hear you wielded it during the battle at the shores."

"I did." My voice cracked, and I swallowed roughly before draping my cloak over the weapon once more.

"Then that speaks of your power."

Frowning, I glanced at the wrinkled material that covered the gold. "I think you give me too much credit. I didn't come away unscathed, you should have seen my hands after the battle. The burns and blisters took days to heal."

Hectoar hummed under his breath while his fingers rubbed at his chin thoughtfully. "If the myths are true, the power of that blade is a fearsome thing to behold. No one had wielded it but the Huntress herself. So, I suppose it would make sense for it to leave its mark on you. However, the person who gave you that blade certainly did not underestimate you in the slightest. They obviously thought it was meant to be in your hands. Maybe you should follow *his* lead and give yourself more credit."

My heart twisted painfully at the words while I swallowed roughly, and I searched for a response, longing to clear the awkward stillness that had suddenly blanketed us.

"Ready?" A delicate hand cupped my shoulder in a welcome interruption, and I turned to Ella as she pressed in closer. "Are you okay?"

"Fine," I managed, though my tone was clipped, and Ella turned her questioning stare to Hectoar. The immortal man, however, remained rooted in place, his eyes roaming over my friend inquisitively. He pulled his hand from his breeches and fiddled with a piece of silver, and I watched as he slid his thumb across the smooth surface all while his emerald eyes studied Ella.

"What?" she grumbled, her hands self-consciously fluffing her curls before her dark eyes darted to my own.

Tilting his head, the immortal lifted his fingers and held the silver out towards us. No, not us, towards Ella, and she snatched the metal from him. Cradling it in an open palm, she inspected it, and I looked at the piece that shone brightly against her dark skin.

It was a coin, though larger than any other piece of silver I had seen, and I waited with bated breath as she flipped it over. Skimming her thumb across the top, she wiped away any dirt and studied the symbol closely. It was a four-pointed star, and the sharp tips had been carefully engraved, each one nearly reaching the edge of the coin while a delicate script filled the empty space between each point.

"What does it say?" I asked, narrowing my eyes at the tiny letters, as if that would help me understand the words of old. Tilting her head, Ella began reading the words one by one.

"Fate, fortune, doom, and…" Her eyes lifted to our host as the last word passed through her lips in a hushed whisper. "Destruction."

"What is this, Hectoar?" I demanded, my voice accusatory as I glared at the immortal.

"A coin of the Jester," he answered, his voice patient, unaffected by my distrust. "I may have my qualms about the God and some of his people, but even I know that in the right hands, this coin can bring the best of blessings."

Hectoar reached for Ella and curled her fingers around the coin before patting her hand gently. I, however, looked to Gaelon in question. He had approached us while Ella had been deciphering the words, and now, I needed his reassurance that this was not some trick.

"Those coins are rare and extremely sought after." He nodded his head as Ella tucked the silver into a pocket. "Many have spent their lives searching, only to come up empty-handed. I'm surprised you'd part with it."

Hectoar shrugged before glancing at my friend once more. "It's not meant for me to keep any longer."

Ella thanked him quietly and then excused herself. Turning, I watched as she pressed a sweet kiss to Elizabeth's lips and then they mounted their horses. Barrick was just behind, shifting impatiently from one foot to the other, his eyes scanning the group carefully before moving to me.

"Skylahr?" Gaelon called, his hand skimming across my arm as he drew my attention.

"Sorry," I apologized and glanced at Hectoar.

"I was advising our Healer to stay out of the western mountains. There is the passage that will take you right through the col that is at the base of the dual peaks. It may be a longer journey to the coast, but it is far safer."

Our travels while rebuilding Elrin had mostly been focused on the north and the villages near the shores, but I had been through the western mountains once before and was sure that we could manage, especially if it meant shortening the journey.

As if Hectoar could read my thoughts, he frowned and gently shook his head. "The sea is not the only thing that is changing, Huntress."

"What does that mean?" I demanded while crossing my arms.

"The Crimson Goddess is no longer a threat, and the earth and its creatures have begun to realize that. Things are going back to the way they were."

Frowning at Hectoar's words, I turned to the Healer. "What does this mean? Tell me in a way I will understand."

Gaelon lifted a brow at his friend and shot him a pointed look. "Out with it, Hectoar, what are you talking about?"

"The western mountains were a wild place for a long time. They were the last piece of Elrin to be explored, and I fear that the creatures who had once been chased off are slowly returning. That could explain what has happened to your vessels as well. Perhaps the beasts of the waters have returned too."

Swallowing, I straightened my shoulders and lifted my chin. "The Seductress may have reigned for centuries, but would she be so powerful to have had the ability to frighten away such great creatures?"

"We don't fully know how her magic works or what all had happened, but when the Huntress was defeated, the earth changed. It mourned its Goddess for a long while, and the Seductress took the opportunity to ravage what was left. She was powerful and her abilities were unlike the others. She can control people and things in a way no other God could—her magic is dark and ancient."

Acid bubbled in my gut, and I swallowed roughly as the bitter taste crept into the back of my throat. I knew exactly how easily the Goddess had been able to take over someone's mind, how simple it was for her to use a broken being as a pawn in her game. She had done it to me. She had taken my heartbreak and pain and twisted it until I was no longer a person I recognized, though only for a short while.

Thankfully I had friends, loved ones, and things to hold on to. If it had not been for them, I wasn't so sure I would have been strong enough to fight back, even with the Huntress's power filling my blood. After all, I never had been living for just myself. Wasn't that what I told *him*? That I lived for others?

"If you really think the route through the mountains is too risky, we will go around." Gaelon's voice beckoned me back to the conversation, and I exhaled roughly before meeting his concerned gaze.

Slumping in relief, the immortal moved, patting Gaelon on the back gently before turning to me. "May your Goddess protect you on your travels, dear Skylahr. Please remind our Healer to write to me once you've reached your destination."

"I will," I promised before eyeing the Healer carefully. "Thank you for your hospitality, I hope to see you again soon."

Hectoar's lips lifted on one side, and then he folded into a graceful bow before me for a long pause, despite my obvious discomfort. "I hope to see you again as well, Huntress."

Chapter 13

The heat of mid spring was unforgiving as we took the road south. We had followed Hectoar's advice and remained on the east side of the mountains rather than going to Celinde and down the coast. Though as I sweltered under the late afternoon sun, I wondered if that route had been worth it. It had been over a fortnight since we had left Beilham, and we were still a long way away from Ritari.

Wiping at my sweaty face with the crook of my elbow, I did my best to ignore the burning chafe along my inner thighs and glanced at my friends. It had been too hot to continue to ride the horses for hours on end, and we had instead dismounted and led them on foot.

"How are you faring?" Ella asked, catching my eyes, and I narrowed my gaze before wiping my face once more. The immortal enjoyed the heat far more than the harsh cold of the north and I envied her right now. Her thick curls had been wrapped stylishly in a teal fabric, and her clothes blew lightly in the warm breeze.

"I think my thighs have worn these breeches through," I grumbled while lifting one leg. Sure enough the fabric was thinning, the cotton nearly translucent now, and I winced as I stroked my fingers across the patch.

"We'll stop here for the night!" Gaelon called suddenly from ahead, and I lifted my eyes to the buildings that scattered across the land ahead of us. I had been keeping track of the days that passed but had not bothered checking where this road would lead us, and I was left unprepared for the familiar rotting wood structures and dusty hills that suddenly surrounded us. Closing my eyes against the onslaught of memories, I could barely feel Ella's hand when she grabbed my shoulder.

"What a shithole. What is this place?" Barrick sighed, and I took in a deep breath before swallowing.

"*Ferrii.*" The word was a hoarse whisper, and the head guard turned to me with a lifted brow, but I could not explain why I had such strong feelings for an abandoned village. I had no words to express what those tattered buildings meant to me.

"Let's set up camp before the sun sets," Gaelon ordered, and I wiped at my eyes roughly when I realized the fog had swelled over and a tear had trailed down my cheek. Embarrassed by my dramatic reaction, I cleared my throat and moved to trail after the soldiers who began to pull the tents from the wagon while the head guard and the Healer scouted the area.

"We could probably sleep in one of the buildings. Barrick said there was a bathhouse in the larger one." Gaelon's voice was soft as he watched me secure one of the tents, and I took a deep breath before turning to face him.

"No." My tone left no room for argument. "You go ahead, I'll stay out here."

"You don't want to bathe and wash your clothes? I never took you for someone who enjoys being filthy." His smile was soft and warm, and I felt the irrational need to run from this conversation. Inhaling deeply once more, I shook my head before swinging a bedroll over my shoulder.

"Skylahr, what is it? What is wrong?" I felt foolish for being so upset, but I couldn't push the feelings away.

"Just a memory, one I would rather forget." It was as honest as I could be, and I was relieved when he nodded his head in understanding before grabbing another two packs. Following behind him silently, I placed the rolls into the newly built tents and waited for my friend to leave the cover of the material before I crawled onto my cot.

It was only early evening, and I could hear the busy movement of the camp as everyone readied for dinner, but I couldn't pull myself out of the safety of the furs of my bed to face them. Curling into myself, I ducked my head to my chin and closed my eyes, willing sleep to come.

I don't know how long I slept for, but by the time my eyes fluttered open, Ella and Elizabeth were quietly breathing beside me and the golden evening light that had filled the tent before was gone.

Pulling the blanket from me, I smiled at my friends fondly. Even in sleep I was cared for, and my heart lifted at their thoughtfulness and their concern that I would grow cool with the evening's drop in temperature.

I creeped my way to the entrance, ducked through the flaps, and secured the ties before scanning the area around me. The fire was just a pile of glowing embers, and the area was quiet with no one in sight other than Barrick, who was lounging on the ground nearby. I could tell from the straightness of his posture he was not asleep, and I crept close to him.

"You should actually sleep, Barrick." I nudged his ribs with the toe of my boot and narrowly avoided the massive hand that shot out to grab my ankle.

"I don't sleep when it's my watch, Huntress, go harass someone else." His voice was gruff, and he rolled onto his back before glaring up at me. "You look horrendous."

"I didn't know you knew words that big," I snapped while self-consciously tucking a piece of hair behind my ear.

"I'm full of surprises. Now go bathe, or change. I can smell you from down here." With that he rolled back onto his side in a silent dismissal, and I glanced over my shoulder toward the bathhouse.

I was certain I needed a wash, and I felt worn down and uncomfortable in my clothes, but I wasn't sure how I could bear being alone in that room that preoccupied my dreams on lonely nights.

"Go on now, Huntress. I don't know what ghosts are haunting you here, but they cannot hurt you," Barrick whispered from his place on the ground, and it felt as if a weight sat on my shoulders.

"You'd be surprised what can break a person." I sighed and turned back to my tent to fetch a fresh pile of clothes.

Shuffling through the doorway, I bit my lower lip as I took in the room. The moon was the only light, its reflection bouncing off the clear water that had filled the stone pool. The walls looked the same, if just slightly more ragged, and it was eerily quiet. Feeling my heart stutter in my chest, I stripped from my clothes before stepping into the cool water.

But the cold did little to settle my nerves, and I could feel the tightness in my chest grow taut as I waded my way into the middle of the pool. I had worked so hard to forget what had happened here, I had spent so many nights pushing away the memories, that now it felt like an emptiness in my soul.

Needing to leave the water, I dunked my head quickly and scrubbed at my skin and hair with the soap that had been left perched on the edge of the pool. Once satisfied that I was clean, I rushed to pull myself from the water and dry off before tossing the tunic over my head.

"Skylahr." Gaelon's voice startled me, and I spun on my heel to face him. He had changed into a loose white cotton shirt and a pair of dark breeches. His hair was a wild mess of curls, and a dark shadow had grown over the sharp edges of his jaw. "I'm sorry for interrupting. I didn't think anyone would be here at this hour."

"Wasn't that your excuse the last time you caught me in such a state of undress at the shores?" I had meant for my voice to be light and joking, but it rattled with emotion. I tugged my tunic farther down and carefully grabbed the discarded towel to wrap around my hips. "I think there is a pattern happening here, Healer."

"It's not intentional," he assured me before turning around, and I took the opportunity to tug on my breeches.

"I'm decent," I called and carefully approached him. Gaelon peered over his shoulder, taking in my damp hair and misty eyes before he sighed heavily.

"Are you alright?" His voice was heavy with concern, and one hand reached for my waist, his fingers grasping the material before pulling me closer. His brows were furrowed, and I lowered my eyes to my bare feet to escape his prodding gaze.

"I'm fine," I tried to assure him, but I knew he saw right through my façade.

"You're not." He lifted a hand and tucked a finger under my chin, raising my head until it was held high, and then he peered up at me carefully. "Can I ask you something though?"

"Of course."

"Are you hurting this way because of him?" His tone was gentle, but I still crossed my arms around my middle protectively.

"Yes." The words were blunt, but what else was there to do but be honest?

"And you still care for him after all this time, even after what has happened." It was not a question, but a realization, and I clenched my eyes shut under the weight of it. Sinking my teeth into my trembling lower lip, I tried to swallow down my pain and nodded my head begrudgingly.

"Yes."

"Does he deserve such loyalty?" Gaelon moved his hand to cup my chin, his thumb grazing across my scar twice before I pulled away. And then before anything else could be said, I gathered my things, and like a coward I fled, running from the Healer, his words, and the memories of *him*.

Chapter 14

Harnessing my ignite had a few benefits, but my favourite by far would be the strength I had no matter how little I slept. My brain was fogged, and I could feel the exhaustion, and yet I was still quicker on my feet than I would have been previously, and I was thankful for it. Especially considering I was so eager to leave this place and its memories.

Mounting my horse swiftly, I turned to Ella and Elizabeth, observing as the latter struggled to put her foot in the stirrup while she rubbed tiredly at her eyes. I smiled fondly, watching for a moment in amusement while she hoisted herself up.

"Think you can stay on, Elizabeth?" I called over my shoulder, and her bleary eyes narrowed at me, her brows pinching together as she settled on her mount.

"Fuck off."

Ella snorted before she could muffle it and smiled at me when a quiet chuckle left my lips.

"Alright now, leave the poor mortal alone, you two," Gaelon called as he finished organizing the soldiers and kicked his horse to the front of the group. We had not seen each other since the night before, and I blushed when our eyes met as he passed.

Sensing my discomfort, Ella and Elizabeth flanked my sides, and I could feel their gazes on my face as they waited for an explanation for the tension between the Healer and me. But instead, I cleared my throat and offered a weak grin in reassurance.

"That's all we get, that grimace version of a smile? Something happened between the two of you, your face gives it away." I hated that Elizabeth was still so good at reading me, and I cursed under my breath before moving my horse into a steady trot. My options were limited—I could stay with my two meddling friends, or I could move to the front, and I inhaled roughly before squaring my shoulders as I closed the distance between the Healer and me.

His dark gaze watched me from the corner of his eye, and I cleared my throat before breaking the tension. "Did you sleep?"

"I did, and you?" I hummed under my breath and nodded before I slowed my horse to a halt, waiting for him to do the same before trying again.

"You are very dear to me; I hope you know that. And I hold your opinion in high regard."

"Skylahr," he sighed, but I shook my head.

"I know I shouldn't feel the way I do. I'm trying to make it stop, truly I am."

Gaelon's brows furrowed, and he spun his horse to face mine.

"Don't ever think I would wish for you to push your feelings aside for anything. I may not understand why you care for him the way you do, but I don't have to. It is not my heart, and I do not judge you for loving someone."

My throat closed, and my heart thundered in my chest. "I never said anything about love."

"You didn't have to. I don't need to hear the words to know that it's true." My eyes burned, and I swallowed around the tightness of my throat. But before I could respond, the echo of hooves sounded from behind us.

"Healer!" Ella shouted as she closed the distance with her arm raised, pointing to the hills ahead.

Coming over the horizon was a small party of men, and I lifted my hand to shield my eyes from the sun as I focused on the incomers.

They did not appear threatening, and I was rather concerned as they swayed tiredly as they approached us.

There were only half a dozen, and by looking at the state of them, they had been on the road for a long while. Their clothes were creased and filthy, some had holes and tears, and their faces were sunken in. Each man looked as if he had not eaten in days, and Gaelon dismounted and rushed to them before I followed.

The man leading the group watched us with wide eyes before he clumsily fell to one knee, and I hurried to his side before urging him back up to his feet. Wrapping my hand around his biceps, I winced when I felt the delicate flesh beneath my palm.

"What's your name, friend?" Gaelon asked before grabbing the wineskin Barrick held out. He opened the top, gently pressed it into the stranger's hand, and directed him to drink with a kind smile.

"Edwin, sir," he croaked while wiping his mouth with the back of his hand before passing the water to his friends.

"And where are you from, Edwin?" Carefully the Healer made his way through the group and assessed each one before focusing back on the man who had now taken a seat in the dirt before us.

"We've come from Bascala, sir," he whispered shakily, his face pale, and I glanced at Gaelon in concern.

"It's a long way from the coast. Have you travelled this whole way on foot?" Gaelon motioned a soldier forward and ordered him to grab some of the rations before kneeling next to Edwin.

"Aye, sir. We had no choice, everything we had was lost." The others ducked their heads, and my heart went out to them when I realized how difficult this journey must have been.

"You said lost? What happened? Did someone ambush you on the road?" It wasn't unheard of for thieves and bandits to surprise unsuspecting travellers, but something in my gut screamed at me this was not the case for Edwin and his comrades.

"Lost to the sea. We had set sail for Honera months ago, but two nights in we were overtaken by—" The man behind Edwin lifted a boot and tried to subtly nudge him, but I had caught the movement and narrowed my eyes in warning.

"Overtaken by what?" My voice came out harsher than I had meant for it to, but the suspicion bubbling in my gut had my defences rising. Shrinking back from my tone, Edwin spared a look to his friend before clearing his throat.

"I don't rightfully know." He paused as he glanced at the green banners before studying my cheek and then cleared his throat and ducked his chin. "I don't know, Huntress."

"What does that mean?" Barrick's voice sounded from just over my shoulder, and he raised a hand to rest on the hilt of his sword before he glared at the stranger. When the man remained silent, Barrick closed the distance between them, casting his shadow over the men. "I asked you a question."

"Barrick, enough," Gaelon ordered my guard, but Barrick's eyes caught mine, waiting for my nod before stepping back.

"I apologize for him." Gaelon watched the head guard with a sharp glare before turning back to Edwin. "I do not know what you have been through, but I want to reassure you, I will not disbelieve anything you choose to tell us."

"I don't know if I could even put it into words."

"Try," Barrick snapped, and I pressed a hand against his arm before ushering him another foot away.

"We set sail on a sunny morning; it had been nothing but clear skies and gentle winds. We had been making decent progress with our journey, but then the tides turned on us. The wind changed in a matter of seconds, and we knew something was wrong." Edwin's face paled as he continued, and I could see the same haunted look the Healer had worn that night in his room. "All hands were on deck; the entire crew was scrambling to ready ourselves for whatever was coming. But nothing could have prepared us, it was nothing like I had seen before, Healer." Edwin inhaled roughly, his lower lip trembling before he continued. "It was a monster, taller than any hill or cliff I've ever known. It was dark in colour and rose from the water as if it had been waiting for us."

I heard Ella gasp, but I had focused on Gaelon's face, waiting for some form of reaction, but the Healer schooled his features and gently clasped his hand on the man's shoulder in comfort. But even the touch of the Healer could not keep the fear at bay, and Edwin gazed at us with wide, terrified eyes.

"Forty good men perished that night." His voice shook with emotion, and the remaining crew bowed their heads in silence. "We were the only ones who managed to find a way to keep our heads above the waves until another ship crossed our path the next morning. As soon as we boarded, we tried to warn our rescuers, but they thought we were superstitious, that we had mistaken the tide for a monster. It only took a few hours to reach shore and then they were happy to be rid of us, nervous that we were sick with sea fever."

"And these men who rescued you, they went back to sea?" I asked in concern.

"We tried to stop them, begged them to reconsider, but they refused. They were determined to reach their next destination. They wouldn't listen, and I did not want to wait around to see any more carnage."

"You did what you could, my friend." Gaelon sighed before rising to his feet.

"I should have done more. I should have never boarded that damn ship to begin with. I had heard the whispers, I just had not paid them any mind."

"What has been said?" I demanded sternly, ignoring Gaelon's disapproving stare. I should have been kinder with my tone, but I was too on edge. I had learned the hard lesson that gossip was not always idle chatter, and by the look on the man's face, he now knew it too.

"The Siren's immortals have started to gather on the sea. It is said that they are migrating along the western coast, and last I heard, they had planned to set sail for a lost island. They seem to think the storms and wrecks are a sign from their Goddess, and they plan to wait for her return."

"And the monster? Do they speak of that?" Gaelon asked with a frown. Edwin took a deep breath before meeting the Healer's eyes and nodding.

"It is said to be her creation, a creature to do her will until she has freed the seas of her enemies."

"Could it be true? Could she truly be controlling the seas from wherever she is with a monster? Could that be what is happening?" Ella asked as her eyes focused on the men who were now huddled around a fire.

"She is the Goddess of the tides," I murmured helplessly. Gaelon's face had remained a blank mask, and he avoided our questioning stares while he tried to get the exact coordinates from the men's journey.

"But I've never heard or read anything of the Siren since the stories of the war, I always assumed she had fallen," Elizabeth sighed.

"We had also never heard of the Chosen but look where we are now. Besides, you heard Hectoar, the version of events we had been taught is not what truly happened," I snapped, only to feel a tug of guilt as she flinched at my tone.

"We should make camp here," the Healer interjected. "I think we could all use the rest, and I don't feel right about sending those men off without a good night's sleep and some food in their bellies." Gaelon folded himself gracefully onto the ground next to me, and I glanced at him from the corner of my eye.

"They said her immortals were gathering. Are there many?"

"Their numbers have dwindled over the years, but there are a few groups of them scattered across the south." My eyes widened in surprise and the corners of Gaelon's lips lifted at the look of bewilderment on my face. "You have yet to meet any made in the Siren's name. Just like their Goddess, they are not ones to aid those in need and did not respond to our calls before the battle at the shores. Though to be honest, I was not expecting them to."

"Are they now allies of the Crimson?" Surely, if they were not, they would have done something for the people who had suffered at the hands of the Seductress's army.

"As far as I know they have claimed to always remain neutral since the war, but that is not to say they have not assisted the Seductress over the years. Fear makes even the best of us do foolish things, things we would have never imagined ourselves doing." His eyes locked on mine, and I realized that he was referencing his own inaction in the past.

"And the Siren? If she did not perish in the war, where has she been all this time?" Ella asked, her face drawn down in worry.

"I supposed hiding away, biding her time until there was an opening for her to strike."

"And when we chased Balor and the Crimsons out, we gave her that opportunity." My teeth clamped on my lower lip in thought as my words settled over us. "Has she been waiting for us to rid Elrin of her competition?"

Barrick tensed, and his brows furrowed before he lifted his eyes to mine. "Where one snake leaves, another is ready and waiting to slither in its place."

"What does that mean for us? Surely she couldn't be worse than the Crimsons and their mistress." Ella's voice was weak and full of doubt, and I felt my own fear curl in my belly at our lack of knowledge.

"She may just be the lesser-known evil. Why else would she have hidden away all this time only to appear once the threat of the other Goddess was gone?" Barrick questioned. I moved my eyes to Gaelon, waiting for a sign that the guard was wrong, waiting for some sort of reassurance, but the wisdom the Healer had always carried seemed to be lost.

"What could she want?"

"What they all want. What she has probably been waiting for all these years." Barrick's voice was quiet, but I could hear the uneasiness in it.

"And what is that?" I asked, though I already knew the answer.

"Power."

Chapter 15

The air had grown heavy with the smell of salt, and I knew that we were close to the sea. Turning to my companions, I observed the toll the journey had taken. The soldiers had grown restless over the last few days, the growing heat of the south making their armour more than uncomfortable. The only one who hadn't complained was Barrick, but I could see that he had also grown weary, though I couldn't tell if it was the sun or the unknown of what we would find once we reached the coast.

"Here," Ella called as she guided her horse next to mine while holding out a wineskin.

"I'm fine, El." I waved her off, but the immortal glared before thrusting the leather at me.

"You look flushed, you're fidgeting in your saddle, and I haven't seen you drink anything all day. You'll be no good to anyone if you faint the minute you dismount." Rolling my eyes, I grabbed the wineskin and took a long drink before passing it back.

"You know how much I hate your mothering, don't you?" Her dark eyes glittered with amusement before she took a swig of water. "Will I have to deal with this for the rest of my life?"

"Even when you are old and grey, Skylahr Reed." Her smile faltered for a second, and her eyes traced my face before shooting a glance at Elizabeth.

I often wondered how Ella felt about being an immortal, especially now that she had someone to love. It was something we never spoke of, but I could see the pain it caused her to think about the future. She would lose us eventually, and what then? Death had never frightened me, but thinking about leaving Ella alone made my heart ache.

"We are nearing Carlon, we should be at the city by sunset," Gaelon called from his mount at the head of the party, and my eyes shifted to Ella's face. The last time we had been in this city, we both had nearly died at the hands of the Crimson. It was not a memory I was fond of reliving, though truly, none of them were.

"Are you two okay?" Elizabeth asked in concern, and I nodded in silence before moving my horse forward, allowing Ella a moment of privacy with her human while I decided to check on the Healer.

"How long will we stay in the city, Gaelon?" Bascala was still a ways away, and Ritari even farther. Carlon may have been near the coast, but they were not known for their ports, and I worried this would be a detour from the path we had planned.

"Long enough to rest and gather more supplies. We cannot continue at this pace without them. Besides, we have no idea who may be travelling through. The city has flourished now that it is not held by Crimsons."

"Do you think we will find something useful? Surely any person who knows something about the missing ships or has seen that creature would not be willing to tell just anyone they come across." I squinted as I scanned the horizon.

"It's a very good thing you and I are not just anyone then."

The city was brighter somehow; the atmosphere was light, and the townsfolk seemed at peace. It was strange to see the gate open and welcoming without the red armoured guards, and I tightened my reins as we filtered past the entrance.

Although it had been a long time since our last travels, my instinct to make myself small to avoid being caught was strong. It felt odd to barge into a city with little care, and I was never really prepared for the wide-eyed gazes that always seemed to lock on my being. Gaelon, however, thrived under the attention. His chin lifted and his spine straightened, and he truly looked like he belonged in a position of power.

Moving my gaze to the crowd that had formed on either side, I scanned the strangers for any cause of concern, but the mass of people seemed thrilled to have the two Chosen within their city walls and cheered and hollered with their excitement.

"Don't worry, the novelty will wear off." Gaelon leaned over in his saddle while giving my shoulder a reassuring squeeze.

"Maybe for me, but you seem to have your pick of admirers." The long line of welcomers was filled with handsome young men and women, many of whom were waving and calling out for the Healer, and my lips lifted in amusement when I noticed his face flush. "You are going to be very popular while we are here."

Ignoring my teasing, the Healer lifted his hand and waved at the crowd before ushering his mount towards the heart of the city. The last time I had been in the city limits, I had been too focused on the task at hand to really observe that there were no grand houses or manners, and I realized that our options for a place to stay were limited to the hills outside the city, or the local inn. I preferred the openness of the outdoors, but I knew that our party had grown tired of sleeping without the basic comforts the inn would provide.

"Will we be safe in there?" I asked quietly while eyeing the rough exterior of the building. Considering it was a prominent city, I had expected more, but it would seem that Gaelon was set on his decision. I sighed as he dismounted before handing his horse off to the stable boy who stood eagerly outside of the barn.

"We have guards, Barrick, and the Huntress's Chosen herself, what more could we want?" Ella asked as she too passed off her mount before helping a wobbly Elizabeth down from her saddle.

"I don't know, perhaps four solid walls and somewhere that doesn't reek of sweat, piss and ale," Elizabeth grumbled as her eyes darted to my face. At least I wasn't alone in my disappointment.

"Alright, you two, that's enough complaining. I need a belly full of ale before I have to listen to any more whining. I don't know who is worse, you or those children who call themselves soldiers." Barrick walked past me in annoyance, but I noticed the palm of his hand had curled around the hilt of his sword and his eyes scanned every inch of the entryway before he decided to duck into the candlelit room.

Following behind my guard, I too gazed across the open space of the inn. There was a bar at the back of the room surrounded by occupied tables, in the corner a group of men played a folky tune on their fiddles and flutes, and nearly every chair was taken. It was obviously a very popular place, and I hoped that with the number of patrons, we could blend in before settling for the night.

"What can I get for you?" The barmaid was a short, plump woman with a knot of red curls and had to be nearing sixty. The lines of her face and weary look showed the hard life she had lived, and I wondered if our victory over the Crimsons had eased her worries at all. Moving to the chairs that sat around the table, we all paused for a silent moment, unsure if we should introduce ourselves.

"Ale for the group and stew if you have any." Barrick's rough demand drew her attention to his face, and she blushed prettily before smoothing her hair.

"Of course. Anything else?" Her hands had drifted to the bust of her apron, and I nearly choked as she tugged it down to expose a large expanse of cleavage.

"No," Barrick dismissed her without another glance, and I coughed into my fist to hide my shock as dark eyes narrowed at me.

"Gaelon is not the only one with admirers it seems." As far as I knew, Barrick had no wife or family, and I was interested to see how he would handle the attention.

"Not interested" was his gruff reply before he dragged one large hand down his face.

"Oh come now, Barrick. You could use some fun, and you found someone who doesn't know you well enough to go running for the hills." Ella giggled as she leaned across the table beside me.

"I hate to disappoint you two, but unless those tits come off and she's hiding a different part under those skirts, I'm not interested."

"Then we will just have to find you a handsome man, won't we?" Ella smiled, but a frown had passed over the guard's face. Ignoring the barmaid, who had returned with our drinks, the massive man stood from his chair and turned for the door. Concern pushed at my gut, and I too made to leave only to come chest to chest with the redheaded woman, who was now gaping at me.

"By Gods, it's you!" Her eyes widened in surprise, and she scrambled to curtsey before gazing up into my face. "You're the Huntress's Chosen!"

Sliding up beside me, Gaelon grabbed at the pitchers of ale before assisting the woman with the stew. Now that she had been distracted by the Healer, I made my move towards the entrance. The streets had quieted with the darkness of night, and I scanned the area, searching for my guard before deciding to check the stables.

"Barrick?" His back was to me while he stroked his gelding's forelock, and I waited with bated breath for him to face me. "I'm sorry if we upset you. I promise we meant nothing by it."

"It's fine." But I could see it wasn't. His shoulders were stiff, and he had yet to look at me.

"Truly, I did not mean to cause you any grief. I shouldn't have said anything."

"I should not be this weak. It has been over a year now since I lost him, and yet even the idea or mention of wanting anyone else rips me open." His voice was thick, and my heart dropped as a single tear escaped the corner of his eye and traced the scar that covered his cheek. The giant man had been nothing but strong and fierce for as long as I had known him, and I was not prepared to see such pain from him.

"Who was he?"

"Ian, my husband." Suddenly, I felt like a fool. Barrick had been by my side for months, and I had never once had the decency to ask about his life.

"I'm so sorry, Barrick." I lifted a hand to rest on his shoulder, but as soon as my palm touched the bulging muscle of his back, he spun on his heel and crushed me against his chest. Shock left me frozen, and I stood with my arms hanging limply at my sides until he pressed me closer. Wrapping my arms around the guard, I let him hold me tightly until his shuddering breaths became steady once again.

"Would you tell me about him?" I whispered against his chest.

"We had been married for eighteen years." Sliding his arms from me, Barrick stepped away and moved to sit on the straw that had been piled nearby.

"What was he like?" I folded myself next to him and leaned against his side as I waited for him to form an answer.

"He was the best part of me. Kind and loving, always welcoming to anyone around. He gave me hell constantly. Forever telling me that I was as approachable as a bear. He was my everything, and by Gods, I miss him."

Stroking a hand down his spine, I offered what comfort I could.

"What happened to him?" As soon as the words left my lips, I regretted them. The strong man who had never once wavered before slumped, and he cradled his head in his hands.

"He was killed six months before your battle at the shores." I wasn't sure what I had been expecting, but that was not it. The north had very heavy laws for those who murdered, and crime of that sort was infrequent, unless done by the Crimsons. And there was only one real reason why they would take the time to kill a commoner.

"He was a halfling," I whispered. It wasn't a question; I already knew the answer.

"He was. Had gone his entire life without being found out. But we had gotten careless as the years passed, and when the Crimsons began to rally, we had been left unprepared. I had headed to Port Huronian to help the townsfolk who had suffered a raid. I hadn't thought we were in any danger. I was a fool."

"You couldn't have known, Barrick." I wished I could ease his hurt, but I knew my words offered little comfort.

"That never eases the guilt or pain though, does it, Huntress?"

"No, it doesn't." Wrapping an arm around him, I settled close and laid my scarred cheek against his shoulder and let the quietness of the night soothe our hearts.

Chapter 16

Barrick stood guard in the corner of the room as our group began to settle for the evening. Most of the soldiers had been put on watch outside the entrance while the rest had found their rooms upstairs. There were still a few dozen groups of men scattered around the room, most of whom were well into their cups. Keeping an eye on the rowdiest of the bunch, I stirred my cold stew with disinterest.

"Excuse me?" a deep voice called from behind me, and my eyes lifted to Ella, who sat across the table, in alarm. Her own dark gaze had narrowed at the stranger at my back, her lips pressing together tightly, and I turned on my stool.

"Yes?" I didn't recognize the dirty blond hair or oversized grin and shifted uncomfortably when his grey eyes roamed my face before dropping down to my body.

"So it's true then? You're the Huntress's Chosen?" His grin grew even bigger, and I swallowed roughly at his sly expression.

"Are you blind or just stupid?" Ella bit out from across the table before pulling herself from her seat when she noticed my discomfort. Leaning forward, she pressed both of her palms into the wood, and I shot her a warning glance.

"Is there something you wanted?" I shifted my weight and peeked around him to see what could have sent him over here, not believing that it was just pure curiosity.

"Well, that is—" He seemed to be having second thoughts and looked towards the immortal before clearing his throat. "I just mean—is it true you gave your maidenhead to a man named Dane after knowing him for just a day?"

The air around us grew quiet, and I could swear the musicians in the corner had stopped their playing, although I knew that there was no possibility that they had heard the man's question. Out of the corner of my eye I noticed Ella straighten to her full height and could feel the rage that seemed to burn through her.

"Why would you ask something like that?" Her voice was calm, steady, but the rage was there, and once again I was thankful to have her as my own tongue felt as if it had swelled in my mouth. But when the man didn't answer immediately her voice rose. "Are you daft? Get the hell out of here!"

Blinking at the immortal, the man stayed rooted to the spot and spluttered out an apology under his breath but did not move. Barrick, who was still in the corner, must have noticed my face and had begun to make his way over with his hand already curling around his weapon. However, he hadn't even taken three strides before a dark fist flew from across the table and cracked into the nose of the stranger.

"She is a Chosen! Who are you to ask her such a thing?!" Ella moved to stand over the man, her slender shoulders lifting with every heaving breath, and I placed a calming hand on her back in reassurance.

"I'm sorry! I'm sorry! I thought he was lying! He's spent months telling anyone who would listen, and I just didn't believe it." The man was still clutching his nose while the blood poured from behind his fingers, and I blinked down at him before searching the room.

Ella too lifted her chin, her eyes darting around the space before she swore under her breath and then strode towards the unruly group of men in the back, not stopping until she stood in front of the man I was familiar with. And then with a quick, graceful movement, her arm cocked back for a second time, and she slammed her fist into his jaw.

Dane toppled backwards off his chair, but Ella did not hesitate and launched herself onto him, her tiny fists striking him over and over until strong arms wrapped around her waist and Barrick hauled her off of her brother. Kicking, she fought the guard's hold all while screaming obscenities at the man who was now being helped onto his feet by his friends.

"She is a feisty little thing, isn't she?" Elizabeth chuckled as she stood beside me, taking a long drink of her wine. "And Gods do I love her."

Moving my eyes to my friend silently, I watched as she finished her cup before wiping her mouth and following the guard out of the building. Ella was still screaming threats at the top of her lungs, and I wiped at my face tiredly.

"This is not quite what I had in mind for our first night off of the road." Gaelon sighed as he approached me, watching Dane clean the blood from his mouth with his shirt before shooting me a questioning stare. "Are you okay?"

I felt humiliated, embarrassed, and exposed. Dane and his friends were all watching the Healer and me, and their prying eyes made my skin crawl. Never once had I thought I would see the man again, let alone now and here of all places. I also had never anticipated that he would go and tell anyone about our single uninteresting night together.

As if the Healer could sense my thoughts, he crowded in closer. "It's what men do, Skylahr. They brag about their victories and their conquests." Gaelon's voice was low and gentle, but my jaw clenched at his words.

"Is that what I was then, something to be conquered?" The words spat out of me viciously, and I grabbed at my forgotten ale before tipping my head back and swallowing it down.

"To a man like that, yes. You will be the only thing of importance he will ever be able to boast about."

I glared at Dane's bloodied face until he ducked his head and turned away from us. "That's pathetic."

"Yes, it is," the Healer agreed.

I rapped my knuckles on the door and crossed my arms while I waited for the heated whispers to stop. After Ella had calmed, Elizabeth had ushered her to their room, and I had bided my time on my own until my impatience got the better of me. Knocking again, I shifted my weight from one foot to the other while chewing my thumbnail. I hoped Ella was not still too upset. I felt badly that she was put in such a difficult position, and regret filled my chest as I waited in the hall.

"Sky?" Elizabeth whispered as she cracked the door. Her hair was a tangled mess, and her cheeks were flushed. Realizing what I had interrupted, I blushed hotly and covered my face with my hands in embarrassment.

"I'm sorry, I was just coming to check on Ella. I should have waited until the morning. I'm so sorry," I repeated.

Grabbing my hands, Elizabeth tugged them down and pulled me into their room before shutting the door quietly. The immortal was in a far better state than her lover. Her hair was wrapped in the silk cover she slept in, and her nightgown was smoothed out. Grinning at me, she winked, and I rolled my eyes before falling into the chair in the corner of the room.

"Are you alright, Sky?" Ella whispered in concern, and I felt my cheeks heat before ducking my chin to my chest.

"I'm mortified but otherwise fine." Wiping at my face, I allowed my gaze to roam across the room while I waited for the churning in my gut to settle.

"You have absolutely nothing to be mortified about," Elizabeth soothed as she reached a delicate hand out to me, and I grasped her fingers gently.

"The entire room heard; everyone down there knows what I did."

My brows furrowed as I glanced at my friends, who perched on the bed with matching frowns.

"What you *did*? I'm not sure I understand." Ella glanced at her human for a pause before her dark eyes searched my face. "You're upset that people know you're no longer a maiden?"

Leaning back into the chair, I shrugged helplessly before dropping my chin. I myself truly didn't understand what it was that I was most embarrassed about. But I knew having people talk about me, having Dane boast about that night, made me feel *small*.

"You know that your"—pausing, Elizabeth searched for the words before clearing her throat softly—"*virtue* has no reflection of your worth, right?"

"And what if it's less about my virtue and more about their reaction? I mean those men could barely believe it to be true. They looked at me as if I should have been a secret kept from the world for Dane's sake. The only reason he told people is because of what I am. You heard his friend; he asked if I was truly a Chosen." The curtain of bronze that had shielded my face was pushed back behind my ear, and soft fingers stroked my scarred cheek before cupping my chin. Tilting it up, Ella waited for my eyes to meet hers before she smiled softly.

"Oh, Sky, when will you learn to see what you are?" She sighed dramatically before kneeling at my feet. "You are a Chosen, yes. But you are more than the title and deserve far better than a man who would only claim you for your power. The fact that you think otherwise makes me want to hunt him down again."

"He's your brother," I chided gently. "You shouldn't have to defend me from him."

Ella's slender fingers interlocked with my own, and she squeezed my hand tightly. "Dane and I share blood, but you are my family, Sky, and he had no right to speak of my sister in any way that contradicted her worth." Fury filled the immortal's eyes, and I tightened my hold on her fingers. "I hope I knocked a tooth out. Let's see him be charming without his smile."

Snorting, I knelt on the ground and held Ella tightly before lifting an arm out to Elizabeth.

"I would be lost without the two of you, I hope you know that," I whispered quietly into our embrace, thanking the Gods for my companions.

"You will never have to worry; we aren't going anywhere," Elizabeth murmured into my hair and I tugged them closer.

The halls were quiet by the time I crept out from the immortal's room, and I held my boots tightly in my hand as I snuck down the stairs towards the warm embers that burned in the fire pit. The room had been vacated, and I sighed in relief as I settled cross-legged in front of the glowing cinders, finding peace in the quiet until a door creaked open and heavy footsteps approached.

"Skylahr?" a deep voice whispered, and I peered over my shoulder to stare at Dane. His cheek had swelled from his sister's attack, and his lower lip was scabbed over.

He somehow looked smaller than I remembered, and I tried to recall why I had found him attractive in the first place. Sure, he was still a handsome man, but there was nothing extraordinary about him, and knowing he was willing to speak about me in such a way in order to gain the admiration of his friends left a bitter taste in my mouth.

"I'm surprised your sister didn't chase you out of this city, Dane." He took a step back at my tone and dropped his eyes to the floor. "What is it that you want now? Surely not another quick, unsatisfying fuck?"

The words surprised me. They had not been what I was planning to say had I run into the man again, and yet something in me was oddly pleased by the look of guilt that crossed his face. I wondered if he had been honest in the details of our tryst. Or perhaps he had exaggerated to make the story better for him. I could not imagine he would be patted on the back for his performance that night.

"I'm sorry I told them about us, it was not a kind thing to do." His words were mumbled, and I lifted a brow at him before turning to face the coals once more.

"Telling people that we had been together is not a reason for me to be upset, Dane. It was your motive for it. I'm sure that night had not even crossed your mind until you found out who I was. You only told them because you wanted to lay claim on the Chosen's maidenhead."

Dane's soft footsteps grew closer, his boots nearing my knee before he paused and let out a long breath. Glancing up at him from the corner of my eye, I watched him stare at the fire pit before seeming to decide to try his luck and sit next to me.

"I am sorry, Skylahr." Rolling my eyes, I shifted a few inches away from him.

"You are sorry because your sister humiliated you in front of the same men you bragged to." Turning my chin, I waited for his eyes to finally meet my own before I lowered my voice in a harsh whisper. "Tell who you want, but at least try to be honest about it. You have more reason to be embarrassed than I do."

Uncrossing my legs, I rose to my full height and lifted my chin high before peering down at him. The glow of the embers was quickly fading, and the shadows grew across his face. But when he remained silent, I turned towards the stairs.

"What happened to Ella?" The guilt in Dane's tone had disappeared, and I recognized the accusation behind the words. "Don't try to tell me that nothing is different, Skylahr. Something has changed my sister. What did you do?"

Tipping my head to look up at the stairs, I took in a deep breath. He was right of course; his sister was not the same halfling he had grown up with. She had lost that last bit of mortality after the ceremony had saved her. But that was not my story to tell, and I would not share her secrets with anyone, not even her brother.

"That's not for me to speak on. If you want to know something, ask her yourself." Moving to the stairs, I grabbed the wooden railing before looking back at him. "And Dane? You address me as Huntress. You no longer have the right to call me anything else."

Chapter 17

The inn was quiet as I finished my bowl of warm oats, and I glanced at the Healer as he spoke to the other patrons who had filtered down the stairs. Gaelon, as always, was warm and welcoming, his handsome face managing to capture the goodness that was in his very soul, and the people flocked to him.

"Sleep well?" Elizabeth asked, interrupting me from my musings as she found the empty stool next to me.

"Shouldn't I ask you that? Though I have a feeling you didn't get much of it after I left." I laughed while her pretty pale face flushed. Swatting at me, she leaned across my body and stole the last piece of bread from the table before popping it into her mouth.

"What are we talking about?" Ella questioned as she sat in the space across from me with a wide smile before focusing on her partner. The two of them were mindless when they got like this, just staring into each other's eyes while sharing secret smiles, and I sighed dramatically before moving away from the table.

"Enjoy your meal, you two," I called before heading towards the door and making my escape to the stables. Barrick was giving the soldiers instructions, and I kept my distance as he lectured them on their duties and his expectations. A few of them had locked eyes on me, and Barrick's attention wavered as he followed their gazes.

"Enough of your gawking. By Gods if I find out any of you put a foot wrong, you will be spending your free time sparring with the Huntress. Let's see how much you like to stare when she's beating you down with a wooden sword." The men seemed to take the threat seriously and scurried away without another glance in my direction.

"Really, Barrick? Resorting to empty threats these days?" His dark eyes narrowed at me for a minute before he strapped his sword to his hip and tightened the fastenings of his chest plate.

"Who said that threat was empty? They could use a good beating and you could use a clear head." Rolling my eyes at the man, I ducked into the stables.

The stalls were surprisingly quiet, and I checked on the horses before glancing over the dimly lit space. The walls had seen better days and the aisle could have used a good sweeping, but it was peaceful, and I exhaled roughly. Taking the opportunity to be alone, I turned to start the morning chores, but just as I was about to pass out the hay, I heard Gaelon call for me.

Wiping my hands across my tunic nervously, I stepped out of the barn, squinted in the morning sun, and eyed the Healer as he whispered to the guard heatedly. Whatever pleasantries he had made this morning had obviously led to him learning some sort of information. I crossed the space between us hurriedly as anxiety bubbled in my gut.

"What is it, Gaelon?" The Healer cupped my elbow gently and pulled me close before checking around us for eavesdroppers.

"I have been told there was a group of travellers who had crossed the city's limits just under six months ago."

"And? Surely they get many visitors here during the warmer months?" My brows pulled together in confusion, and I searched his handsome face for a clue as to what I was missing.

"Yes, but this particular group came just before the incidents began on the waters and were apparently searching for any information on the Siren and the Gods of old. They even asked for a tour of the Temple of Fate and Fortune."

"What did they find?" I asked, noticing that Ella had come from the inn and was armed as if she was ready to repeat her last visit to the temple.

"They were refused entry, but that same evening an intruder had managed to find a way in and ransacked the library. The priests are certain everything has been accounted for, but if they were that determined to get in, then I am sure this was not just a bit of curiosity. Perhaps there is something that could answer our own questions." Ella was nearly bouncing with excitement, and I glared at her for a pause before turning to the Healer.

"And are they planning on denying us entry as well then?"

"Of course not." Gaelon tilted his head in confusion, and I lifted my hand to gesture to the immortal beauty.

"Then why does Ella look like she's prepared to scale the walls again?"

Ella glowered at me, and I shrugged.

"Ella is coming along because she found the last scriptures you had been searching for, correct?" I supposed that was true even if it was only a fraction of the story, and I nodded my agreement. "And those scriptures were meant to be hidden, or so I am told."

"Yes, I was told the same." I thought back to how angry the Lupine alpha had been when I had confronted him with his portrait. He had said that we should have never been able to find that page, and yet Ella had managed to in a matter of minutes after I had hoisted her through the window of the temple.

"So, given that information, I'm inclined to believe that Hectoar was right in giving her that coin." My brows lowered in confusion while Gaelon cupped the immortal's shoulder. "It would appear that perhaps our little immortal here is not just a halfling, but a halfling in the name of the Jester." My eyes widened as my focus turned to Ella.

"What does that mean?" she asked with a whisper as her gaze searched the Healer's face.

"Given your uncanny ability to find things, I am willing to bet that you, Ella, carry the talent of luck and chance." Gaelon gave her shoulder a squeeze before turning to find Barrick, and Ella's eyes followed the Healer.

"Are you okay, El?" I asked as I stepped close and wrapped an arm around her shoulders.

"You don't think it's possible, do you, Sky?" I smiled down at her in reassurance.

"Why wouldn't it be? You didn't think you were just that special, did you? Of course there was a higher power behind all of your coincidences." My lips pulled as my grin grew, and I pushed her away from me playfully. "To be honest it makes me feel a little better knowing that you had something more on your side."

"Oh, because being the Huntress's Chosen was inadequate compared to my ability of being able to find a tiny scripture." She rolled her eyes while swatting at my shoulder half-heartedly.

"Are you two ready?" Barrick called to us as he approached, and I noticed he had not only armed himself with his sword but also a pair of daggers.

"Preparing for something, Barrick?" I questioned while gesturing to the multitude of weapons.

"Always. You would do well to remember that and perhaps take notes."

"What is the need when I have you around?" I teased, but his face never lifted into the half smile I usually received, and I swallowed roughly as he held my stare.

"Because there may be a day when you are unprepared, and I am not there." His voice was quiet but cold, and my stomach turned at the sound. "Never forget who you are and what people would be willing to do to get a hold of you. The only person you can truly trust to save you is yourself."

Without another word he turned his back to me and led the way to the temple, though I remained frozen in my place, wishing so badly I could find the words to tell him I had already learned that lesson.

The Temple of Fate and Fortune was much more extravagant in the light of day, and I scanned the intricate carvings that littered the walls as Ella searched the scriptures that were now piled on the table in the middle of the room. Along with the carvings, the walls were lined with stained glass, and the room was filled with dancing colours that I would have basked in had it not been for Ella's frustrated groans that would sound every few minutes as she searched page after page.

"Nothing?" Gaelon asked from his place at the far wall where he had been pulling book after book before tossing them on the table.

"Am *I* the only one reading these because you think the Jester's blood will help me find something?" Ella snapped as she rubbed her face in irritation.

"No, Ella, you and *I* are the only ones searching the pages because we are the only ones who can understand the tongue of old," Gaelon reminded her softly while lifting the book in his hands. Ella glared at the leather-bound pages while the Healer focused back on his task, and I gave her a reassuring nod when her eyes caught mine.

"Ella, why don't you stretch your legs?" I offered before shooting a pointed glare to the Healer, who had opened his mouth in protest. "Go for a walk and come back with a fresh mind."

Taking my advice, the immortal stood and stretched her arms above her head before offering me a grateful smile. "I saw a priest in the front hall. I think I will ask him if there is anywhere else we can search."

Nodding my head, I watched as her form sauntered out of the library and down the cobblestoned hall. We had been at this for half a day, and I knew I wasn't the only one whose patience was starting to waver. I waited until Ella's footsteps were nearly silent before turning to Gaelon.

"How long do we plan on doing this, Gaelon? This library has thousands of scriptures. We can't possibly search every page, and Ella has to be exhausted." Tossing the book he was reading onto the desk, Gaelon turned to me with a frown before exhaling roughly.

"You're right. Maybe we will just have to make our way along the coast and hope we will find more answers there." Gathering the piles of books from the desk, I began to put them back onto the shelves, awkwardly fumbling as the silence grew. Sensing my discomfort, the Healer moved to help me, his hands grabbing the pile from my arms, and I blinked at him as he smiled softly.

"You know, you are a good friend, Skylahr." The words surprised me, and I tilted my head in confusion.

"What brought that on?"

"You three are always looking out for each other, constantly aware of what the other needs. Even just now with Ella, and it's always that way with the three of you." He had turned to face the shelves, and I noticed a pink hue had filled his cheeks.

"That's what family does, they look after one another." I shrugged before clearing my throat self-consciously.

"Family," he whispered under his breath. "Is there room for one more?" His tone was teasing, but I could see the sadness in his eyes, and I wondered if he had ever had a family of his own before Hectoar had found him.

"Of course, Gaelon, always." Turning to me, Gaelon wrapped one strong arm around my waist and tugged me closer. I was unsure how to respond until I felt a subtle tremble vibrate across his shoulders. Feeling a tug of guilt, I pulled him closer to me and wrapped both of my arms across his shoulders. When was the last time someone had just held him or offered him any sort of comfort? Had he been feeling isolated and lonely for decades?

Just as I was about to ask, we were interrupted by the sound of footsteps running across the stone floor. We sprung apart just as Ella burst back into the room, her slender arm held above her head with a book clutched in her grasp.

"Oh! Sorry, was I interrupting?" Her eyes were wide with innocence, but I could see behind the façade and glared at her as another flush crossed my face hotly.

"Ella? Did you find something?" Gaelon asked as his eyes focused on the leather-bound book she still held above her head.

"Yes, well, I'm not certain, but I think so." The immortal lowered the scripture and then took a step towards us. "I found the priest, and he said a number of scriptures had been damaged after the last visitors. Some had been in a worse state than others and were currently being repaired."

Taking another step forward, the immortal slowly crossed the stone floor and then opened the leather-bound cover. "Now why would they bother destroying books?"

"They were in a haste to find something," Gaelon suggested and then he frowned. "Or hide it."

"That is exactly my line of thinking," Ella agreed and then carefully set the worn pages onto the table and gestured for Gaelon to take a look. The Healer bent over them, scanning the parchment quickly only to flip the page.

But there wasn't another page. In fact at least a dozen had been sloppily torn from their places, and his face paled as he flipped through the remaining pages once more. But just as he was about to shut the book, Ella's dark hand grabbed his wrist.

"Wait," she whispered and rifled through the book one last time before stopping. Placing her finger at the centre of the parchment, she slid the book closer to Gaelon. "There."

I could barely make out the faint outlines from where I stood and shuffled closer to see what had caught her attention.

Sitting in the middle of the page was a near invisible map of Elrin, though none of the minor towns or cities were listed, and to the left of it was a shape I didn't recognize. It was north, nearly neighbouring what would be the Lupine territories and was placed on the very edge of the page. But the strangest part of the image was not only the fact that it had not been in the atlas Elizabeth had found in Noordeign, but that there was a faint black circle around the island.

"What is that?" I asked as Gaelon's long finger traced the black ink.

"Skohyn, the island of torment."

Chapter 18

"Skohyn? I've never heard of it," I whispered to Ella as Barrick and Gaelon led us back to the inn.

"I've only heard the name once or twice in passing and never in a way that made me believe it truly existed," she whispered back while keeping a close eye on the men, though I knew Gaelon could hear us given his heightened senses as a fellow immortal. "And none of Elizabeth's maps have it marked."

Turning towards us, Barrick motioned for us to continue through the doorway. I watched as the Healer sneakily handed the book to the guard before following, and I tipped my head in question.

"Later," he promised as he passed and then instructed my head guard to prepare to leave by nightfall before heading up the stairs.

"That's not suspicious or concerning at all," Ella muttered under her breath as she focused on the now-closed door of the Healer's room. "I guess we better pack because it seems as if we are leaving."

"There you are, you two! I've been waiting all day." Wrapping her arms around our shoulders, Elizabeth gave a long squeeze as she guided us towards the table that had been set with breads and meats. The smell forced a long grumble from my stomach. "I figured you would be hungry and I'm glad I got this ready in a hurry. We better eat now; I doubt we'll have another meal like this on the road."

I kept my eyes trained on Gaelon's wooden door even as I tore into the warm bread and shoved it into my mouth. After finishing the meal, we helped load the wagons and did one last final sweep through the inn to be sure we hadn't forgotten anything before mounting our horses.

"Any idea why we are leaving now rather than in the morning?" Elizabeth grumbled in irritation, and I shook my head while keeping my eyes on the back of the Healer. Other than avoiding my gaze, he had behaved completely normal once he had finally emerged from his room, and I waited for the opportunity to catch him alone.

"At least we mostly avoid the heat this way." Barrick sighed and Ella nodded in agreement.

"Huntress?" Gaelon turned to face me and inclined his head, a silent invitation to ride with him, and I nudged my horse forward. Once we had managed to distance ourselves a few yards, I turned to the Healer with a lifted brow.

"Whoever beat us to the temple found exactly what they were looking for, that is obvious." He pulled the book from his saddle bag, gently tore the map from its place, and cautiously handed it to me.

Holding it in front of me, I scanned the page. "And they think Skohyn is of importance?"

"It is circled in the only book that has missing pages." Gaelon sighed.

"And what does the book say?" I handed back the map, steered my horse closer to his until our legs were nearly brushing, and waited until he had pocketed the drawing once more.

"Nothing that I would immediately deem important, but the last page remaining mentioned a calling or a summoning. Or perhaps it was in regard to an instrument. It is in a different dialect than I am used to and was hard to decipher."

"So what then, we go to Skohyn rather than continuing down the coast?" I wondered out loud with a frown.

"Skohyn is called the island of torment for a reason, Skylahr. The legends say it is a place full of magic and deception. I do not know a soul who has located it and returned."

"Well, someone must have, Gaelon, or we wouldn't know about it," I argued and then halted my horse before rubbing my eyes.

"If Skohyn was significant enough to break into the temple, then perhaps we should go there first and not waste any more time. Ritari and Lord Deavion can wait."

"I agree that the missing pages and the mark on this map shows that things are too coincidental to not be of significance, but we have no idea who did this or why, and we cannot set sail based on a whim. To be honest, I am surprised you would even suggest that we do so."

"It's not as if the decision to ride south was based on much more than a *whim*," I snapped before realizing what I was implying, and Gaelon's expression hardened.

"I wasn't aware you felt that way."

Rubbing at my face tiredly, I sighed. "I just meant I didn't know how little information we would have, and I thought we were seeking answers. This is the closest—no, the *only* thing we have found of any true consequence."

"We came south because we were called on and we are needed," Gaelon argued. "And after my last journey, I have learned to not be so rash in my decision making."

His dark eyes never wavered from my face, and a tension tugged across my chest. "Skylahr, I would have thought you had learned that lesson as well, but it appears, even after all of the loss and grief you have suffered, you have not." Kicking his horse, Gaelon took off towards the gates of the city, and I felt my heart drop when I realized that I had only added to the Healer's guilt.

Gaelon had not acknowledged me for days now, and I knew the strain between us had been the focus of the group. The soldiers assumed it was some form of a lovers' quarrel while Ella and Elizabeth reassured me that I had not been in the wrong to question the Healer. But their words of affirmation did little to quell the shame I felt, and I so badly wished I could have approached my concerns in a different way.

"You look like you could use a spar." Barrick's voice pulled me from my thoughts as I sat next to Ella as she ate her dinner, and I glanced up at him when his boot nudged my own.

"Barrick, I'm not really in the mood." Tucking my knees to my chest, I leaned forward and rested my chin on the joints as I blinked up at the guard.

"Even more reason to agree." Bending at his waist, he tucked one massive hand under my arm before hauling me to my feet. "Pouting with your friends won't solve anything, Huntress."

"And sparring will?" I grumbled as I pulled my arm free from his hold.

"No. In fact, given your lack of sleep and shitty attitude, it will make you feel worse because I am about to knock you around." Stroking his beard in thought, he paused before grinning at me. "But at least it will make me feel better. Watching you mope about is getting on my last nerve."

Catching the dull sparring sword he tossed my way, I followed the guard away from the group and took position as he pulled his armour off piece by piece. Once free from the metal, he lifted his own blade at me in challenge, and I raised a brow.

"Feeling that confident in your skills today? Are you sure you don't want a helmet?" It appeared that Barrick was done with my talking, and he lunged forward with his blade, forcing me to dodge his attack. He generally started off with a slower move, and I frowned at him.

"Stop scowling and do something. A moving target is much more of a challenge, and I am not here to play." Annoyed by his persistence, I focused my weight and skillfully moved forward with an attack, holding my arms steady as his own blade clashed with mine.

This was a dance I knew well; it was a rhythm that my body had memorized, and the melody of it made my blood sing. This was what I was good at, this was what I had been born to do. Fighting was my destiny, and as I surrendered to my instincts, the spar had reached its crescendo, ending with Barrick at my mercy.

"There you are." He panted from the ground while pushing the tip of my sword away from his face. "That is the Huntress I have been waiting for. Welcome back."

Smiling down at the guard, I helped him to his feet and dusted him off. He was right to push me; I felt better than I had the whole journey and was finally clear-headed. Stepping away, I went back into position and nodded my agreement for another round.

Much like the last, Barrick held on for only a few dozen strikes before I had bested him once again. But as always, he stood, dusted off, and readied himself for me once more. It was a routine we had mastered, and though I usually felt a small amount of remorse when I watched him rub at his back or the marks I had left, I knew there was no place he would rather be.

Thankful didn't begin to describe how I felt for the guard after the time we had spent together. He had given me back something I had thought left me when my father died, and though he wasn't a replacement, I couldn't help but feel as if he had been sent to me.

"Alright. That's enough for me. I think it's time we settle for the night, Huntress."

Peering over my shoulder, I noticed the small audience that had gathered and flushed under the scrutiny before passing my sparring sword to my opponent.

"When is that blush ever going to go away? By Gods, girl, you still turn as red as you did the first day I met you."

"I hope never." Elizabeth laughed softly as she tugged me to her. "She wouldn't be our Sky without it."

Pulling away from the immortal, I searched for the Healer's face, hoping I would see that soft smile I had grown so fond of. But he was nowhere to be found, and my shoulders sagged at the realization. He was always the first to watch our sparring matches when he had the time, and not having him in the crowd just solidified the space that had grown between us.

"He sent me over here to collect you. Says we should rest while we can. Apparently, he's aiming to reach Bascala by tomorrow."

The ruckus of the market echoed around us, and I watched in amazement as hordes of people pushed and shoved their way to the carts that were overloaded with fish. The noise was overpowered only by the smell, and I lifted my tunic to cover my nose.

"Never been to a fish market before?" Barrick laughed as he pulled down the fabric that concealed the lower half of my face.

"We don't really fish in the north; we don't have the weather for it, and no one was stupid enough to brave the frigid, temperamental waters in Noorde Point. It was always venison or rabbit, and honestly, I think I prefer it." I grimaced, watching as a net of fish opened into an empty barrel with a sickening slapping sound. "Definitely prefer it."

"Nothing is better than roasted fish with salt and a side of crab." Barrick watched the shipments come in with a longing gaze, and I lifted my tunic over my nose once more.

"I will take your word for it."

Bascala was not a large village, about the size of Noorde Point, though it felt as if many more travellers made the journey here compared to the north. Shuffling forward behind Barrick and Gaelon, I pulled my hood farther down to cover my face. The heat of spring may have been an issue before, but today the ocean winds pulled every which way, and it had been raining since the morning. Luckily though, the poor weather meant I could conceal my face from any inquisitive eyes, and I gazed down at my feet while dropping my shoulders.

"Stop making yourself small," Gaelon whispered from in front of me, and the sound of his voice had my chin lifting instantly. He had not spoken to me since leaving Carlon, and I blinked at him in surprise before giving him a gentle nod. "You are a Chosen, you are not meant to hide or blend in. Carry yourself with pride, even if it is not your own. Take the pride others feel when they look at you and know that you are nothing but extraordinary."

I chewed on my trembling lower lip while my eyes misted at his sincerity, and I took his words for what they were, a peace offering.

"As are you, Gaelon." His dark eyes seemed to lighten at the reassurance, and he smiled softly before moving on.

"Thank the Gods," Ella groaned. "Took you two long enough to kiss and make up." Elbowing her in the ribs, I followed the men up the steep steps towards the rest of the town. The market was just off the road and near the port, but the rest of the village sat high on the massive rock cliffs that overlooked the ocean.

Enormous waves crashed against the jagged stone, and the spray nearly reached the brittle wooden buildings that covered the land above. Squinting against the wind, I turned to look across the view and stopped short at the sight.

The whitecaps were not just massive in size, they also seemed to change direction every few minutes, and the clouds above swirled in a pattern that could only be described as vicious. Dark greys and greens moved this way and that, twirling around each other as if a painter was churning the two colours together, and I felt an unease bubble in my gut.

"Come along!" Gaelon shouted over the whistling gusts that surrounded us, and I glanced at the horizon for one last long moment before following the Healer.

Chapter 19

The townsfolk rushed to shelter as the storm grew, and I pulled Ella and Elizabeth along, ignoring them as they cursed at me for my long legs while they struggled to match my pace. Managing to reach the cover of the town, I glanced at my friends while Gaelon led us to the tall central building.

"This is the manor of Bascala," he explained. "Lord Orrick is an old, foul man; you would do well to watch what you say around him and do your best to avoid conflict," he warned with a pointed stare at Ella.

"Why is he only looking at me?" Ella grumbled after the Healer had turned to the door, and I coughed in my fist in an attempt to hide the chuckle that had escaped me. Placing a hand against her back, I pushed Ella forward and nodded my head at the servant who had welcomed us in. But my gesture was obviously not what was expected of me, and the man took a step back with a slack-jawed expression before hurrying around the corner.

"This is not Noordeign, Huntress, it's best if you ignore the staff. If you need something I will find the chamberlain. And you don't ask, you demand. These people are beneath you," Barrick whispered firmly while avoiding my eyes.

"Says who?"

"Says tradition, Huntress." The title was sneered in a gruff voice, sounding more like an insult than a triumph, and I narrowed my eyes at the stranger.

He was nearly my height, but his rounded belly and thick neck made him seem larger. I moved my eyes across his luxurious robes that were decorated more brilliantly than anything that hung in my wardrobe back in Noordeign. Atop his balding head sat a pointed gold crown that was littered with emeralds and pearls, and I wondered how he managed to find such treasures when his town looked as if it had spent the last decade falling apart.

"Lord Orrick." Gaelon drew his attention away from my face and waited until the man's pale grey eyes met his own before offering a slight incline of his head. But the man did not reciprocate the gesture, and instead moved his gaze back to my face with an expectant glare. Ella, who had remained beside me, scoffed under her breath. But the noise hadn't been quiet enough, and those expectant grey eyes turned into an icy glare without pause.

"What was that, you little wench?" The words slithered from him like a serpent, and immediately I shifted in front of the immortal before squaring my shoulders.

"Mutter another insult and it will be your last." My voice was unwavering, and it felt as if for the first time since he and I had locked eyes he realized just how accurate my title was. I may not know the ways of nobility nor be what he had expected, but I could be just as lethal as my Goddess given the right motivation, and protecting my family was reason enough to threaten him.

No one moved for a long pause, and then a burst of laughter broke from Orrick and his fingers curled around his bulging stomach while his crown nearly toppled from his head as he threw it back in joy. Stunned, I glanced at Barrick as his hand slowly slid from the hilt of his weapon before he turned to the Healer in confusion.

"By Gods, you may be the Huntress's Chosen after all," he wheezed as he wiped at his eyes. "You looked ready to take my head just now." My jaw tightened as I refrained from confirming just how accurate he was, and I glanced back at Ella. Her own dark eyes were burning with anger, but when she met my gaze, she exhaled roughly, and I gave her a gentle smile before moving my attention to Elizabeth. She had shuffled closer, her pale hand tangled with her immortal's, and she looked as if she was ready to flee back out the doors.

"Come in, come in!" Orrick waved us over and then turned to the hall behind him. The manor itself was in a poor state; the walls looked ready to crumble at any moment, and the floor was cracked and chipped. There were no paintings hung, no artwork of any kind, and the halls seemed cold and barren as we passed through.

"Tell me, how are the Chosen ones of Elrin? I bet you're enjoying your victories and admirers!" Orrick laughed to himself, and Gaelon offered a polite smile, but I remained silent as we finally entered the dining hall. The long stone table was filled with mountains of fish and seafood, the piles nearly ready to topple over if not for the lack of space between each dish. I wrinkled my nose at the smell as the lord of the manor waddled his way through the room.

Following the group, I moved to the empty seat left of Orrick's and realized that I could not even see Gaelon, who had sat across from me. I frowned at the headless scaled bodies that blocked my vision. Ella, who had taken the chair next to me, looked just as repulsed, but Barrick's eyes shone with excitement, and I waited for his dark gaze to finally meet mine before making a face at him in disgust.

"To my honoured guests." Orrick lifted his golden goblet high above his head. "I am privileged to have you here. Let us feast together as brethren would!" He tipped his head back, rivers of wine sloshing over his rounded cheeks before sliding down his neck. I leaned into Ella carefully while he was distracted.

"Hear that, El? You went from wench to honoured guest," I whispered just loud enough for her heightened hearing, and then glanced at Barrick, who had filled his plate with half a dozen long tentacles. "At least one of us will not go hungry."

"Tell me, Huntress, where are you from?" Orrick ordered as he cracked the pair of crab legs that had been piled on his plate before slurping the meat out of them.

"Noorde Point." My tone was still harsh, but the man paid no mind and reached for another piece of shellfish.

"I've never heard of it. I bet you don't have delicacies like this up there." His face shone with the evidence of his meal, and my stomach turned as he lifted his arm to wipe it on the beautiful robe he still wore. The front of him was splattered with wine, and tiny bits of food had covered his lap. "But I'll bet you've heard of me, eh?"

Though I was not able to see Gaelon, I heard him clear his throat distinctively, and the instruction was clear: he wanted me to sing this man's praises. But I was not dishonest, and I had no answer for the man. I had never heard of Bascala let alone the lord of it. So instead, I leaned back in my chair and tilted my head in confusion. "I'm sorry, Lord Orrick, I must confess I have not."

His eyes narrowed at me in suspicion, and he chewed loudly before pointing a wet finger. "You lie. Surely you have heard of the only human lord in Elrin."

Prior to the battle, the lords and ladies of Elrin had all been immortals, most belonging to the Seductress, but now that the Crimsons had been defeated, more and more vacancies had come up, and we had filled them with the best possible candidates, not caring if they were immortal or not.

"Actually, my lord"—I ignored the warning kick from under the table and smiled at Orrick—"there are now half a dozen human lords and ladies of Elrin. The Healer and I appointed them ourselves. Each one was hand chosen. In fact a vacancy has just come up in the north, and there are a number of mortal women I would love to see fill the role."

Orrick choked on this mouthful of food, and my smile turned predatory as his face reddened from lack of air. I pushed back from the table, strode to the man, and slapped his back roughly with my palm, using enough force to knock him forward into his plate. "Careful now, I would hate to have to replace another."

I peered over the golden crown and focused on the Healer's dark eyes that were now burning with warning. But I refused to listen to this man brag about himself as if he were a God while others suffered. Just looking at the staff that had lined the room, I could see the longing on their faces as they watched their lord indulge in his never-ending hunger. I could tell that they went to bed hungry even though there was enough food on this table for not only them, but for villagers who were probably wasting away in the alleys of town.

Lifting my chin, I felt the heat of my conquered ignite simmer under my skin, and I gave the Healer my own warning look. I would not be reprimanded for this. Not this time. Not for insulting this poor excuse of a leader. I was rash, I was imperfect as a Chosen, but in this circumstance, I knew that I was right.

"Now then." I moved back to my chair while catching Ella's prideful smile. "We actually came here hoping you could answer some questions, Lord Orrick."

Patting his chest, he continued to inhale deeply, and I waited until I had his full attention. Those grey eyes that had just begun to soften were sharp and accusing once again, but I paid them no mind. Sipping on the wine that had been placed in front of me, I held his stare, assuring him that I was the one who currently ruled this room.

"We heard rumours that you've had some trouble on the waters here." I was careful with my wording, sure to not divulge too much information. "Have you heard anything about that?"

Orrick turned to the Healer before glancing around the room, and I followed his eyes, taking note that the staff had begun to fidget in their positions. A sign that even if the lord would not be honest, the people of this town knew something was amiss. Orrick grabbed the cloth that had been left unused next to his plate and dabbed at his face before folding his hands on top of his belly and leaning back in his chair.

"I'm not sure I know what you speak of, Huntress."

I used my legs to turn my seat just slightly before bracing my elbows on my knees and leaning forward. "No? You've heard nothing?"

Orrick shook his head and raised his shoulders in a shrug.

"But, Huntress, if there are rumours spreading all the way up to the north, they must be very interesting. Boring gossip never makes it that far." Orrick smiled, and I laughed under my breath, ignoring the sound of Gaelon shifting in his seat as he prepared to interrupt me at any moment.

We had come here for answers, and if the lord refused to speak to the Chosen themselves, then I was sure there would be severe consequences for any townsfolk who decided to reveal what they may know or have seen, and we would leave this place empty-handed.

"My concern is really for you, Lord Orrick." I took another long drink of wine, ignoring the narrowed eyes that watched my every move.

"Your concern is unnecessary, I have everything a lord could dream of." His voice was heated, and I nodded silently while I gazed across the piles of food.

"I see that. How lucky you are to have such wealth. But here is where my worry lies," I sighed dramatically while pretending like the room had not grown very still. "If those rumours were to be true, and Bascala or any of its trading partners were to be having trouble, I would assume that eventually it could escalate."

"Escalate?" he repeated with a scoff, and I nodded my head.

"Yes, eventually the market would slow, ships would stop attempting to make the journey, and what would happen if yours continued to perish?" I wondered out loud. "By then you would need assistance, and the north, well, you know what little knowledge we have about the comings and goings of a grand village like yours. But *if* we were asked to return, wouldn't it seem like a wasted effort considering we had already come all this way, and you refused to tell us anything that could potentially aid you?"

Orrick lifted his forgotten fork and pointed at me in challenge. "It is said that you are not versed in the ways of court. I heard that you like to play warrior and are as empty-headed as any idiot guard."

Barrick, who had been silent this entire time, cursed under his breath and rose from his chair with enough force to tip it over. But I held my hand out, cautioning the guard to remain where he was. "You are correct, Lord Orrick; it appears rumours do have to be interesting to spread so far. I hope you are not too upset that those ones proved to be false."

"You play the game well, Huntress, I will give you that. And I know better than to challenge an opponent who has me backed into a corner." Smoothing his filthy robe, the lord seemed to take a pause as he gathered his thoughts. "Things have not been right on the sea for nearly a year now, but occurrences have been more frequent in the last two months. I won't bother to bore you with the details as I can see now that you know what has been said to be out there."

"We do," I agreed.

"Then you know that there is no stopping it. But if you are determined to try, go to the tavern. There you will find a woman named Mira. She has been on the sea her entire life and is a well-known sailor here."

Standing from my chair, I tipped my chin and glanced across the table at Gaelon. His dark eyes were light with surprise, and his lips lifted in a soft smile before he too rose from his seat, gesturing that the rest should do the same, and then we moved towards the hall.

But just as I reached the threshold of the room, I turned on my heel and glanced back at the man with a hard stare. "Orrick, you would do well to remember how kind my friends and I were even after you insulted my sister and my intelligence. If I were you, I would follow our example of kindness and share your delicacies with your staff and people."

His eyes widened at my unspoken threat, but my attention was drawn to the shocked faces of the staff. Nodding at them, I gestured to the table and remained in my position until the last of them had scurried out of the room with an armful of fish.

"And if I hear anything about you punishing them for what I just allowed, I will make sure it is you who starves."

Chapter 20

"I have been in more taverns in the last two years than I have in my entire life," I grumbled as I pulled my hood over my hair and stepped carefully around a pile of vomit that littered the ground outside the building. My teeth chattered against the chill in the air now that the adrenaline that had been pumping through my veins had slowly dissipated, leaving me shivering and drained.

"You are trembling," Elizabeth said worriedly as she grabbed at my hand, and I squeezed her fingers in reassurance while glancing around self-consciously, concerned that my shaken form and pale face had drawn attention.

"Honestly, how do you go from being the fierce Huntress one moment to a quivering mess the next?" Barrick wondered out loud, and I wrapped my arms around myself in uneasiness.

"I can be fierce to do what I have to for others, Barrick. But you don't spend your entire life trying to twist yourself into something people will accept just to forget how it felt to be cast aside once you have managed it. I can't unlearn a lifetime of insecurities in a matter of months just because you have all decided that my title means those memories should no longer matter."

I had never divulged the ridicule or loneliness I suffered in Noorde Point to my guard, and I watched as his mouth pulled into a frown and his eyes shone with sympathy.

Gaelon, who had led us to the tavern, turned to me and placed a strong hand on my shoulder in comfort. "You handled yourself brilliantly, Skylahr, and you got us more information than I could have hoped for. I am sorry I doubted you. Orrick is not an easy man to intimidate, and I do not think anyone could have done a better job." Pulling his hood from over his head, Gaelon motioned for us to stay put and ducked through the doorway.

The winds continued to whistle through the roads of the village, and I turned slightly and used my body to block Ella and Elizabeth from the misty gusts while we waited. After what felt like ages, the Healer finally reappeared with a heavy frown.

"Mira's ship has yet to dock, and looking at the water now"—he paused while he searched out the massive waves that were visible between the buildings—"she most likely will not be attempting to come this close to shore until the storm passes. Especially with those cliffs."

"Staying with Lord Orrick is out of the question," Ella said while nudging me with a grin. "And the tents will be impossible to construct with this wind."

Glancing up at the rotting wooden planks of the tavern wall, I sighed. "I've stayed in worse. We should alert the soldiers though; they must be freezing in the market."

Barrick had volunteered to round up the party while the four of us settled into our rooms for the night. The tavern was drafty, the smell of stale ale and fire filled the air, and I sighed in exhaustion while I took in my room. The bed that was pushed against the far wall was a foot too short, and I fingered the damp, worn sheets with a wrinkled nose.

Draping my cloak across the mattress, I curled onto my side and tucked my knees to my chest while the wind and rain pounded against the walls. The tiny space under the door flickered with the light from the hall, and I watched as shadows passed while the rest of the group found their beds. The tavern itself was quiet, unlike the last we had visited, but something about the room brought a flood of memories to my mind, and if I closed my eyes and focused, I could swear I felt *his* body next to mine.

The longing for him had never truly disappeared, but the ache it left had been soothed with time. Now when I pictured the chiselled angles of his face, I was left with wanting rather than pain and regret. Part of me had wondered if I still thought of him because I clung to the memories of what he made me feel before it all crumbled around me, because he had been the first to ever truly pique my interest.

But now that so much time had passed, I knew it couldn't be *just* that.

Rolling onto my back, I closed my eyes and stretched my limbs out. I could see him there, his face above mine while those molten silver eyes watched my every expression. I could smell him, the scent of pine and cedar with a hint of smoke, and if I truly focused, I could hear his voice whisper my name.

Normally at this point I would be fighting the urge to stroke my skin and move my hands across my body as he would. This time, however, a burning sharpness prickled at the backs of my eyes, and I blinked up at the ceiling as a single tear rolled down my cheek and across my scar while the loneliness set in.

"You look like hell," Barrick muttered around his mouthful of bread, and I glared at the guard before falling into the seat next to him. Wrapping my hands around the warm cup of tea, I willed the warmth to seep into my bones while I waited for everyone else to wake.

"They weren't your usual nightmares last night, were they?" the guard asked quietly, and I closed my eyes as my shoulders slumped and shook my head. "I didn't think so, I haven't heard you call out that name before."

"Has Gaelon told you the plan for today?" I asked, hoping to change the topic of conversation.

"He wants to head to the docks and wait for this Mira." Barrick sighed while pushing a plate of bread at me.

"How do we know she will return?" The storm last night had been awful, and given the way it had come on so suddenly I was sure I would wake to news of another ship disappearing mysteriously.

"You have such little faith, Skylahr." Gaelon's voice sounded from behind me, and I felt guilty for speaking my worries out loud. We didn't need any more negativity on this journey, and I glanced at the Healer with an apologetic smile.

"One of us has to be cynical, it brings balance to the group." I shrugged and Gaelon rolled his eyes.

"You certainly are good at it, and I do hate to disappoint you, but I have already confirmed with the barmaid that the woman we are searching for has already made it back to port."

"Then it seems I was wrong to worry," I admitted and offered the Healer my plate in a peace offering, while ignoring Barrick's narrowed gaze.

"You should eat, Huntress. You didn't touch anything last night, and you'll feel worse if your stomach goes empty any longer." I had planned to dismiss his cautioning, but the thought of having to resort to fish when the hunger became too much had me shoving the stale piece of bread into my mouth clumsily.

"Good Gods, Sky, no need to choke yourself, I'm sure we'll find more bread." Ella laughed as she and Elizabeth made it to the table. I swallowed down my mouthful before taking a long sip of tea to ease its journey.

"Death by bread, what a horrible and boring way for the Huntress to go," Elizabeth joked, and I rolled my eyes at the snickers that followed.

The docks were nearly empty by the time we had wandered down to the port, and I wondered if it was because the sailors had taken advantage of the better weather and set sail or if something more ominous had happened to the ships that would have docked.

Scanning the shore, my eyes landed on the sole ship that rocked on the soft waves in the distance. I carefully led the way across the wet wooden planks until we had reached the end of the dock. Gaelon had confirmed that the ship with faded blue sails was in fact the one we had been waiting for, and I glanced at the Healer.

"Well, now what?" I had never been to a fishing village and had never truly thought about how a ship would reach shore but now realized the sea beneath us was probably much too shallow and the crew was forced to anchor farther in the depths of the water.

"We take one of these." Barrick pushed past me and pointed at the rowboat that had been tied to the dock. Managing to step into it with a surprising amount of grace, Barrick then held out his hand and helped the rest of us get into place and untied the rope.

My fingers grasped the wooden edge as we approached the massive ship, and I swallowed the queasiness that had already begun to swirl in my gut. Glancing at my friends, I noticed that Elizabeth also looked pale, and I offered her a grimace before I was pulled to my feet by the guard.

"Up you go, Huntress." He pushed me gently towards the rope ladder that hung in front of me, and I grasped at the rough material before hoisting myself up. Time seemed to slow, and my heartbeat echoed in my ears as I carefully climbed up the ship's side until finally reaching the railing. I had never been afraid of heights, but my inexperience with being on the ocean had left me shaken, and I took in a deep breath when my boots had found purchase on the wooden deck.

"Can I help you?" Turning on my heel, I backed away from the gleaming blade that was pointed at my neck and lifted my hands in surrender. The weapons master was a short little thing, with wide hips and a round face. Her wild blond curls would have placed her at my shoulder, and I took in her massive black hat and beaded necklaces. She looked no older than five and thirty, and I gave her what I hoped was an apologetic smile before glancing at the thin man at her side.

"I'm sorry to board unannounced." I looked at the Healer, who had just hoisted himself over the rail, but my attention was immediately pulled back to the woman when I heard her surprised gasp and the clanging of her sword colliding with the wooden floor.

"It's you." Her blue eyes were wide, and she hastily bent at the waist before gesturing to the man to do the same.

"And you're Mira, the sailor?" I asked, but the words seemed to have struck a nerve, and the thin man's spine straightened before he turned to the blonde and then he moved his hands around rapidly in what seemed to be a pattern, almost as if he was repeating my question somehow. The woman's eyes followed the fluid movement with ease and then she turned to me with a narrowed gaze.

"Captain actually." My brows rose in surprise, and her jaw clenched in response. Saving me from offending her again, Gaelon stepped towards us with a charming smile, and I watched in amazement as his own fingers lifted.

"Sorry for the mistake, Captain." He paused, though his hands kept moving in what appeared to be a dance of sorts. "We had only just learned of you last night from Lord Orrick, and with the storm, we had little time to ask any more questions."

Mira watched his fingers closely before sneering. "Orrick is a bastard," she spat and I laughed under my breath.

"Yes, he is," I agreed with a nod of my head. "He also seems to have a habit of underestimating women." A flurry of movement came from the Healer's hands once again, and I watched as the tension slowly left Mira's tan face. The Healer took a step forward and offered a palm for the captain to shake.

"And what can I do for the two of you?" she asked, ignoring Gaelon as she moved to retrieve her sword.

"We are here to ask you about what has been happening on these waters." The man who had been next to her had also moved towards the weapon, but he froze just as his fingers touched the hilt, and then his eyes lifted to my face.

"What would either of you know about that?" Suspicion laced his words, and I looked to Gaelon for guidance.

"We know that something unexplainable has been happening to

the crews who have set sail along this coast. The storms and the tides have been irregular, and any who may have survived cannot fathom what they have seen." Gaelon's face had paled, his voice had grown shaky, and I could see the way his own experience had haunted him.

"You've seen it." It wasn't a question. Mira assessed her friend closely before turning to us once more.

"I've seen it," Gaelon confirmed.

"Then you know whatever it is must have returned last night," the man whispered.

Nothing about the storm the night before had been natural, and I had assumed that something was amiss, but I had not heard the chilling cry Gaelon had described in Noordeign, and no one spoke of a monster this morning.

"We had been heading to port last night when the tides changed, and the sky turned that sickening green. From what I've heard, those are the telltale signs of its return."

Glancing across the gentle waves and grey skies, the man took in a deep breath and then looked at his captain. "Captain Mira ordered the crew to anchor down half a day's journey up the coast, and we waited for the storm to clear before setting sail. But one of the expected ships had not changed their course in time, and word is they found pieces of the wreck this morning."

"Any survivors?" I whispered.

"No, there rarely are. Whatever this is, it takes pleasure in the lives it steals," he replied.

"Then we need to find a way to stop this from happening again." The words poured out of me before I could stop them. The captain's blue eyes studied my mouth very carefully and then her head tilted.

"And you think you could?" Of course, I knew how impossible it sounded but I would not sit idle and wait for another answer. So, I squared my shoulders and nodded at Mira before asking her the only question that weighed heavily on my mind.

"If not us, then who?"

Chapter 21

The crew boarded the ship with wary eyes, their attention immediately drawn to us as we stood silently behind their captain while she greeted them with a few flicks of her fingers. Gaelon was the first to move; his warm eyes and calming presence seemed to soothe the strangers' apprehension and soon they huddled in closer, enraptured by every word the Healer spoke.

Once again admiring his way with strangers, I remained rooted in my spot next to Barrick as we kept our distance. We did not have the charisma of the Healer or the pleasant appearance of Ella and Elizabeth, both of us too hard and imposing to feel welcoming to those who were already wary of us, and I dipped my chin and lowered my shoulders when I caught the eyes of a few of the crew.

"Stop that, she's deaf, not blind and she can see the way you keep trying to crawl into yourself. You aren't exactly giving them the confidence a Chosen should have," Barrick whispered harshly at me, though his words were loud enough to be heard and the gruff sound spooked our spectators.

"Barrick, I am just trying to look less imposing. We need their help, so perhaps you should make the effort to be pleasant and less"—I waved my fingers at him impatiently—"this."

"This? What does that mean?"

"You look like you are ready and waiting to run someone through,"

I sighed.

"That's just my face." He lifted the hand that was not resting on his weapon to stroke his beard. "But I am always ready, if the need should arise."

Nudging him in the ribs with my elbow, I focused my attention back on the Healer just in time to see him wave me over. I softened my jaw, attempting to shift my face into what I hoped was a gentle smile, and stepped next to Gaelon.

"I have spoken to Mira and her crew at length. The latest wrecks have been north of here, though there is no exact location. Whatever is behind the attacks seems to move constantly." The strangers who stood in front of me looked nervous, and my eyes flickered around the group before landing on the captain.

"How many?" I asked, my voice sharper than I had meant for it to be, and I swallowed before trying again. "How many have you heard of?"

"Too many to count," one of the men whispered with a thick voice, and I turned to the Healer in concern.

"Captain, the Huntress and I want to fix whatever is happening on these waters, but we do not know where to start nor have the means here to do so. By the time our own vessels from Noordeign reach a southern port, it will be too late for many more souls." He signed the words to her as he spoke them, and I held my breath as I waited for her reply.

"What are you asking of me and my crew, Healer?" Mira's blue eyes were narrowed, and I glanced at Gaelon before trying my hand.

"Based on what we had been told, we had assumed the attacks were more isolated and had planned to travel to Ritari. That was before we found this." I swallowed thickly, my gaze roaming across the crew, and then I held my hand out towards the Healer.

Gaelon's dark eyes glanced down at my pale fingers and then lifted, and I waited as he searched my face. Seeming to find whatever it was he was looking for, the Healer then exhaled roughly and slipped his hand into the fabric of his cloak before passing me the folded piece of parchment.

"During our travels, we came across a group of men who had come from here. They said that they had been on their way to Honera when their ship was attacked. Perhaps you heard about that?" I asked, waiting for Gaelon to finish interpreting my words.

Mira's jaw clenched and then she lowered her chin. "It was said that they were raving mad. That they had caught the seasickness."

"But you don't believe that." Her eyes moved from Gaelon's hands to her crew before she shook her head softly.

"I did at the time. They were the first survivors any of us had come across but now..." She paused as she inhaled sharply. "Now I can't help but to believe in what they saw."

Humming under my breath, I swiftly unfolded the parchment and then held it out for the captain to take.

"And what do you know of Skohyn?" Murmurs moved across the men like a gentle wave, and I fidgeted while I waited for her stare to meet mine one more.

"I had spent most of my life never hearing that name and now it is all anyone can talk about."

"How so?" Gaelon asked as he stepped forward.

"Over the last while, more and more travellers had begun to come to the shores. At first, we had assumed it was because of the victory over the Crimsons and now people felt safe." It made sense, after all it seemed as if a weight had been lifted from the people of Elrin, and I myself had seen the changes across the country. But Mira did not appear convinced.

"That is until we noticed their banners," she muttered quietly.

I could feel Gaelon's eyes on me, but I kept my focus on the captain.

"What banners?"

"The sapphire ones with the Siren's trident," Mira answered hoarsely.

"And these visitors carried them?" Gaelon asked while his hands moved.

"Carried them, wore them. Some even had themselves branded with the emblem." I could tell she struggled to keep her eyes from my cheek as she responded.

"And these people spoke of Skohyn?" Barrick's voice rang out from behind me, and I glanced at him from over my shoulder.

"At first, they said nothing, came and went without so much as a word. But as more of them arrived, it was easier to overhear conversations, to learn a secret or two, and that name was almost always spoken between them."

"And you think that is where they went?" I wondered.

"It is," Mira confirmed.

"And do you also believe that they may know what is happening on these waters?"

Her bright blue eyes darkened as they watched Gaelon, and then she lifted her chin towards me. "Not just know, I think they are responsible for it."

The air left my lungs, and my chest tightened as I looked at the Healer worriedly. Noticing the sudden wave of panic, Gaelon grabbed my hand and squeezed my fingers reassuringly.

"The Huntress and I can ask another captain; we can search for another crew. But you know these waters, and you know that it's only a matter of time before more men perish. If you truly think Skohyn will have our answers, then that is where we need to go, and I am hoping you will aid us and agree to sail—"

Mira held a hand up, signalling the Healer to stop, before she gazed out across the quiet sea. "I will not answer for my men, but I will take your request into consideration and discuss it with them."

Impatience and frustration ate away at me, but I knew it was the best we could hope for, and I ignored the Healer's warning stare as I bowed my head slowly.

"No matter what you decide, I am pleased to be able to say I met the fierce Captain Mira of Bascala, and I hope to hear of your many voyages for years to come."

Making my descent, I refused to look up at the deck until I was securely seated next to Barrick. Gaelon had followed behind, his dark eyes questioning as we organized ourselves in the small boat. But I remained silent, waiting until my guard had begun to row before glancing up at the ship. Just as I had predicted, the captain was leaning over the rail, her eyes focused on my face, and I raised my hand, waving goodbye.

"That was not what I had expected from you, Skylahr." Gaelon tipped his head before glancing up as well. "I thought you would have demanded an answer."

The thought had crossed my mind, but there was something about Mira that I could understand in a way Gaelon could not. She was a woman doing her best to make her way through a world dictated by men, and at the end of it all she wanted what I had often longed for. She wanted the power to make a difference.

"Demanding wouldn't have worked." I shrugged. "So I gave her something better, something I don't think she will refuse."

"And what is that?" Barrick asked as his arms continued to move steadily.

"A future," I whispered while looking up at the blond curls once more. "A future to be something greater than those around her."

It had been two days since we had left Mira, and the certainty I had of her agreeing to help us had begun to waver. We still had not heard from her, and my worry that we would have to find another ship to help us grew. In fact, Gaelon had already started to send messages to those he trusted, asking for aid as we planned our next move. He had written to every lord who had vessels to spare and requested that they gather as we continued to piece together what exactly the Siren's people had been doing over the last few months.

So far all we had learned was that there were no more than two hundred who had come together, nowhere near what I would deem an army, but enough to raise suspicion, and they all seemed to be devoted to their long-lost Goddess. In fact, many had paid the smith in town to create shields and other items with her sigil on them.

That had worried Gaelon, and I couldn't help but notice the way my own stomach churned at the news. However, apparently none of these men or women appeared to be soldiers, nor were they violent in any way, and the villagers had not seemed concerned, though they were fascinated by these new visitors. They had even helped them dye the white sails of the three ships they had secured to blue, thinking nothing of what that colour could mean nor imply, though Barrick had easily voiced his thoughts on that and had called them mindless radicals.

Sighing from the stress of the last two days, I closed my eyes against the cold wind and then glanced down at the harbour from my perch on the bluff. Tucking my knees to my chest, I squinted at the familiar boat and then watched the docks for any sign of the captain.

The market was quiet today, and when it seemed as if every last person had found their way home, I pulled my legs in closer, resting my chin on them while I moved my gaze across the waters. The cliffs of Bascala were massive things, giving me a perfect viewpoint of the ocean and port, though their sharp edges would lead to a messy fate for anyone who stumbled or slipped on the thick green grass that covered the tops. Leaning forward just a touch, I glanced down at the pointed rocks that poked their heads from beneath the waves.

"Yes, a messy fate indeed," I whispered to myself before shuffling back, and then I glanced towards Mira's ship once more, hoping she would somehow feel my stare and come to a decision under the pressure of it.

"Are you hoping you can hear her thoughts or something?" Elizabeth called, and I turned, watching as she lifted the hood of her cloak over her dark hair.

"What are you doing out here?" I asked with a frown while my eyes scanned her pink-tinged cheeks. I worried that she may catch a chill from the damp wind.

"Coming to collect you of course. You've been sitting out here for over an hour!" Falling to her knees, she carefully scampered towards me and then pressed in close as her teeth chattered. "The wind is freezing up here!"

"You are supposed to be a northerner," I reminded her with a gentle laugh and then wrapped an arm around her shoulders.

"I hate to say it, but I think I prefer the south. Though not this part, the wind is far too cold on this coast," she admitted sheepishly, and I glanced down at her with a raised brow.

"Ella will be thrilled to hear that. I'm sure she'll be packing your things the moment we return to Noordeign."

"If we return."

My spine stiffened at the words, and then I pulled away just slightly to give myself a better view of my friend's face.

"Elizabeth," I admonished. "Why would you say such a thing?"

Her dark eyes did not meet mine, and instead she wormed her way closer, not settling until our sides were pressed together. Her lashes fluttered closed as she sighed softly.

"It's nothing, it's nonsense really," she reassured me, but I could practically feel the fear seeping from her body.

"You know I would never let anything happen to you, don't you?"

Elizabeth hummed under her breath, and her lips lifted in a sad smile. "I know, Sky."

Sliding back, I turned to face her fully and then lifted myself onto my knees before cupping her shoulders. "Nothing will harm you; I won't allow it."

"I know," she promised again.

"And when we are done here, you and Ella can do whatever it is that will make you happy. Travel and see what the world has to offer, find somewhere warm where the sun is always out and be together."

"And what of you?" Elizabeth asked quietly.

"Ella is your home, but Noordeign is mine now." I sighed. "I suppose I will spend the rest of my days arguing with the lords of the court and beating Barrick down in the training yards and reading the letters from my sisters who spend their time going on grand adventures while staring at each other longingly. At least I won't have to watch the pair of you lovesick fools then."

Elizabeth's smile grew for just an instant, and then her face became concerned. "That sounds lonely for you, Skylahr."

"How can it be when the people I love would be so happy? That is all I want for my life," I assured her. "Now how about we find something to eat?"

"That is actually why I came here in the first place." She pulled herself to her feet and reached out a hand for me to take. "Rabbit stew has been prepared especially for you, and Gaelon has the captain's answer."

"I have written to Lord Deavion with our change of plans and have made sure to alert the other coastal cities and villages that they are to turn away any visitors who are carrying the trident sigil," Gaelon explained softly as he gently stirred his stew. "I have also cautioned them not to enter the waters for the time being. Luckily it is spring, and there should still be enough provisions for the people to manage for now while we stop any trades."

"But how long can that go on for?" I asked anxiously.

"I'm not sure. I don't think we have ever had trades stop completely. But right now we don't have much of a choice, and Mira said it would take us a few weeks to reach Skohyn based on the map we found in the temple. That is if the weather is good."

"What about the other worry?" I whispered while keeping my eyes downcast.

"Mira says she can recognize the signs well," Gaelon promised, but I frowned.

"What good will that do us if we are in the middle of the sea?"

The Healer sighed roughly and then his shoulders curled inwards. "It's the best we can do for now, Skylahr."

"There is no other option, is there?" I wondered out loud.

"We could continue our travels south and hope that we learn more while we wait for word about another attack," Gaelon suggested.

"Or we could wait here, send a crew out to search the waters for Skohyn."

"That certainly sounds safer," I murmured under my breath.

"If that is your choice, I will not judge you for it," the Healer promised, and I lifted my chin and examined his face.

"What would be your decision?" I asked.

Pressing his palms against the tabletop, Gaelon leaned back in his seat and then his gaze bounced from me to our comrades and then towards the window that overlooked the port. His handsome face was tense in the fading sunlight, and I held my breath while I waited for his answer.

"I know what lies out there. I have seen it." His voice shook just slightly, and his eyes scanned the horizon. "But if what Mira said is true, if the immortals of the Siren are gathering on Skohyn, it must be for a reason. I know that this beast and its attacks are not random. Why else would they have started around the same time the gatherings had begun?"

"You want to go." The words were soft, but I knew the truth behind them. I knew his answer.

Sliding his dark gaze back to me, he swallowed and then ran a hand through his curls. "I have to."

"Then it's decided."

"Skylahr," he began with a shake of his head. "You do not have to come; I would never expect you to follow me blindly."

"It's not blindly, Gaelon. I know the risks," I reminded him. "And besides, you should know better than that by now." I reached across the table, placed my hand over his, and then gave his fingers a gentle squeeze.

"I will stand by your side, no matter the circumstances," I promised.

"Why?" he asked, his voice breaking, and my mouth lifted in a soft smile as I shrugged.

"Because that's what it means to be part of a family."

Chapter 22

Gaelon's jaw was tight as the boat crashed through the waves, and I gripped the railing with all my might as I fought to keep upright against the force of the ocean. Mira, who stood on the top deck, watched us with doubt, and I struggled not to recoil under her sharp gaze, feeling her skepticism even from this distance. She had finally agreed to take us to Skohyn, though not without the promise of a hefty payment and assurance that should things not go well with the Siren's immortals, we would flee rather than call on her crew to fight.

"Are you okay?" the Healer asked, his sharp gaze focused on my white knuckles that curled around the wood.

"If something were to happen, how long can survivors last out here when it's like this?" I swallowed down the sharp taste of bile and closed my eyes as I tried to push away the thought of getting sick.

"It depends on many variables, I suppose. But nothing is going to happen. There have been no signs of any danger and we will take every precaution." His words did little to reassure me, and I bent at the waist to rest my forehead against my hands.

"Sky?" Ella called from behind me, and a gentle hand stroked down my spine while she waited for me to straighten. "I brought you something."

Glancing at her from over my shoulder, I studied the green leaf pinched between her fingers and then raised a brow in question. "It's mint. It won't cure the seasickness, but it will help."

Reaching behind me blindly, I grabbed at the leaf and shoved it into my mouth with a wince. The thought of ingesting anything made me want to curl into myself, but the sharp flavour did seem to help, and I sighed in relief as my mind was finally occupied by the taste.

"Who would have thought you'd be this susceptible to such a human ailment. Elizabeth and Barrick are doing just fine."

"I am human, Ella," I reminded her. "Even if I have conquered my ignite." Though I had immortal qualities, my body was still human, and I was reminded rudely as my stomach churned sharply. I had never sailed before, but I was an avid rider and had never experienced any sort of motion sickness, so I was surprised that I was suffering so badly.

"The waves may settle soon," Gaelon offered, but my anxiety rose as our ship continued over the whitecaps that rocked against us.

"Why not come to the cabin? Elizabeth and Barrick are looking at some of the maps the crew found while they have supper."

My gut twisted painfully at the thought of eating, but the maps piqued my interest, and I turned to Gaelon with a raised brow.

"You go ahead, the waters are not bothering me. In fact I enjoy the sea air." He smiled softly as his curls blew in the heavy gusts of wind.

I relaxed my hold on the rail and moved my tongue around my teeth, searching for the sharp taste of mint before I took one unsteady step towards my friend. Noticing my struggle to make my way across the wet deck, Ella moved and wrapped a slender arm around my waist with a laugh.

"You look like a little fawn," her melodic voice rang out above the wind. "All legs and no idea on how to use them."

Scoffing, I rolled my eyes but could not find it in myself to pull away from her support as we headed to the cabin. Entering the dimly lit room, I braced myself against the door as I swallowed the bitter acid that had crept up my throat once more, and then I looked to the pair who sat at the small, rickety table tucked in the corner.

"Sky, are you alright?" Elizabeth asked worriedly as she crossed the space between us. "You look ghastly."

"Yes, thank you for that," I grumbled as I pressed past her and then hurriedly moved to the now-empty chair before the ship could rock roughly once more.

"Don't worry, Huntress," Barrick called from his place across from me. "If this map is true, we only have just over fortnight or so left before we reach the shores of Skohyn."

"Is that meant to comfort me?" I snapped, closing my eyes tightly as the room shifted again.

"I suppose it wasn't helpful, was it?" He laughed softly and then he grabbed the wineskin and held it out to me.

"Drink," he ordered. "If you get enough into you, you won't remember to worry about your stomach."

Normally I would have refused, as I was never one to overindulge, but my desperation to rid myself of the constant queasiness outweighed any of my usual protests. Grasping the soft leather, I removed the cap and then tossed my head back before guzzling down a mouthful of wine.

"And you said wine doesn't work like that." Ella snorted as she watched me take another long swallow.

Wiping my mouth with the back of my hand, I then glared at the immortal. "If I can keep it down, you can remind me you were right in the morning."

Days melted into each other as more time passed at sea, and the vast open ocean had begun to make me feel stir-crazy. The scenery was the same, our daily routine was the same, and the worry that we may run into a creature of the water began to seem like an impossibility. After all there had been no sign of any other life on the waves. We had yet to even find another ship or crew, though that may have been because of Gaelon's warning. Surely his letters would have reached their destinations by now.

"It looks like we may get a storm tonight," Gaelon murmured worriedly from beside me as we leaned against the railing, and I lifted my eyes to his face before glancing up. The clouds that had filled the sky had begun to deepen in colour, and I swallowed roughly as the winds grew stronger around us.

"Just when I finally got my sea legs," I groaned and then turned to peer at the captain.

But Mira's attention was also captured by the rolling clouds that had begun to cover the night sky, and then a loud crack of thunder rumbled from above accompanied by a flash of lightning, and her eyes widened before she glanced down at us.

"Healer!" Mira yelled from her perch. "Get below deck and stay there!"

Suddenly shouting began amongst the crew, and they scattered, grasping ropes and ties while their captain barked orders at them. My friends gathered around the Healer and me in confusion, and we watched as the sailors seemed to organize themselves, preparing for something I didn't understand.

Without argument, the Healer pressed a hand against my back and herded us towards the stairs that led below. I clutched the rail, my body tipping as a wave crashed against us, its spray reaching the deck, covering the wood with water. I nearly toppled over from the force before grabbing a hold of Elizabeth, who came to find us after hearing the thunder. Pulling her along, I ushered her down the slick stairs before turning at the sound of my name. Quickly Ella and Barrick hurried towards us, and I held a hand out for the immortal and helped her step down before following behind, and then I glanced around the dark space we had been directed to.

It felt cold and damp, and the smell of rotting food and wet wood wafted in the air. Rusted buckets were placed under streams of water that passed through the cracks of the ceiling above, and I scanned the space for a candle to light and something dry to use as a cloak for Elizabeth, who was huddled next to Ella shivering.

But my search was interrupted as the tide collided with us again, and the crew above began to shout at each other while their frantic footfalls ran back and forth above us. Turning to Gaelon in concern, I waited for his eyes to meet mine while Barrick wrapped his cloak around my human friend with a quiet reassurance.

"What do we do? Is there nothing we can do to help?" I asked urgently, but both Gaelon and Barrick shook their heads while crowding in close as the ship groaned against the waves.

"None of us know our way around a ship of this size, and I don't want any of us to be in the way." The guard gave my shoulder a gentle squeeze, and I sighed in resignation. Grabbing my hand, Elizabeth led me to the rows of furs that were organized across the floor in makeshift beds. Once the two women were settled, I knelt next to them and curled in close, praying that the storm would pass.

We had been huddled in the dark for hours as the ship rocked back and forth, and each movement had sent my heart racing until the motion settled into a gentle lull. A small amount of light now streamed through the entranceway above the stairs. I carefully pulled my arm from under Ella's head, making sure not to wake my friends, who had just fallen asleep, and then I crept my way up the steps and narrowed my eyes at the crew that had gathered at the edge of the ship. Whatever had captured their focus had left them unaware of my presence, and I slowly approached, for once thankful for my height as I peered over their shoulders.

The dark waters of the ocean were smooth and still, the only interruption being the ripples that our ship created, and I moved my gaze across the glass-like surface, waiting for something to appear. When the crew continued to lean over the railing, I searched the deck for their captain and found her leaning against the main mast.

"What happened? Where are we?" I asked as I approached. Her eyes were focused on my mouth, though the rest of her face remained tight with nervousness.

"I don't rightly know." She turned to the open waters and swallowed. "I'm not sure how long we have been drifting, but the winds took us off course and waves were never-ending. And then suddenly, the whitecaps just stopped, and the storm cleared. It is almost as if they had been figments of our imaginations."

Then her deep blue eyes moved to her crew. "They thought they had heard something in the waters, though I wouldn't pay them any mind. We haven't slept and the strain of that storm could cause even the calmest of men enough stress to fog their minds."

My brows pulled as I frowned at the captain, but I said nothing and returned to my place near the crew. The sea had remained still and quiet, but the air around us seemed to grow heavy. Tendrils of fog lifted from the surface, the wisps moving and twining together in a mesmerizing dance. It was as if I couldn't pull my eyes from the mist, and I felt spellbound as my feet shuffled closer.

Once I had reached the edge of the deck, I realized there was a noise coming from the sea. It was a voice humming, the sweetest song I had ever heard, and I closed my eyes as a longing filled my chest. Grasping at the railing, my body leaning forward of its own accord, I pressed my waist against the wood as I gazed down below.

The melody had grown louder, and I was entranced by the gentle ripples that spread around us. Completely consumed by their movement, I hadn't noticed that the fog had thickened, and the open ocean was no longer visible. In fact, I hadn't noticed anything until it was too late.

I rose up onto the toes of my boots and curved over the rail, one of my hands outstretched towards the sea to capture whatever it was that called to me. I extended my arm, fingers wiggling as I grunted in effort. The crew that had gathered did not offer any help, and too seemed lost in their own minds as they stared blankly at the waters that I reached for.

Growing frustrated, I shimmied closer, lifting off of my toes and balancing on the rail all while I searched the waters. And then suddenly something appeared. A deep grey webbed hand shot out of the sea, its cold wet grip grabbing onto my wrist before hauling me overboard. I had barely managed a scream before I crashed into the icy waters.

Chapter 23

Darkness surrounded me, the depths of the water becoming more suffocating as I was dragged farther into the sea. My pale fingers that had reached for the waves now seemed to nearly glow as they extended towards the surface. My other hand was still trapped by its captor, and the tightening of its grip drew my attention towards the grey limb that had locked on to my wrist.

Long, thin, shining fingers encircled the joint, their knuckles linked together by a nearly translucent web, and I followed the shimmering skin up towards the creature's shoulders. Its head was turned away from me, but I watched the fine silver hair flow as it pulled me along.

And then, as if something had finally snapped, I came to my senses and began to struggle. My long legs thrashed towards the monster, and I swung my other hand at its grip, my fist colliding with the cold flesh roughly. The impact was enough to draw the attention of the creature, and the silver hair swirled violently as it finally turned to face me.

Its jaw was square and protruding, and its thin blue lips pulled back in a snarl, displaying its sharp teeth in all their glory while its black eyes narrowed. Lurching back in fear, I struggled with more force, my entire body thrashing with all of my strength, and I kicked my foot towards its boney torso before aiming for the long, scaled tail.

Widening its jaw, the monster pulled me close, and a horrendous screeching noise echoed around us, the sound creating a ringing in my head that left me dazed. I squeezed my eyes closed in pain, swinging blindly at the creature once again while my lungs burned for air, but it was no use, and I was dragged deeper into the abyss.

Glancing up at the surface one last time, I watched as the light from the sky seemed to dim, and just as I was about to say my silent goodbyes, a point of a spear rushed towards us. The creature hadn't seemed to notice the soft gleam of metal, and I shifted to the left at the very last second as it hit its intended target, the tip lodging into the shoulder of the arm that had held me captive. Surprised by the weapon, the monster released my wrist, and I took the opportunity to kick away from the creature before escaping to the surface.

I had never been a strong swimmer as a child, and as my lungs began to beg for air, my limbs slowed in their efforts. But before I could succumb to the exhaustion, another body crashed into the waves headfirst, and then one massive hand reached out towards me, the thick fingers extended until they grabbed a hold of my tunic, and then I was tugged forward as Barrick swam towards the surface.

Breaking through the waves, I gasped for air, panting as I sluggishly treaded water. Barrick's hands cupped my jaw as his eyes searched my face with worry.

"Skylahr, are you alright?" It was the first time he had ever called me by my given name, and though I knew it was an odd thing to focus on, I smiled at the familiarity and nodded. Pushing my hair out of my eyes, the guard double-checked that I was unharmed before linking our arms together.

The once-calm waters had begun to turn, and my heart raced as our bodies were pulled by the current that surrounded us. Tugging me closer, Barrick began to swim, though there was no way of knowing if we were heading in the right direction as the fog had thickened and the ship was nowhere to be seen. Keeping our heads above water was growing increasingly difficult as the whitecaps grew bigger, and I tightened my arm around Barrick's.

But I was too late, and suddenly we were pulled under another wave. I struggled to right myself under the water, my hands reaching for the guard, and I squinted in the dark, searching for a sign of Barrick when my fingers couldn't locate him. But I was alone with nothing but the empty darkness, and I swam to the light above me.

"Huntress! Skylahr!" I heard Barrick call as soon as I broke through the surface, and I spun in circles as his voice grew increasingly panicked. But the waves continued to rock into me, creating more confusion each time I managed to escape their clutches, and my head spun.

"Skylahr!" Barrick's voice roared again, the sheer volume indicating he was near, and I sobbed in frustration as I fought through the water and fog, pushing myself towards his screams.

My body was exhausted, my skin stung as the temperature bit at my flesh, and I could feel my energy waning. Panting in exhaustion, I prayed to my Goddess, to the Protector, to anyone who would hear me, and cried out for Barrick in desperation.

"Barrick! Barrick, please!" I sobbed as I searched frantically for some sign of the massive man.

"Sky—" His voice rang out from behind me, and I spun, watching in terror as the scarred face I had grown so fond of disappeared into the sea. Using every ounce of strength I had left, I kicked my legs and swam to where he had vanished before taking in a lungful of air and diving down below.

The ocean had grown even darker with the thick cover of fog, and I scanned for any sign of the guard before swimming deeper, forcing my body as far as I could until a flicker of something caught my eye. I could barely make out the form, but as I closed the distance, I noticed the glint of silver metal and I knew it was Barrick's blade.

Realizing I would not have enough air, I rose to the surface as fast as I could and then forced myself down towards the glittering metal. Once I was near, I could finally see Barrick's form, and watched as his massive body twisted against the pull of a long, thin grey arm that had wrapped around his neck. It was similar to the one that had dragged me off the boat, but this creature had pale yellow hair and a hook protruding from its shoulder.

I clasped Barrick's hand before tugging, but the creature tightened its hold, squeezing its elbow around the guard's thick neck. I watched horrified as Barrick's dark eyes widened in panic. Reaching for his belt, my fingers slid across the smooth metal of his weapon, but I couldn't pull the blade from its sheath, and my desperation rose as his dark eyes began to flutter.

Looking for another way to pull him from the monster, I curled my fingers around the boney limb that had trapped my guard and heaved. But even though the flesh of the monster looked frail, its strength was unwavering, and the joint pressed even tighter against Barrick's pale flesh. Knowing that I was running out of time, I leaned forward and grasped the hook that gleamed against the grey skin and pulled as hard as I could.

The screech that left the jaws of Barrick's captor immediately alerted him, and his dark eyes finally focused on mine before he clawed at the arm that had loosened. Once he had managed to fight his way from the limb, he grabbed a hold of me, but I had been too distracted by my relief that I had not noticed the webbed hand had clutched his dagger and unsheathed it before lodging the blade into his torso. Bubbles streamed from the guard's mouth as he shouted in pain, and I froze, watching as the monster pulled the weapon from his side before moving to pierce him once again.

Terrified, I grabbed the slender wrist before it could wound Barrick once more and used both of my hands to pry the fingers from the hilt. But the hand never wavered, and the curtain of pale yellow hair danced in my vision as the distance was closed between us. Then suddenly the square jaw filled with pointed teeth was latched onto my shoulder, the incisors closing around the curve as they tore open my skin.

Swift pain burned across my shoulder, and I lifted my hands to tug at the thin hair, leaving me unprepared for the blade of the knife. The tip wedged into my ribs and I gasped in pain, which allowed my mouth to be flooded with water. Clenching my teeth together, I forced myself not to inhale and used my feet to push against the belly of the creature and away from its clutches before blindly searching my torso for the handle of the weapon. My fingers slid against the cool steel, slipping twice before I managed to get a good grip. However, once I was sure I had a solid hold, I tugged, grinding my teeth in pain until it was free, and then I swung.

The move was sloppy at best, but the monster had not been prepared, and I watched with satisfaction as the dagger found its home in the black iris. Twisting my wrist, I pushed the weapon deeper into the socket, making sure that it had done its job and killed our assailant before finally looking for Barrick. But the guard had disappeared, and I raised my eyes to the surface, my gut dropping in horror when I saw his unmoving form floating above me.

Keeping the knife in my hand, I rushed to Barrick, my body crashing through the surface as I panted for air. His face was pale, his eyes unfocused, and I whimpered while I tugged him closer. I lifted his head, cradled his face against my shoulder, and clenched my eyes shut, willing the tears away. Crying would do nothing for my friend, and I shuffled him around until I had a free hand and then tapped his cheek. When he did not respond, I swung with more force, the pads of my fingers striking his bearded face with a sharp sting, and the man lurched forward, his legs kicking out while his arms flailed.

"Barrick! It's just me, it's me," I reassured him with a rough voice and waited for his brown eyes to meet mine before offering him a grimace of a smile.

"Huntress." His voice was weak, and I tugged him closer to me.

"Why are you so massive?" I sobbed as I tried to drag us farther through the fog.

"You need a guard bigger than you," he whispered hoarsely. "How would it look if the soldier in charge of your protection couldn't even meet your height?"

Scoffing half-heartedly, I searched the fog for our ship, but the vessel was nowhere to be seen, and I swallowed down my cry of frustration as I struggled to keep us afloat. After adjusting my hold around Barrick's waist, I realized a warmth had coated my hand,

and I glanced down. My pale, wrinkled fingers were coated in blood, and they shook as I prodded at the torn tunic and flesh of his body.

"Stop your poking, Huntress, it stings."

"What happened to Skylahr?" I asked with a thick voice while I tried to distract him from what I was sure was a serious injury and carefully placed my palm over the wound. But Barrick didn't answer, and I looked at his face with worry as he tried to catch his breath.

The waters had calmed, but the frigid temperatures made my mind feel hazy, and I grew more concerned as Barrick's lips trembled, the flesh turning a violet colour. Holding him tightly, I continued, forcing my body to move even though it begged me to stop.

But I would not fail him.

We crossed what felt like miles of ocean and slowly the fog began to lift, its thick curtain fading until I could finally see our surroundings. The sun had sunk, and the sky was littered with bright burning stars, their reflections bouncing off the water. I prayed that this would not be the last clear night of our lives. I begged the Gods that they would allow us both to see another.

I wanted to hold my friends again, I wanted to laugh with Ella and smile with Elizabeth. I wanted to smell the northern forest.

I wanted to see *him* again, just once more.

Lost in my regrets and disoriented from the cold, I hadn't noticed the ship approaching until the ripples of water interrupted my thoughts, and I turned to face our rescuers. The sails were a darker blue, and its size was double that of Mira's. On any other occasion I would have been cautious about accepting aid from strangers, but this was our only chance, and I thanked the Huntress under my breath before paddling towards the ship.

"Barrick." I jostled the man on my shoulder and waited for his eyes to flutter. "Help is here. Can you move?"

"Aye, I can move," he assured me, and as we neared the ship, I noticed the crew had gathered and tossed a rope ladder over the rail.

Helping the guard to the side, I waited for his shaking fingers to grasp at the rough cords and then used both of my hands to hoist him up. His movements were slow and sluggish, and I held my breath as he made his way up the side of the ship. Each step forced my heart to pound harder in my chest as I waited for him to slip and crash into me, and I trembled with fear as the guard struggled with each movement.

Finally reaching the top, I grunted in effort as I pushed Barrick onto the deck, ignoring the burning pain in my side and shoulder as the cold winds and salt from the sea ate at my healing wounds. Once I was certain Barrick was safe, I finally hoisted myself onto the wet wood beside him, my body shivering as I caught my breath.

Moving onto all fours, I ignored the way my knees wobbled as they held my weight, and I coughed violently, retching up the last of the sea water before my eyes opened and I noticed black boots had edged their way into my vision.

Struggling to rise from my hands, I straightened my spine and peered up at the dark eyes that glowered at me. The man was young but had a stern face, and his eyes were narrowed with suspicion. I lifted my hands up, shrinking back on my heels, and shot a worried glance to my injured guard as he groaned, struggling to move from his back.

The stranger turned to Barrick before he gave an order, but it was not one I understood. When neither of us moved, he grabbed the silver handle on his belt and unsheathed his blade, using the tip of the weapon to press against my chin.

Again, he gave the order, but I blinked helplessly at him, my hands still in the air as I searched his crew for help. But the other men who had gathered kept their distance, their eyes burning with careful curiosity as the stranger barked words at me once more, the order ending with one I recognized.

Puore.

Growing frustrated, the man stepped forward, putting more force behind the weapon, and I turned my head to avoid the blade, unconsciously baring my scarred cheek to the crowd. The clanging of metal hitting the deck echoed around us, and I turned my chin, no longer afraid of being cut. The stranger's eyes widened in fear before he scrambled to pick up his sword and snarled the name I knew would surely doom us both.

"*Seductress.*"

Chapter 24

Rough hands hoisted me to my feet while my captors ignored my struggles, and I tried to free myself while I watched four others drag Barrick across the wood. His face had grown even paler, and his head lolled to and fro as they jostled his limp frame around before sinking down the stairs below deck.

"Please, you have to help him," I begged hoarsely over my shoulder at the rest of the group, who glanced at me with cold expressions. But the men remained still, watching as a pair of their comrades pulled me across the floor, my boots slipping over Barrick's blood and seawater before I too was dragged down the stairs.

Towed down the narrow hall, I was directed to the left and then pushed past the iron bars and onto the cold wet floor of the cell. Barrick was crumpled in the corner, his eyes barely open as he peered at me, his left arm crossed over his middle, blood sliding its way between his fingers.

I scrambled to my knees and crawled to him, cupping his cold cheek before I pressed my hand over his. The air seemed to leave his lungs, and my lower lip trembled as his eyelashes fluttered. I turned my head, glancing at the men through the steel.

"Please." The word was a sob, and I lifted my blood-covered hand to show them how serious it was before pleading once more. "He's badly hurt, I need a healer. *Please.*"

"*Healer?*" the young man from the deck above repeated, his tongue rolling over the word while his brows pinched, and he shook his head before lifting an accusatory finger at me. "Seductress, Crimson."

After tucking Barrick's arm across his torso, I turned to face my captors. "I'm not. I'm not one of them." My hands pressed against my chest as I shook my head earnestly. "I'm a halfling, a halfling of the Huntress."

They whispered amongst one another at my declaration, their voices too low for me to hear, and their expressions unreadable. I knelt there, head bowed while I waited for them to decide if I was being truly honest.

"Please, I'm not a Crimson and my friend needs help, right now."

Barrick whispered my name in warning, but his voice was faint, and panic struck as his hand slid from his side before dropping to the floor lifelessly. Unwilling to remain in my place, I clambered to my feet shakily and grasped at the bars.

But my forward motion spooked the group of men, and they jumped back, gripping their weapons before shouting at me in warning. Ducking my head, I curled my fingers around the bars and tried once more to plead for my companion.

"*Please.*"

A firm voice called from behind the men, and I glanced up at the newcomer as the group parted for him. His hair was long, the black braid reaching his waist, and he was dressed in a floor-length robe of fur, the colour a brilliant white. He was slender in build, only a few inches taller than Ella, and I waited as he spoke to the men with a stern voice. Whatever was being said seemed to placate all but one, and the youngest eyed me warily before shaking his head in disagreement.

Fury filled the newcomer's face, and he grabbed the man before turning his back to me. My eyes that had been focused on his face were immediately met with the sagging snout and eyeless face of the wolf that draped across his shoulders, and the sight of it made my stomach roll as I pictured another being.

"*Isla.*" Her name had pressed through my lips before I could stop it, and suddenly the heated argument ceased, and all eyes turned to me. The fur-clad man stared at me with interest, his dark gaze roaming my face until he turned to whisper to the men. Scattering from their places, they all seemed to move at once, collecting things for the stranger before unlocking the door.

With his chin lowered, he entered the cell, his face a mask of calm as he approached, and I glanced at the supplies being deposited on the floor before sagging in relief. The stranger took the glass bottle that was handed to him before he closed the distance between us.

Once he was within arm's reach, his fingers lifted to the tear in my tunic, his warm hands palpating the healing skin roughly. I shrugged from his touch before turning to Barrick. "Help him first."

Dark eyes moved to my guard, his gaze soft as he observed the crumpled form of my friend with a frown. His voice was gentle and slow, but I understood nothing and grasped the hand that had examined my shoulder before tugging him towards Barrick.

"Help him first." The man followed and sank to his knees before lifting Barrick's face, and then his eyes shot to mine, his gaze doubtful. Folding myself beside him, I lifted my shaking hands to Barrick's side and raised the tunic. The wound was still bleeding, and a tan finger traced the edges before carefully examining its depth.

I glanced at Barrick's face, waiting for a reaction, but he remained silent, though his eyes fluttered open. I swallowed roughly and turned to watch as the man uncorked the bottle before lifting it to Barrick's mouth.

"Is it tonic?" I asked as he carefully poured the liquid into Barrick's parted lips. The guard winced as he swallowed before coughing roughly, and my eyes widened in concern. "What are you giving him?"

Turning to me, the man lifted the bottle to my mouth and nodded his head. When I hesitated, his brows pinched, and he pressed the bottle roughly to my lips with an order.

"What is it?" The smell wafting from the glass was vaguely familiar, and I sniffed the opening before narrowing my eyes at it.

"Licur." The word had just rolled off his tongue when my mind was flooded with memories from another time. A time when I had sat in a padded seat across from the Lady of Denimoore while she poured glass after glass of the dark liquid.

Growing impatient, the man nudged the bottle at me once more, and I grasped the neck of the glass before taking a swig. It burned the back of my throat before settling in my belly, and I took another long drink before pressing it against Barrick's mouth.

"It's bloody disgusting," he croaked weakly as he peered up at me through heavy lids. "That's nothing like our ale or wine. I want no more of that shit."

Ignoring his protest, I lifted the bottle and watched as the guard swallowed another mouthful. Within a few minutes a flush crawled across his pale cheeks, and the stranger poked at his wound before making his way back to the pile of supplies. He gathered an armful of things, crossed the cell once more, and laid the tools out in front of him.

Sensing my gaze, he lifted his eyes and shooed me away before gesturing to Barrick's other side. Stepping over the guard, I knelt across from the stranger and watched as he removed the white fur from his back before he grabbed Barrick's hand. Waiting until the guard peered at him, the man bowed over their joined hands and whispered a stream of words with his eyes closed before he gestured towards me.

Not understanding, I remained frozen in my spot and held my breath as he stretched across Barrick before taking my hand. Once he had a strong grip on my fingers, he continued, his eyes falling closed once more, and then he moved our joined hands to Barrick's lap before releasing us.

My fingers had been ready to slip out from Barrick's own, but he suddenly clenched his palm and groaned out in pain. The man across from me frowned, his eyes focused on my guard's side as he began to work, and I nestled closer to Barrick as another pained groan tore from him.

"It's okay." The words were not nearly as reassuring as I had meant them to be, and I watched in concern as Barrick grimaced again before his head lolled. Nestling closer, I moved my shoulder under him, ignoring the startling cold skin of his face against my neck as his forehead rested against me.

The man continued to work, his hands constantly moving, and every so often I would catch his worried glances as he gazed up at my guard before focusing back on the wound.

"Will he be alright?" I knew he didn't understand me, but sitting in the quiet as the ship rocked against the tides was gnawing at my patience, and my hand trembled under Barrick's. The stranger sat back on his heels before tearing the tunic from hem to neckline. Pulling the rest off carefully, he then lifted the discarded white fur and carefully draped it across my guard before his dark eyes met my own.

With a dip of his head, he stood, clearing the rest of his things before crossing the cell, and I scrambled to my feet as he reached the door.

"Wait," I called, my voice hoarse. "Thank you."

He watched me for a long moment before dropping his chin down again in acknowledgement and then he was gone, his form retreating up the stairs while his comrades closed the heavy iron door with a resounding slam.

Barrick's skin had warmed as the hours passed, though his face had remained ashen while he slept under my watchful gaze. I tucked the fur around him once more as the deck above us rattled with movement. All had been quiet since our cage had been closed, and I turned my attention to the stairs, my stomach churning as I waited for the men to reach the bottom.

The group seemed less hostile, their faces not quite as stern, and I remained in my spot next to my guard while they approached. The youngest of the group lingered in the back, his arms crossed as he watched the healer from the night before unlock the door.

The man stepped towards us and squatted next to Barrick, his hand resting against the pale skin of my friend's forehead for a moment before he moved his focus to Barrick's side. I watched closely for any sign of concern, and after a pause his dark eyes lifted and he offered me a small smile.

Relief flooded my chest, and I felt my shoulders sag now that the weight of my worry had lessened. Returning his smile, I blinked away the fog that had filled my vision while he moved to his feet before beckoning with his hand for me to do the same. When I didn't immediately follow, he motioned impatiently with his fingers once more, and I glanced at the waiting party before scrambling to my full height.

The men had remained on the outside of the bars, their attention solely focused on us as the healer approached. He grasped my wrist and I fell into the space behind him, allowing him to drag me to the iron door before I pulled my limb from his clutch.

"No." He may have helped Barrick, but it wasn't enough for me to trust him, and I backed away a step before the young man pressed through the open door with a dagger drawn.

All at once commotion broke out through the group, their voices raised as they argued with one another, some drawing their own weapons while others seemed to try to calm the situation. I remained behind the bars, watching with concern as the disagreement grew in volume only to suddenly stop at an order that was barked from the stairs.

It was the captain; his voice had rung out through the space around us, and his crew lowered their gazes as his heavy footfalls echoed through the room. His face was unreadable, but the steady hand that sat on the hilt of his blade on his hip was an unmistakable sign. We were to comply with his orders.

Swallowing roughly, I edged closer to the door, my body shielding my guard while I held his stare. The healer slid to my side, his voice calm and quiet as he spoke to his leader, though the captain never looked away from my face. After a long, silent pause, he responded gruffly before turning on his heel and marching up the steps.

The man beside me motioned with his hand once more with an order. The tone was still quiet, but I could hear the plea and I knew what my refusal would mean for me and my guard. So, I stepped past the bars of the cell, my spine stiff as I weaved through the group of men before climbing the stairs to the upper deck all the while preparing myself for the fight of my life.

Chapter 25

The wind was cold as it blew against me, and I shivered while I crossed the ship. The men led me silently towards the stairs of the upper cabin, and I glanced back at the group who remained behind, their eyes hard as they watched me climb each step until I had reached the top. I grabbed the cold copper handle, pushed the heavy wooden door open, and stepped into the room.

The captain sat at the head of the table, his leather boots crossed at the ankles where they rested on the surface, and his gaze remained focused on my form as I shut the door behind me.

"Sit," he snapped, and it took a moment for me to realize I understood the order before I approached the table. I pulled the heavy chair across the rug before folding myself into it with caution.

"Eat." His foot kicked at a bowl that had been placed in front of him, the force tipping the dish over, spilling the rolls of bread across the table. I caught one before it could tumble from the ledge. My fingers sunk into the softness of it as tension filled my body, and I lifted my eyes to his face before bringing it to my lips.

I should have felt the pangs of hunger by now, and yet my gut churned at the feel of the bread on my tongue as I chewed it carefully. The captain remained unfazed by my suspicion, his expression never changing while I finished the roll. We remained in tense silence for a long while before he slid his feet from the table and leaned forward.

"Who are you?" I had been careful not to disclose my title or name when we had been rescued, only declaring my blood of the Huntress when he had accused me of being a Crimson. Gaelon and Barrick had engrained the importance of concealing my identity to anyone who may be unaware, especially if I were to ever be caught on my own, and now, I was thankful for the lesson.

"I'm no one." I could tell immediately that he did not believe me, and he stood from his chair, bracing his palms on the table.

"Don't lie." His voice was filled with rage, and I clenched my jaw as he leaned forward. "Who are you? I won't ask again."

"Nadine," I stumbled over the name, unsure of why hers had been the one I had chosen. "My name is Nadine."

The captain tipped his head to the side, his gaze sharpening before his lips lifted in a smirk. "Is it now?"

Panic filled my chest as he straightened and I pressed farther into my chair as he rounded the table. His fingers moved to his belt stealthily, the tips stroking the dagger that rested there for a moment before a loud pounding interrupted us.

Turning to the door, the captain grumbled under his breath, his long legs striding across the space before he pulled it open to reveal a massive man I had not yet seen. Stepping aside, the captain welcomed the stranger into the room and then glanced at me with a smile.

"This is Valis, he is here to get some answers from you." The man's head nearly touched the ceiling, and dread filled my veins as he tossed a pile of chains onto the table, and then his dark eyes locked on to my face.

"Now before we begin, tell me your name once more."

I clung to the lie and swallowed roughly before lifting my chin in defiance.

"Nadine."

"Very well, do your very best work, Valis, and find me when you are done." The captain laughed softly and then left us alone in the room. The quiet click of the door seemed to echo in the space around us.

The stranger's eyes had not left mine, and he held my gaze

prisoner as he took one step forward, then another, and then one of his enormous hands was grasping my jaw with a heavy grip. Using his thumb, he pressed my lower lip down and then tilted his head as he studied my lower teeth.

"Pretty and white," he murmured softly. "I wonder how easily they will come out."

Struggling in his hold, I wrapped my hands around his wrist, using every ounce of strength to pull his hand from me, but it was to no avail, and he chuckled under his breath while reaching for the chains on the table. The metal clanged as they slid from the wooden surface and then the heaviness was twisting around my torso, pressing me against the back of my chair roughly. Certain I was secured, he then took my hands and tied down my wrists to the arm rests before taking a step back.

"Have you been tortured before?" he asked with keen interest, and I trembled.

"You have," Valis decided. "Good, perhaps this will be easy then."

"I wouldn't bet on it," I snapped, and he threw his head back and laughed.

"You think a fight would upset me? I would prefer it; the victory always tastes sweeter if I have had to earn it." He reached for his belt and then pulled a simple dainty silver chain from his waist. He coiled the ends around his fists and held it in front of me.

"I noticed the faded marks on your wrists, I see you have some experience with the immortal's enchanted steel." My fingers flexed as I tried to pull my hands through their binds, but it was no use, and Valis bent his knees so that we were face to face.

"Let's begin, shall we? It's not a well-known form of torture. Most prefer dunking heads in water or taking fingers, but I have mastered the careful skills it takes to use this." He stepped forward, his hands moving to either side of my head, and then the cool chain pressed against my throat. At first the metal just kissed the skin, but slowly pressure was added, and my eyes watered as my windpipe was crushed under the force while my skin broke under the jagged edges of the chain.

"Usually men stand behind their prisoners; it is easier to do from that angle. But I like to watch my victims panic." My mouth opened as I gasped for air, but it was no use, and Valis smiled as he watched me struggle. But just as black began to cloud my vision, the chain was gone, and my head fell forward as I drew in a heaving breath.

"Now, what is your name?" he asked, though I could barely hear the words over my dizziness, and I coughed roughly in response.

Growing impatient, he grabbed my face once more and tilted my chin. "Your name, girl! What is it?"

Gnashing my teeth together, I snarled at my captor but did not answer, and he threw my head back, slamming it into the hard wood of my chair.

"Fine, have it your way." He had moved quickly in his frustration, and the strength he had come at me with sent my chair tipping backwards. He followed me to the floor, straddled my hips, and smiled down at me before starting his torture once more.

Stretching out my fingers, I attempted to claw at his sides, to do anything that might force him off of me, but it was no use. He lifted the metal from the torn flesh of my throat, allowing me to take in another breath or two, and then shuffled forward, pressing his knees into my hips tightly. However, the movement had brought his belt closer to my fingertips, and they traced the cool leather hilt of his dagger carefully. Watching his face, I waited to see if he noticed my discovery, but his dark eyes held nothing but joy as he observed me fighting for air.

"I think once more should do it," he muttered to himself, and just as he leaned forward, I curled my fingers around the dagger and pulled. Figuring I had just begun to struggle, he paid me no mind, and I took my chance and angled the blade before using as much strength as I could and shoved it into his side.

At first, he did not react, but when I pulled the blade from him and stabbed him once more, he finally flew back, his hands clutching at his side where the weapon was still lodged.

"You stupid girl," he snarled at me as he tugged the dagger free.

"You'll pay for that."

Bending down, Valis grabbed the back of my chair and brought it back onto its legs. My head spun at the sudden change, and I glanced down at my hands, hoping I would find some way to release my chains. However, as I scanned my fingers, it was then that I saw my left hand was coated in his blood. I pulled my elbow into my side, and my hand slipped against the metal. Clenching my jaw, I tugged once more, and this time my fingers slid past the cuff.

Not noticing my sudden freedom, Valis came at me once more, towering over me with his dagger in hand, and I held my breath as the distance between us closed. And then at the very last second, I lifted my hand and pressed two fingers into his wounds with as much strength as I could muster. Howling in pain, he fell backwards, and the door flew open as the captain and two crew members burst into the room.

"What is going on in here!?" the captain shouted as he looked between me and Valis. "Good Gods, man, did she actually manage to wound you?"

"That one is not what she seems," Valis snarled as he pointed his bloodied blade at me. "She is something else entirely. I can sense Mòrbàs in her."

Shrinking away from the obvious insult I did not understand, I glanced at the leader nervously.

"Come now, she's just a girl," the captain argued, though his eyes studied me carefully with interest.

"Release me and I'll show you just what kind of a girl I am," I snapped. A dark brow lifted, and then the captain tipped his head before humming softly.

"Alright, let's see what you are made of." He ordered his men to release me, waited until I stood, and then he unsheathed his sword before handing it to me. Once he was certain I had a solid grasp on the blade, he looked to the massive man and directed him to arm himself. "Well, get to it."

Valis held his weapon steadily, and I watched as he braced his weight and then he charged. Prepared for his attack, I manoeuvred myself around the room carefully, defending myself from every blow all while attempting to gain an upper hand. The man fought with skill, his balance and speed obviously that of an immortal, and he was nearly a head taller than me, but I could see that he was not as well practiced as I would have assumed, and he often left himself open as he swung with far too wide of strokes.

Moving in, I took the next opportunity he presented, and I tilted my blade so that the sharp side was angled away before hitting him in the torso. It wouldn't be a bad injury, but it was enough to startle him. Reeling away, he panted for breath and glanced at his leader with uncertainty.

"What are you looking at me for? Go on," the captain ordered, and Valis strode towards me once more.

Batting his attacks away more easily this round, I waited until I had an upper hand once more, but this time, I swung at his sword hand and nicked the flesh of his forearm before swinging again. Hitting his shoulder, I watched as the blade cut through the fabric of his tunic, and then I came at him again, this swing aiming for his neck.

Sensing what was to come, Valis fell to the ground, his weapon forgotten, and he bowed his head in defeat.

"I yield." Freezing, I held my blade, ready for a trick, but when he remained on the floor I looked at the captain.

"That was quite the sight, girl. Where did you learn to fight like that?" he called from the door, and I glared at him in response.

"Fine, don't tell me. But go on then, you have unfinished business." He motioned me forward with a flick of his fingers, and I remained rooted in my place.

"Finish what you started," he ordered, his brows pinching at my shocked expression.

"But he has yielded, he is unarmed." He stepped forward, his rough fingers grabbing my own, and he uncurled my hand from my blade. Tsking at me in disappointment, he then turned to his man and pressed the tip of the weapon into his chest.

Valis gasped roughly, the sound a wet choking noise, and I closed my eyes against the acid that burned the back of my throat. The captain turned on his heel, strode to me, and then leaned in close.

"Showing mercy to your enemy is a fool's decision," he whispered in my ear, his breath warm as it hit the cool skin of my face. "You would do well to remember that."

Turning to the other men in the room, he growled out an order, and the younger of the two moved forward, picking up the iron chains before taking my hands. Twisting the metal around the joints, he gave them a testing tug, and then pulled me forward towards the door.

"Now that I've seen you with a blade, I will be taking every precaution. I suggest you be on your best behaviour. Selian here won't hesitate to take matters into his own hands if you decide to be a problem before we dock, *Nadine*." The name rolled off of his tongue, and I knew that using it had been a mistake when Selian turned to his captain with wide eyes. He yanked on the chain, pulling me from the room before ushering me back below deck.

Barrick was still against the wall, though his eyes were open and wide with panic as he watched me descend the stairs. I offered him a grimace that I tried to mask into a smile. Pulling me forward, Selian directed me into the cell before slamming the door shut.

"Puore," he snarled, then spat at my feet, and with one last glare, he headed back to the stairs.

"What happened? What did they do?!" Barrick asked, his voice shaking with worry. His eyes roamed across my face before tracing the injured skin of my neck and then they widened.

"I'm fine," I promised, but I knew he didn't really believe me.

"Did they torture you?!"

"They wanted information from me," I whispered. "But I gave them nothing."

"Brave girl," my guard praised before wincing as he tried to sit up.

Unwilling to watch him struggle in pain, I dropped to my knees next to him and placed a gentle hand on his shoulder. "How are you?"

"No worse for wear it would seem thanks to that healer. Though I don't know why they would bother wasting supplies on us." Barrick shifted restlessly and I watched with careful eyes until he settled. I turned on my knees, dropped onto the floor, and rested my back against the wall.

"What do you think they will do with us?" I whispered.

He glanced at me from the corner of his eye, his focus roaming across my face before dropping to my neck once more.

"I'm not so sure I want to know."

Chapter 26

I wasn't pulled from my cell again as the days passed, but my chains remained, and the skin had begun to chafe under the heavy weight. Sighing, I lifted my hands, wincing at the sharp sting as I pressed a piece of apple into my mouth.

"You've gotten better at managing with them," Barrick grunted as he observed me, and I chewed the mushy, bruised fruit slowly before tipping my head back to rest against the wall.

"I suppose I have finally mastered the skill of eating and removing my pants when I need to take a piss," I grumbled.

"Thank the Gods for that," Barrick agreed. "I will guard your life, Huntress, but I draw the line at helping you with removing your breeches."

Inhaling deeply, I closed my eyes and then shifted to glance at my guard. "How long do you think it's been since we were pulled from the water?"

"At least a sennight, though I think longer." I had prayed that I was wrong with my guess and my mind was playing tricks on me, but if Barrick thought the same then it must be true.

"Where do you think we are headed?"

My guard shuffled close, pressing his shoulder into mine, and I sighed as his warmth seeped into my side. "There's no way to say for certain, but given the drop in temperature, I would guess north."

It made sense, of course, these men spoke words I recognized from my last travels through Elrin, and it could only mean that they would be from the same place as the immortals from my past. But they were far crueller than those Lupines had been, though perhaps the captain had been pretending this entire time and he truly did know my identity after all. Maybe their leader hated me enough to order this kind of treatment and that is why they had been so determined to learn my identity.

Maybe this was his revenge.

Lost in my thoughts, I hadn't noticed the opening of the door at the top of the stairs, and I jumped when the sound of Selian's footsteps echoed around us as he rushed down the wood steps. The young man's face was hard with a frown as he approached the cell, and it was then that I noticed the black cloth in his hands. Leaning against Barrick, I eyed him warily while he opened the door, and then he motioned for me to stand.

"He's bold to come down here by himself," Barrick whispered angrily. "He seems to think you'll let him hood us without a fight."

My instincts were screaming for me to charge at the young man, to use my height and weight to my advantage and try my hand at an escape. But Barrick was in no condition to help, and there was an entire crew above to worry about.

Giving my guard one last warning glance, I stood, bowing my head for the man as he opened the material. Once blinded by the black, I stayed still, listening as Selian barked an order at Barrick. The air remained quiet, though I could feel it grow tense, and I turned my head towards the guard.

"Stand up and don't fight him, Barrick." I could picture the nasty look he was giving me, and I sighed before whispering, "Please."

Succumbing to my request, he moved, and I listened carefully as metal clanged from where they stood.

"Barrick?!" It didn't sound like a weapon, and he hadn't made any noise that would alert me to danger, but I remained anxious as I waited for his answer.

"Just cuffs, Hu—" He caught himself before clearing his throat. "They're just cuffs."

My relief did not last long as the chain connecting my wrists was pulled, and I was tugged to what I guessed were the stairs. Reaching the upper deck, I took in a deep breath as the sun warmed me, the sounds of gulls and loud chatter filling the air, and I lingered, waiting to feel Barrick at my side before I followed along while Selian herded me forward.

We were led down a ramp, hurried by the crew as they grew impatient with our fumbling steps, and then I heard the rough voice of the captain, his orders stern as we were directed through what I had to guess was a market of sorts. I could hear the shocked gasps, the whispers of strangers as we struggled to weave our way through the narrow space. I curled my shoulders, ducking my head even though they could not see my face.

We followed blindly for what felt like a long while, though it could have been my nerves that seemed to make time drag on. Every few steps I would lean to the right, brushing my shoulder against Barrick's to be sure he was still there. His breathing had grown laboured, and I could tell his pace had begun to falter as we clumsily climbed the flight of stairs we had been led to.

Reaching the top, I stuttered to a halt, turning my body as the crew began to shout at my guard, who remained below me. He groaned in pain, and my stomach sank as I slid my boot to the edge of the stairs, prepared to clamber down them to help him.

But even if I managed to reach Barrick, I had no way to aid him with my vision blocked and my hands cuffed. Shifting from foot to foot, I waited anxiously until I finally felt his presence beside me once again, and I shuffled closer until our sides were pressed together.

"Are you alright?" My whisper was laced with concern when I felt him lean heavily into me.

"Just—" He paused with a wheeze. "A little winded."

My worry grew as he struggled to catch his breath, and when a hand pressed between my shoulders, I dug my heels in, trying to buy my guard some more time.

"Move." The captain's voice was low and deadly, and fear curled in my belly as I pushed forward. The noise from the market had quieted, and I could no longer feel the sun on my face as we entered what I guessed to be a building of sorts. The stone beneath my feet was smooth, and there was the sound of doors opening before me.

The fingers between my shoulder blades were persistent in their force, and my feet faltered when hushed whispers echoed around me, and then suddenly, the captain grabbed my shoulder. The pressure was heavy as he directed me to my knees, and I shook with nerves while I heard Barrick scuffle with our captors before cursing at them.

"Bastards!" His voice was gruff, though free of fear, and I wondered how he had managed that as he fell by side on the floor. Quiet laughter had broken out across the crew behind us, the noise only adding to my unease until a deep voice snapped at the men and then the air grew quiet.

Footfalls grew closer, their sound echoing in my ears as the person approached. I moved my body slightly in front of my guard, attempting to shield him from the pursuit of the stranger. At my movement, the feet hesitated before stopping altogether, and the man spoke lowly to the crew, the words foreign but his voice *so* familiar. The command was repeated once more, but when no one answered, the cloth was tugged from my head.

The sudden change of light was blinding, even from behind the curtain of bronze waves, and I winced before glancing down. I blinked through the burning of my eyes, and my attention was caught by the leather boots that had edged their way into my vision. The toes were clean, the black polished, and I noticed the perfect way the dark breeches were tucked into the tops before I moved my focus higher. My eyes traced the long strong thighs, and then moved on, and I had to rock back on my heels and tip my head to follow the strong torso up, and up and up. An impressive golden chest peeked out under the neckline of the navy tunic, and my heart hammered behind my ribs as I took note of the strong square jaw before my eyes lifted higher.

And then they met molten steel.
A burning silver.
Kalian.

Chapter 27

I had forgotten just how truly imposing he was, and I took in the broadness of his shoulders before noticing the dark shadow that covered his sharp jaw. His hair was longer too, the ends curling around his ears, and I scanned across his devastatingly handsome face, exploring every change, drinking him in.

His own eyes had moved, drifting to my torn tunic, and his attention focused on the shredded cotton and then rose to the tender skin of my neck before shifting to the crew behind me. His burning silver gaze was murderous for a long moment before it flickered back to me, and I adjusted under his scrutiny, raising my cuffed arms to my chest before my eyes caught the flexing of his right hand. His long fingers had stretched by his side, lifting in my direction before curling in on themselves tightly.

"Which one of your crew harmed these prisoners, Captain?" His voice was vicious though just barely audible, and I shrank away from the tone as I pressed against Barrick.

"It wasn't us, my lord, we found them this way." The captain had fallen to one knee beside us, his head bowed, yet I could feel his gaze as he glared at me from the corner of his eye.

"You found her with her neck like this?" Kalian asked, the words filled with rage as he peered down at the man beside me.

"Valis—"

"Valis is your man, is he not?" Kalian snapped. "He follows your orders, which means you gave him the command to do this to her."

The captain stood shakily, wiping his palms on his thighs. "Yes, my lord." His voice cracked nervously. "I had no choice; the girl would not give us her name."

"And so you had her tortured, Torris?" the alpha spat. "Where is Valis now? Bring him to me."

"I cannot, my lord," Torris whispered.

"And why is that?"

Torris wrung his hands together. "He is dead."

Kalian's expression did not change at the news, but his eyes did flicker to me briefly. "How did that come to be?"

"The girl managed to wound him during his questioning—"

Kalian lifted a hand, silencing the captain. "Of course she did, what else would you expect from the Huntress's Chosen?"

The captain's eyes widened before shooting down to my face. "She— But—"

"Are you telling me you had no idea, Torris?" Kalian crossed his arms over his chest while one black brow rose. "Certainly word of her existence reached you on the waters?"

"But she's marked—" Torris cleared his throat roughly. "I only mean to say is that she is not what I had thought…" I could feel the tension rise in the Lupine, and Torris moved his fingers to his belt frantically. Grabbing on to the set of keys, he crashed to the ground beside me and moved to take my wrists. But the jerkiness of his movements made me flinch, and I pressed farther back into Barrick. Seeing my fear, Kalian shot forward, one hand curling around the captain's throat before pushing him to the floor with a snarl.

"*Do not touch her*," he whispered, those silver eyes angrier than I had ever seen them. My heart stuttered at the sight.

Kalian swiped the forgotten keys from the floor and knelt before me, his gaze now soft as he held one massive hand up while he waited. I felt like I couldn't breathe, like the air had been pushed out of me, and I trembled as I slowly moved my arms, carefully placing my right hand into his own.

His skin was rough under my touch, and my quivering increased at the warmth that spread through me as Kalian gently turned my hand, exposing the lock on my wrist before carefully inserting the key. The metal snapped open, and he laid my palm on my thigh before lifting the other hand. Once I was free, his fingers stroked the skin of my wrists and then his attention moved.

He cupped both sides of my neck, his thumbs pressing at the underside of my jaw, and he tilted my chin carefully before he inhaled a deep, shuddering breath. Gazing down at him, I watched as his eyes took in the pale skin of my throat, and then the soft pads of his fingers traced a gentle line across the flesh.

"I will have his head for this." He seemed to be whispering the words to himself, and with one last stroke of his fingers he stood and moved towards Barrick. Kalian removed my guard's hood and tossed the fabric aside, and Barrick's eyes slid to mine in question, though they still appeared glossy and unfocused.

With the slightest dip of my head, I reassured him all was well, and he allowed the Lupine alpha to remove his cuffs, though he glared at him in suspicion. Ignoring my guard's hostility, Kalian stood once more and held my gaze for a pause before turning on his heel without another word.

Gaping at his retreating form, I sat stunned, only moving my attention when a low groan pulled from the man next to me, and then suddenly the room was filled with chaos and commotion. A swarm of strangers circled us, their faces filled with concern as they checked us over, and the crowd became daunting as person after person asked me a multitude of questions, their voices overlapping each other so loudly that my head spun.

"Give the woman some space!" a deep voice ordered, and my shoulders slumped when Keyno's gentle smile appeared from behind the strangers. "Hello, Hazel."

My lower lip trembled, quivering like a child's, and I smiled as tears clung to my lashes. "Hello, Keyno."

My voice was weak, pitiful even, but the man took no notice and crashed to the floor in front of me. He cupped my face with his hands, his thumb skimming the rough skin of my scar before he tugged me forward and enveloped me into a strong embrace.

"What are you doing here? Where is your Healer?" he asked as I clung to him.

"Oh Gods, Keyno." The mention of Gaelon had panic pressing against my chest. "We have to send word to Gaelon somehow! They're probably still at sea looking for us. We have to tell them we're okay before they venture too far!"

His big hand rubbed my shoulders gently in reassurance. "We will find a way to reach them, but for now let's be sure you two are alright."

Barrick's painful groan grabbed my attention, and as the men carefully lifted my guard from the floor, I scrambled to follow.

"Slow down, they're taking him to our curer," a voice scoffed, and I glanced at the familiar frown. Leena was just as stunning as I remembered, her face regal and unwavering, though her eyes did not hold the hostility they used to.

"Halfling."

"Leena." I dipped my chin in greeting. There was no embrace, no fond smiles between us, but I was grateful for the subtle warmth in her eyes, and she shooed the men away from me before turning to her mate.

"I will take it from here, Keyno. Go check on that brooding brother of mine and make sure he doesn't go on a rampage. He was practically shaking with rage and the captain's head may not be enough to quell that anger. I really don't want to lose an entire crew to his wrath."

Keyno nodded, and with one last pat on my back, he left us.

"Come on, let's go find you some new clothes and something warm to drink." And with that I was led from the room and into the familiar halls of Denimoore.

Leena had escorted me to the far wing of the castle, opposite to the one I had stayed in before, and I glanced around the unfamiliar hall in confusion as the Lupine pushed a door open before gesturing for me to enter. Stepping through the threshold, I eyed the lavish chambers carefully, and she watched me with a frown.

"What is it?" she asked, and I sank my teeth into my lower lip as I gazed at the bed in thought. I should not have had a preference to where I stayed, I had no right to request anything, and yet this room felt cold, foreign even. I crossed my arms around my torso while I tried to soothe my sudden unease.

"Well, spit it out."

"I just assumed I would have my—*the* old room is all." Her brows pinched, and she frowned at me before running her hands through her long hair.

"I had thought you would be thankful for an escape from old ghosts." Leena's voice trembled just slightly, and I studied her for a long moment.

"Do you think a change of rooms will offer me that? Will I really be able to hide from them in here?" Her dark eyes moved to the open window, and she blinked at the glass.

Her shoulders stiffened, and then she dropped her voice. "Maybe you're right, maybe you can never truly escape from some things. But it is worth a try, isn't it?"

This was not the Leena I knew. This woman before me seemed to be a broken shell of herself, and I longed to reach out and comfort her. To hold her, even if it would be a weak attempt at keeping her pieces together for just a little longer.

"What is it you are running from, Leena?" It was a bold question, one I did not expect her to answer, but the beauty glanced at me before sighing and then she moved to the door. Grabbing the handle, Leena stopped, and her chin lowered as she studied the floor for a pause. Seeming to collect her thoughts, she sighed roughly and then lifted her head.

"What we all flee from eventually." Her voice was strong once more, and her eyes bore into my own. "The memories of a past we cannot change."

The bed was just as comfortable as the previous one had been, and I pulled the sheets up to my chin before settling into the soft feather-filled mattress. The room was bright with the light from the moon, and I held my breath as I searched the canopy above me.

Sleep should not have been difficult to find now that I was somewhere familiar, and yet I couldn't help but jump at any sound, my mind unable to calm even though I was safe.

Safe.

The idea felt foreign now, and I wondered when was the last time I had felt that way? I was unable to stop my mind from picturing that dusty floor, the furs sprawled across the wood as his arms curled around me, pulling me to his chest—

No, there was nothing *safe* in those memories.

Forcing myself to lock those thoughts away once more, I gave up on sleep and swung my legs over the side of the bed before searching for the pair of boots that had been left for me. I found them tucked in the corner, grabbed the fresh pair of breeches that had also been set aside, and changed.

Satisfied that I was a bit more presentable, I glanced at the mirror that hung on the wall. My face looked no worse for wear, though the skin had lost some colour. However, as I moved my head side to side, I couldn't help but notice the angry red line that stood out against the pale flesh of my throat. By now it should have faded, but given the scars I still carried from my previous run-ins with immortals, I assume that this too would stay with me now.

"What's one more?" I asked myself with a frown, and then I turned from the glass and hurried from my room.

The boots were dry and warm though ill fitting, and my toes folded uncomfortably inside the leather as I strode through the empty hallways before rounding the last corner and entering the library. The walls were lined with shelves from floor to ceiling, each perfectly organized, and I moved my gaze over the spines before glancing at the far corner. Leena sat perched in a cushioned chair, her face blocked by an old, worn book, and I cleared my throat.

"I'm sorry, I didn't think—" Leena's face remained hidden, but she lifted one slender hand, her pointer finger rising at me, and I rolled my eyes as I waited.

Her softness from earlier was already forgotten apparently.

Shuffling my feet, I let my attention roam across the room until the sound of the book snapping shut rang out, and then I crossed my arms while watching the immortal carefully lay the book on the table next to her.

"Join me," Leena ordered before gesturing to the empty chair across from her own. I tried not to flush as the Lupine studied me silently while I strode across the distance.

"Keyno has already sent hawks out with word of your well-being in hopes of reaching your Healer, and your guard is being tended to."

"Thank you," I whispered and then I cleared my throat. "Barrick thought we might have been with Torris for some time. Has there been any word of the Healer's whereabouts in the last little while?"

Leena's head tipped just slightly for a pause, and then she frowned. "To be honest, we had no idea either of you had left the northern capital."

"We had not planned to make it well known," I muttered quietly.

"Are you able to tell me why you left Noordeign? Surely the comfort of the capital was better than travelling through the western channel. And how did you come to be stranded in the middle of the sea by the way?"

"We had set sail in Bascala, planning to travel north," I offered weakly. "We had been a few weeks in when we ran into trouble."

"Sea-maidens." Leena nodded. "You and your guard are lucky to have survived."

Lifting my chin, I gazed at the immortal beauty. "Sea-maidens, is that what they were?"

Dark eyes rolled and she sighed in exasperation. "Of course, what else would they be?"

I had always imagined that the maidens of the sea would be like their illustrations in the fables I used to read. They had been depicted as striking figures with long golden hair and soft features, not at all like what had attacked us. "Now will you tell me how you ended up overboard and in the water?"

"I didn't do it on purpose, Leena." I sighed while crossing my arms. "I don't even remember why I had moved towards the rail in the first place."

Leena's dark gaze sharpened and then she shook her head, exasperated. "Good Gods, halfling, have you never heard of the sea-maiden's song? Why on earth would you step foot onto a ship if you have absolutely no knowledge of the ocean?"

My cheeks burned under her scrutiny, and I clenched my jaw as I narrowed my eyes at her. "It wasn't for leisure, I can assure you."

Leena snorted and then pressed into the back of her chair before lifting a slender brow. "But Bascala? Why go all the way south only to turn around?"

"The plan had been to go to Ritari to aid the people after they had lost a number of trading ships."

"Yes, we too have had a number of losses."

"Then it seems we all have been affected by the wrecks." Leena's eyes narrowed and then she leaned forward onto the arm rest of her chair.

"Affected by the beast you mean," the Lupine guessed, and my brows rose in surprise. "Why do you think our best ship was out there? As soon as word reached Kalian about the lives perishing, he had sent word to Torris and his crew. Luckily, he listened to reason, or he would have been out on those waters himself."

I sank back into my chair at his name and studied my toes.

"The two of you are cut from the same cloth, you know. Both ready to take on the world with little care for your own preservation." She rolled her eyes with an annoyed huff. "So maybe you can answer me this: why are you always ready to sacrifice yourself?"

I thought on her words for a pause, and I decided there was no hurt in being as honest as I could be. "My worth has always been determined by what I can do for others."

"And who decided that? Do you think that's true just because that's how you see yourself?" Unable to answer her, I bit my lower lip and crossed my arms around my torso while my shoulders hunched.

"That's not how *he* saw you." Her voice was quiet, timid even, and I blinked away the sudden moisture in my eyes as they widened in surprise.

"You're wrong," I argued half-heartedly. "That's exactly how he saw me. Why else would he have lied to me for so long?"

"He was forced to make an impossible choice. One that he had made long before he met you." Leena sighed before she glanced around the room. "If sacrificing one single person could bring your family and village back, what would your choice be? If one soul could save hundreds, would you do it?"

I knew my answer. I had thought long and hard on that very question over the last year, but I wasn't ready to be honest, and instead shook my head. "I don't know."

"You're lying. I don't even need to see your face to know that you would. I heard your screams for your parents. I was there." Wincing at her claim, I wiped at the tear that had found an escape out of the corner of my eye.

"So how can you hate him for making the exact same choice you would have?" Her voice cracked before she turned to face me, her eyes careful as I swallowed roughly.

"Leena," Keyno called from the doorway, his voice stern and full of warning while he narrowed his eyes at his mate. "Skylahr needs to rest. Perhaps we should leave her be, my love." The two Lupines had locked eyes, seeming to have a private conversation, and I waited silently for the outcome.

Sighing, Leena ran her fingers through her hair in frustration before standing from her seat and crossing the room. Wrapping a powerful arm around her shoulders, Keyno glanced at me with a warm smile.

"You should rest, Skylahr." When my lips opened to protest, he shook his head with a soft laugh. "There is nothing else for you to do. Your guard is in capable hands, and if your friends are out there, my hawks will find them."

He pressed a sweet kiss to Leena's hair and gazed down at her for a pause before eyeing me once more. "There is nothing more for us to do, and tomorrow you can go back to your worrying, but for tonight, try to find some peace in the quiet."

My attention focused on Leena, who had paled at his words but nuzzled her face into his chest, and I tilted my head at the man. "Good night, you two."

I didn't have the heart to tell him that quiet in these walls would only bring back memories, and just like his mate, I longed to run from them.

Chapter 28

Rolling onto my back, I blinked up at the ceiling before looking at the window for a long, silent minute. It was still dark out, no sunlight in sight, and I pulled myself from the bed once more, grabbed the throw to wrap around my shoulders, and then tiptoed through the hall.

Rather than heading back to the library, I went the opposite way and wandered aimlessly through the castle until I turned around another corner. Lifting my gaze, I froze and took in the long line of statues, their faces angular and their eyes unseeing. Each one had similar features, and my eyes moved from one face to another before stopping at the second last stand that sat empty.

Tilting my head in confusion, I took a step closer before glancing around, and it was then I realized where I was. The stone wall across the hall looked no different than the rest, but I could picture a curtain of black hair fanning across the stone while a breathy voice called out. I felt my face heat at the memories.

Leena was right—this place was filled with ghosts better off forgotten.

Tightening my fingers around the wool that covered my shoulders, I fled down the dark corridor until I finally found the long hallway I had often thought about. The crisp, clean white snow was missing from the rooftops below, but the view was still just as beautiful as I remembered, and I inched my way closer to the window before lifting a hand and pressing my palm against the cool glass.

The mountains were still mighty, their tips reaching past the clouds, and the village that sat below was quiet in the moonlight. I scanned the little homes and shops before I glanced down, tipping my chin to my chest as I took in the castle grounds. The yards were clean and manicured, the shadows of the trees covering the perfectly green lawn, and I traced the smooth grass until movement caught my eye.

A massive black form curled in on itself, its fur ruffled from the gentle spring breeze, and I held my breath when his head lifted, his long snout turning to face the stone wall he lay against. I followed his eyes, trying to see what it was he had been searching for. But nothing seemed amiss, and I stepped back from the window and glanced down the hall in the same direction, imagining the corridors in my mind before tracing my steps back.

My heart stuttered sharply in my chest, and my eyes widened when I realized he was below the room I had been given.

Moving forward once more, I closed the distance between myself and the window, nearly pressing my nose against the glass as I watched. As though he felt my gaze on him, Kalian rose, sitting back on his haunches as he gazed up at the window of my room before his body seemed to fold in on itself, his shoulders slumping as his head bowed, and my stomach dropped at the sight.

This was not the mighty Lord of Denimoore, the Alpha of the Lupines.

The Protector's Chosen.

This was not the man I knew.

Sliding to the floor, I curled on my side, pillowing my head with my hands as they tucked under my cheeks, and I watched while he lay under my window in the quiet of the night and I wondered if he could hear the pounding of my heart.

A gentle nudge to my shoulder woke me, the leather-clad toe pressing against my body until I rolled onto my back and blinked up at the handsome face of Keyno. His arms were crossed, the muscles bulging beneath his thin tunic, and one black brow rose at me in question.

"We do have more rooms if yours was not to your liking." One long hand reached towards me in offering, and I rolled my eyes before pulling myself to my feet.

Narrowing my bleary gaze at the man, I scanned his smiling face for a pause before my eyes drifted past his shoulder and down below to the soft green grass. There was no sign of the black wolf, and I moved my attention across the yards until Keyno's warm hand clasped my arm.

"What are you searching for?" His own eyes never wavered from my face, not casting a single glance at the glass wall, and I stiffened under his watchful gaze as he tipped his head. "Or rather who?"

Pulling away from his touch, I pressed my hands against my tunic, smoothing it carefully while I cleared my head. Keyno was far more observant than he let on; most missed his watchful eyes and the careful way he noticed everything in his surroundings. His easy smile and warmth skillfully disguised his intelligence, and I wondered if that was his greatest weapon.

"I'm not looking for anyone," I grumbled, but he knew better and shot me a sly smile before taking a step back.

"Well, if you are done lying on the floor, you can follow me to the tower. I was just informed my hawk has returned." My initial annoyance was immediately forgotten as my eyes widened.

"One has returned this quickly? Is that a good sign?" My chest was heavy with nerves as Keyno ignored my question and turned on his heel, remaining silent while I followed him through the halls of Denimoore.

The tower was located on the north side of the castle, an area I had never ventured to before, and I took in the blank stone walls before following the Lupine to a dimly lit passageway. Keyno stepped forward to the heavy wood door, lifted the solid metal bar, unlocked the entrance, and then stepped through, his arm stretched back to hold it open just long enough for me to follow before it slammed shut.

Shuffling forward, I trailed Keyno up the first few steps, not realizing how daunting the climb would be. The winding staircase was steep and dark, and the tower walls seemed to close in tighter the farther we climbed. Panicked by the lack of space, I lifted my arms, my fingers sliding against the stone, searching for purchase as my feet faltered, and I gawked at the man ahead of me who easily climbed two stairs at a time with more grace than I could have imagined.

"Are you alright back there, Hazel?" His voice was light with amusement, and had I not been too afraid to lift my eyes from my feet in fear of tumbling backwards, I would have shot him a nasty glare.

"Why is there no railing?" I complained as I cautiously took the next step.

"Why would we want to help those who would try to intercept our letters?"

My brows furrowed in confusion. "Do you have so many secret correspondents for that to be a concern?" A great booming laugh echoed around us, the sound bouncing off the stone walls, and although I was annoyed, I couldn't help but smile at the sound.

"No, but the tower offers the best vantage point of Denimoore and the grounds. It would make an excellent lookout for anyone hoping to seize the castle. Not to mention our enemies' use of valkhags; they can easily carry thirty men and this tower is the perfect perch. However, rushing down these stairs would be a careless mistake, and without a railing to aid them, it may even be fatal."

It had never occurred to me that the people of Denimoore had devised a plan to keep enemies out, or rather at bay, and I couldn't picture the Lupine capital falling under siege. The very idea that someone would attempt it seemed impossible.

"Wait, what are valkhags?" When I had repeated Keyno's words in my mind I realized I hadn't understood that one.

"What on earth do they teach you mortals in the south?" he

grumped under his breath. He finally reached the perch and then turned to offer me his hand as I followed behind him. "I understand never seeing one, but surely you were taught about the beasts of old who ruled the skies for centuries?" I shrugged my shoulders helplessly as his brows lifted in surprise.

"They are great winged beasts from the Elrin mountains. Once thought to be the sacred creatures of the Gods, but over time more and more were captured, their bodies harnessed, and spirits broken so that they could be used as weapons. Many were ridden by the Crimsons during the war and used to kill hundreds of our own people."

"If they are used by the Crimsons, why have I never heard of them?"

"The numbers dwindled after the war, and those remaining in the wild fled the continent, hiding in the mountains of Seadraid." Keyno turned to the opening and approached the edge, arm out as he gave a long, loud whistle. I held my breath when I heard his hawk call back.

It was a great beast of a bird, nearly a quarter of the size of its master, and had Keyno not been immortal, I bet he would have crumpled under its weight. Its feathers were deep black, almost purple in the sunlight, and its talons had to be bigger than my hands.

Lifting his free arm, Keyno stroked its head with a fond smile, and I nearly shrank back from the pair when the hawk turned to face me. It wasn't the long-hooked beak that had frightened me—no, it was the empty sockets that sat on either side, deep holes of black where its eyes should have been.

"I thought you said it was a hawk?" The eyeless face had not turned away, its attention still focused on me, and I took a step back.

"Well, his name is Hawk." Keyno shrugged with a smile. "But he's a hafok."

"And should I know what that is as well?" Keyno stroked Hawk's feathers once more, then focused on the parchment tied to one of its legs.

"No, these beasts only reside this far north and only half a dozen have been accounted for. Hawk is the only one who has bonded with a human as far as I am aware." Keyno unrolled the paper and scanned the page before moving his arm to the window.

Hawk stretched his wings wide, the feathers nearly reaching the opposing walls of the tower. He flapped them twice, and I closed my eyes against the gusts of wind, and then he moved to the ledge and dove headfirst from the window. Watching his beast soar across the yards before lifting himself into the clouds, Keyno blindly reached his hand towards me, the paper clasped between his fingers.

"It doesn't appear that they've reached any northern shores yet." His voice was soft as he closed the distance between us and cupped my shoulder gently. "But the moment they do, we will know. In the meantime, you and your guard are welcome to stay here. It will give him time to heal."

Frowning, I took the parchment from the Lupine and opened it. The handwriting was that of a stranger, and I scanned the scribbled words, confirming that there had been no sightings of my friends along the northern coast of the Lupine territories, but word would be sent south.

"You do not need to stay; your guard may be unable to travel but that doesn't mean you can't," Keyno said, his voice full of sincerity. I supposed he was right. I could perhaps leave Barrick here while I searched the coast for the Healer and my friends, but where would I even start?

"Where would I go, back south? Back to Noordeign?" Keyno shrugged and then glanced out the window towards the grounds. "No, I can't return without them, and I would be better off staying in one place until they have received word of my whereabouts."

"That could take weeks," Keyno whispered, and I knew even *that* was optimistic. We had no way of knowing if they were even alive to receive his letters.

No, I couldn't think that way. I couldn't assume the worst; it would do nothing for me.

"Well, even if you are better off staying in one place, are you sure you want to remain north? Are you certain you want to stay here?

We could find a place in the village for you." I stared at the Lupine, waiting until he finally turned to face me before crossing my arms.

"Am I not welcome here?"

Keyno shook his head. "You know you are, but I just want you to be comfortable."

"Are you worried about my comfort or someone else's?" His usually warm face filled with tension, and he rubbed at his jaw as he seemed to try to find the right words.

"He's had a hard time, Hazel." I couldn't stop myself from rolling my eyes, and Keyno's frown deepened.

"*He's* had a hard time, really?" I scoffed.

"I am just being honest."

"Well, next time keep your honesty to yourself, I don't want to hear it." Turning from him, I grabbed on to the railing and all but slid down the narrow stairs, ignoring Keyno's call of my name.

Chapter 29

"You look like shit." Startled by the hoarse voice, I lifted my head and closed the door softly as Barrick stared at me through one bleary eye. After leaving the tower without any word of my friends' whereabouts, I decided to check in on my guard, too worried to wait any longer.

"Honestly, Huntress, I think you look worse than I do." Sighing heavily, I fell into the chair next to his bedside and wiped my face in exhaustion.

"Not possible," I grumbled, not bothering to look at Barrick as I sighed once more.

"Well, if you want to live in denial, I suppose that's your choice, but mind telling me why you're hiding in my room? Shouldn't you be socializing with our hosts?"

"I'm not hiding, I'm checking on my guard." My lips quirked and I snorted when Barrick rolled his eyes in exasperation.

"Denial *and* avoiding my questions, your specialties." He struggled to pull himself up and was panting by the time he had settled against the headboard, but he still mustered the energy to narrow his eyes at me. "Come on now, girl, don't waste my time. What has you hiding in here with me? Has something happened?"

I had been ready to give another excuse when a quiet tap sounded from the door, and I took the opportunity to escape my guard's scrutiny as I moved to greet the visitor. I pulled on the handle and swung the door wide, and Leena's brows lifted in surprise.

"Skylahr," she greeted and then glanced over my shoulder toward Barrick. "I didn't think you would be here, I thought you were with Keyno."

"Apparently she's avoiding someone, hence her hiding in here with me." Turning my chin to my shoulder, I glared at my guard, though he didn't seem the least bit concerned, and then I opened the door for our visitor.

"I'm not avoiding anyone," I grumbled under my breath while I crossed my arms. Leena gave me a pointed look before stepping towards the bed.

"Right, well, I'm feeling right as rain," Barrick grunted, but I noticed his wince when he shifted, and I frowned in concern.

"I will have one of the lady's maids bring some tonic for you." The guard rolled his eyes but did not argue with the imposing immortal woman. "And then your lady can come have tea with us and let you rest."

"I think I better go fetch some refreshments for Barrick instead," I suggested, and Leena's dark gaze moved to me as her mouth lifted in a smirk.

"Maybe your guard was right, you are hiding away." I wanted to argue, I wanted to deny it again, but I wasn't sure I could do so convincingly, and instead I stepped out of the room, unable to face the immortal's knowing gaze for another moment. Sensing that this was my chance to escape, I took it, and rather than turning left to take the route to the kitchens, I instead went right and headed towards the armoury and training yards, praying that it would be empty.

The way was familiar, even after all the time that had passed, and my fingers twitched in anticipation, eager to feel the hilt of a sword in their grasp once more. Glancing at the solid stone building, I sighed in relief when I realized no one else was around, and I nearly skipped through the door when I saw the sparring swords.

After taking my pick, I strode back to the yard and turned towards the dummies, ready to soothe that familiar burn in my spine by beating the straw-filled bodies into dust. Rolling my shoulders, I took in a deep breath and braced my weight.

"Hazel," Keyno called, and I glanced at him for just an instant before I charged at my opponent.

Within a few moments, the burlap body was falling apart, its stuffing coating the grass beneath it, and I smiled to myself before moving onto the next one, not caring that Keyno was still watching me from the fence that surrounded the yard. Lopping off one arm, I slashed and cut the torso until it no longer resembled a body and then moved onto the third.

"You know they won't fight back!" Keyno shouted so that I would hear him over my grunting. "I'm not sure I see the point if your skills aren't even being tested."

I lowered the sword and let my arm hang at my side, and then I wiped at my brow with the back of my free hand. "Are you offering?"

His lips lifted into that familiar smile, and he stuffed his hands into the pockets of his breeches. "I think I'm the one to blame for your piss-poor mood. Maybe I deserve a good beating for speaking out of turn earlier."

"You didn't," I admitted. "I am a guest here and I would do my best to remember that before I let my temper get the better of me."

"Don't worry, Hazel, I can handle your temper," Keyno promised and then jogged to the armoury to grab a blade for himself.

Keyno entered the ring, stood across from me, and then lifted a hand and curled two fingers, beckoning me forward. I accepted the invitation, and we began our dance. My blood sang at the familiarity of it, though I had to remind myself to rein in the amount of force I used.

Focusing instead on the enjoyment I found in our sparring, I allowed Keyno to lead us around and around. Our feet moved swiftly across the straw-covered ground as we fought, and his face brightened into a smile.

"You've gotten better, your movements are smoother, even if you aren't truly trying," Keyno remarked proudly, and I paused at the sentiment. Taking advantage of my distraction, the Lupine brought his blade down on my own, knocking it out of my grasp, and I narrowed my eyes at him.

Laughing, Keyno shrugged. "You shouldn't let my praise go to your head so easily."

"That was rude," I argued as I bent to pick up my blade.

"You say rude, I say strategic."

Blowing a strand of hair out of my face, I went after the Lupine once more, though we had both been too distracted by our banter to notice the way the soft earth had begun to mix with the straw, and just as he fought off my attack, his foot slipped, and he went tumbling to the damp earth. Not able to stop myself in time, my foot caught on his and I fell forward, my torso landing heavily across his own as I tried to keep the edge of my sword away from us.

Taking a second, I gasped for air, and then I turned to look at the Lupine with a smile. "Was that strategic as well then?"

His own face brightened, and he chuckled. "I—"

"Keyno." The voice was low with warning. Stilling, both of us turned our heads cautiously towards our audience.

Kalian's hands were braced on the top rail of the fence, though I could see the white of his knuckles from here. It almost appeared as if the wood was bowing from the weight of his grasp. Following the golden skin of his hands, I watched the way the muscles of his forearms flexed, and then I peered up at his face.

His jaw was tight, and those brilliant silver eyes were bright with anger, though I couldn't understand why. He had nothing to be upset about, yet I couldn't help but notice the way his attention was solely directed at his brother.

Moving under me, Keyno placed a careful hand on my shoulder, his movements slow and cautious. But when the sound of splintering wood came from the alpha, he froze once more, and then pleading dark eyes glanced at me.

"I think we better call it a day," Keyno suggested. "And I don't really feel like losing a hand, so perhaps you could get up without my assistance."

Blushing hotly, I swallowed and then staggered to my feet unsteadily while those molten eyes watched my every move. Deciding to forget about my discarded blade, I hurried from the yard, doing my very best to ignore the way my pulse pounded through my veins.

"Where have you been?" Rolling my eyes, I used my hip to shut the door behind me and roughly dropped the tray onto Barrick's nightstand before toeing off my muddy boots. The guard glanced at the pile of food for just a moment before he eyed me closely and then grabbed for the fruit tart. "This is some place; I've only had food like this during important celebrations."

Picking at one of the pastries, I sat in the chair once more and lifted my feet to rest on the edge of his bed. "The kitchen was stocked full today, there must be something happening this week."

"Is that where you've been this morning? Hoarding all the good treats for yourself?" His dark brows lifted while he messily shoved the remainder of his tart into his mouth, and I nudged him with my foot before wrinkling my nose.

"No, I was giving you some time alone to gather your strength so that you can continue to pretend like you are fine even though we both know you aren't." Barrick scoffed, sending crumbs tumbling down his beard, and my face twisted in annoyance. "Were your manners always this bad or did you just pick this up?"

"You know what I think?" One long finger pointed at me before the hand reached for another tart. "I think there is more to this place and that boy than you've let on."

My cheeks flamed under his security, and I pulled my feet from his bed before tucking my knees to my chest.

"Boy? Who are you calling a boy now? Everyone here is an immortal, they are centuries older than you," I pointed out, resting my chin on my knees.

"The pretty one with the eyes," he grumbled around the food in his mouth before grabbing another helping.

"You think he's pretty?" I teased, ignoring the glare he sent my way at my deflection.

"You never speak of your time before your crowning; anything I know has been from Miss Ella and Elizabeth, and now I'm wondering why that is." He was right, of course, though we were close, we never truly opened up to each other until recently, but there were still things I preferred to keep to myself.

"I think you should concern yourself with getting well and not with whatever you think you need to know about my past here." Stretching my legs, I crossed my ankles and then ran my palms over my thighs nervously.

"Past here?" he questioned with a furrowed brow, and my eyes caught his as I felt myself pale.

"Please, Barrick," I begged. "I really do not want to talk about this."

"Okay," he relented. "But, Huntress, if that changes—if you need someone to hold your secrets, I'm right here. I will be right here, ready to carry whatever it is you need me to." His face was warm, earnest even, and yet his eyes held worry.

Dipping my head, I swallowed roughly before attempting a soft smile. "Is that part of the position of being my guard?"

"No, but I have always been an overachiever." His lips lifted in an answering grin. "I will guard you, your life, your heart, and your secrets. Always."

"Of that I've never had any doubt. But please, Barrick. It's Skylahr, not Huntress. Not to you."

His dark eyes warmed as colour filled his cheeks and his chin dropped in what almost seemed to be bashfulness. "Alright then, Skylahr."

Chapter 30

"Our curer says your guard needs at least another fortnight or two in bed," Leena sighed as she sipped her wine. "And we still have not received any news on the Healer."

My chest grew tight, and I chewed at my lower lip. "What do you think that means?"

"Skylahr, it may not mean anything. It has been a day, and though Keyno's hafok is fast, the rest of the hawks will take time to reach their destinations," Leena assured me, but it did little to quell my nerves.

"When you say destinations, where are you speaking of?" Leena's brows furrowed. "I know you sent them to those you trust in Elrin, but what about other places?" I asked, unsure if I should even bother with my suggestion.

"Other places?" the immortal asked, clearly not understanding what I meant. "What other places would you want me to send word to?"

"I told you we had originally planned to go to Ritari before stopping in Bascala and then we had sailed north."

Brushing her dark hair over her shoulder, Leena shifted in her chair until she was all but leaning across the table between us, and then she flicked her hand, gesturing for me to continue. "Yes, and?"

"We were going north, but not to another village in Elrin." I paused and then took in a swift inhale. "We were on our way to Skohyn."

Leena's face was unreadable as she stared at me, and I shifted under her gaze as the silence stretched on between us for a few long moments.

Unable to stand the quiet any longer, I ducked my chin to my chest and gazed down at my feet before clearing my throat. "Well, are you going to say something? Anything?"

"I am trying to figure out why you and the Healer seem to wish for a quick death."

I lifted my eyes to peer up at her but quickly regretted it once I saw the scathing expression painted across her face.

"What about that plan has made you so angry, Leena?" I snapped.

"Good Gods, you are a reckless girl," she muttered under her breath. "Skohyn is a dangerous place, surely your Healer told you as much."

"Yes, he may have mentioned it."

"It's a place of the old world, a place of the Gods," she explained. "What could possibly be there that is worth your life?"

"The Siren's immortals have gathered on that island."

"Who told you that?" Leena asked with a tilt of her head.

"The captain who had agreed to sail with us."

"And you did not think for a second that perhaps it was a lie? That maybe she was tricking you?" If I was honest with myself, no, the thought hadn't crossed my mind.

"She believed that those immortals were behind the sudden appearance of the monster, and if that is true then we needed to find them, and that was the only name that was spoken when we asked of their location."

Leena lifted her glass and drank greedily, though her eyes never left mine from over the rim, and I waited impatiently for her to finish. The immortal drained the remaining wine with one last swallow, and then she placed the glass on the table next to her before moving from her seat.

She paced back and forth across the space in front of me, all while muttering to herself, though her voice was too low for me to understand what she was saying, and I watched with interest.

"Leena, what is it?" Seeming to remember my presence, the immortal turned to me, but her eyes were still bouncing around the room. "What?"

She didn't answer and instead straightened her spine before glancing at the lady's maid who was carefully stepping out onto the terrace. Noticing the immortal's stern gaze, the young woman lowered her own and curtseyed while addressing Leena.

"Supper has been served, my lady."

"Thank you." Leena dismissed her with a wave of her hand, and then she ran her fingers through her long black hair. "We best be going before Keyno comes searching for us."

"Oh, no." I began to shake my head. "I will take dinner with Barrick."

"You will not," Leena argued.

"Leena, please," I pleaded, and her face softened just slightly.

"He won't be there," Leena promised with a roll of her eyes. It should have been a relief, and yet I was still worried about the other face I had seen only once since my arrival.

"And Nadine?" The immortal had the nerve to look confused, and the expression made me feel foolish for even speaking the name.

"What of her?" Scoffing, I lifted a hand to rub at my temple as I peered up at Leena.

"Well, I'd rather not see her either," I admitted.

"You won't have to," she assured me.

"She'll be with him then? You promise?" I prayed that she was right and not just placating me so that I would agree to eat with her.

"No, she won't be with him." One brow lifted at me, as if I should understand what it was she was trying to get across.

"Leena, take pity on me," I grumbled. "I know they're mated so where will she be? Just tell me."

"They're not mated, Skylahr. Nadine has not been in Denimoore since our return from the shores."

"What?"

"Kalian broke off the betrothal. He has had no one else since *you*."

I was left reeling from Leena's news, and I followed behind her silently as I replayed her words over and over in my mind.

He has had no one else since you.

Surely she was wrong, or misinformed because Kalian had been promised to Nadine after he had shattered my heart, and there was no possible scenario where she had not been warming his bed. No, Leena was mistaken, and I would not allow myself to be fooled.

Hardening my resolve, I entered the dining room and scanned the vacant chairs quickly before taking the spot across from Keyno. The Lupine male had paid us little attention as we entered, and I gazed at him, wondering what had soured his mood before spotting the small bloodstains on the front of his tunic.

"Are you alright?" I asked, my eyes wide as I scanned his face for any sign of injury. Leena moved to him, her long, delicate fingers cupping his jaw before lifting his chin so that she could examine him more closely.

"Fine," he murmured quietly as his mate traced her fingers over his handsome face.

"What happened?" the immortal beauty demanded, and her mate grabbed her wrist before pressing a soft kiss to the palm of her hand.

"He was just feeling a bit territorial is all," Keyno explained and then he turned to me.

"What?" My attention bounced between both Lupines in confusion, but Leena just shook her head and then sank into her seat.

"Tell him if he touches you again, I will cut off his precious bits and feed them to your hafok," Leena whispered sweetly with a small grin and then leaned over to press a kiss to Keyno's cheek.

Smiling at her, Keyno returned the gesture, and then his focus moved back to me, and he lifted a bowl of boiled potatoes towards me. Prior to the talk with Leena, I had been starving even after having a number of pastries with Barrick, but now my stomach protested at the thought of food.

"I think I will retire for the night." I sighed as I stood from my seat, and the immortals glanced at each other worriedly.

"Hazel, if we have upset you—" Shaking my head, I interrupted Keyno and wiped my palms across the front of my tunic nervously.

"No, it's been a long day is all, and I would like to check on Barrick before getting a good night's rest." I did my best to appear poised and unbothered, but I knew neither were falling for it.

"Well, I hoped we could talk more about what you told me." Leena frowned, and as her eyes moved to Keyno quickly, and he looked at her with concern.

"What more was there to discuss?" I asked, frustrated.

"Well, I don't know, maybe the fact that you think that the Siren's immortals are the ones to blame for this beast that seemingly came out of nowhere."

"What?" Keyno's eyes widened in shock as he stared at me.

"And that they have gathered at Skohyn," Leena continued.

"Skohyn?" The man's face paled, and given that fact that his mate had had a similar reaction, I wondered if my rather unconcerned reaction to Gaelon's warnings of the island had been unfitting.

"Do you think it's possible?" Leena wondered nervously.

"I'm not sure what to think," Keyno confessed. "But I can't help but feel that there must be some truth to it. The fact that it is being said that they are gathering at the shrine of their Goddess can't be by chance."

"The shrine of their Goddess?" I asked. "Is that what is there?"

"Yes, originally her place of worship was hidden amongst the island, but it had grown too dangerous for her people to travel to over time, and they were given the Siren's cove as their capital before the war."

Taking a step forward, I braced my hands on the back of the chair I had been sitting in and peered down at Keyno. "Dangerous? How so?"

"It is an ancient place, full of the magic of old."

Nodding, I motioned to Leena. "Yes, she said as much."

"And a place like that would be a safe haven for things that no longer have a place in our world now," Keyno explained.

“Things? What kind of things?” Panic bubbled in my belly as I thought of my friends who may have still been on their way to the island.

“Dark things, horrible things. Things most do not speak of.” They were half answers and riddles, and I crossed my arms as I grew more anxious.

“What do we do?” I demanded, now terrified that those I love were venturing into a place far more dangerous than they had thought.

Leena was the one who answered. “We need to tell Kalian first, see what he thinks of your theory.”

“And what of Gaelon and my friends?” My body trembled as I spoke the words, and both glanced at me with concern before Keyno lowered his eyes to the tabletop in front of him.

“We pray to the Protector that they are far from there.”

Chapter 31

I watched Barrick's chest rise and fall steadily as I perched on the chair next to him. Leena and Keyno had left to find Kalian, though they had wanted me to come along, but I had been too much of a coward to follow. I wasn't ready to face him. Not yet, not with all of this hurt and anger and confusion that still blanketed me like a constant shadow.

Leena had said we were cut from the same cloth, that given the option to save my parents and people, I would have made the same choice he had, my feelings for *him* be damned. And deep down I knew there was truth to that.

But I still could not use her logic to stop those gaping wounds from opening. Instead, my heart remained frayed at the edges, bruised and bloody as I pointed all of my guilt and anger towards him. After all, that was far easier than admitting the alternative.

"Foolish idiot," I whispered while pressing my forehead against my knees, hugging them tightly to my chest.

"I hope you are not talking to me," Barrick grumbled as his head turned in my direction, and I lowered my legs before leaning towards him.

"How are you feeling?" I asked and then turned to pour him a cup of water.

"Like I could use a solid night's sleep without you muttering to yourself like a madwoman." He scowled but still took the offered cup from my hands and drank the contents.

"I'm sorry I woke you." My guard lifted onto his palms and pulled himself until he was sitting against the headboard.

"It's too late for apologies now," he responded while rubbing at his eyes tiredly. "But you could tell me who you were busy insulting."

"I was talking to myself," I admitted sheepishly as my face burned.

"Ah." He nodded. "That makes far more sense."

My mouth parted in shock, and I swatted at his shoulder gently. "I was right, your manners are long forgotten."

Ignoring me, my guard carefully turned on his side, though his face twisted in pain, and I hovered over him worriedly. He had been healing well now that he was being taken care of properly and resting in far better conditions. But the stab wounds had been deep and exposed to the sea, and I knew that an injury like that on a mortal man could take ages to heal right, especially if he was not careful to not strain the area.

"Lie still, won't you?" I scolded, and my guard growled in frustration as he fought to get comfortable. Barrick stopped moving and then glared up at me.

"Stop ordering me about!" he snapped.

"I will do as I please." I scowled at him. "You need to rest."

"And I would have an easier time doing so if you were not my constant companion," he growled. "Why don't you stop being a coward and face whatever it is you are fleeing from."

"Why do you continue to say things like that? I am not hiding, I'm not fleeing, and I am certainly no coward."

His deep brown eyes held mine, and then he laughed under his breath. "Never in my days would I think you were both a coward and a liar."

The words were sharp as they hit their intended target, and I stood to my full height before peering down at him. "How could you say such a thing?"

"Because I told you that I would protect you, even if it meant protecting you from yourself, and I can see now that you need someone to say it."

"Say what?" I demanded while a surge of anger burned through me.

"You have been in pain since the day I met you, and I had no idea as to why. I had heard the rumblings at court, of course, but had not put that much weight to them." That annoyed expression of his slowly melted into something else, and my stomach rolled once I realized what it was.

Pity.

"But now being here, I can see that they were right. You are *bleeding* for that boy and yet you refuse to acknowledge it." Falling back onto his pillows, he sighed softly. "Leave a wound like that long enough and it will fester."

"What would you have me do, Barrick?" I whispered, unable to keep my voice from trembling.

"I would tell you to figure out what you need to heal and then do so," he answered. "It's either that or you cauterize it."

Not understanding, I wrapped my arms around myself and blinked past the tears that had filled my eyes. "Meaning?"

"Meaning you seal away whatever it is that you feel, and you never think about it again. You force yourself to forget it."

"Right." I nodded and then I moved to straighten out his blankets, all while ignoring the careful way he watched me.

"But, Huntress." He grabbed one of my hands and held it tightly. "I would say you should be careful with which choice you make. I think you and I both know you do not need to carry any more scars."

The hall was dark as I left Barrick's room, and I wondered how the talk with the Lupine alpha had gone. Chances were he had been just as frustrated by the plan the Healer and I had decided on as his siblings were. Being overbearing and disapproving seemed to be qualities all Lupines shared, and I sighed, readying myself for another lecture when I saw them next.

Quietly tiptoeing across the smooth stone floors, I took in the mighty walls of the castle and finally noted the subtle changes from my last visit. Gone were the vases of flowers and warm details that had once covered the open spaces. In fact, the rooms had seemed bare, almost if they had been neglected, and I frowned, wondering what had changed as I descended down the stairs and towards the library.

Certain sleep would escape me once more tonight, I had decided not to bother with returning to my chambers. I stepped into the grand room, basking in the soft moonlight as I took in its impressiveness, and then I carefully closed the doors behind me. I knew from my previous stay that many of the books were in the tongue of old, and though I could not understand them, their portraits and illustrations were unlike anything I had ever seen, and I figured I could use the distraction.

I grabbed the tinderbox left on the centre table, brought it to the fireplace, and carefully lit the fresh logs that had been left before moving to the shelf in the far corner. Tracing the worn leather spines, I skimmed over the row of books until I found one that caught my interest.

Huntress.

The perfectly curved letters were faded, the once-shimmering gold now flat and dull, and yet the single word had taken the air from my lungs. I carefully pulled the book from its place and sought out the chair closest to the window. Glancing down at the leather cover, I smoothed my hand across its surface and inhaled sharply before readying myself to open it to the first page. However, just as my fingers curled around the leather case, the turning of the door handle sounded in the room, and I froze, holding my breath as my skin tingled and I waited for my visitor to greet me.

"I didn't think you would be in here." His voice was soft, gentle as if he was attempting to approach a skittish animal, and I swallowed roughly before glancing over my shoulder at him.

"I hope you don't mind?" I asked while lifting the book to show him what I had found.

"A little late to be asking that, isn't it?" That damn smirk had curled across his lips, and for a moment I saw a glimpse of the man I had met all those months ago, though now it felt like a lifetime away. The last time we had truly spoken to each other had been in the shelter of that tent. When he had been lying across that bed, both of our hearts broken while he tried to mend whatever it was between us.

"It's better to apologize than ask for approval, right? That's what my father used to say at least." I shrugged awkwardly.

"Smart man." His smirk grew, his stunningly handsome face striking me frozen once again, and my pause had allowed a heavy silence to filter into the space around us. He cleared his throat, and his silver eyes roamed around the room before he straightened his tunic and then took two steps closer.

"Which book is that one?" His chin lifted, indicating to the one I held in my hand, but his gaze found mine, and I felt heat fill my cheeks before I dropped my eyes to the pages.

"I think they're scriptures of the Huntress."

"Haven't you heard enough about her over the past year?" He tilted his head to the side, and then he closed the remaining space between us and folded himself into the chair across from my own. The light from the window bounced off his dark hair and tanned skin, and my breath caught as his silver eyes glimmered under the soft glow.

"Honestly?" I moved my attention back to my lap before flipping through the pages. "I feel like I've hardly learned anything."

"What do you mean?" Leaning forward, he lifted his arm, fingers stretching until the tips had reached the page, and he hesitated for a minute, waiting until I nodded before taking the book from my lap.

"I know that the Huntress is the Goddess of creation. She is the guardian of the land and animals. Fierce and strong and all that nonsense. She was a warrior of sorts of course—"

"Of sorts?" Kalian's eyes had widened, and the bewildered expression would have been comical if I hadn't been so taken off guard. "She was *the* warrior. She was cunning and strong. No other God could compare to her in combat. She was the defender of justice!"

"Of course." My teeth sank into my lower lip for a pause, and I watched as the Lupine alpha flipped to the middle of the book.

"I don't know what things they have been spewing in the south, but the Huntress was the mightiest one of them all." He passed the book back, and I looked at the portrait in front of me.

The statue in the square of Noordeign had been one of beauty. The clay had been carved so meticulously, creating a woman who was not only captivating, but also stunning.

However, this picture in my hands looked nothing similar to the face I had memorized since my crowning.

She was long limbed and strong, her hips wide under her armour, and her eyes were not the sparkling sapphires I associated with her face. The blue in the portrait was like looking at ice, hard and cold, and I wondered which depiction was correct. My fingers traced her, the pads smoothing over the harsh lines and angles of her face, and I blinked down at the Goddess.

"Kalian?" Leena's voice called from the door, and my heart lurched as I glanced up at the Lupine alpha. His eyes, however, had focused in on his sister, and his face settled into a mask void of emotion while he sank into the back of his chair.

"I'm sorry, I should go," I whispered as I suddenly came to my senses.

Leena's attention bounced between me and her brother, and her mouth pressed into a thin line before she nodded. "Yes, it is late, and I seem to remember you wanting to retire early."

"Right, of course, I'm sorry." Scrambling from my place, I went to move around Kalian, but just as I passed, his hand shot out and his fingers curled around my wrist. Gasping at the sudden touch, I stiffened while his thumb stroked across my pulse point.

"Wait," he whispered before standing, and then he was right in front of me, so close my chest nearly brushed against his. "Take this with you. Maybe you can learn a thing or two, or at least find some enjoyment from the pictures."

He lifted the book and pressed it to my torso, holding it there until I took it, and then he stepped back and moved his attention to Leena. The two seemed to have a silent conversation, and I grew more anxious as time went on without either of them speaking a word. Deciding to give them the privacy they obviously needed, I cleared my throat and then glanced up at Kalian.

"Thank you," I whispered shakily as I held the leather-bound pages up.

"Don't thank me," he growled, and when I took a step back at his tone, his shoulders sagged, and he lowered his eyes to the floor.

"Don't thank me," he repeated softly. "It is the least I could do for you, Huntress."

My heart ached as it pounded in my chest, and I glanced at Leena, unsure of what I should say or do. But she wasn't paying me any attention; those dark eyes were locked on her brother, gazing at him sadly.

Dipping my head, I took a step away from him, and then another, and another, not stopping until I had safely made it to the solid wooden doors, and then I pressed them open, just wide enough for me to slip through.

"Kalian," I heard Leena sigh as I pushed them shut behind me and then I held my breath, waiting for his reply.

"Not tonight, Leena, please." His voice shook in a way I had never heard before, and I closed my eyes while cradling the book to my chest, as if the pressure of my own touch would nurse the soft throbbing that had seemed to settle there.

And then I did what Barrick had accused me of.

I fled.

Chapter 32

Sitting cross-legged on my bed, I flipped through the book I had taken the night before and studied the illustrations. Some were familiar, of course, especially those of the manors of the north I recognized, though they had obviously grown over time and no longer looked as humble as they were depicted on the pages. I also became more accustomed to seeing this new version of my Goddess. Her harsh scowl and heavily muscled body were no longer foreign, and her portraits almost seemed to ease something within me.

I turned to another page, my brows furrowing as I glanced over the worn parchment. There were sigils I recognized, the burning heart, the stag's antlers and bow, the Lupine shield, the four-pointed star, and the moon and sun belonging to the Healer of course. But there was also the Siren's trident, though this drawing included an added detail of a shell tucked behind it. I frowned at it before moving onto the next page.

"Skylahr," Leena called through the door, and I shut the book before standing from my bed. Opening the door slowly, I nearly gasped at the sight of the immortal.

Her normally glowing golden skin was dull, and her hair was a tangled mess that hung around her shoulders. Stepping out of her way, I invited the Lupine in and watched as she sat on the edge of my bed.

"Leena?" I asked worriedly, unsure of what to say or how to broach the subject of her appearance.

"How did you do it?" she whispered with a hoarse voice.

"Do what, Leena?"

"How did you continue to live after seeing what you have seen, after losing all you have lost?" she answered. "I saw you fall apart and watched as you put yourself back together. I have heard you cry out in the night for your father, and yet you would wake the next morning ready to take on the day and all while remaining kind. How do you do it?"

I didn't understand where this was coming from. Nothing had happened the night before that would lead to this conversation, and it seemed so odd that she would want to discuss this now.

"You have suffered losses as well," I pointed out, and her mouth pulled into a deep frown.

"Many over the years," she agreed. "My three half brothers to the war, though I never knew them, so I'm not sure if I can really claim those. But I have grieved my father, then my child. Next came my mortality and now my mother."

"I am sorry," I offered, not knowing what else I could say without risking upsetting her.

"I have not stayed kind; I have hardened over time," she whispered. "Though I'm not sure I ever was kind to begin with."

"Why is this on your mind now? Has something happened, Leena?" I questioned.

"Nothing my brother would want me to tell you about." She sighed and then cleared her throat. "I said some things last night that I shouldn't have after you left, and he retaliated of course. You know how his words can cut you to the bone."

"A skill you both share, if my memory serves me right." Leena flinched at that, and I wished I could take back the words almost immediately. "I'm sorry, that was unkind."

"It looks like we taught you well." Leena laughed softly, and then she sighed. "Last night I dreamt of her for the first time in months.

It was so real that when I woke, I could have sworn I could sense her presence."

"I'm sorry," I whispered again. "I too have experienced that, and it always hurts terribly when you realize it was just your mind playing tricks on you."

"So what do you do?"

"I fight." I shrugged. "Sparring usually does the trick. There is something about having a sword in my hand that makes everything else fade away."

"I don't much feel like being bested by you today," Leena murmured.

"What of Keyno? Perhaps he can take your mind off of things." The immortal raised a slender brow at me, and my face grew hot when I realized how that suggestion sounded.

"I didn't mean—" But Leena snorted before running a hand through her tangled hair.

"No, you're right, sometimes that works. You should try it," she admitted with a sly smile. "But I'm afraid Keyno is not very pleased with me either. He thinks I crossed a line last night."

I moved slowly, hesitating for a moment before sitting next to her on my mattress, and then I glanced at her from the corner of my eye. "Did you?"

"Probably, but I still think it needed to be said."

"I've come to realize that usually when people feel that way, the things they want to say are often hard to hear." I thought of Barrick's own speech from the night before. "And the words almost always hurt."

"Even if they're the truth?" Leena asked.

Humming under my breath, I nodded. "Especially if they're the truth."

"Keyno thinks I should give him space to lick his wounds before trying to talk to him again, which is probably a wise decision. I don't want us to say anything else that cannot be taken back."

"So, what will you do instead?" Her eyes moved around the room until they landed on the book I had discarded near my pillow, and she carefully picked it up from its place before opening the cover.

"I'm assuming you still cannot understand the tongue of old?" I shook my head, and Leena shuffled back and then tucked her legs under her. "Then I shall tell you what this says, that way you don't have to stare at the pictures and imagine what the words are."

Friendship had never been something I expected from Leena, tolerance maybe, but never more, and I had to force myself not to show my surprise at her offer as I slid farther back across the blankets. Crossing my legs, I settled uneasily and glanced down at the book in her lap as she began to read.

"'The Huntress, mother of all earthly creations, wielded the golden blade otherwise known as Goldsbane, which was forged in the fires of Vinmare. The blade was infused with the Goddess's own magic, similar to the other Godly weapons and instruments—'"

"Other Godly weapons?" I asked with interest.

Leena's eyes scanned the page and then the next before looking up at me. "There's not much else about that, I'm afraid. It moves onto the story of the Forefolk."

"But the other Gods have their own weapons?" I asked.

"Most did, I believe. The Protector's shield hangs in my brother's chambers," Leena confirmed. "The others I do not know about besides the trident of the Siren, though its location is unknown."

"And there is no mention of a beast?" Leena frowned and shook her head. "Anything about Skohyn and why her immortals might gather there?"

"None, unfortunately any mention of the other Gods is brief. We, of course, have more scriptures, but they are of the Protector and our beginnings. I'm not sure you will find any of the answers you seek here."

"I don't know what to do, Leena." My head hung in defeat, and I took in a deep, shuddering breath. "What do I do?"

"We will have news soon, Skylahr, and as soon as we do, we will find a way to reunite you with your Healer and friends," the immortal promised.

"And what of the sea? How will we stop a creature we know nothing about?" The feeling of helplessness weighed heavily on me and I sagged under its load.

"I don't know," Leena sighed.

"What would happen if we don't?" I inquired nervously. "What would the consequences be?"

"Our trades would continue to diminish," Leena started. "At first it may not be such a hardship, but our winters are difficult, and the people will suffer if there is no access to the southern coasts. They will lose many of the things most need to survive."

"But we did not venture out to sea in Noorde Point and we still managed."

"Your village may not have had trades with the southern cities, but the large towns you exchanged with did," Leena explained. "If the entirety of the north is cut off from the south, they will eventually begin to perish. Not to mention the southern cities who depend on their fish markets and the money brought in by trading."

She was right, of course she was, but how I wished she wasn't.

"I'm sorry, I had wanted to distract the both of us from our worries," the immortal apologized.

"Unfortunately, distractions never last." I shrugged, and Leena chewed at her lower lip in thought.

"What do you say we give sparring a go?" Nodding, I moved to my feet and allowed the immortal to lead the way, the book of scriptures and our problems forgotten, at least for now.

Keyno was already in the yards as we approached, and we both paused, watching as he lifted his bow before letting the arrow loose.

The metal tip hit its intended target, but the man frowned and then glanced over his shoulder at us.

"I think he's still upset with me," Leena whispered, and my eyes slid to hers in question. I had never seen Keyno upset with his mate and wondered what it must have taken to make him this way.

"I'm not," Keyno promised, but I didn't believe him, and by the looks of it, neither did Leena.

"Then you wouldn't mind a quick spar." The immortal beauty gave me a wink and then moved her attention back to Keyno.

"I suppose not, but only with you." He grinned and then curled an arm around her shoulders. "I would like to save myself from another bloody nose, and Hazel's guard has been asking for her this morning."

Panic slammed into me, and I searched the man's face for a hint as to why Barrick would need me. "Is he okay?"

"Fine, or so he says," Keyno assured me. "But he mentioned something about needing to apologize to you."

"I'm guessing he said something he thought you needed to hear?" Leena asked as she curled into her mate's chest.

"Something like that." I nodded. "I better go see him before he does something stupid like try to get out of his bed by himself."

Though Keyno had said Barrick was fine, I still hurried across the yard and nearly ran to the castle. Entering through the back doors, I turned for the spiral staircase that would lead me to the guest chambers, but I had not been paying enough attention, and as I rounded the bend, I slammed into another body.

"Easy there." Tipping my head back, I glanced up at his handsome face. His searching gaze roamed across my features and then lowered to my throat before he looked up once more, but this time his eyes were filled with worry. "Are you alright, love?"

"Don't," I snapped as I carefully stepped down to the stair below me in order to create space between us. "Don't call me that."

"Apologies, Huntress." He dipped his head though that mask was back. "Force of habit."

"Is it not time you unlearn it?" I asked, but the façade remained. Deciding to ignore my question, Kalian moved to the side and pressed himself back against the wall before gesturing for me to continue on my way. Taking the invitation, I passed the Lupine, but just as I reached the top of the stairs, Kalian called for me once more.

"Huntress." I turned my chin to my shoulder and glanced down at him. "Forgive me for my slip-up, I did not mean to upset you."

Something twisted at the sound of my title, and that anger and hurt I had been holding on to burned in my chest.

"It's a bit late for apologies now, isn't it?"

Chapter 33

Weeks had passed since my last awkward encounter with Kalian on the stairs, and I had yet to see him again, which was probably a mercy. I felt badly for the way I had snapped at him, but I wasn't sure I could muster the courage or the want to apologize, and I was sure I would lose control of my anger again if we had another similar meeting. Pushing those thoughts away, I peered at the bearded man who was lifting the glass vial to his mouth, and I felt relief at the soft pink that had filled his face.

"Your colour is looking better," I observed as Barrick sipped on his tonic, though I couldn't help but laugh when his nose wrinkled at the taste.

"I'm glad to hear it. Hopefully that means I don't need much more of this shit," Barrick complained as he finished what was in the vial. I took it from his fingers and then placed it on the table next to the empty plate.

"And I see you've been sneaking more pastries," I chided. "You can't exist purely on sweets and cakes."

"Are you here to help me or mother me?" my guard muttered grumpily, and I rolled my eyes before offering him my hand. Wrapping his fingers around mine, Barrick pulled himself from the bed and stood, though he wobbled just slightly, and I moved closer so that he could lean against me as he got his bearings.

"Barrick, are you certain you want to try this now? Maybe you should rest another day. I know it has been over fortnight, but the curer said it may take more time."

"It's been nearly a month!" he growled. "It's been nearly a month since our arrival, and if I stay in that bed any longer, my ass will melt into it." Sighing, I took his hand and lifted it, curling his arm around my shoulders while I wrapped my own around his waist.

"Fine, but we are only going to the chairs on your balcony," I grumbled as I shuffled us towards the door.

"Have any of the hawks returned yet today? Have we had any news on the Healer?" Barrick grunted as he slid onto his seat, and I swallowed before shaking my head.

"There has been nothing," I whispered, my voice breaking while my eyes misted over.

Barrick exhaled roughly as he gazed across the mountaintops. "And what of the beast?"

"There still have been no definite sightings, but Leena said there have been two wrecks reported, though the number of occurrences has slowed substantially. However, that might be because crews are far less likely to risk going out on the water."

"I know we will hear of the Healer any day now, and then we can continue on our journey to stop any more attacks from happening," Barrick promised, and I fell into the chair next to him before cupping my face in my hands. "Now, now, none of that, Huntress. Do not lose hope now."

"The more time passes, the more I feel like I am failing, Barrick," I admitted helplessly.

My guard shook his head with a frown. "You are not failing. Venturing out onto the sea would certainly lead to your death, and the Healer will be told you are here waiting for him. Leaving now would just put off your reunion for even longer. There is nothing more we can do right now."

"He's right," Leena's sweet voice called from Barrick's room, and I glanced through the open doors at her. "For now our hands are tied, but sitting here stewing on it will do you no good."

"What do you suggest instead?" I asked.

"Keyno and my brother left two days ago for the north to check on the smaller villages," Leena explained. "They're not due back until late tonight. Which means you no longer need to tiptoe around the castle." Barrick laughed under his breath, and I narrowed my eyes at him before moving my focus back to the immortal.

"I thought we could perhaps visit the village together," she proposed with a shrug. "Might do you some good to have a change of scenery for a bit."

The idea did not truly hold any appeal to me, but I also did not want to ruin this new delicate kinship between Leena and me, and so I nodded in agreement before turning to my guard. "Will you be alright for a while?"

Barrick rolled his eyes and then waved one of his massive hands in my direction. "Just go already."

"Fine," I grumbled. "But do not try to get back into the bed yourself. You need someone to help you."

"I will send one of the servants up to check in on him," Leena promised, ignoring the way Barrick scoffed in annoyance.

"Tell them he is not to have any more desserts either." His dark eyes widened as he turned his attention to me. "In fact, I think we should probably remove them entirely from his diet for the next while. He needs something far more nutritious."

"Yes," Leena agreed. "I think perhaps broth and boiled carrots for tonight."

"And certainly no more ale," I added before smiling at my guard. "You really must get better if you want all my mothering to stop."

Barrick crossed his arms over his chest, and it almost looked as if he was pouting, and then he turned back to the mountains. "Enjoy your time, Huntress, do not hurry back."

The village of Denimoore was still just as stunning as I remembered, and I slid from my horse before looping the reins over the post. Glancing around the cobblestoned streets, I watched as the people went about the afternoon in the warm summer sun, and Leena dismounted before moving in next to me.

"Did you spend much time here during your last visit?" she asked, and my eyes slid to her. "I will be honest, I can't say I paid that much attention to your comings and goings then."

One of my brows lifted at her words. "I suppose that's true, the only time you really paid me any mind was when you were insulting me."

Her stunning face pinkened, and she lowered her chin sheepishly. "I guess I never apologized for my behaviour then."

"No, you haven't. Nor have you ever told me what I did to make you hate me so." Leena turned her face from me, and I waited as she seemed to gather her thoughts.

"Would you accept that it was just me being protective of my family?" Snorting, I shook my head.

"We both know that's not it. It may be part, but you were vicious. You enjoyed hurting me with those sharp words of yours."

"You said it was a talent," she pointed out.

"I think the word I used was *skill*," I reminded her. "But to be honest, it no longer matters, you don't need to explain yourself to me. Let's just move past it."

"You have yourself a deal, Skylahr Reed." Smiling softly at her, I dipped my chin and then followed as she turned to the road before us.

The people of the village seemed just as captivated by the immortal beauty as I had once been, and I wondered how it felt to be looked at with envy and awe rather than bewilderment. The Lupine, however, didn't appear to notice any of the glances directed at her as she continued to stride down the alley.

"There is a swordsmith just there." She lifted a slender hand and pointed to the end of the road. "He makes fine weapons if you would like to go have a look."

"I'm not sure I have a need for a new one." I shrugged. "Not right now at least."

"Right, of course." Leena winced. "A foolish suggestion, I guess."

"No, not at all," I disagreed. "I appreciate it, but maybe there is somewhere else we can go to take my mind off of things?"

"How do you feel about mutton and ale?" she asked, her dark eyes hopeful.

"Lead the way." And she did just that.

The inn of Denimoore was far lovelier than any other I had been to, and I looked at the stonework of the building as Leena paused at the walkway that led to the door. It was relatively quiet, only the soft sounds of chatter and a quaint melody of a flute could be heard from behind the walls, and I sighed, suddenly anxious about entering along with the Lady of Denimoore.

"What's wrong?" the immortal asked, but I didn't know how to tell her. How could I explain my nervousness of being seen with her, of being compared to her? How would I say it in a way that she would understand and not pity me? I couldn't, and so I decided to lie instead.

"Nothing," I promised, though my voice was weak, and she frowned in response.

"We can go back, have tea in the library or spar," she offered, and I shook my head.

"No, I've beaten you too many times already," I joked. "Let's go in."

She paused for another moment, as if she was checking that I was certain, and when I nodded, she stepped through the door with me close on her heels.

The chatter quieted as the beauty entered the room, and I watched from my place at her back as all eyes glanced her way before looking up at my own face. As predicted, their eyes widened, but no one looked at me with judgement or disdain, and I exhaled slowly as my shoulders loosened.

"Hello, my lady," a barmaid greeted Leena with a soft smile. "Will your mate be joining you today? I know how much he enjoys our apple tarts."

"Not today, Gretchin." The immortal shook her head and then placed a gentle hand on the woman's shoulder. "How is your little one doing? Have his teeth come in?"

I watched Leena with interest as she spoke so kindly to the woman, and I realized, for the first time, that she truly resembled her mother in more than just her looks. The barmaid offered the Lupine a curtsey and then directed us to a table.

We slid onto the stools and waited for the woman to bring us both a cup of ale, and I smiled as she laid a plate full of apple tarts at our table as well. The other patrons had gone back to their business, no longer paying us any mind, and I felt myself begin to relax as the soft tingle from the ale settled into my belly.

"Keyno will be sad to have missed this." Leena smiled as she licked her fingers clean of apple.

I took another sip of my drink before carefully forming my question.

"Where did he go?" Her brows lifted towards her hairline as she leaned back from the table.

"Where did *they* go, you mean?" Leena corrected. "You don't need to pretend like my brother doesn't exist, Skylahr, I will try to not bother you with any of my questions just because you mention him in passing."

Embarrassed, I wrapped my hands around my cup and then nodded.

"They went north to check on our own villages along the shores. One of the lords wrote to Kalian about the loss of a ship. He had gone against our advice and allowed his men to sail, but they have not returned."

A silence blanketed us, and I knew she too felt the same fear and panic that was churning low in my gut. Lost in our worry, neither of us noticed the soft footsteps approaching until Leena's eyes narrowed at the person behind me and I grew tense at her expression.

"Hello, Leena." The voice was low and polite, but the Lupine sneered at our visitor as she answered.

"Nadine."

I continued to keep my back to the woman, my shoulders curling as I made myself as small as possible, hoping that Nadine would not bother with me. But of course, I would not be so lucky, and I heard her as she moved past me and then I slowly lifted my eyes.

Nadine was just as stunning as she had been, though her fine gowns had been replaced by a simpler dress, and her hair was swept back into a neat braid. Any of the jewellery she once wore was also missing, though I noticed a simple gold band on the fourth finger of her left hand.

"Ah, I see your pet has returned." Nadine smirked, her dark eyes hardening as she glared down at me.

"Mind your tongue," Leena warned, but the woman ignored her.

"I thought I had seen the last of you." Crossing her arms, Nadine lifted her chin with a scowl. "I didn't think you would be so desperate as to come crawling back. I really thought you had more pride."

"Puore!" Leena snapped as she rose from her stool, and one of my hands shot out, reaching across the table to grab her slender wrist. Inhaling sharply, Leena rolled her shoulders and then sat back down.

"That insult no longer holds any weight, my lady," Nadine scoffed and then she lifted her left hand. "I'm a mated woman now."

"Married, not mated," Leena corrected. "I heard about your sham of a ceremony. Tell me who was it again that agreed to take my brother's scraps?"

"Leena," I cautioned, but neither woman paid me any mind.

"Torris, the captain of the Protector's fleet." Nadine smiled confidently, and I paled at the name before glancing worriedly at Leena.

"And tell me, where is your husband? Have you seen him since he returned?" the immortal asked with false interest, and I swallowed roughly when Nadine paled. "Because last I heard my brother was calling for his head."

Nadine's mouth parted, and her eyes bounced between the Lupine and me. Realizing she had surprised her brother's previous lover, Leena smiled, obviously pleased with herself before continuing.

"That's what happens when someone decides to harm the Huntress. That's what he will do for the woman he loves."

Chapter 34

My heart stuttered and my lower lip trembled at the immortal's words, but I was unable to say anything. Nadine took a step back, her jaw clenching as she glowered at Leena. Unbothered, the Lupine lifted her ale and sipped, and then, when no one moved, she squinted up at the woman.

"Are you still here?" she asked, her expression bored, and my own face heated in embarrassment when I noticed we had caught the attention of the other customers.

"Leena," I warned once more, but my voice drew the attention of Nadine, and she turned those furious dark eyes on me.

"I do not need *you* coming to my defence, you great beast!"

Leena was fast with her movements as her hand reached for the knife she had used to cut the tart, but I was faster, and my own grabbed her wrist before pinning it to the table and then I stood. Keeping my hold, I turned just slightly towards Nadine and shook my head.

"I think it would be best if you leave this place *quietly*," I instructed. "Before I decide to let her at you for that insult."

Heeding my advice, Nadine backed away one step and then another and then finally turned for the door, but not without first sending one more glance our way. Once I was certain she was gone, I used my free hand to pull the knife from Leena's fingers and then shook my head at the immortal.

"Was that necessary?" I asked.

Rolling her eyes, she grabbed a tart and took a bite before tilting her head. "Which part?"

"All of it," I snapped. "Though I mostly meant provoking her about Torris and then grabbing the knife."

"She had a right to learn of her husband's fate, and she should know where Kalian's heart lies." Leena shrugged. "Though I have no idea why she is acting as if he hadn't been the one to tell her as much over a year ago."

"Leena," I sighed, and then rubbed at my face tiredly.

"What?" She held her hands up as if she was the one who was frustrated. "He did."

"Whether he did or didn't, that is not the point."

"Actually"—she lifted a finger to point at me—"it kind of is."

Deciding I did not have the bravery to have this conversation sober, I lifted my cup and tilted my head back as I swallowed down the rest of my ale, and then I grabbed Leena's. Ignoring her protests, I finished hers as well and sighed.

"Well, that was impolite," she grumbled and then motioned for Gretchin to come with more.

"Leena," I began. "Whatever happened between me and your brother before is over now. What he once felt for me is—"

"Still feels," she corrected, and I shook my head.

"Leena," I tried again. "What he felt was not real love. Saying otherwise is doing no one any favours, and I would very much like to drop the subject. Besides, you told me you would not bother me with your questions." Her mouth opened in protest, but I lifted a hand.

"*Please*," I begged.

"Fine," she relented. "We won't discuss it, or him. Instead let's have our fill of ale and tarts before you go back to torment your guard once more."

A pitcher was placed on the table between us, and the immortal filled our cups once more before dishing out more desserts. The ale I was interested in, but my appetite had left, and we both sat quietly as we became lost in our memories.

"Didn't we have horses?" I asked as I stumbled into Leena and then laughed when she wrapped an arm around my shoulders.

"We did." She snorted, her face bright with amusement as she peered up at me. "I had someone walk them to the stables when we left the tavern."

"Oh." I hiccuped, and the high-pitched noise made me blush.

"You are drunk," Leena laughed. "Very drunk."

"I am," I agreed, and then I glanced at the long line of stone stairs. "I think I need a rest before trying to climb those." I swayed as I tried to point at the steps, and then I bent forward, pressing my hands to the ground before shifting onto my backside.

"Are you okay?" the immortal asked as she squatted in front of me, and I swatted her hand away from my face before smiling.

"I'm drunk." Hiccuping again, I pushed my hair away from my sweaty face and then frowned as I looked up at the Lupine. "Can I ask you something?"

"What is it?" she asked, her eyes suddenly wary.

My frown deepened. "Why are you making that face?"

"Because usually drunk questions are the ones people are not brave enough to ask sober."

Humming, I thought on her words and then nodded. "Well, I'm going to ask anyway. When you came to my room that one morning, when you looked like shit—"

Leena scoffed and then stood with her hands on her hips. "I did not look like shit."

I snorted and then lifted a brow. "You did. I can promise you, you did."

"Fine." She rolled her eyes with a huff. "I looked like a mess, now ask your damn question."

"You said you mourned your child, what did you mean?" Leena's face grew pale, and her gaze lowered to her feet. She almost seemed to shrink under the weight of my question, and my stomach twisted at the sight.

"When I was in my twenty-sixth year I became immortal, but it was also when I lost my child." She closed her eyes and took in a deep breath. "A stillborn girl."

Sorrow slammed into my chest, and I moved forward to hold one of her hands. "Leena, I am so sorry."

"It was a long time ago," she whispered, but I shook my head.

"That doesn't matter. You are allowed to still feel the loss no matter how much time has passed. You are entitled to that." Her eyes opened, though the rest of her face remained drawn, and she nodded.

"My body did not recover from the birthing bed, and I too lost my life, but my mother was able to bring me back. That is when she performed my ceremony."

"That must have been impossibly hard." Leena sank onto the ground next to me.

"Harder than you can imagine," she whispered. "I did not want to be saved then, I wanted to be with my daughter."

"Did she have a name?" I asked, though I was not sure if I had the right to.

"Isla. Her name was Isla, after my mother."

My lips lifted into a sad smile, and I unsteadily moved forward, curling an arm around her shoulders as I embraced her awkwardly. At my touch, the immortal stiffened for a pause and then wrapped her own around my waist before slowly pulling away.

"Come now, halfling, we better get to bed."

The kitchen was spinning by the time I reached it, and I grabbed on to one of the shelves to steady myself. Certain I would not fall over, I continued on my way to the table in the middle of the room and glanced at the baskets of rolls and jams that had been prepared for the next morning.

After our long journey back to the castle, Leena excused herself and headed to bed. I probably should have done the same, but the smell of freshly baked bread would not leave me, and I was certain I was slowly starving to death.

I grabbed one of the rolls, shoved the entire thing into my mouth, and sighed happily as I chewed. Eyeing the jar of pear jam, I then grabbed for another and ripped it open before looking around for a knife. Not finding one, I glanced at the doorway to make sure no one was around and then opened the jar and dipped my finger into it. Happy with the amount, I messily spread the sweet topping over the roll before biting into it and then sank to the floor.

"What are you doing?" a voice called from behind me, and I paused midchew and looked over my shoulder.

There was Kalian, in all his glory, casually leaning against the doorway with his arms crossed over his magnificent chest, and the only thing I could think to say was: "What are *you* doing?"

"You're drunk," he muttered with a shake of his head, and I lifted my finger to my mouth before sucking the pear jam from it.

Certain my skin was no longer sticky, I pulled my hand from my mouth with a loud pop and nodded. "I am."

"You should go to bed, or you'll regret it in the morning." That was all he said as he turned to leave the room, and I bristled at his dismissal as I scrambled to my feet.

"So, is that it then? Is that all that's left between us, silent stares and quick departures even after what you did?"

Kalian spun on his heel to face me once more, the muscles of his jaw working.

"What more would you have from me, Huntress? You do not want to hear anything from me, least of all my apologies." Stalking forward, I stood toe to toe with the great Lupine Protector.

"Some honesty," I snarled. "I would have honesty from you. For once."

"Honesty," he repeated, his voice low and deadly. "Fine. Why did you tell Leena there was no love between us?"

"There isn't, because that's the truth," I whispered and then corrected myself. "There wasn't."

"Lies," he snapped. "That's a lie."

"You would know one when you hear one, wouldn't you?" I accused, and he looked at me as if I had struck him.

"I made a *mistake*," he argued. "I should have told you about the bargain I made, I know that now. But that does not take away the rest of it."

"You really believe that?" I asked, incredulous.

Running a hand through his hair, he grabbed at the black strands in frustration. "It's the truth."

"And how am I supposed to decipher what is true and what isn't with you?"

"So, I made a *single* wrong choice and now everything, every word I ever spoke to you, is a lie? Is that what you have decided?"

Yes, it was exactly what I had chosen to believe even if he refused to admit it to be fact.

"Fine, so you think you love me," I spat. "But that is only because you think that is your fate! You think we have to share a destiny because of our Gods! You think we need each other."

"Fuck fate!" he snarled. "I don't love you because I have to! I love you because I choose to! And I don't need you, I *want* you."

"You're blinded by your desire to repeat history. You want the Huntress!" I shouted, lifting my arms into the air in frustration.

"Blind? Is that what you think I am?" He shook his head and then ran his fingers through his hair again. "I'm not blind, Skylahr. I see you for exactly what you are, and I don't love you despite of it, I love you *because* of it. I don't want the Huntress, I want you. I want your temper and your stubbornness. I want every imperfect piece of you. And I know how that sounds. I know you find the idea of someone loving you to be impossible, but that doesn't mean everyone else feels the same." My mouth fell open, any retort I had ready disappeared, and instead, I lifted onto my toes and pressed my mouth to his.

At first, he stood frozen, though his lips were warm and pliant under mine, and I lifted a hand to tangle into his hair at the nape of his neck. Curling my fingers into a fist, I pulled him down and ran my tongue across his lower lip gently. That seemed all he needed to spring into action, and he groaned into my mouth before bending slightly and then my thighs were cradled in his palms as he lifted me from my feet.

Moving farther into the room, he carried me to the table and then carefully lowered me onto the wood before securing my legs around his waist. Now free to use his hands, he slid them up the length of my thighs, squeezing the flesh of them softly before cupping my hips. The tips of his fingers snuck under the hem of my shirt, and I whimpered as the warmth of his skin seeped into my own.

Pulling my mouth from his, I panted as I worked to catch my breath, but Kalian continued, his attention moving to the edge of my jaw, and he pressed soft kisses to the skin there. Happy he had covered every inch, he bent his knees so that he could continue his journey and began to suck at the skin just below.

Too caught up in the heat simmering in my belly, it took me a moment to notice that he had softened his attentions and now his mouth was ghosting across the narrow scar that curled around my throat.

It was soft and sweet, the touch of a man in love, and my chin wobbled as I scrambled to grab on to the lust that had been burning through me just seconds before.

Tangling my hands into his hair once more, I pulled his face to mine and pressed a bruising kiss to his mouth before forcing his head back. Watching as those silver eyes burned, I finally said the words I had kept hidden away for what felt like ages.

"I want you."

Chapter 35

"You're drunk," Kalian said again, and then he was pulling my arms away from him and I frowned.

"So?" I asked, not understanding why he was suddenly stepping out of my reach.

"You need sleep," he whispered, and then took one of my hands before helping me from the table.

"I need you." His eyes fluttered closed, and his nostrils flared while his jaw clenched.

"Huntress," he groaned, and then those silver irises were peering down at me. "I am trying to behave myself."

"Don't bother with all of that," I argued. "I told you I wanted you, so have me, *take* me."

"No," Kalian whispered. "Not like this, not when you don't know what you're saying."

"I know what I'm saying," I argued and then moved to close the distance between us, but I had misjudged the space and stumbled to the left just slightly.

"Bed, *now*." The order sent a shiver down my spine, and I grinned up at him, pleased to see he changed his mind.

Noticing my hopeful expression, Kalian rolled his eyes and clarified, "To sleep."

Crossing my arms, I scoffed, and Kalian's jaw clenched. "I'm not asking you; I'm telling you."

"Or what? Will you take me over your knee and give me a good swatting?" I challenged, and Kalian's mouth lifted into a smirk.

"I see that threat has stuck with you even after all this time." His grin grew. "Tell you what, ask me nicely when you are sober, and I will make good on it."

"I—" Seeming to run out of patience, the Lupine alpha stepped forward and bent at the waist before grabbing my legs. Keeping a firm grasp on me, he forced me over his shoulder and then stood to his full height, taking me along with him.

"What are you doing?!" I shrieked as I hung over his back, and Kalian turned from the kitchen.

"You didn't want to listen," he sighed, and I slapped his back in protest when he jostled me about.

"Put me down!" I screeched, angry that he would have the nerve to treat me this way, but the immortal man ignored me as he turned for the stairs, and I pounded against the hard muscles once more. "Put me down!"

"Keep making that wretched noise, and you'll wake the entire castle," Kalian warned.

"I don't care!" I snarled, and he laughed.

"You don't care that they will see you all flushed and wanting?" he asked. "You don't mind that they'll see the desire you have for me, the desire that you try so hard to hide away?"

"You are an arrogant bastard," I growled and he tsked at me.

"My parents were married, actually," he said. "And as arrogant as I may be, I am nearly certain you will not remember any of this in the morning, Huntress."

Entering my chambers, Kalian kicked the door behind him and then moved across the room with ease before dumping me onto my bed. Blowing the strands of my hair out of my eyes, I glared up at him with a scowl.

"You knew my name once." His eyes softened as he peered down at me, and then he grabbed one of the throws before draping it over me.

"And I still know it now," he assured me, and I blinked at him, though the motion slowed as a sudden wave of exhaustion slammed into me.

"Will you not use it?" I asked as my eyes fluttered closed.

"I don't think I have the right to, not anymore," he whispered, and I felt the blanket lift to my chin before it was tucked around me.

"I think I'd like to hear it from you, just once," I muttered quietly. "Just once more."

I heard his sharp inhale but my eyes remained closed, and then I told him my own truth, the one I had been desperate to keep hidden. "I've missed you."

The room had grown quiet as sleep began to set in, and just as I was pulled into slumber, I heard his answer. "I've missed you too, Skylahr."

Groaning, I rolled to my belly and buried my face into the pillow below me. My head was throbbing, though to be honest, everything ached. I groaned again as a bitter acid crawled up the back of my throat.

"Good Gods!" I cried, though the sound was muffled, and I clenched my eyes shut against the wave of nausea.

"I don't think the Gods can help you," Leena laughed from somewhere behind me, and I lifted one hand from under the blanket and waved her away. "Come now, Huntress, it's well into the day."

"Leave me be," I moaned, but Leena just laughed softly and then the pillow was being pulled from beneath my head.

"Come now, Skylahr, get up. Keyno brought you back a gift from their travels." Normally I would have perked up at that, but nothing would have excited me at that moment, and instead I reached for the wool blanket and lifted it over my face. "Get out of bed, get some water into you, and your healing will do the rest. You'll be right as rain in no time."

Turning over, I carefully sat up and then squinted one eye open at the immortal. "You have been spending too much time with Barrick."

"He and I get along." Leena shrugged, and I snorted.

"Probably because you two are some of the most unapproachable people I have ever met," I snarked and then stood from my bed.

"I think that is an over-exaggeration," she murmured and then scanned me from head to toe. "But no matter, I'm glad to see you up. There are some rolls and jam waiting for you in the dining hall. Though the cooks noticed the pear seemed to have been tampered with. You wouldn't know anything about that, would you?"

My face flushed hotly as flashes from the night before flooded my mind, and I swallowed before shaking my head.

"Odd." Leena shrugged though I noticed the knowing look in her eyes. "Well, we will be waiting for you."

Nodding, I crossed my arms and watched as she moved to the door. Reaching for the handle, the Lupine beauty paused and then turned back to me.

"Perhaps you should bathe first—you smell like a tavern floor." My cheeks heated once more, and I nodded.

"And be sure to wear something with a high neck, you have a mark." She stroked the skin under her jaw. "Just here."

The rose water had apparently been just what I needed, and I sighed in relief when I realized the bright light of the sun that filtered through the windows no longer irritated my head. Tucking my damp waves behind my ears, I made my way to the hall, and ducked my chin when both Keyno and Leena turned to me as I entered the room.

"Morning, Hazel. You're looking well." Keyno smiled knowingly, and I glared at his mate, annoyed that she had told him about my condition this morning.

"Thank you," I snapped sarcastically before taking a seat. I grabbed an apple, ignoring the basket of rolls and assorted jams, though my eyes did linger on the half-empty one.

"We received two hawks today," Leena began, and my eyes lifted to her face. "Neither spoke of your friends, but one did mention a halfling who has been looking for you."

"A halfling?" I asked, confused.

"Apparently you've met once before." Leena shrugged.

"Unfortunately, that does not narrow it down. I've met many halflings over the last year and a half. There was no name mentioned?" The immortal shook her head.

"No, but she was adamant about speaking with you, and apparently has convinced Lord Ewen to give her a horse, though he has sent three of his men along with her."

My brow furrowed. "She is coming here?"

"Yes, I agreed to give her an audience on your behalf. I hope you don't mind."

"Of course not, but I wonder what it is she needs."

"Who knows," Keyno answered, and then he lifted the package onto the table and slid it across the tabletop. "I suppose we shall see, but in the meantime, you have these to preoccupy your time and mind. Might be better for you than the ale from the inn."

Choosing to ignore him, I pulled at the twine that held the package together then carefully peeled the parchment away.

"Books?" I asked, and then my eyes caught Keyno's.

"They are still in the tongue of old, of course, but there are a lot of portraits, and one of us can read them to you should you desire to know what they say," he promised.

"Thank you, this is a very considerate gift."

Keyno glanced at his mate and then rubbed at his neck sheepishly. "They're actually not from me."

"Oh," I whispered and then the room grew awkward.

Leena reached across the table to pick up one of the books, and as she flipped through it, she cleared her throat. "He had a meeting with some advisors in the throne room, he may still be there."

I shouldn't have wanted to see him, and I certainly should not have been touched by his thoughtfulness, and yet it seemed as if my mind and heart were in a battle of wills. Glancing at the two books that remained in front of me, I thought of my options.

We could carry on the way we had been, avoiding and ignoring each other unless absolutely necessary while I waited for Barrick to heal or for news of Gaelon.

Or I could explain to him that no matter what our past might be, I could not trust him with my heart, and I was not willing to. That I may have said things last night I didn't mean, and we would need to find a way to live amongst each other until it was time for me to leave.

Deciding, I stood from my chair and turned from the pair of immortals before pausing at the doorway.

"The throne room?" I asked, though I did not look back at them.

"At the end of the hall and to the left. You'll see the doors with the Protector's sigil," Keyno answered, and I swallowed roughly before making my way.

Chapter 36

"What are you doing, Skylahr?" I whispered to myself as I leaned my forehead against the solid wood. What was I doing? Making the same mistake over again? Not learning from the hurt and heartbreak I had already suffered? Shaking my head softly, I tried to clear my mind and then I pressed on the door.

The room was bright with the afternoon sun, and I gasped as I took in its splendour. On either side was a wall of massive arched windows that overlooked the mountains of the Lupine territories, and there, in the centre of the room, sat a stone throne, and behind it hung an enormous silver banner of the Protector.

"Huntress?" Kalian called as he turned from the two men he was speaking to, and I tried very hard not to frown at my title.

"I'm sorry," I apologized. "Am I interrupting?"

"No, not at all." He left his advisors and approached me slowly, carefully, and I crossed my arms around my middle as I studied him.

"I came to thank you." My voice came out hoarse and weak, and I flushed before clearing my throat.

"Thank me?" One black brow rose, and I realized he thought I meant for the night before.

"For the books," I clarified.

Taking one step closer, he lifted a hand as if he meant to touch me but then thought better of it, and then he let his arm hang at his side once more. "I thought I told you not to thank me?"

"Well, I'm doing it anyway," I grumbled.

Lifting a brow, he shook his head. "Fine, then you're welcome."

His eyes held mine, and I felt the longing from last night begin to seep into my bones once more. His gaze darkened as he caught sight of the mark he had left under my jaw, and then his tongue darted out to lick his lower lip.

"Was there anything else you *needed*?" His word choice was not by chance, and the air left my lungs roughly as my skin tingled in the most pleasant of ways.

"Yes." The words slipped from me before I could stop them, and I watched as silver turned molten.

"Leave us," Kalian called to the men, though he hadn't bothered to lift his gaze from my face.

"But, my lord—" one of them called from their place, obviously confused at their dismissal.

"Leave us!" he growled, his voice rising and leaving no room for argument.

Both men scurried off, though neither of us bothered to watch, and when the door slammed shut, one of Kalian's hands tangled in the back of my hair before he dragged me to him.

His tongue was warm as it slid over mine, and I trembled under his touch when his free hand curled around my hip. Backing us farther into the room, Kalian guided me towards the throne, and when the backs of my knees hid the edge of the seat, he pressed me down into it.

"This is where you belong," he whispered, his lips still caressing mine, and then he took a step back and sank to his knees. "And this is where I belong."

My eyes widened as I peered down at him, and he bowed his head under my stare. "Being on my knees before you is an honour, one I do not deserve, and yet I can't help but beg for it."

Taking in a deep, shuddering breath, he then lifted his chin, and his eyes watered as he gazed up at me.

"I am sorry, Huntress," he choked out. "I am sorry for lying. I am sorry for breaking your trust and for making you believe that I did not love you. I am sorry that I have caused you pain. I hate myself for it."

My own eyes began to burn, and I held my breath as his head bowed once more. "I am also sorry that I made you believe that my love for you is not my own but what I think I should feel. That could not be further from the truth."

I thought back to the night before, remembering every word of his confession, and then I swallowed roughly.

"So let me swear here and now, on my knees, that what I feel for you is my love and mine alone. You have my heart, and now I offer both my body and soul. Take them, do what you want with them, but call them yours. *Please.*"

Unable to form the words he wanted to hear, I instead bent forward and cupped his face in my hands before dragging his mouth to mine. Kissing him thoroughly, I prayed that he would forget this pledge and settle for what I was offering. The only thing I could stand to give him now.

"Huntress," he moaned into my mouth, and I tugged on the black strands until he tipped his chin.

"Skylahr, call me by my name," I demanded and then kissed him once more.

Grabbing at my thighs, Kalian dragged me to the edge of my seat and then he brought his trembling fingers to the laces of my breeches before pulling his mouth from mine. "Is this okay?"

"Yes." I nodded, too impatient to say anything else, and he grinned before he pulled at the knot. Once the front of the fabric loosened, Kalian then curled his fingers over them and gave a gentle tug before pressing a kiss to the soft flesh beneath my navel.

"Lift your hips, sweeting," he whispered, and I followed his instructions, carefully rising from my seat as he pulled my breeches over my thighs and down my legs. After freeing one foot from a pant leg, he then moved to the other, growling under his breath when they caught on the toe of my boot.

"You'll rip them if you tug much harder." I laughed, and Kalian grinned as he finally freed my other foot. He paused, his eyes holding mine captive as the heat returned.

"I want to taste you," he whispered, his hands sliding up my thighs before he applied the gentlest pressure to the insides of my knees. I parted my legs for him, eager to feel his mouth on me.

Taking my silent invitation, Kalian pressed a kiss to one knee, then the other, and then slowly worked his way up, constantly switching from my left leg to my right, making certain to shower both with equal attention. Once he hit high on my thigh, he paused and nuzzled against the skin there before closing his eyes, and I realized that was where I had been cut when I had fought the Crimson captain outside of Carlon. When I had told him that love was the most powerful healer, and in return, he had pressed a kiss to my wound and said I was healed.

Carding my fingers through his hair, I allowed him to press one more kiss there, and then I directed him higher.

"Impatient, are we?" he asked, his voice vibrating against my skin, and I sighed before opening my legs wider.

Not waiting any longer, he took his first taste from me, and I moaned as his tongue finally passed over my core. It was better than I remembered. My hips rocked into him as his hands clutched at the soft flesh of my thighs, and then he lifted them over his shoulders and tugged me farther forward, completely burying his face into me.

"Kalian!" I gasped, my head tipping back against the back of his throne, and he hummed, obviously pleased to have coaxed such a reaction from me. Doubling his efforts, he slid one hand from my leg and carefully pressed a finger into me while his tongue flicked over my clit.

"Oh Gods," I cried out again, my hands moving from his hair to the arms of the throne as I clenched down on his finger. "Kalian!"

Lifting his chin, he smiled at me though he continued to use his hand to press against my inner walls. "What do you need?"

I was close, so close to my release, and I whimpered softly, "More."

Happy to oblige, Kalian pressed a second finger into my cunt and then laved his tongue across me once more, all while studying me closely. "Are you nearly there?"

"Yes," I sobbed softly.

"Good."

Picking up his pace, Kalian fucked me with his fingers, and just as his mouth closed around me once more, my back bowed, and I cried out his name beneath the silver banner of his God.

Slumping against the wood behind me, I watched as the Lupine lifted his head from my knee, and then he pressed his two fingers past his lips and cleaned them carefully.

I was still shaking, my muscles twitching under my pale skin. Kalian reached behind him for my breeches, and then he carefully pulled them up over my boots. I frowned as he hiked the fabric higher over my legs, and then he stopped, waiting for me to lift from my seat once more.

"What are you doing?" I asked, not understanding why I was getting dressed rather than him getting undressed.

"You can't very well wander the halls with a bare ass," Kalian laughed, and I rolled my eyes before tying the laces.

"But don't you want to…?" I gestured to the front of his breeches. His cheeks pinkened, and then my eyes lowered to the darkened fabric below his laces.

"Oh." I had to sink my teeth into my lower lip to keep myself from grinning, and Kalian's blush darkened.

"No better than a green boy half my age," he grumbled, and I snorted loudly.

"I think even boys half your age might have more control than that," I joked, and Kalian rolled his eyes before surging forward to kiss me.

"Not when they are knuckles deep in a creature as magnificent as yourself," he argued, and I pushed him from me and then stood on shaky legs.

Passing by him, I moved to the doors and then called out, "You tell yourself whatever you need to so you can sleep at night, Protector."

The portraits in the new books Kalian had brought me were bright and beautiful, and I carefully turned each page with the lightest touch I could manage. I had yet to see anything of great interest, but I still appreciated the skill and artistry it took to paint such images. Glancing at the sigil of my Goddess, I took in the tiny details of the stag's antlers and flipped to the next one.

It was the Siren's seal this time, and once more there was the deep blue with the trident and the shell behind, though this drawing had the conch angled just slightly, and there was a loop of tiny pearls coming from its base. Studying the shapes once more, I then moved onto the burning heart, the same one that marked the skin of my cheek, and I glowered at the crimson-red page.

"Enjoying your gift?" Leena asked as she stepped into the library, and I nodded but remained silent. "I hear it's not the only gift he gave you."

My head lifted and I stared wide-eyed at the immortal beauty. "Pardon?"

"It seems you were very vocal with your appreciation." Leena smiled slyly, and my cheeks burned as I understood her words.

"I have no idea what you're talking about," I lied as I lifted the book up to hide my face.

"Well, I'm glad for it." Leena sighed and then sank into the vacant chair. "The tension was slowly suffocating us all."

"Leena," I grumbled, peering at her from over the pages, and she held her hands up in surrender.

"Sorry, sorry." She laughed. "I suppose if you don't want to talk about this drunk, you most definitely do not want to when you're sound of mind. I will keep my words to myself."

"Somehow I doubt that," I snapped and then glanced down at the book once more.

"So," she began. "Does this one have any interesting pictures?"

"Are you actually interested?" I asked with a raised brow.

"No," she admitted honestly. "But you don't want to hear what I *actually* have to say."

Placing the book down onto my lap, I rubbed at my eyes tiredly and then lifted a hand, gesturing for her to continue. "Fine, Leena. Just say it and be done with it."

"I suppose I just want you to know that despite my teasing and my interest, I did tell him time and time again to leave you be." That was not what I had been expecting, and my brows furrowed as the woman fiddled with her fingers. "I know how much he has hurt you, and though I can't say I disagree with his decision to make a deal with the Crimsons to protect our people, I wish you had not been wounded by the choice."

Clearing her throat, Leena lifted her attention to the window. "After all, he lied to us as well about being the Chosen. He and my mother had kept that from us, and it hurts to know he was able to do it so easily."

"He thought he was protecting you, I guess," I whispered, and she nodded softly.

"That was his reasoning for you as well." She shrugged. "But being protected with a lie is no better than being hurt with honesty, and in the end, the truth always comes out anyway."

"Yes, that has a way of happening, doesn't it?" I wondered as I too looked out at the brilliant mountains that surrounded Denimoore.

"It does," she agreed. "Which is why I hope you see his feelings for what they are."

"Leena," I whispered weakly.

"He has lied, and he has told the truth," she continued. "And his feelings are true, Skylahr."

Chapter 37

Another day passed without any news, and though the Lupines reminded me that these things take time, that even if the Healer and my friends had returned safely to shore, the hawks may not have reached them yet, my worry continued to grow, and distractions that had worked were getting harder to come by. In fact, it had now been just over a month since Barrick and I arrived, and I had broken multiple sparring swords, ruined every training dummy ten times over, and had my fill of trying to learn the tongue of old.

The only distraction I had yet to test out again was Kalian, and he had all but disappeared since our time in the throne room. I had not seen more than a passing glance of his handsome face, and I wondered if I had done something to upset him. After all, he had fallen to my feet and declared his love for me, and I had said nothing in return. Not to mention the fact that apparently his sister had attempted to dissuade him from seeking me out.

Sighing, I pressed my back against the rough bark of the tree I sat under, and lifted my eyes to the night sky. I could just make out the soft twinkling light of the stars through the leaves, and I glanced down at the lantern I had placed on the grass beside me. I had planned to look through the last book Kalian had brought me, but the want was no longer there, and so, I lifted the metal cage and blew out the candle before turning to the stars once more.

The night was warm, surprisingly so, especially considering how far north we were, and I slid my hands under my tunic to grab the wrap that covered my chest. Giving up gowns and boned stays had been easy, but I still found my breasts often got in the way, and binding them was the best solution. In the cold it added an extra layer of warmth, but in the summer the fabric grew itchy and irritating, and now that I was alone in the dark, I took the opportunity to unwind the tight fabric.

"Much better," I sighed happily as I closed my eyes. However, now that I was no longer focused on the light above me, I realized how quiet the night had grown. Squinting at the surrounding area, I scanned the dark as my hair stood on end, and I couldn't help but feel as if I was being watched.

"Hello?" I called out, shivering as the air stilled, and when no one answered, I moved to stand.

Seeming to sense my fear, whatever it was that hid in the shadows moved, and I held my breath as I heard the rustle of leaves. I was unarmed and alone, and I pressed back against the trunk, trying to decide if I should attempt to climb it when I noticed the flash of silver.

"Kalian?" I whispered, hopeful that my eyes were not playing a trick on me, and I heard an answering rumble, a deep growl that I knew well, and then he appeared.

He was stunning as an immortal man, but his wolf form was nothing short of glorious. His black fur was slick and shining as it blew in the gentle breeze, and though his back came an inch or two past my head, his movements were smooth and graceful.

Approaching me cautiously, he lowered his head and I waited, watching silently as he closed the distance between us.

"Have you been spying on me?" I asked, unimpressed that he would hide away where I couldn't see him, and he rolled his eyes before shaking that massive head.

"So, you just happen to appear the minute I unwrap my binding?" It was my eyes that rolled this time, and his snout lowered. "Usually I would be glad to not have to hear your witty remarks, but this conversation is truly feeling a little one-sided."

His body shivered and shifted, and I watched with keen interest as the fur disappeared into smooth golden skin, and then his handsome face was peering down at me.

"You think I'm witty?" he asked, that deep voice of his oddly similar to his wolf's growl, and my lips parted at the sound.

"You really are desperate for compliments, aren't you?" Tipping his head back, he laughed, and I studied the way his muscular shoulders moved.

"Only from you," he added as his laughter quieted.

Flustered by his answer and his nudity, I cleared my throat and then glanced back at the forest he had come from. "What are you doing out here?"

"I couldn't sleep, so I went for a run." His eyes moved to the forgotten lantern and book.

"I'm not sure I understand the idea of *running* for pleasure," I admitted as I bent to retrieve the items.

"It's to tire me out," he said, and then his voice lowered once more. "Though if I'm looking for a more *pleasurable* way to do so, I'm far more partial to fucking."

My fingers slipped across the smooth leather cover as his words registered, and then, as I slowly straightened, I asked, "Is that an offer?"

The Lupine alpha appeared to be caught off guard, and I waited, tilting my head to the side as I examined him closely, wondering if I had overstepped. Perhaps the throne room had been a one-off. Maybe his lust had been satisfied with that one little tryst, though if I was being honest, it had only intensified my own.

Searching my eyes, he took a moment to answer, though his lips opened and closed twice, almost as if the words were on his tongue and then he changed his mind. "Do you want it to be?"

"Yes," I admitted honestly, and I gasped at the way his eyes darkened at the words.

"Thank fuck," he groaned, and then he kissed me.

It was searing, and rough, and the force of it had me backing into the bark once more, though I paid no mind to the wood scratching at my skin through my tunic. I was too consumed with how Kalian's massive hands cradled my face as if I was the most precious thing in the world, or the way his lips seemed to mold to my own.

Realizing my arms still hung at my sides, I carefully wedged them between us and ignored the way Kalian jumped when my knuckles grazed him as I untied the laces of my breeches. The threads loosened just slightly, but I needed more space to pull them through the holes, and when I reached to guide the Lupine back just a step, his own hands grabbed mine as he broke our kiss.

"Wait," he whispered, his mouth now grazing my forehead as he panted against my temple.

"Did you want to take them off?" I asked, not understanding why he had stopped me.

"Not here," he whispered, his warm breath blowing across my hair. "Not outside on the ground like I'm some rutting beast."

"That actually sounds rather appealing." I could see it, me on my belly as my cheek rested against the cool grass, and Kalian on his knees behind me, his hands grasping at my hips while his head tipped back towards the stars.

"Not now," he growled out. "Not for the first time."

"It's not our first time," I reminded him.

"It's the first of sorts," he whispered, and I lifted my chin to peer up at him.

"Fine, if not here, then where?" He took half a step back, just enough that his warmth was no longer seeping into me, and then he took my hand.

"I want you in my bed," he answered, "in my room, where no one else has been."

"You already know I want you," I muttered. "There's no need for falsehoods."

His mouth pulled into a frown. "What do you mean?"

"I know you've had other women, Kalian."

His brows pulled together as he frowned. "Not in *my* room, not in my bed."

"But Nadine—"

"Never stepped foot in there," he interrupted.

"But—" I shook my head, not believing his words, and his hand cupped my jaw, his thumb stroking across the raised flesh of my scar.

"Not once was she in that room, Skylahr," he swore. "No one but you ever will be."

There was something about that, about being the only woman to be in his bed, that made me nervous. It felt *intimate*, far more intimate than I wanted, but I was too desperate for him to disagree or to think about another place we could go.

"Lead the way," I ordered, and his eyes softened for a moment before he turned for the bushes nearby. He pulled a pair of breeches out from the leaves and then hastily stepped into them before reaching a hand out for me.

Grabbing the book and lantern, I then moved forward and slid my palm against his. Squeezing my fingers, he smiled tenderly and then pulled me towards the castle.

The door seemed to open inch by inch, almost as if time had slowed, and I swallowed at the sudden nervousness twisting in my belly. This was what I wanted, this was what I had been longing for, a distraction of sorts. And yet it felt like so much more than a distraction, it felt almost *pivotal*.

Stepping into his room, Kalian towed me along and then gently shut the door. The fireplace was empty, but there were two dozen candles sprinkled across the room that gave off a soft glow, and I inhaled sharply before glancing at him.

He, however, had yet to look at me and instead turned to place my book on the nightstand. Keeping his back to me, he sighed roughly, and his body seemed to quiver.

"Are you alright?" I asked, suddenly worried that he was having second thoughts.

"Perfect," he answered as he faced me, and I lifted my chin when he crossed the space between us. Carding his fingers through my hair, he tilted my head back and then pressed a sweet kiss to my mouth. Lost in him once more, I let him guide me back, my steps unsteady as he herded me to the massive bed that sat in the middle of the room, and when we reached the edge he pulled from my embrace.

"Skylahr," he began, and I shivered at the sound of my name coming from his lips. "I—"

But I knew what he was going to say, and I wasn't sure I could hear it. Not here, not now. And so instead, I hastily grabbed the hem of my tunic and pulled it over my head. Letting it slip from my fingers, I watched as it pooled on the ground and then I gazed at him.

Silver eyes moved from my face to my neck and then down, and I felt the heat of them, even from a distance, as they examined every bare inch of me.

"You've changed," he said softly. "You've gotten stronger."

Once I may have turned away at the words, but he said them with such wonder, as if he was in the presence of the Huntress herself, that I couldn't help but feel desired.

Moving to me, he lifted his hands and cupped my shoulders, letting the tips of his fingers skim across the heavy muscles there before tracing them down my back, and I shook as the rough skin of his palms smoothed over my flesh.

Reaching my hips, he then directed me to sit on his bed, and I followed his guidance. I sank into the soft mattress, pulling myself across the soft furs until I was propped up by the pile of pillows. Taking in a shuddering breath, Kalian gazed at me from the foot of the bed, and I leaned back, letting him take his fill.

"By Gods, you are incredible," he groaned as he placed one knee on the bed, then the other and then he prowled across the surface, not stopping until his hips were cradled by my thighs.

Gazing up at him, I felt my heart clench at the way his silver eyes glowed in the candlelight, and he lifted a hand, stroking his knuckles from my temple to jaw before lowering his face to kiss me.

It was slow and gentle, as if he was trying to say everything he felt with this single touch, and I whimpered into his mouth as my blood heated.

"I need you," I whispered when he finally pulled back, and he fell forward, resting his forehead against my collarbone for just a moment before his hands were at his breeches. Discarding them quickly, he then grabbed at my own and pulled them down my legs with one smooth movement.

Now bare, he returned to his previous position between my thighs, though I could feel his hand skimming down over my lower belly. I inhaled sharply as his fingers slid through the slickness of my core.

"You're soaked," he whispered, pressing his face into my neck, and I widened my legs before canting my hips towards his touch.

"Please," I whispered, my toes curling in the furs beneath me as his thumb circled my clit, and he scraped his teeth against my neck when he felt me shiver.

Dipping two fingers into me, he carefully stretched me open, and I gasped as they curled against my front wall, searching for that spot that made me forget my own name.

"Kalian," I panted when they finally found it, and his teeth clamped onto my shoulder as I lifted, desperate for him to let me finish.

"Fuck, Skylahr," he grunted when I cried out again, and then those fingers were sliding from me, and I whined at the loss before my eyes fluttered open.

"What is it?" I huffed, not understanding why he had stopped.

"I'm not sure I can hold off much longer," he admitted as his face flushed, and I glanced down at him, taking in the weeping head of his cock.

"Then don't," I suggested as I lifted my knees so that they closed in around his ribs, and he groaned at the invitation.

Sliding one hand over my ass, he tugged me closer, though it seemed impossible, and then he was cradling the back of my knee, holding it against him while his other hand guided his length into me. The first thrust allowed only a few inches in and he paused, cursing while his body trembled. I curled my fingers in his hair while the other hand stroked down his spine.

"Kalian," I whispered, ducking my chin towards my chest so I could get a better look at his face. "You're shaking."

"I'm okay," he promised, and then he was grasping my fingers, weaving them with his own before pinning my hands on either side of my head, and then his forehead touched mine. "I know you don't want me to say it, but I need you to know."

I gazed into his eyes, watching them soften as he looked down at me, and then I nodded, suddenly desperate for the words. "Tell me."

"I love you."

Lifting from the pillows, I crashed my mouth into his and wrapped my legs around his hips, pushing my heels into his ass. Taking the encouragement, he pressed the rest of his cock into me, and my body tightened as he filled me completely.

I couldn't tell where I ended and he began as he moved within me, his rhythm remaining slow and steady but oh so *deep*. Almost as if he couldn't bear to be parted from me, not for a single second, and my legs closed around him as he brought me to the edge.

"I love you," he panted again, his fingers tightening around my own.

Though I couldn't repeat the words, his admission filled my chest with warmth, and my eyes moistened as his own peered down at me. He released one of my hands and slid his fingers over my hair, smoothing the bronze strands back, and then his fingertips traced my cheek, taking the time to cover every detail of the sigil with his touch before he was pushing against the flesh tenderly, directing my head to the side.

Now having full access to the mark, he lowered his lips and pressed one kiss to it, then another, and another, all while whispering of his love for me. And when he was done and his mouth finally met my own, I fell over the edge.

Chapter 38

Tucking my head beneath his chin, he wrapped an arm around my waist and pulled me close, not settling until I was all but draped over him. He tightened his hold, securing me to his side, and then reached for the book left forgotten and placed it on the ridges of his muscular torso.

"This one took me ages to find," he murmured before pressing his lips to my temple, and then he flipped to the first page. "Most of the history books and scriptures focus on the Divine Triad. They don't bother with much information on the others. This one was written by Thomos the Cunning, one of the Jester's first followers."

"Was he part of an ancient house as well?" I asked as the Lupine turned the pages.

"I suppose it depends on who you ask." Kalian sighed. "The followers of the Gods of old did not acknowledge the families the Second appointed. That was just the beginning of the tension between the two groups."

"When did it start?" I asked. "Gaelon had said the reign had been most peaceful until the Seductress had set her sights on the Protector."

Snorting, Kalian shook his head. "Of course the Healer's Chosen would see it that way. They never see the ill intentions of others until it's too late. The animosity between the Gods and their people had been brewing long before the first man charged, and the war itself lasted for over a hundred and thirty years."

"That long?!" I gasped as I pulled from his shoulder to peer up at him.

"I'm sure for the Gods it seemed like no time at all. That's just a fraction of an immortal life."

Lowering my cheek to rest on his shoulder once more, I glanced at the curved words I didn't understand and waited for Kalian to begin reading.

"The sigils of the Gods were chosen carefully, each representing their weapon, instrument, or gift. Though the depiction of each varied across the lands of Elrin. The four-pointed star of the Jester had included a copper coin, though it was later changed after the temple of Fate and Fortune had been built. The trident of the Siren was later altered to include her horn. The heart of the Lover—"

"The Lover?" I interrupted as I gazed down at the page, studying the plain crimson heart. "Where are the swords? Where are the flames?"

"This was written before the war," Kalian explained. "At that point she was known as the Lover, and the crossing swords and flames were not added until the battle began. Surely you knew that they had thought her the Goddess of love before her ambitions became known."

"I did," I answered. "I guess I just never thought I would find anything that referred to her in such a kind manner."

"She had everyone fooled," Kalian growled and then he hastily flipped the page. The next symbol was that of his God, the mighty Lupine shield of the Protector, and I curled into him as his thumb skimmed across the portrait before I glanced at the wall where the shield hung.

"So, the shield represents his name, of course," I guessed, and Kalian nodded.

"His name and his gift," he whispered.

"Gift?" I asked, tipping my chin towards him. "You mean the wolves?"

"He not only had the ability to take on the form of the great white wolf but was also immune to the dark magic of the Seductress. The story says that is how he was able to resist her when she set her sights on him. It is said that he also was able to protect his people from being manipulated by her. A barrier of sorts, I suppose."

"Like yours?" I asked, thinking back to the shining curtain that blanketed the border of the Lupine territories.

"Yes." He nodded.

"How does it work, your barrier?"

Kalian lowered the book onto his stomach and then lifted his eyes to the ceiling.

"I am not sure I really know," he answered. "When the Crimsons had begun their search for the Chosen, I had been desperate to protect my people. I had been willing to give up anything if it meant keeping them safe. Somehow that twisted into a shield of sorts. It's a magic I never understood but I am thankful for it."

"So it's a part of you then?" Kalian nodded again.

"The men I had tasked with keeping Denimoore safe when we were at the shores said that it had begun to dissolve when I was injured." His voice was low, but I could hear the worry. "I guess if I die, it dies with me."

The room fell silent, and I shuffled my way onto his chest, pressing my ear against the solid muscle until I could hear the beating of his heart.

"What else does the book say?" I asked, not wanting to dwell on the way my blood felt cold at the thought of the world without him, and the Lupine alpha began to read once more, his deep voice soothing away my worries until I finally found sleep.

When I woke again, the room had gone dark, and I turned my chin to my shoulder, glancing at the man who had curled around me. One strong arm had curved over my body, the length of it allowing his hand to hold my own that lay under my cheek, and he was pressed so tightly to me that his chest forced my body to rise and fall with each of his breaths.

Taking the opportunity to study him, I realized besides the length of his hair, nothing else had really changed. Gone was the shadow that had grown over his jaw when I had been forced to my knees at his feet, and other than the fact he was not recovering from a battle, unlike the last time I had seen him sprawled across a bed, he did not truly look any different.

He had said I had changed, and I had, of course. I would be turning four and twenty in the fall, and I had been through more in the last two years than most humans dealt with in their entire lives. I had more scars, both on the outside and in, and though I had grown stronger, I had also aged, as all mortal beings do.

But Kalian had not.

I slipped out from the weight of his arm, slid from the bed, and searched the floor for my clothes. I found my tunic and pulled it over my head, making sure it came down to cover the curve of my ass before grabbing the book Kalian had cast aside before he had woken me up only to roll me under him once more.

I moved to the dark fireplace, knelt on the deep grey fur, and fiddled with the kindling before lighting a flame. Blowing on the burning parchment and twigs, I waited until the logs caught and then I crept closer. Opening back to the heart of the Crimson Goddess, I glared at the beauty of her simple seal until I could no longer bear it, and then I snapped the book closed once more.

"Skylahr?" Kalian called in alarm as he sat up in the bed, and I stood in concern when I noticed his bleary eyes searching for me.

"I'm here." His shoulders slumped in relief, and I padded across the stone floor. "I'm right here."

"I thought you had left, or maybe that I had dreamt it all," he whispered, running his fingers through his hair, and I knelt on the bed, cupping the back of his neck gently.

"I'm here," I promised for the third time, but he shook his head softly.

"Not for long," he whispered. "Soon we will hear from your Healer, and you will leave."

"I will have to," I sighed. "Once I know where they are I will travel there, and we will continue on our way to Skohyn."

"It's too dangerous," Kalian growled.

"If the Siren's immortals are the reason for the beast, then we don't have a choice. It has to be stopped, and I have wasted enough time here."

"Wasted?" he repeated, his jaw clenching.

"Kalian." I rubbed a hand over my face. "My friends are still out there somewhere, I can feel it in my bones, and now that Barrick is nearly healed, we need to find them. No hawk has returned with their location so I need to go south myself."

"And if you're wrong? If they are not out there?" Kalian asked, his face unreadable.

Swallowing at the sudden pain in my chest, I lowered my eyes and gathered my thoughts. "Then I will finish what we had set out to do. I will find a way to stop the Siren's followers and their beast and will bring peace to Elrin once more."

"Fine," he snapped and then he was dragging me onto his lap, his fingers tangling into my hair as he captured my mouth with his own. Parting my lips with his tongue, he deepened the kiss, and I straddled his hips before coiling my arms around his neck.

We stayed like that for what felt like ages, both hungry and needy for each other, and when I finally needed air, I pulled from him and slumped against his chest.

"Fine," he said again, though his tone was much softer. "But I am coming with you."

"Kalian," I began, but he quieted me with another kiss.

"I am coming with you. This responsibility is just as much mine as it is yours, and I will not leave you to carry this burden. We will share the weight."

Kalian

Chapter 39

"I see you didn't listen to a word I said." Leena's voice interrupted the quiet of the room as she rested her hip against the door frame, and I peered at her from over the reports I had been reading. My sister's face was impassive, and the well-practiced expression would have fooled most, but I knew better, and I lowered the parchment before leaning back in my chair.

"Hello to you too, sweet sister." Crossing her arms, she narrowed her eyes at me, and I smirked, pleased with myself for cracking her façade so easily.

"I'm just wondering what the hell you are thinking, Kalian?" She stepped into the study, quickly shut the door, and then stood on the other side of my desk, her dark gaze narrowing as she waited for my answer.

"I'm thinking a great many things." I shrugged. "Things such as what is for supper, what I will do with those men in the village who have been spewing filth about Skylahr, and how badly I wish to have her wrapped around me right now."

Leena's pert nose wrinkled in disgust, and then she turned to the window, bracing her palms against the ledge as she peered at the grounds below.

"What is it, Leena? I thought you'd be happy for me."

"What made you think that?" she asked, glaring at me from over her shoulder. "I have spent the last month asking you to stay away from her."

"See, that is what I do not understand," I sighed and then crossed my arms over my chest. "You try to sway me from getting too close, but then you take the time to assure her that what I feel is real. That my love is true."

"And that is why I asked you to stay away after she and I talked. I'm not sure it is a love that she truly returns," Leena snapped, and I swallowed roughly at her words.

"Well, obviously you are wrong considering last night." My voice was hoarse, and I could hear the slight tremor in it.

"Kalian, fucking and love are not the same thing, you should know this by now. In fact you should be an expert in understanding the difference," she growled and then rubbed at her temples. "Listen, you hurt her. You can see it, I can see it, we all see it. It's there every time she looks at you. I have tried to get around it and determine what it is she feels for you. But any time I try, she crumples into herself, and I am reminded of the girl I saw leaving your tent last spring."

I shook my head. "You're wrong. It's not like that anymore, she has forgiven me."

"Has she?" Leena asked. "Has she truly? Has she even said the words?"

My head bowed as my chest constricted, and Leena sighed softly before crossing the room. She rounded my desk, stood next to my chair, and placed a comforting hand on my shoulder.

"I am just worried," she said softly. "I worry for both of you."

Shrugging out from under her touch, I stood from my chair and paced across the floor. "Just be forthright, Leena. What is it that you are suggesting? What are you asking of me?"

"I would ask that you give her up," Leena whispered, and I froze, staring at her with wide eyes. "But I know that is pointless, so because you can't, I am asking that you guard your heart."

"Leena," I breathed, and then I moved to her and wrapped my arms around her carefully. "You do not need to concern yourself with me."

Pulling from my touch, she gazed up at me with a frown. "You and I both know that is a lie. You don't have a lick of sense when it comes to her, and that can lead you to make idiotic choices."

"It won't," I disagreed.

"It already has." One slender brow lifted. "Or do you always punch someone in the face just because he was on the receiving end of her smiles?"

I glowered at her as shame filled my chest, and she ran her fingers through her hair before turning from me once more.

"You're jealous and angry and that won't get better when you inevitably leave with her. In fact, I think it will only get worse when the Healer joins you."

"We have yet to receive any word of him," I pointed out, and Leena tensed.

"And you're pleased about that?" she asked.

"Of course not!" I exclaimed, angry that she could think such a thing. "I don't wish any harm on him or her friends. I never have."

"Even if he's the one she truly loves now?"

"Especially if that is what she feels for him," I said softly. "I would never wish for her to have to grieve another person she cares for, and I will keep praying to the Gods for their safety."

"But you also plan to continue to warm her bed in the meantime," she concluded, and my face flushed.

"If that is what she wants," I answered with a shrug, and Leena's shoulders fell.

"Kalian, is that really wise?"

"Probably not," I whispered. "But I will take whatever parts she wants to give me; I do not have the right to ask for anything more than that."

"This will end badly," she warned, and I let my gaze roam around the room, reluctant to look at her face and unwilling to admit that I had already come to that conclusion.

She was glorious as she swung the sparring sword at Keyno, and I watched from my place on the terrace, smiling fondly as she beat my brother into the dirt.

"Apparently he did not learn his lesson," Leena remarked as she leaned against the banister next to me, and I glanced at her from the corner of my eye. "You don't plan on hitting him again, do you?"

"Did your mate even tell you what it is he said to me to deserve such a beating?" I asked in annoyance.

"I have no doubt he goaded you." Leena nodded, a fond grin pulling at her lips as she watched Keyno stand once more. "But to let him get under your skin so easily, well, I just expected more from you, brother."

"The pair of you." I shook my head in frustration. "Let me just say you deserve each other. I hope you annoy one another for the rest of your days."

Patting my back, Leena tipped her head and offered a sweet smile. "Why annoy each other when we have you?"

Slapping her hand away, I moved from my place and hurried down the stone steps that led to the yard. Keyno's face had begun to harden as Skylahr danced away from him gracefully, and I paused in my pursuit, watching as she blocked another blow from him before sliding away. She had gotten faster, more confident in her technique, and I could see the difference in her movements now that she was no longer holding herself back for the sake of my brother's ego.

Keyno growled at her, his frustration beginning to show, and as the spar continued, his attacks grew sloppy. Holding my breath, I waited for her to take her opening and smiled when I saw her eyes catch it. Coming down from above, Skylahr collided with his own blade, and the force sent his weapon to the ground, and then she was pressing the edge of silver to his collarbone, waiting for him to say the words.

"I yield," Keyno growled begrudgingly, and Skylahr's answering smile was blinding as she held a hand out for him to take.

"Were you holding out on me the last few times we've done this?" Keyno wondered as he bent down to retrieve his blade. She shrugged as she panted for breath.

"I didn't want to lose my sparring partner." Rolling his eyes, he clapped her on the back, and her chin tilted towards the sky as a deep laugh rumbled out of her.

There was such an ease between the two of them, and I felt a twist of bitterness as he pressed a hand to her back before guiding her to where their wineskins lay. Not noticing me yet, Skylahr fell to the ground and stretched her legs out in front of her before taking a long swig of her water.

"Hello, Kal," Keyno called, though he didn't bother to look at me, and I scowled, annoyed that he would announce my presence.

I had hoped to observe her for just a moment longer, but now I could already see the difference in her body. The way her posture straightened or how the heavy muscles of her shoulders and back tensed at my name. I was sure those brilliant hazel eyes that had been shining like stars were also now dull, the walls she had built around her heart already rising, and I hated that she felt the need to protect herself from me.

No matter how much I may have deserved it.

"Looked like you took a thrashing, Keyno," I answered, my mouth lifting into a smirk as his dark eyes caught mine.

"I wouldn't go as far as to say that."

"I would." Sky smiled just before pressing the wineskin to her lips, and my brother's mouth fell open.

"I see how it is," Keyno grumbled, and then he tucked his wineskin under his arm. "I shall go find my mate, at least she appreciates me."

"Keyno," Skylahr started. "I hope you know I do appreciate you a great deal."

"Yes, brother," I added with a laugh. "She values having the opportunity to pummel you into the ground."

Hazel eyes finally met mine, and I swallowed as they narrowed at me.

"Seems to me you'll be the one getting knocked around this round, Kal. I hope you enjoy yourself." Stepping out of the ring, he turned to the terrace where his mate was still watching, and when the air filled with awkwardness, I wished I had kept my mouth shut.

"Do you want to smack me around?" I asked, unsure of what else to say. "Because you can. I wouldn't stop you."

Rolling her eyes, Skylahr took another drink and then rested her head against the fence. "It won't be nearly as fun if you just stood there and took it. Maybe you should run around a bit, make me chase you."

"So you want to work for it then? Delayed gratification and all that?" I asked, one brow lifting as I smiled down at her. Her face heated and then something else crossed over her expression, something akin to regret, and I felt my heart drop at the sight of it.

"That's— I'm—" she stuttered out, and then she was standing, wiping her hands over her thighs as she glanced around the yard. Gone was the confidence from the night before. The obvious need for me that burned in her eyes had disappeared in the light of the sun, and I could see her slipping away.

"I was kidding, Sky," I tried, offering her a soft smile. But she didn't return it and instead continued to search for an escape.

"I should go see my guard. I have yet to do so today."

"Sky—" I started, but it was too late. She was already fleeing, and I watched as she stumbled her way to the castle.

Rubbing at my jaw, I waited until she was gone from sight and then exhaled roughly. "Fuck."

Chapter 40

"Is Hazel not eating with us?" Keyno frowned as he cut into his venison, and Leena lifted her wine glass, peering at me from over the rim.

"She took supper with her guard," my sister answered, but I could see she had more to say on the matter.

"She mentioned wanting to check on him after your spar," I said before she could continue, and then I lowered my eyes to my plate, though I no longer felt an ounce of hunger.

"Odd timing if you ask me." Leena tilted her head. "He seemed like the farthest thing from her mind until you showed up. Funny how that happened."

"Funny indeed," Keyno agreed as he chewed, though his mouth was lifted at the corners.

"I fail to see any humour in it," I grumbled, and the couple's eyes met for an instant before my sister was leaning back in her chair with a thoughtful look on her face.

"I've never known you to be so repugnant to a woman before." Leena laughed softly. "What did you say?"

I scowled at her for a moment and then pushed my plate away. This was uncharted territory for me; I didn't know how to proceed with Skylahr. If I pushed too hard, she would run. If I let her be, she would continue to build those walls around her, and I would never be able to breach them.

I had thought that the night before was a new beginning for us, but I had obviously misjudged what she felt. Not once had she said the words back to me, and though I told Leena I would be happy with whatever parts she gave me, I couldn't help but long for more.

"Kal," Leena called, her eyes now filled with worry. "I'm sure she was just concerned for Barrick. The two are very close, and she has been worried about his healing."

"But he is nearly mended now?"

"He is." Keyno nodded. "He is a stubborn old thing. Wouldn't listen to anything our curer had to say, but our Hazel was able to knock some sense into him on occasion."

"What are their plans now then? Have they changed?" I was sure they hadn't; Skylahr had been too set on them to bother to hear any reason.

"If we have not heard of the Healer by the end of this week they want to travel the coast themselves. They fear that perhaps our messages have not been received, and they are hopeful that they will find answers."

"What do you two think?" I whispered, worried that they shared my fears.

"It is possible, perhaps they are safe and sound and are looking for Skylahr as well," Keyno started. "But surely we would have heard something by now if that was the case. Even if our letters were intercepted or had been missed somehow, there would be word of them."

"Have you told her this?" I asked, my heart clenching as I thought of Skylahr's face when she realized that chances were her friends were dead.

"No, I've been able to convince her that it may still take more time to learn of any news," Leena said but her face was drawn with guilt. "I didn't want to see her give up hope."

"And what of the immortals and Skohyn? What of the beast?"

"There have been no other sightings of the beast, but vessels continue to disappear. As for the Siren's immortals, they are not meeting along the shores of Elrin any longer. All accounts say they had set sail, and unless they too have fallen victim to the sea, then they have gathered elsewhere."

"And you think the Healer was right with his assumption? You think they could have travelled to Skohyn?"

"Yes." Keyno nodded. "It was just a moon after the first ship with the Siren's sails left that the beast was said to appear, that cannot be coincidence. They must be the reason for it."

"So, what do we do?" I asked, though I already knew what I wanted.

"Now that we have some idea on a destination, I would send a ship, warn the crew of the risks, but offset it with the reward. Have them go to Skohyn and investigate and then secure a hostage for questioning."

"How will they make it there if the beast is still at large? Will they not just end up like the rest?" Leena asked as she sipped her wine.

"Then we send two ships, three even. Send them out from multiple ports and have each one take a different route," Keyno suggested. "As great as this creature may be, it cannot be in two places at once."

"And if what we think is true? If they have assembled there and are responsible for summoning the creature?"

"Then we take up arms and go to war. There are no more than a few hundred, or so our allies say, and they have yet to find their Chosen. As far as the Siren herself, well, she is still as absent as she has been since the war."

"What do we tell Skylahr?" I asked, my stomach filling with dread.

"This time?" Leena turned her eyes to me, and then they narrowed. "The truth."

Skylahr had been difficult to find later that evening, and when I had entered the guard's chambers, I immediately noticed that the man's face appeared ashen. Leena had decided to be the one to discuss our assumptions with the two, her conscience growing heavy after having dismissed Skylahr's fears over the last few days. I had offered to do it myself but she refused, feeling that it was her responsibility.

"My sister has visited you, I gather?" The guard nodded gruffly, and I bowed my head. "How did she take it?"

"Not well," Barrick whispered, his dark eyes sad as he looked at the empty chair next to his bed. "A part of her knew, I'm sure, but I don't think she wanted to admit it. Neither of us did."

"I am sorry. I too had been hoping for word of their safe return from sea." Barrick's brow lifted but he remained silent, and I shoved my hands in my pockets as I shuffled my weight from foot to foot. "Do you know where she has gone?"

Barrick's frown deepened, and he fell back against his pillows tiredly. "Had it not been for that tonic I keep having shoved down my throat, I would have gone after her, but that shit makes me dizzy."

"It is meant to put you to sleep, and by the looks of it, they're giving you enough to calm a horse." I lifted my chin at the vial left on his bedside table.

Lifting a hand, he waved me off and then pulled the furs up to his chest. "She's most likely beating something or someone. It's how she processes her feelings best."

Of course that's where she'd be. I felt like a fool for not assuming so, and I turned for the door.

"She will not want to be coddled," her guard warned. "But perhaps she should be held. She needs comfort now more than ever."

"I don't think she will allow me to do so without a fight," I admitted, and Barrick hummed under his breath.

"Probably not," he agreed. "So let her fight you. Let her scratch and scream and claw at you. Let her feel it all and then, when she is done, pick up the pieces and put her back together."

"You're certain I'm the one who should be doing that?" I asked softly.

"No," he admitted and then ran a hand over his black beard. "But I think you're the only one who can."

I could hear her grunts of frustration the minute I stepped onto the grass, and I frowned at the way her breath hitched between them.

She had been crying, or was still crying, and I closed my eyes as my heart clenched.

"Fuck," she gasped, the word coming out of her in a rush, and I hurried towards the noise.

She was kneeling in the dirt, a hand clasped to her shoulder and a river of red slipping through her fingers.

"What happened?" I demanded. I fell to the ground next to her and she turned her head, peering up at me with wet eyes. My heart cracked as I took in her tear-stained cheeks.

"I swung too hard and nicked my shoulder." She sighed, and I grabbed her hand, pulling it away so I could examine the wound.

"Sparring swords should not be this sharp." I frowned, wiping away the blood from the now-healing cut.

"It's not a sparring sword, I grabbed one of the others from the armoury." My gaze moved from her shoulder, then to her face and then to the trunk of the tree she had apparently been hacking away at.

"A dummy wouldn't suffice," Skylahr explained, and I hummed before picking up the blade and moving it farther away.

"Do you feel better?" I asked, though I knew she did not.

"They can't be dead" was all she whispered, the last word ending in a choked sob, and I lowered my head. "They can't be."

"We don't know anything for certain," I tried, and she sniffed before her shoulders shook with another whimper. Shuffling forward, I tucked a hand under her chin and tipped it. Using my other, I carefully wiped away the wetness from her skin, taking gentle care around the mark on cheek before stroking my thumb across it.

"We don't know anything for certain," I repeated. "Until we do, you can pray, and you can hope. Don't give up now."

"Leena doesn't have any hope," she spat out bitterly and I sighed.

"Leena isn't you." I shrugged with a half-hearted smile. "She does not have the same stubbornness or perseverance. She does not stand tall when the odds are stacked against her."

"What kind of lashing would you receive if she heard you say as much?" Skylahr wondered as she rubbed her nose against the back of her hand. I smoothed her hair out of her face, my fingers catching one of the pieces before rubbing the blunt end between the pads.

"Perhaps you could do me the favour of not telling her?" I smiled softly and she nodded, her eyes searching my face, and then she was surging forward, her mouth seeking mine as her own hands wrapped around my neck.

Giving in to it for a moment, I allowed myself to respond, my lips moving against hers as she kissed me roughly. But I couldn't ignore the salt I tasted, and I let it continue for another minute before cupping her jaw and pulling back.

"What are you doing?" she asked, her brows furrowing as her attention moved from my eyes then to my mouth and then back again.

"I didn't come out here for that," I assured her, and I watched as that wall rose again, and she began to lean away from me.

Desperate to stop her from shutting me out, I cupped the back of her neck and pulled her forward until her forehead rested against mine. Holding her gaze, I took in a deep breath and then wrapped my other arm around her shoulders. "Let me hold you, just for a little while."

Those brilliant hazel eyes watered at my touch, and as predicted she pressed her palms against my chest, shaking her head as she tried to pry herself away from me. But I held fast, my hold tightening before I dragged her to me. Placing her face into the crook of my neck, I shushed her, whispering whatever words I could think of that may bring her comfort, though I was sure she could not hear me over her cries, and I closed my eyes.

"It's okay, I'm here," I promised, at first unsure if the words eased anything, but when her fingers clutched my tunic and she pressed herself against me, almost as if she could not get close enough, I repeated them. "It's okay, *I'm here.*"

Chapter 41

"The two of the ships are due to leave tomorrow morning, the third the following day. If the sea cooperates, they could reach Skohyn in a little over a week." Keyno's eyes were focused on the crackling fire, and I nodded my head as I sipped at my glass of licur.

"Thank you for getting that organized so quickly," I muttered as the liquid burned the back of my throat. "What did you have to offer them?"

"A very large sum and a promise of an audience with the Protector's Chosen."

"That's it?" My brows lifted in surprise.

"And titles for the captains."

"For all of them?" I clarified, and Keyno rubbed at the back of his neck awkwardly while nodding.

"And the first one to return with what we asked will be the new admiral of the Lupine fleet."

"A designation well deserved, I suppose." I swallowed another mouthful and then placed the glass down carefully before leaning into my chair and closing my eyes.

"How is she?" Keyno whispered, concern heavy in his voice.

"Hurting," I answered. "I don't know if she was ready to hear it."

"She was never going to be ready to hear it; no one is ready for hard truths."

"We don't know any truths for certain, Keyno," I reminded him. "I know what the chances are that they are still alive, but the Healer is a Chosen of the Gods. If anyone can beat the odds, I'm sure it's him."

Keyno remained silent, but doubt was written all over his face. Deciding to ignore it, I moved across the room to grab another bottle of the amber-coloured liquid before settling once more. I poured another hefty glass and passed the decanter to my brother.

"Will you try to convince her to stay until our men return?"

"I don't think I could." I sighed. "And if she chooses not to, I will accompany her south."

"Kal," Keyno began, but I gave him a pointed look.

"I can't send her south and sit by wondering where she is or what is happening. I can't, I *won't*, so don't ask me to. Not again."

Keyno moved forward, bracing his arms on his knees, and just as he was about to respond a rough knock came from the door. Our eyes met in confusion, and I glanced at the door once more when another knock rang out, and Keyno shrugged before standing.

He pulled open the heavy wood and then moved aside, and Barrick stepped into the room, his face impassive as he stood near the entrance. Realizing he was waiting for an invitation, I got to my feet and gestured for him to come in before grabbing another glass. I filled it, passed the guard the delicate crystal, and lifted a brow when he glanced at the licur uncertainly.

"Have you not acquired a taste for it?" I asked, amused.

"No, my lord." He shook his head and then lifted the drink to his nose. "I don't think I ever will."

"Kalian is fine," I corrected him and then took the glass from his fingers before handing him a bottle of wine instead. "Just be careful with this, it will not mix well with that tonic."

"Don't worry about me, I'm made from stronger stuff than most," he assured me and then sank into Keyno's vacant chair at my direction.

"Are you well?" I wondered, scanning his face for any sign of pain or discomfort, doing my very best not to linger on the ruined half.

"Right as rain." He nodded and then pulled the cork from the bottle and took a sip. "But it seems that sleep will not come tonight, and I wanted to be sure that the Huntress was alright."

"As well as expected, she plans to leave Denimoore as soon as you are ready." Barrick nodded.

"Yes, I figured her patience had run thin, and if I'm being honest, so has mine." Those dark eyes slid to mine quickly and then he lowered his chin. "Not that I don't appreciate the hospitality or kindness you have shown us. Without you, I would most certainly be dead."

"Most certainly," I agreed. "The sea-maidens are not known for mercy unfortunately."

"Then I'm glad I have lived to tell the tale of my experience with them."

"You will be famous in the north," I remarked with a grin, and the captain laughed quietly.

"That's never really been a goal of mine, I'm afraid. And besides, by the time we return I'm sure the story will be less interesting."

"I wanted to tell you that we have organized three vessels who will head to Skohyn in the morning. They have been ordered to learn how many immortals have assembled there and to bring back a man for questioning. We will learn what part they played in the summoning of the beast."

"Does the Huntress know?"

"Not yet, I wanted her to try to get some rest. But we will tell her first thing in the morning, and then she can decide what she would like to do."

"If our friends are really gone, she will be wanting retribution," Barrick warned softly, and I nodded.

"And I'm prepared to give her that."

"They left today?" Skylahr confirmed, her hands on her hips as she looked between Keyno and me.

"They did, and they should reach the shores of Skohyn within a fortnight. As soon as they do, they will send the hafok with word."

"And then what?" she asked, her face pale and her eyes bloodshot.

"If we get word that your friends are there, we will leave immediately," I promised. "If they aren't, we will wait for the men's return. They have been instructed to bring a hostage back with them, and I will be sure to get the answers to your questions."

"So, in other words, you don't think I should bother searching the coast, is that what you are saying?" Skylahr whispered, her shoulders hunching.

"I'm not sure if there is any reason to." It was harsh, but honest, and her teeth sank into her quivering lower lip.

"I see." I didn't want to hurt her, I didn't want to smother the hope I told her to hold on to just the night before, but I would not tell her another lie. I would never make that mistake again.

"So, more waiting," she concluded.

"Not much more," I promised.

"If the Siren's immortals do in fact control the beast, and my friends fell victim to it, I want whoever is responsible to be held accountable."

"They will be," I swore, and she nodded.

"Fine." Turning on her heel, she left my study, and my brother's brows rose before he glanced at me nervously.

"She's angry," he noted.

"She has every reason to be. She has lost a great deal over the last year."

"As have you," Keyno pointed out.

"Yes, and if Balor was still alive, I would be just as angry."

"Balor wasn't the only one to blame for your mother." My jaw clenched as I turned to Keyno.

"And if there is ever word of that Crimson bitch, I will hunt her down and tear out her throat myself," I snarled. "But we now have a new enemy, and that must be our focus."

Both Barrick and Skylahr had been persuaded to have tea with us, though the guard seemed disinterested in the concept and had eyes only for the plate of sweets and pastries that was provided, and I watched in amusement as he shoved an entire tart into his mouth.

Skylahr, obviously noticing where my attention was focused, elbowed her guard in the side gently while her face flushed.

"Barrick, it's a miracle you don't choke when you stuff your face like that."

"Leave me be, I am still recuperating," he grumbled, though he took a small bite of the next one he had lifted to his mouth.

"Interesting," Leena muttered. "You spend all your time convincing us that you are well enough to leave your bed and that you are fine, but the minute we mention your love for dessert you are suddenly still healing."

The gruff man's face pinkened, and his eyes fell to his lap shyly at my sister's words.

Quiet blanketed the table, and as I reached for the milk, I noticed the sound of hurried footsteps. Standing from my chair, I turned to the doors and waited for the men to round the corner.

"What is it?" I took in their worried expressions nervously and felt Skylahr's presence as she stood beside me.

"We have visitors, my lord." The taller of the two bowed quickly. "A halfling and a mortal. They are just outside the barrier and are asking to speak to the Huntress."

"Do you recognize either of them?" Sky asked in a rush, but the man shook his head.

"I can't say for certain, but no, I do not think so." Her face fell and then Leena stood.

"This halfling, did they say who they were or where they came from?"

The men looked at each other and then the other stepped forward.

"South, my lady. She thought you may have received word of her travels from Lord Ewen, that you may be expecting her. As for her name, it's unique, one that is not known here. A Sadie or a Sellney."

"Selbie?" Sky asked, her eyes wide.

"Yes, that's it." The guard nodded.

"Who is she?" I asked, turning to Skylahr.

"A halfling I met last summer while we journeyed across Elrin after the battle. I have not seen her since, so I'm not sure what it is she would need, but she is no threat."

"Bring her and the mortal here," I ordered. "We will see them in the throne room." Bowing once more, the men turned to the hall, and I glanced down at Sky as she chewed on her lower lip.

"What is it?" I asked, stepping close until her shoulder brushed my chest, blocking her from the others, and her eyes lifted.

"Selbie left Beilham a while back, but there was no mention of her needing or wanting to see me then. Something must have changed in the time since she's left, and if she was willing to travel such a long way with just one other friend, whatever happened must have been serious."

"What do you think her reason is?" Leena asked, her brows furrowed.

"I don't know, but I can't help but think it's not good."

Chapter 42

The anticipation was making Skylahr anxious, and she fidgeted, smoothing her tunic and pulling at the hem as we waited. Feeling my stare, she turned to me, and I offered her a soft smile and then lifted my hand towards the throne.

"Sit," I ordered, ignoring the quiet gasps coming from my family as they stared at me wide-eyed. She flushed but shook her head.

"That is your place, not mine," she whispered, and my smile fell, pulling down in the corners.

"I have already told you that it is," I replied. The words were quiet but full of warmth, and her flush grew. Taking in a deep breath, she shook her head once more, and my shoulders fell in defeat as I moved to the throne. Just before I sank to the seat, I glanced back at Skylahr and tilted my head towards my shoulder, a silent direction for her to stand at my side.

Inhaling sharply, she took her place, and then the massive doors were opening. I waited as two figures entered the great room. The first was one I didn't recognize, though I assumed her to be the halfling named Selbie. Her dark skin glowed under the sunlight that filtered through the massive windows. She looked no worse for wear, and she tucked her cloak behind her shoulders before glancing at her comrade.

Turning my attention, I noticed the small pale hands that lifted the hood and then dark shining brown hair was falling forward. Skylahr gasped, her eyes widening as the human's bruised and swollen face lifted, and I realized it was the same girl who had been at the shores, Skylahr's friend from home. Leaping from her place, Sky ran down the steps and rushed to the human, wrapping her arms around her before lifting her from the ground.

"Good Gods, is it really you?" Sky sobbed, carefully tucking the girl into the crook of her neck.

The mortal cried quietly, her face hidden away against the scar on Sky's throat, and she held the small woman tighter. However, after a minute she seemed to notice the girl's quivering and what sounded like a gasp for air, and Sky set her down gently. Too weak to stand, the human crumpled to the floor in a heap, and Skylahr followed her, kneeling on the stone before wiping at the tears on the girl's face, and then she palpated the swelling around her bruised cheekbone.

Flinching at her touch, the human grabbed Sky's fingers and pulled them from her before meeting those brilliant hazel eyes.

"I sure am happy to see you," she whispered hoarsely, and Sky sobbed out a laugh.

"Not as happy as I am to see you, Elizabeth. Tell me, how do you keep managing to surprise me like this?"

She shrugged weakly and then rubbed at her nose. "I guess this is twice now," she sighed. "Maybe I will be lucky enough to manage a third."

Tucking a strand of hair behind her friend's ear, Sky exhaled roughly once more and then peered up at the woman who had accompanied Elizabeth.

Selbie's own dark eyes had watched the entire scene carefully, and Skylahr smiled at the halfling, her face filled with warmth and gratitude. But the stranger did not return the expression, and as her face hardened, Sky turned to her friend in concern.

"What happened?" she demanded, and Elizabeth's eyes filled with tears before she lowered her head.

"Their ship was commandeered," Selbie offered with a soft voice, and Skylahr wrapped an arm around Elizabeth carefully as she shivered.

"We were looking for you," the human said. "After you and Barrick went overboard."

Sky shuffled closer and rubbed Elizabeth's back soothingly as she waited for the rest of the story. "We had heard Mira's shouting and the splash and knew something was wrong. But when we started for the stairs, we noticed it, that sweet song wafting through the walls of the ship, and the sea-maidens' voices were so enticing, we could hardly remember why we had been worried in the first place. Thankfully Mira had remained unaffected by their song, and when she saw us emerge from below deck, she had us stuff our ears with pieces of cotton before we began to pull the crew from the rail. But then more and more came, swarming us from every side, and I was sure that we had met our end."

Unwilling to watch from a distance any longer, I moved from my seat and carefully crossed the room until my shadow loomed over the women on the floor. I placed a wary hand on Sky's shoulder, not tightening my hold until she leaned back against my legs, almost as if she was needing whatever comfort I could offer her. Seeming to gather her strength, Sky then turned back to Elizabeth and waited while the mortal licked her split lower lip.

"Luckily, the cloth worked, and once we had woken the rest of the crew from their trance, they were able to find a dozen or so bows and managed to scare off the pool. But when the fog lifted you were nowhere to be seen, and we had no idea where we had drifted to." She sniffed again and then glanced down at her lap as she picked at her nails. "It wasn't much longer until the Siren's immortals found us, though to say they were disappointed would be an understatement."

"Disappointed?" I repeated, my fingers tightening in Sky's tunic, and it was then that Elizabeth seemed to notice my presence.

"Yes." She swallowed nervously. "They were looking for the Huntress's Chosen. They were looking for you, Sky." Not understanding, I glanced between the two friends and then my attention lifted to the halfling as she cleared her throat, and I immediately noticed the way the air around her felt heavy, like it was occupied by some unspoken power.

"They had heard that the two Chosen had been planning to set sail to Skohyn. Apparently, the lord from Ritari had passed along that information happily. It appears as though that his ask for help had been a ploy all along in hopes to draw you out from the north."

"Why?" I asked, my voice harsh as I peered into the halfling's dark eyes.

"Because the blood they took from her in Noordeign was not enough."

"You always said they had an obsession with the Huntress's blood," Elizabeth murmured quietly and then corrected herself. "Your blood."

"How did—" Sky began and then her eyes widened, like the answer suddenly came to her. "The attack before Bloomingdae?"

"It had been one of the Siren's followers, it seems," Selbie confirmed.

"And do we know what they needed her blood for?" Leena asked from beside the empty throne, and Sky looked back up at Selbie.

"The magic of the Siren's horn requires the blood of the man who first conjured the Second Gods." Skylahr pulled herself and Elizabeth to their feet and wrapped a steadying arm around her friend before focusing on the halfling once more.

"Horn?" she asked in confusion. All the scriptures I had read and the ones we had read together had never mentioned a horn of any sort. But as I thought back to the words of old, I realized the word *instrument* had been used, and multiple times at that.

"The conch shell on her banners, that is her horn." I could feel Skylahr's eyes on me, but I paid her no mind; I was too focused on the other detail I had stupidly overlooked.

"You said it needed the blood of the man who conjured the Second Gods, so why would they take hers?" I asked.

"It seems that the man who ventured to Vinmare to conjure the Second Gods was Caedell of House Reide, Skylahr's ancestor," Selbie answered. "The spelling of the name was probably changed after the shame he brought to his family. Especially considering they were a house of the Huntress. But even with the alteration, it does not change the fact that his blood runs through her veins."

I struggled to relax my face into the emotionless mask I had mastered, and I knew Skylahr could somehow still feel my surprise. Swallowing, I put that information away for now and then asked my next question. "And this horn, what does it do?"

"Well, it summons the Siren, of course."

No one moved, no one spoke, and we all watched Selbie carefully as she tucked her hands into her pockets. Not put off by the sudden attention, she moved her gaze from person to person, and then Leena finally stepped forward.

"Perhaps we should have the rest of this conversation elsewhere, brother," she suggested. "Somewhere more private."

Nodding, I peered down at Sky and then glanced at Elizabeth, my face softening as I took in the state of her. Her pale skin was littered with bruises, and one eye was nearly swollen shut. Whoever had found them had not held back, and a wave of rage washed over me as I pictured those immortals harming such a helpless being.

"I will have the curer come to see your friend and will ask for the kitchens to prepare something to eat. Meet me in my study as soon as you're ready."

"Why did we never think of her last name?" Leena asked as she leaned against the mantel of the fireplace, and Keyno moved in behind her, placing a gentle hand on her shoulder before pressing a kiss to the back of her head.

"It never mattered, nor does it now," I answered quietly, and my sister spun to face me.

"It doesn't matter?" she asked, bewildered.

"No, it doesn't," I replied, and Leena raised a slender brow.

"It *matters*, Kalian," my sister argued. "It matters because the conjuring of the Second was the beginning of the end for our Gods, and Skylahr is related to the man responsible."

Rolling my eyes, I moved to the window and leaned against the wall next to it, letting the warmth of the sun seep into me before lifting my gaze to my sister once more.

"Related?" I shook my head. "She is no more a Reide than I am."

"What are you talking about?" Leena snapped.

"It was her father's name."

"What is your point?" She ran a hand across her face in frustration.

"Her father who was human, Leena," I explained. "A father who loved, cherished her, and raised her. But not a father who actually sired her. That blood does not run in her veins."

"Then who is her father?" Keyno asked while his arms crossed over his chest.

"Apparently an immortal of the Huntress, but she doesn't know for certain, and pushing the subject won't help. It's a sore spot for her," I advised and then turned to the door when I realized I could hear the soft footfalls coming from the hall outside. Opening it wide, I invited the halfling through, and then Sky, who had Elizabeth in her arms. I rushed to pull a chair close, waiting for her to lower her friend into the seat before turning to her in question.

"The curer suggested she stay off her ankle as best she could, and I was in too much of a rush to watch her limp her way here," she explained and then turned her worried gaze on her friend. "She wouldn't tell me much more about what happened until we were all together."

"I'm not sure I can tell the story twice," Elizabeth explained with wet eyes. I nodded sympathetically, and then everyone settled into their places before she began.

"When they realized only the Healer was aboard, they began their questioning. Many of the crew remained strong and stoic, but as the days continued, more and more succumbed to the pressure. The problem was, however, no one knew where you were." Elizabeth looked up at Sky, and her face paled as the guilt hit her.

"Eventually there were only a few of us left. Gaelon often took the brunt of it. They tried to find new ways of pulling answers from him, but he said nothing. He didn't even scream when they—" She stopped and clenched her eyes shut. "Ella too suffered quietly, until they set their sights on me. Then she would plead and beg—"

Her words broke off in a sob, and Sky rushed to hold her, wrapping her strong arms around the girl as she rocked her back and forth.

"After days of this they finally decided we would tell them nothing, and I'm assuming they disposed of the remaining crew. When it came to me, however, they thought it would be a great game to listen to Ella's threats. She told them that you would come for the people responsible for our deaths, and I suppose that is exactly what they hoped for." She took in a long, shuddering breath and then sniffed. "So they unshackled me and tossed me into a boat before lowering me to the sea, and then they said if I made it back to my Huntress then it was our God's will and I should tell her of our friends' fates."

"How did you survive?" Leena asked, her hand clutching her mate's.

"A group of fishermen who had decided to venture out against their lord's warnings found me two days later. I was lucky no storm or creatures found me, though maybe it was less to do with luck and more to do with the fact the immortals wouldn't bother with a measly human."

"*They* wouldn't bother?" Sky asked. "What do you mean?"

"We were right, the immortals on Skohyn raised the beast from the waters. And not only that, but they also control it."

Chapter 43

"What of Gaelon and Ella?" Sky murmured softly, her eyes filling with tears that she desperately tried to blink away.

"I don't know for sure, but I am fairly certain they took them back to Skohyn." Elizabeth sniffed, ignoring her own tears that were now trailing over the bruises on her face.

"Do you think they would let them live?" Skylahr asked with a trembling voice, and my heart ached at the sound.

"If they were smart, they would keep them alive." It was Keyno who spoke now, and all eyes turned to him. "They will want a bargaining tool, a way to convince Hazel to come to them. The only way they are sure to do so is to make a deal for her friends' lives."

"Why make her go there?" Leena began. "Why wait for her on that island?"

"The island is a safe haven for them; they are familiar with it and its creatures and know visitors are not likely to find an upper hand should they decide to attack. Not to mention the fact that they can't leave Skohyn if they want to summon their Goddess; their horn cannot be removed from its place," Selbie answered. "They don't have the magic needed to do so."

"And how do you know this?" I asked suspiciously as I took her in, and when that power crackled, I knew. "You are a halfling in her name."

"I am." Selbie nodded, though her face grew tense. "But make no mistake, I do not side with them. I do not agree with what they have done."

"Why should we believe you?" Leena snarled, moving from the fireplace to stand before the three women.

"If I was lying, why would I come all the way here? Why would I risk telling you all of this? If you didn't believe me, it would be my head, and if you did and the others found out I was here, then my life is still at stake."

"So what, you came all this way to warn us against your own people and you are fine that this may lead to their end?" Leena scoffed, shaking her head in disbelief.

"I have spent my entire life in hiding from immortals, and yes, when I first heard that some of the Siren's people were gathering, I wanted to be a part of it," Selbie explained. "But that was before I knew what their plans were, before I was aware that they were willing to harm innocents to gain power. I am not willing to trade one evil for another, and so I came here in hopes of finding help."

My sister's gaze slid to mine, her dark eyes full of doubt, and I frowned, ready to press the halfling for more only to be interrupted by Skylahr.

"You three can decide to believe her or not, I don't care what your decision is, it makes no difference to me," Sky snapped, and then she stood and lifted those hazel irises to my face. "You sent three ships to Skohyn; the wisest time for me to follow would be now. Those men could aid me in bringing my friends home."

"Now just wait a minute," Keyno pleaded. "You can't seriously be thinking of running right into their clutches. Why not wait to see if our crews are able to bring your friends back? Or if a Chosen must go to negotiate, why not send Kalian? Then we do not risk them getting their hands on you, and it would be nothing for Kalian and a crew of men to handle considering there are, what, a hundred of them?"

"The numbers on the island may be few, but you forget that these men control the sea that is between you and the Healer," Selbie whispered. "They will not allow just anyone to pass, and even if some of your men manage to reach the shore, they would still need to survive the island itself. Besides, like you said, they need the Huntress; they will not make a deal with anyone else."

"Then it's decided," Skylahr said, her chin lifting as if she was daring us to challenge her. "I will leave for Skohyn at first light."

"With what ship?" Leena asked, her jaw clenching as she glared at the Huntress, and I could see worry hidden under the anger in her eyes and wondered when my sister had grown to care so strongly for her.

Clearing my throat, I glanced at Leena, praying she would not fight me on this. "She will take one of ours."

"Kalian, we have already sent three of our best," Keyno reminded me, and I turned my attention to him.

"Then it's a good thing we have an entire fleet, isn't it?" His mouth snapped closed as he crossed his arms. "We will take one of ours at first light and send out another three. Now go, gather whatever men we need and do not question me again on the matter."

"Yes, my lord." Keyno gave me an embellished bow and I glared at him as he straightened, not impressed by his attitude but unwilling to say anything, at least not at this time.

Storming from the room, Keyno left us with Leena chasing his heels, and when the door slammed shut, I sighed as I hung my head.

"Kalian," Skylahr began softly, coming to stand at my side, but I disregarded her worry and looked at her friends.

"The rooms next to the guard are empty, and I will have them prepared for you both. There will be warm baths drawn and food sent up." Standing shakily, Elizabeth attempted a curtsey, and then looked to Selbie, waiting for her to do the same.

Lowering my chin in return, I exhaled softly and then my eyes sought her out. "If you would excuse me, there's much to do before tomorrow."

The fire crackled quietly in the silence of the room, and I sighed as I sipped my wine, watching the flames as they danced in the dark. Keyno had left to get everything organized for the voyage tomorrow, and Leena had hidden away in her rooms, leaving me alone with my fear and worry.

Perching on the edge of my desk, I rubbed a hand across my jaw tiredly. A quiet knock came from the door, and I looked over my shoulder as Skylahr stepped into the room before shutting the door quietly.

She looked better; her face was less pale and her eyes were brighter, though I could still see the tension she carried, almost as if the weight was pressing down on those strong shoulders of hers. Feeling my gaze, she glanced at me nervously from the corner of her eye and then picked up the bottle on the desk before filling her own glass. She brought it to her mouth, and we both ignored the tremor in her hand as she swallowed the liquid in one gulp. I lifted a brow.

"If you're going to drink like that, why dirty a glass? You might as well just take it right from the bottle."

Her eyes narrowed as they locked on me, and she grabbed the wine once more before pouring another glass, though this time she barely tilted the bottle and we both watched the red trickle out of it slowly. Happy with the amount, she swallowed it down in the same fashion as before.

"I can get another bottle," I offered but she shook her head.

"That's not what I came for." Her voice was rough, nervous even, and I stood, grabbing her glass and the bottle before placing it on my desk. Now without having anything in her hands, she fiddled with her fingers as she chewed on her lower lip.

"What *did* you come for?" The words rumbled from me, and those striking eyes glowed in the firelight.

"You do not need to come with me tomorrow," she whispered. "They are not your friends, and you owe them—you owe *me* nothing."

"Is that it then?" I asked. "You came here to tell me I owe you nothing, when we both know that isn't true."

"Kalian…"

"And even if it was, do you honestly think those simple words would dissuade me?" I rolled my eyes and took a step forward, cupping the back of her head, letting my fingers weave through her hair before tipping her face up towards mine. "I do not follow you out of obligation, or whatever other fucking idiotic notion you have convinced yourself of. I follow you now, and will follow you always, for the rest of my days, because you have the only thing that matters."

"What are you talking about?" she asked with a frown, and I curled my fingers into a fist before pulling her to me, and then I bent to rest my forehead against hers while I peered down at her.

"You have my heart, Skylahr." Her eyes fluttered closed at my confession, but her face twisted, almost as if she was in pain. However, before I could say anything to remedy the hurt my words seemed to cause her, she lifted onto her toes and pressed her mouth to mine.

Long gone were the days of soft kisses and gentle caresses. Every time she kissed me now, it was almost as if she looked at it as a battle, and I had no choice but to allow her to take her victory.

Let her have it, I thought to myself. Let her have whatever she wants as long as she continued to press herself into me like that, like she couldn't bear for us to be parted.

Skylahr stepped back and dragged me along with her, turning us around until the backs of her legs were pressing against the solid wooden desk, and then rose on her toes just slightly so she could perch on it. Opening her thighs, she pulled me into the space between them and then lifted her knees so that they were tucked against my hips.

I rocked forward, moaning as my hardening cock pressed against the solid muscle of her thigh, and her lips lifted at the sound. Shuffling farther onto the hard surface, she arched her back, and I sucked her lower lip into my mouth before nipping at it with my teeth and then continued my journey across the edge of her jaw.

Her skin was warm and soft under my mouth, and I traced my

tongue down her throat, pausing when I got to the skin of her scar. The colour had faded, and the texture was not nearly as rough, but I hated that she would carry another. I hated that anyone would dare to blemish her in such a way.

"No, that does not belong here," she grumbled as her hand cupped my jaw before she pushed me away. "I do not want pity or softness, not now."

"Pity," I repeated. "Is that what you think this is?"

"Isn't it?" she snapped.

"Good Gods, Skylahr! Why must you always assume the worst?!" I snarled. "It's not fucking *pity*, it's anger! It's rage! I'm furious that someone would dare hurt what is *mine*!"

Her eyes widened in shock and then she spluttered, "Yours?"

"Mine," I repeated. "You are mine and I am yours. Wholly. Completely. And nothing you could say will change that."

Her gaze hardened and her mouth pressed into a thin line, but I would not hear her disagreement, not now, and I kissed her once more. Sliding my tongue along hers, I decided that this victory would not be hers after all, and I kissed her until I grew dizzy and then I pulled from her and grabbed at her hips.

Tugging her from the desk, I spun her around and then pressed a firm hand between her shoulders as I coaxed her down. Skylahr didn't fight me as she bent across the surface, and when she glanced over her shoulder at me, I paused.

"You are not looking for softness tonight?" I checked, and her lashes fluttered while a blush covered her cheeks. The sight of it had me growling. "Answer me."

Her mouth parted with a gasp, and then I watched as her fingers stretched, her hands turning into claws as they scratched at the wood while she shook her head.

"You want me to fuck you? Rut into you like an animal, is that it? Is that what you would have of me?" This time she nodded, and I grabbed a fistful of hair once more and tugged her head back. "Then say the words, sweeting."

"I want you to fuck me. Take me until I can't remember my own name and then fuck me some more." My blood heated, and I released the bronze strands before smoothing a hand across her spine. Upon reaching the waist of her breeches, I tugged the material down until they fell to the tops of her boots, and then I kicked her feet apart.

I stroked the backs of my fingers across her thighs, smirking when she shivered, and then I moved my attentions higher, sliding the tips across the soft skin of her ass before finally seeking out the wet warmth between her legs. Her whimper was barely audible, but it was enough to make my heart race, and I leaned forward, bracing one hand next to her face while I gently pressed into her tight heat with the other.

I could feel the little puffs of air against my wrist as I stretched her open, and her mouth widened as she moaned when I ran the tips along her wall, finding that soft little spot that made her squirm. Thrusting back into me, she pressed down on my fingers and I tsked under my breath.

"Patience, love," I scolded her, but she whimpered again, the sound high and needy.

"I want you in me." Leaning farther forward, I pressed my chest to her back while I brought my lips to her ear.

"I am in you," I whispered as I stroked into her roughly.

"Your cock, Kalian," she panted. "*Please.*"

Unable to do anything but comply, I pulled my fingers from her, waiting until those stunning irises met mine from over her shoulder, and then I brought them to my mouth. "Not pear jam, but just as delicious."

She was so far gone, too desperate for release that she didn't even bother to blush at my words. I pressed a kiss to her temple, then another to her ruined cheek and then one to the corner of her mouth while my damp fingers pulled at the laces of my breeches.

Once they slid to my knees, I grabbed the back of Skylahr's tunic and tried to lift it to her shoulders, but the material was already stretched as far as it would allow with her arms resting by her head.

Growling under my breath, I fisted the cotton with both hands and then tugged, ripping the material down the middle before pushing it from her skin.

Admiring the way her muscles moved under her pale skin, I pressed my mouth to a shoulder blade, then the other and up over a shoulder before resting my nose against her scarred cheek. I closed my eyes, stepped forward, and then lined myself up before flexing my hips. The first inch pressed into her with ease, but I stilled anyway, allowing myself to get lost in the feel of her, and Skylahr grunted, rising onto her toes as she tried to push back.

"Easy, love," I groaned, holding her hips tightly.

"More," she demanded in response.

"I need to go slowly this way, it's a tight fit," I cautioned her, but her nails scratched at the desk, and she shook her head.

"You promised, no softness." Exhaling roughly, I grabbed one shoulder while the other hand cupped her hip, and then I slammed forward, pressing the rest of my length into her. All of the air seemed to leave her lungs at my thrust, and I would have been concerned had it not been for the way she rocked back, grinding into me as she clamped down around my cock.

"Again. *Please*," she pleaded, and my lips ghosted across the skin of her ear as I smiled.

"You beg so prettily for me, love," I whispered, and then I repeated the action, pulling from her slowly only to thrust back in with force. Her whimpers grew in volume until she was calling out for me, and I had never heard anything so fucking *lovely* in all my life.

The muscles in her thighs began to tremble, and her cunt clenched desperately, as if she was trying to keep me from leaving her. Deciding she had suffered long enough, I brought my fingers to my mouth and rolled my tongue across them before wedging that hand between the edge of the desk and her hips. Finding her clit, I stroked her tenderly, keeping the rhythm soft and slow while I filled her over and over again, and then she was there, falling over the edge and dragging me along with her.

Collapsing onto her back, I nuzzled into her hair and closed my eyes as I fought to catch my breath. My heart still thundered and my own body shook, but my senses returned, and I carefully pulled from her as slowly as I could before picking up my breeches. After tying the laces once more, I bent to retrieve her own and pulled them over her legs before stepping away.

"Are you alright?" I asked as she turned to face me, and I noticed her unmarked cheek was bright pink from being pressed against the desk.

"I'm alright," she promised, and then her chin turned to her shoulder, and she frowned as the halves of her tunic began to slide down her arms. "Was that really necessary?"

"You said you didn't want soft," I reminded her with a smirk, and she rolled her eyes before she reached one arm around to her back and gathered the two pieces together.

"You'll need to replace this by tomorrow. I do not have any to spare," she growled.

"I'll be sure to bring trunks full, that way I can shred as many as I want."

Skylahr glowered at me, though I could see the heat in her eyes, and I lifted a brow, daring her to say something about my brilliant idea.

"You are certain you want to come?"

"I am." I nodded. "Will you fight me on it?"

Skylahr shook her head. "Not this time. I think I might need all the help I can get, and I'm not willing to let my pride get in the way of saving my friends."

"We will save them," I promised, and Skylahr nodded but lowered her eyes to the floor, and just as I reached out for her, she ducked away from my touch.

"Good night, Kalian," she whispered and then she left the room, the door clicking shut softly behind her.

Chapter 44

The smell of salt in the air was dampened by the drizzling summer rain, and I pulled my hood over my head, letting the deep navy wool shield my face as the men grabbed our trunks before carrying them on board. Leena and Keyno were standing off to the side, whispering quietly to each other, and I glanced at the dock, making sure that the women had not yet arrived before sighing.

This was a conversation I had been dreading. I knew my face must have shown my apprehension, because Leena's expression hardened when her eyes met mine.

"What is it?" she asked, and Keyno moved in beside her as his jaw clenched.

"I've decided that you two shall stay here," I murmured, readying myself for my sister's anger.

"What?" Her voice was barely audible, and I rolled my shoulders before reaching for her hands.

"You two are staying here," I repeated.

"Why?" Leena questioned, her anger and confusion evident in her tone. I looked at her mate, hoping he would be willing to side with me, but he too looked just as displeased with my choice.

"Because I need to know that I left our home in capable hands." I squeezed her fingers gently. "Mother is not here anymore, and you and I are all that is left of our family, Leena."

Her lower lip trembled just slightly, and I looked to Keyno. "And I would never trust anyone else with my sister's heart or safety. You are the only one who I can depend on."

"Kalian." Keyno swallowed, lifting a hand to cup my shoulder. "What if something goes wrong? What if—"

"Then you both will continue on." Leena's face paled and then she shook her head. "You will, you will live, and you will do what you must to protect our people, just as our mother would have."

Wrapping an arm around her, I pulled her to me and pressed a kiss to her hair and then glanced at my brother. "I do wish you luck dealing with her all by yourself though."

Pushing at my chest, Leena scoffed and then stuck her tongue out at me, and I was glad to see the sadness gone from her face. I stepped back from the two when I heard the soothing voice of Skylahr, and I turned, watching as she followed her guard, who had lifted Elizabeth to his chest before carrying her across the slick wood of the deck.

Noticing my frown as she closed the distance, Skylahr shook her head and gestured to the human in her arms. "She won't listen to reason, and Barrick refused to let me carry her."

"Don't start with that shit again, Skylahr Reed," Elizabeth snapped, unwrapping her arm from the guard's neck so that she could point a finger at her face.

"It's not safe and you are injured," she said softly, trying to appease her friend.

"Ella is there, and where Ella goes, I go," Elizabeth growled, her little face looking fiercer than I had ever seen it.

"I know you are worried, and I know you want to help but—" The human began to struggle in the man's hold, and Barrick carefully lowered her to her feet, his eyes widening when Elizabeth turned on Skylahr.

"I would never, *ever* ask you to stay behind if it was him." A thumb was jerked over her shoulder in my direction. Skylahr's face reddened as she glowered, and it took everything in me not to grin in triumph.

Refusing to let her eyes meet mine, Skylahr crossed her arms across her middle and then lowered her chin as she gazed down at her friend with concern. "Elizabeth, I'm a halfling, I heal."

"I know that," Elizabeth grumbled. "And I know that I am not as fast or as strong as you. But I can't wait here and wonder. I need to go with you, I need to be there."

"It's dangerous." Sky's voice grew more confident, but Elizabeth wouldn't hear it.

"It is, but I have you and I know you won't let anything hurt me. You promised, remember?" Skylahr's shoulders slumped in defeat, and she looked at Selbie and then Barrick before her eyes met mine. Holding her gaze, I gave her a single nod, making my own promise that I would look after them as well.

"Fine," Skylahr sighed. "But you will listen to whatever order Kalian or I give you." The human nodded before Skylahr could even finish her sentence, and I moved my eyes to Selbie.

The halfling stood with a straight back, but next to Skylahr she seemed quite small, and I took her in appearance under the overcast sky. Her dark skin was a stark contrast to the woman next to her, and I examined her pretty face and closely shorn black hair. She was probably about five and twenty, though there was something about her eyes that made her seem older, and the power of her ignite was a heavy presence that seemed to blanket her body.

"Are we ready then?" Sky glanced up at me, interrupting my observation, and I turned to the boat, checking to see if the crew had boarded before answering.

"Yes, it seems that way." Grabbing my sister, I hugged her tightly and then did the same to Keyno.

"Be safe," Keyno whispered.

"What he really meant to say is don't be an idiot," Leena corrected, and then she brushed past me to wrap her arms around Skylahr. I didn't know who was more surprised by the action, me, or the Huntress.

Returning the embrace, Sky patted Leena's back awkwardly and then was scooped up by Keyno. Bending backwards, he lifted her an inch off her feet and then pressed a quick kiss to her unmarked cheek.

"Say hello to the little one and give the Healer my regards. Tell them we will have the best wine in Denimoore ready for their return."

"I will," she promised, and then she stepped from his arms and grabbed Elizabeth's hand before leading the two women and her guard up the ramp.

I watched until they boarded safely, and then turned back to my family. "If the hafok returns before we are due to arrive, send him directly to us. I would like to end this with the least amount of bloodshed possible, and if our men beat us to the Healer, then perhaps we can force them to surrender peacefully."

"You think they'll give up the chance to rule the seas? They have the beast."

"I'm not sure they will think that the beast is worth their lives. I want to do this without violence, but if they refuse, I will do what I have to," I promised.

"Please just use whatever brain you have up there." Leena gestured to my head. "You and Skylahr are likely to end up killing yourselves like the two well-meaning, self-sabotaging idiots you are."

"That is quite a sweet farewell, sister," I snarked with a roll of my eyes, and then with one last kiss to her cheek, I boarded the ship.

The halflings and mortals were all anxious as we sailed across the calm ocean, their previous experiences obviously hanging over them like a dark cloud. I watched as Sky said good night to her friends before closing the door to the cabin, and then she was moving across the deck, though she seemed to sway a bit. Noticing the light sheen of sweat and the way her face appeared sickly pale, I met her halfway and placed the back of my hand against her cheek.

"No fever," I remarked softly, resting my hand against her forehead, and she batted it away.

"I'm not ill," she snapped, and my lips lifted into a smirk.

"You certainly look ill." Huffing, she blew a strand of hair out of her face, and I caught the piece of bronze before twirling it around my finger.

She pulled the lock from my grasp and then glanced at the soft waves. "I do not do well at sea."

"Really?" I asked in amusement, and she glared at me before shrugging.

"The constant rocking motion makes me feel sick," she admitted begrudgingly. "I've tried most remedies, ginger tea, mint leaves—nothing seems to really work."

"What about fucking?" I grinned slyly as the flush moved from her cheeks down to her chest.

Scoffing, she turned from me. "How would I know? Who would I have fucked last time?"

"The Healer?" The name slipped from my mouth before I could stop it, and I winced at my impulsiveness.

"You think Gaelon and I have done that?" Her brows lifted as she looked at me from the corner of her eye.

"Have you?" Now that the topic was out in the open, I couldn't keep my curiosity to myself.

"You sound rather jealous, Kalian," she pointed out, and I crossed my arms before nodding.

"I am," I confessed. "I am jealous of anyone who has been given a piece of your heart. Why do you think I punched Keyno in the face?"

"I was hoping that had nothing to do with me," she sighed. "It seems like such a stupid thing to fight over."

"Not to me," I disagreed. "Your smile, your laughter, hell even the way you look at me some days, like you want to rip me to shreds, is enough for me to survive on."

"Good Gods, you are dramatic," Skylahr scoffed.

"I was aiming for poetic." I grinned again, though this one was less sly and more sheepish, and then my smile faded, and I tilted my head in question. "When will you start to trust my words? What will it take for you to believe me?"

"What if I say it will never happen? What will you do then?" she wondered, and I took a minute to think on it before answering her.

"Then I will do everything in my power to prove to you that you can let me in."

"And if I decide that I want you to let it go? To let me go?" The idea made my heart ache, but I knew what measures I was willing to go to for her.

"Then I would do it. Say the words and I will do it."

I held my breath, waiting for them, but they never came. Instead she took a step closer and pressed a soft kiss to my mouth.

"Do you really think fucking will work?" Caught off guard, I repeated her question twice over to be sure I had heard her right, and then I grabbed her hand and pulled her in close.

"No way of knowing for sure unless we try."

Skylahr was warm as she tucked herself into me, and I smiled down at her when she nuzzled into my chest before pressing a kiss to her hair. The sea had remained calm, no storm, no sea-maidens, no war cry or beast, and though I had promised not to let her sleep after our vigorous round of fucking, I knew the farther we were from shore the less she would rest, and I wanted her to get as much sleep as possible.

Shifting her slightly in my arms, I kissed her once more and then slipped from under her. I tucked the blankets around her body, making sure she was settled, and then grabbed my breeches before tugging them on. I reached for one of the barrels of water, filled the wash basin on the table, and then unpacked the razor and oil before sinking into the chair.

"I thought I told you not to let me sleep," Skylahr grumbled, apparently woken up by my movements, and I watched her in the mirror before wetting my face.

"You needed it." I shrugged, not bothering to turn in my seat to face her when I lifted the razor to my jaw.

"Should you really be doing that while we are on the water?" She frowned, and I paused mid stroke.

"Why, are you worried for me?" I smirked, and she stood from the bed before wrapping the blanket around her naked body, and I let my disappointment show on my face.

"I'm worried you'll ruin your pretty face and then we'll just have to put up with your obnoxious mouth without the distraction the rest offers." Reaching behind me, I grabbed the blanket and tugged until she was close enough that I could pull her onto my lap.

"You didn't think my mouth was obnoxious when my tongue was buried between your thighs," I reminded her while wrapping an arm around her middle.

Skylahr's face turned that adorable shade of red, and she swatted at my shoulder but did not move from her perch, and I carefully adjusted her on my lap before beginning once more. "Worry not, I have had years of practice and my hands are steadier than most."

It was slightly more difficult navigating around her, but I wasn't willing to have her move, and so I took my time, watching my reflection from over her shoulder. Satisfied with my job, I tilted my head back and forth, making sure I had gotten all of the shadow, and then Skylahr lifted her fingers to my hair.

"You've let it grow out," she whispered as her hand carded through the black strands, and I pressed a kiss to the scar on her throat and then her ruined cheek.

"Gives you something to hold on to while you ride my face," I murmured against her skin, and I felt the flesh beneath my lips heat.

Lifting my eyes to her reflection, I noticed the way one bronze brow arched in response as she pouted. "Do you find joy in scandalizing me?"

"Maybe," I confessed. "But I mostly enjoy watching your skin turn that brilliant shade of red. I like to think of it as my own colour. We should call it Kalian's pink."

Rolling her eyes, Skylahr pulled from my arms and picked up her clothes before dressing. Sure she was as put together as she could be, she smoothed her hair and then cleared her throat.

"I am going to see whereabouts we are and check on my friends." Sliding my tongue over my lower lip, I took in the fluffed bronze waves and the marks that littered her collarbones.

"Be sure to tell them you found a remedy for your sickness." She didn't dignify my comment with an answer, but I was lucky enough to see that flush darken before the door slammed.

"I have a question." Elizabeth frowned as she picked at her food a little while later, and Sky looked at her uncertainly. "How will we make it to the island? What if the beast comes after us on our way?"

"It is a possibility," I sighed, my chest tight with worry. "We will need a diversion."

"What kind of diversion?" Skylahr's voice was quiet and trembling, and I reached for her hand under the table and gave her fingers a squeeze.

"Ideally, the other three ships are making the same progress. Their arrival along with the others we had sent out before our departure will be enough of a distraction that the beast will not focus on us."

"And when we reach shore?" Elizabeth asked. "Are you not worried at all about the island itself?" I was. Of course I was. I would be an idiot not to be. I had heard the legends of Skohyn, the island of torment. Over the years the tales had even reached Denimoore, some more gruesome than others, but all ending with the same warning: men who journeyed there never returned.

"The island itself will be difficult to navigate, I am sure, but I have no doubt we will make it through." My eyes turned to the human, and I smiled softly at her. "I am amongst two of the fiercest warriors I have ever seen. Do not forget that I was with you at the battle of the shores, Elizabeth. I have no doubt that you will help us with whatever we face."

My pleasant words were enough to placate her fears for the time being, and Skylahr gave me a small, grateful smile, which I returned. Turning to the mush of warm oats and dried meat, I swallowed down a few bites and then sipped on my wine as the three women chatted quietly.

However, just as I lifted the final forkful to my lips, I felt a warm palm on my knee. I glanced at Skylahr from the corner of my eye as I reached beneath the table. Entangling my fingers with hers, I held her hand tightly, ignoring the way my heart warmed at the show of affection and her own pale cheeks pinked at my touch.

Chapter 45

The night sky was darker than I imagined it would be at sea, though perhaps I had just grown used to moonlight that bounced off the mountaintops or the bright white snow that shone, even on the darkest of nights. The sea was nothing like the north; the vast open ocean was a mirror, but the tiny stars that littered the sky offered no light in their reflection. As I gazed out at the dark nothingness, I prayed.

I prayed to the Gods of old for wisdom, for guidance, but mostly for mercy. I prayed that they would protect Skylahr and watch over her friends.

I didn't bother praying for myself.

"The sea has been agreeable, my lord," the captain called from the quarter deck, and I looked up at him and gave him a nod. "I would expect for us to be there within the next two days if it continues to be this way."

That was both a relief and a discomfort. I so badly wanted to reach the shores; I wanted to see the sadness and worry Skylahr had been carrying lifted from her. But I couldn't help but acknowledge the sense of foreboding that grew stronger as more time passed.

"You feel it too?" Selbie asked as she approached, and I looked at her from over my shoulder. "What do you think it means?"

"I'm not sure we want to know." I exhaled and waited for her to stand next to me.

"But there is something you are wanting to ask me," she stated plainly.

"You are a clever girl." I chuckled under my breath, ignoring the way she bristled at the words.

"Well, are you going to ask me, Protector? Or are you going to continue to watch me from afar, deciding if I am a threat or not?"

"I can promise you, you are no threat to me." My words rumbled from my chest, and I lifted my chin, peering down at her until she looked away. "Tell me again why you are turning on your own kind?"

"My own kind? Is that what they are?" She shook her head as she laughed dryly. "My own kind who turned a blind eye to my suffering and the suffering of the other halflings for years. Who would not risk their lives for any one of us, even when you and the others gathered at the shores. But now they seek to overthrow the peace you fought for? Those are not my people."

"But Skylahr is?"

"Yes." She nodded. "She fought for those who could not fight for themselves. She did the impossible and wanted nothing in return. She is what a leader, a ruler—no, what a *Chosen* should be."

"She is," I agreed. "She is all of those things."

"Then you know why I want to help her, why I want to stop the Siren's immortals who have risen against you. I cannot watch them fill the place of the Crimson Goddess; I won't let that happen."

"You think that is their plan?"

"I think that has always been their plan. I think they have just been biding their time until the moment came, and now they want to resurrect their Goddess and rule in the Seductress's stead."

Seeking out my own distraction from the conversation I had with Selbie, I quietly made my way to her cabin, praying that I would not be caught. I truly did not have the patience for pleasantries right now. Nearing her door, I lifted my hand to grab at the handle when

I heard a quiet creak. I glanced over my shoulder, my eyes catching Barrick's as he glared at me disapprovingly.

"It's late," he murmured, and though the man was centuries younger than me it still felt as if I had been caught by a guardian of some sort, and I still blushed at his knowing stare.

"It is," I agreed, clearing my throat before my mouth lifted in a smirk. "Sleep well, sir. I will be sure to."

After throwing open the door as quickly as I could, I entered her room, leaned against the thick wood, and then I studied her. She was lounging back on her bed, her legs crossed at the ankles with a book of maps balanced on her chest, and I smiled at the sight before moving across the room.

Standing at the foot of the bed, I waited for those hazel eyes to meet mine, and then I tugged my tunic over my head and stepped out of my boots before resting one knee on the mattress. Skylahr lowered the atlas and peered at me from over the pages and then lifted a foot to press against my chest, stopping my pursuit.

"Breeches too," she commanded, and my brows rose, though I happily followed the order. Watching me untie the knot, she tugged her own down her thick legs, throwing them to the floor once she was free from the material, and then she crawled to me.

"I want to try something," she said softly, that crimson flush deepening as she glanced down at my hardening cock, and I cupped her chin carefully in my palm before stroking my thumb over her lower lip.

"Anything," I promised.

"I want to try— I want to use my mouth." She huffed out a deep breath in frustration and then her eyes met mine. "I want to taste you, if that's okay." The words were not purred out in a seductive manner nor were they confident, but something about the soft request had me trembling.

"You don't have to," I whispered, but her chin lifted, and I could see heat fill her eyes.

"I want to." She swore and then she glanced down at my length once more. "But I'm not sure I know how to do it. I'll need you to guide me."

Swallowing roughly, I fought to catch my breath and then nodded. "Alright."

Moving from the bed, she directed me back a step and then began to lower herself to the floor, but I grabbed her shoulders, halting her movements. "Wait a minute."

Reaching past her, I snatched one of the pillows from the bed and tossed it to my feet. Glancing at the floor, she parted her lips in surprise, and I ducked my face, catching her mouth with mine for a heated kiss, and then I threaded my fingers through her hair.

"Are you sure?" I asked once more. "I don't want you to think you are obligated, or that I expect anything from you."

"Kalian," she sighed in frustration, "I am about to kneel at your feet and wrap my mouth around your cock. Do you want to keep discussing it, or can I start?"

"And here I thought you were unsure about the whole thing." Not bothering to respond, Skylahr sank to her knees, shuffling a bit on the pillow before looking up at me, and then she wrapped a hand around my length. It was not soft and delicate like most women's; it was warm, rough, and calloused from years of farm work and holding a sword, but nothing had ever felt so fucking good.

Taking a deep breath, she started, but the first stroke was slow and a little too soft, so I reached down to curl my fingers around her own. "Tighter, like this."

Chewing at her lower lip, she watched the motion carefully and then nodded, and I grasped her hair once more, groaning as she mastered the rhythm. Growing more confident, she slid forward and pressed a single kiss to my head, letting her tongue graze the underside just slightly before closing her lips around me.

"Holy Gods." My head fell back as I groaned, my fingers tightening in her hair, but when my hips pressed forward too quickly, Sky whimpered and then retreated.

"Shit," I cursed and ran my fingers over her damp lower lip.

"Sorry, I'm sorry."

"It's fine, I just wasn't expecting it." Her hand fisted me once more as she peered up at my face. "Can I keep going?"

"Please," I begged, and her answering smile was sly before she continued. As always, Skylahr was a quick student, and soon that heat at the base of my spine grew, and I opened my eyes, blinking down at her as she hollowed out her cheeks.

"I'm close," I warned, but her eyes narrowed in determination, her pace quickening, and then I was spilling into her mouth with a pathetic little whimper while my thighs trembled.

"Good Gods!" I panted, my fingers now smoothing her hair back behind her ears, and she smiled, obviously satisfied with herself, before licking her lower lip.

"I'm not sure our Gods would be pleased to have you calling for them at a time like this." She laughed softly, the sound warming my heart, and I bent forward, grabbing her jaw before I urged her to her feet so I could kiss her.

"I think you're mistaken." I grinned against her lips as I wrapped an arm around her waist and then lifted her from the ground. "I think they would be applauding that performance."

Her face burned while I carried her to the bed, and I gently tossed her onto the blankets. "But I think it's time they hear from you."

Chapter 46

It had been days since Skylahr had last come to my bed or invited me to hers. Days since she had reached out for me. Days since I last touched her skin or kissed her lips or even held her, and now I frowned as she paced across the deck nervously, constantly gazing out at the waters as we neared our destination. I suppose the distraction I was able to offer had worked, for a time, but now she had closed herself off from me, from all of us.

"She's always been this way," Elizabeth whispered from beside me, and I examined her from the corner of my eye. "She shuts the people she loves out when she feels like things are slipping from her control."

"What can I do?" I itched to go to her, to grab her shoulders and drag her to me before holding her tightly, but I was sure that would do nothing but earn me a blackened eye.

"The only thing you can do is be here." Elizabeth shrugged. "She'll come to us when she's ready."

"You're sure?" I asked doubtfully, and those dark eyes moved to me, her healing face unreadable as she examined my own closely.

"What are you worried about?" she wondered, and then she exhaled roughly. "You think now that she's turned you and your attentions away, you won't get her back."

"I know that our time together was fleeting, I just thought I would have longer," I whispered, my attention turning to the Huntress once more.

"I can't say anything for certain in regards to what she will decide after this is all over..." Elizabeth paused, her own focus now captured by Sky's movements. "But I can tell you she still feels something for you, and those feelings have not wavered or weakened over time, even when she wished they would."

"Has she said as much?" I wanted to believe her, I was desperate to, but I had repeated my love for Skylahr over and over again without receiving a response. She had never once said the words back.

"No," Elizabeth confessed. "But I still know it to be true."

"I wish I was so sure," I admitted, and then noticed that Skylahr had paused her pacing, and both her and Selbie were looking towards the misty horizon.

Following their gaze, Elizabeth and I turned to the sea and scanned the waves, noticing the shapes in the distance. We were still too far to know for certain what they were, but based on the way the crew on the deck had grown quiet, I could only assume we were near.

"It certainly doesn't look like a place of legends." I frowned as I squinted at the fog.

The human nodded. "Let's hope the other myths are just as disappointing."

I could now admit that I had been wrong in my assessment of the island as we sailed through the narrow channels between the massive sea stacks. The mist had not lifted but rather grew heavier, and I lifted my hood over my head as I gazed at the mighty rocks that surrounded the island.

The stones were a deep black, their edges rough and sharp from the waves that had eaten away at them over the years. Tipping my head back, I took in the way they reached for the sky, almost as if they were desperate for the warmth of the sun, and I wondered how long it had been since they had felt it.

"No wonder most men do not make it back to Elrin," Sky whispered in wonder as she too seemed entranced by the pillars.

"It would take a very skilled captain to weave their way through," I agreed, and then I moved my attention to the island itself. "Thankfully we have one."

"I think we should be more grateful for the fact that your magic worked. I don't think we have been noticed yet," Elizabeth said as she pointed to the island, and I nodded.

From what I could see there was not a soul in sight, and I finally felt some of my worry disappear as we neared the shores. We had made it without drawing the attention of the immortals or their beast; our plan had worked. I turned to Sky, ready to celebrate, when I heard it.

It was a screaming noise, high in pitch and so loud my teeth vibrated as it surrounded us. I bent in half as I lifted my hands to cover my ears, and then I looked to the captain in panic. But the man was also struggling under the noise, his own eyes clenched shut as a massive gust of wind took the sails, and then the ship rocked roughly as a wave rammed into us.

Slipping across the wet wood, I struggled to get my feet under me, and then I turned to Skylahr, reaching for her as she too stumbled to the floor.

"What was that?!" she yelled over the wind, her eyes wide with panic as she searched the deck for her friends.

Both women and Barrick appeared to be okay, though they were obviously shaken, and Skylahr gathered the women close and turned to her guard just before another wave collided with us. This one was so large the whitecaps poured over the side of the ship and then we were drifting sideways, the vessel losing its path until it crashed into one of the sea stacks with an echoing crack.

Holding my breath, I watched as the silver sail blew against one of the stone towers, the material catching on its sharp edge, and then it was ripping, the fabric shredding as we rocked once more until the ship finally settled on a slight angle against the black rock.

Cursing under my breath, I moved towards the sea stack, though

I had no idea what I planned to do. However, as I reached the edge, I could hear the soft humming, the sweet sound echoing around us, and though I did not feel the same legendary pull, I knew what it was.

"Put your hands over your ears!" I screamed, glancing down at the water just in time to see the flash of scales.

"Cover your ears!" I repeated, backing away as I grabbed the dagger on my belt. I was not positive how my magic would work when it came to their song, but I wasn't willing to take any chances, and as more of them swarmed I tried to think of a plan.

But I was too slow. It was too late; the shouting had already begun. Some of the men were screaming orders at each other as they struggled to protect themselves from the flurry of spears that were now being hurled at us while others had been too close to the edge and were plucked from the ship only to be pulled down into the dark waters below.

"What do we do?!" Skylahr yelled, her voice panicked as she tugged her friends closer to her before squatting low, and I searched the deck for something useful.

"Get the nets!" I gestured to the bundles lying near the women, and Skylahr grabbed a hold of them before crawling to me, only faltering when one of the men crumpled to the floor next to her, his face covered in blood from the spear that had pierced one of his eyes.

"Hurry!" I called as I turned to one of the lanterns that had hung near the door of the cabin. Reaching me, Skylahr held out a shaking hand, and I snatched the nets from her before crouching near the rail. Glancing over the wood, I took in the number of sea-maidens and then threw the mesh over the side.

Holding my breath, I waited for it to catch, ignoring the screams of the creatures as they flailed against the web, and then I opened the bottom of the lantern into the waters, watching as the oil spread across the surface. But it was not enough, and I turned to Skylahr once more.

"I need more oil! Grab whatever lanterns and torches you can find and bring them here!" Sky nodded and turned to the cabin, slipping on the blood that now spilled across the deck as more and more of my men fell.

Catching onto our plan, Barrick carefully guided Elizabeth and Selbie back into a corner of the boat where they would have the most shelter and then followed behind Sky. The screaming continued from both the men and the sea, and I swallowed down the burning acid that had crept up the back of my throat while my head pounded from the sound.

"Here!" Sky ran to me, her arms filled with a dozen glass lanterns, and I took them from her before tossing them over the side. The glass shattered against the scaled bodies, and then I took the burning wick I had held on to and waited for Barrick to bring me the torches he had found. After lighting each of them, I held his eyes for a second and nodded, and then we stood, bracing ourselves against the rails before tossing the flames over.

The thick oil caught immediately, the fire spreading over the surface, and the sea-maidens struggled, their bodies thrashing as they attempted to escape their fate.

"We can't stay here!" I screamed, bracing myself as another gust of wind blew into us, making the ship groan from its force, and I grabbed Skylahr's pale hands as I pulled her along with me to gather the surviving men.

"We have to get off this ship before the fire spreads!" The remaining three men looked nervous but nodded grimly. "Go down to below and fetch whatever rations and items you can manage. We will get the smaller boats into the water on the other side of the ship and take them to shore, but we must hurry. The fire is spreading, and I am sure more sea-maidens will be on their way."

The men dispersed all at once, and I turned to Skylahr, lifting my fingers to the buckles on the silver armour she had dressed in at sunrise. Frowning, she batted my hands away, but I grabbed her fingers, forcing her arms to her sides before starting again.

"If something happens it will be difficult enough as it is to swim without this weighing you down." Her face paled and then she began fumbling with one shoulder while I focused on the other, and we removed the breastplate before handing it off to one of the men.

Ushering them to the side of the ship, I waited for the men to pull at the thick ropes, dropping the boats into the rocking waters, and then the ladders were unrolled, and I helped the women begin their descent towards the sea.

Once Selbie and Elizabeth were seated, Sky lifted a leg over the rail, ready to start her own climb down, when I surged forward and cupped her face in my hands. Pressing my mouth to hers, I kissed her roughly and then stroked my thumb across the scar on her cheek.

"Sit down and arm yourselves. Have everyone face out towards the water, and keep an eye on all sides. It will all be fine," I promised, even as I choked on the smoke and smell of rotting flesh, and Skylahr nodded shakily. Holding my breath, I waited until she had reached the boat, and then I ushered Barrick forward, waiting until he was halfway before I followed.

I rushed down the rope ladder, took the guard's offered hand, and then fell into my seat before grabbing the two pairs of oars. I handed one set to Barrick while I took the other, and we began to row, cursing as the tide knocked us about.

It seemed to go on for hours, the sea never resting as we neared the shore, but just as the bottom of the boat began to scrape against the sand, that sickening cry that made my hair stand on end sounded again.

"Where is it?!" Skylahr yelled, frantically searching around us, and then she was throwing herself over the side and racing towards the shore.

"Skylahr!" I screamed, tossing the oars to my feet before jumping into the frigid water and following her.

Ignoring my calls for her to stop, she continued running across the sand and towards the rock and moss before us. Scurrying up the steep incline, she all but crawled on her hands and knees, scrambling towards the edge that overlooked the water, and then she stopped, her dripping wet cloak billowing in the wind as she stood tall, and it was then that I could see it.

Just past her shoulder I could make out its shape: the massive stone body that towered over the sea stacks and the vivid glowing orange eyes that scanned the waters. Throwing its head back, the creature screamed again, the noise so loud that the earth below my feet shook, and then it was lowering an arm, and its enormous hand swung at something on the water before lifting it to its face.

Watching it carefully, I recognized the silver sails that hung between its fingers and finally realized what it had plucked out of the ocean. It was one of the other ships I sent out in hope of creating a diversion. I grabbed Skylahr's shoulders, leaning against her as the creature closed its fist, crushing the ship and its crew to dust.

"Good Gods," she gasped, her body trembling under my hand. "It's real."

The monster screamed once more before collapsing back beneath the waves, the weight of it forcing the whitecaps to triple in size, and we stood there, watching the entire scene unfold in silence until we heard Elizabeth and Barrick calling our names. Turning to the path we had taken, I watched as the two women and the guard ducked against the wind, and I pulled at Skylahr, turning her away from the waters to face me.

"We need to get to the shelter of the trees and make camp before the immortals come looking." Skylahr didn't seem to hear my words, the shock of what had just happened obviously too much for her to absorb, and I took her face in my hands, forcing her eyes to meet mine. "It will be night soon and we cannot navigate our way through this island in the dark."

Her face was pale, and her eyes were wet, but she didn't fight me as I dragged her into the cover of trees.

Chapter 47

We waited at the treeline for what seemed like ages, our eyes searching the shore for one of the remaining boats, but there was no sign of the other men, and clouds of smoke billowed from the ship we had abandoned.

Knowing that we did not have much more time to wait, I scanned the sea once more before turning to Barrick. The guard looked just as disheartened as he squinted against the wind, and then he glanced back at the women, who were huddled together amongst the trees.

"We should find whatever shelter we can for the night," he suggested, and I sighed, scanning the waters one last time before nodding.

"Still no sign of any others?" Skylahr asked, her lower lip trembling, and I shook my head. "I'm so sorry, Kalian."

"It is not your fault," I assured her while cupping her shoulder, noticing immediately how cold and wet the cotton was.

"We should go a distance in," Barrick recommended, his eyes darting to Elizabeth as she shivered, and I frowned at the human. The dropping temperature would be unpleasant but would not cause me to fall ill, but she, however, would easily catch a chill.

Nodding, I looked back at the guard. "Take down as many branches as you can to cover the ground. It will help with the mud, though we will need to find a way to get warm."

"A fire would be too risky in the dark," Sky interrupted as she tucked her friend under her arm. "I learned that lesson the hard way."

My chest constricted when I realized what she was talking about, and I thought back to when I found her dangling from the rafters, her body swaying as the immortal taunted and tortured her. Swallowing roughly, I approached her and then directed the women into the trees.

"No fires," I promised as we ducked through the brush.

Finding a decent-sized clearing between the trees, we began to layer branches, covering the mud as best we could before the women fell to the ground in a heap, and Barrick watched as they nestled close. Shivering between the two halflings, Elizabeth blew on her hands in an attempt to warm them, and Skylahr watched her every move worriedly.

I pulled my tunic over my head, dropped it to the ground, and then began to tug at my laces until they unknotted, and Barrick's dark eyes widened in panic as I hooked my thumbs under the material.

"What in the hell are you doing, boy?!" he snarled, moving to stand in front of the women as if he meant to block them from seeing me.

"Trust me, in a minute you'll be thanking me for the show." I winked. "Just be sure to keep those breeches with you or you'll be far more scandalized than you're about to be."

Toeing off my boots and stepping out of my breeches, I turned from the group and then closed my eyes. Letting myself feel that fire, the one so similar to the ignite I conquered when I was a halfling, I waited until it flooded my veins, and then I felt those muscles shift and my bones change. It was quick, no more than a second, but it was still pure agony.

Falling forward onto my paws, I panted for a moment, waiting for the trembling to cease, and then I looked down at the guard. Barrick's eyes were wide as he gazed up at my face, and I let my tongue loll out of my mouth before running it across his bearded cheek.

"Fuck off!" he snapped while lifting his arm to wipe his face, and I yelped at him in response before moving past him.

Carefully approaching, I hovered a foot or two away from the trio, not wanting to spook Skylahr's friends, and she smiled softly at me before reassuring the women. "It's alright, he won't hurt you."

Waiting until she nodded, I then moved in behind and fell to my belly, pressing myself against them until they sank into my fur. I wouldn't be as effective as a fire, but I would be able to keep them warm, and Elizabeth sighed before she buried her face into my ribs.

"You're so soft," she hummed tiredly, and I exhaled before nudging my nose under Skylahr's arm. Understanding my request for affection, she huffed impatiently but still stroked the fur between my ears.

"You're no better than Reif when you're like this." My tail thumped at her words, and she tweaked one of my ears in response before leaning close. "Just promise me you won't piss on Barrick's boots."

The sky had not cleared as the night went on, but there had been no war cry coming from the sea or any other sounds. There were no creatures, no immortals, and I kept my eyes focused, constantly scanning the trees for any signs of threats that may appear. But none came, and when Barrick's snores finally began, I let myself relax.

"Maybe a fire wouldn't have been that bad. Surely if there was anyone near, they would hear that man. There is no possible way they wouldn't notice all that racket." Skylahr laughed quietly but made no move to wake her guard, and I nuzzled into the softness of her belly before resting my chin on her lap.

"I am sorry about your men, Kalian," she said softly. "I am sorry you have had another loss."

More than one, I wanted to say. There were two ships we saw being taken over by creatures of the sea, but what about the first three I had sent here? There were no signs of them, and somehow, I knew that they too had perished.

"Do you still think Gaelon and Ella are alive?" she asked, the words catching in her throat, and I rolled my head against her stomach once more, offering as much comfort as I could.

"Don't give up now, Huntress," Barrick called from his place across from us while squinting open an eye. "Those two are made of stronger stuff than you give them credit for."

Sniffing, Sky nodded her head and began her petting once more. Watching her carefully, the guard sat up and rubbed at his face tiredly before focusing on me.

"You should get some sleep, Protector," he suggested. "I can take the next watch."

I wanted to argue, of course, tell him that his hearing and other senses were dull compared to mine and I didn't need nearly as much rest as he did. But the soft strokes of Skylahr's fingers and the warmth the three women provided had begun to lull me into a state of exhaustion, and I growled quietly in answer before closing my eyes.

The conditions the next morning had not improved as the rain began as soon as the sky lightened, and I shook my fur out before shifting once more. Remaining in my Lupine form may have been ideal for hunting and tracking, but I wasn't able to communicate with the others, and the growing restlessness of the group had made me too antsy to remain as a beast.

"If they have the Healer and Miss Ella, where would they keep them?" Barrick asked, his eyes bouncing from each face until they settled on Selbie.

"I don't know," she confessed. "I have never been here, and I did not follow the others to the coast before they travelled."

"Kalian, what do you know of the island and the temple once used to worship the sea Goddess?" Skylahr whispered.

"I know that there was once a grand temple constructed here, but as far as where, that I cannot say." It was not what she wanted to hear, but it couldn't be helped.

"Okay, so where would we begin?" It was Selbie who spoke this time, but I was too busy watching the way Elizabeth had turned to the east, not bothering to even look at the halfling.

"What is it?" I asked, and the human jumped and then her brow furrowed.

"The immortals who commandeered the ship often spoke to one another before they began their interrogations. It was always in the tongue of old, but they often repeated a word. It sounded like *cruinllach*."

"The summit," I translated, and then I lifted my head to the mountain peak that was visible past the trees. "They must be talking about that."

"It would make sense." Barrick frowned as he too turned his eyes to the cliff. "It would be a difficult place to reach, which would allow the immortals to keep the scriptures and this horn of theirs safe. Probably allows the person a great view of the ocean as well."

Taking in a deep breath, Sky grabbed my fingers, and I interlocked them with my own, showing her that I was here, that I was by her side. Gazing up at me from the corner of her eye, she offered me a gentle nod and cleared her throat.

"Then that is where we go."

Chapter 48

"This is a Godsforsaken place," Barrick cursed as he continued to blow at the kindling he had yet to actually light, and I pulled on my breeches before tossing Sky the animal I had caught. I wanted to say it was a rabbit, but to be honest, I couldn't be sure. I had never seen anything like it before. It was the size of a small pig but had the ears and the fur of a rabbit, or a squirrel maybe, and Sky looked at the body with interest before she rolled it onto its back.

"Think it will taste like rabbit?" Elizabeth asked, her nose wrinkling as Sky began to skin it.

"We'll never know if he doesn't figure out how to get that fire lit," Selbie grumbled, and Barrick stood with his arms crossed.

"First you lot decide that a fire is a bad idea, and now you complain that I'm not doing it fast enough. Make up your damn minds."

"It's daylight, we probably won't draw that much attention right now, and we will keep it small." Elizabeth shrugged before she looked to me, and I nodded.

"Yes, we'll keep it small," Selbie agreed and then glared at Barrick. "That is if we ever get one. We might starve first."

"It's not so easily done, halfling," he spat, and she snorted in reply.

"I offered to do it, but you refused. Apparently, you have something to prove." Selbie rolled her eyes, and I looked between the two of them before dropping to my knees. I took the dagger from Sky, pushed her bloody hands away, and tilted my head to her friends.

"I'll finish, you just focus on keeping those two from killing each other." Skylahr glanced at her friends from over her shoulder and then dipped her chin.

"I think I'd rather do this," she whispered sheepishly, and I laughed under my breath before nudging her with my shoulder.

"Don't be a coward," I chided and her mouth parted.

"Me a coward? What about you? Coming over here like some scared little boy, needing me to deal with two people who are hundreds of years younger than you." She was right, but it didn't change my mind, and I nudged her again.

"Go," I pushed, grinning when she huffed in frustration.

"Fine, but you owe me," she grumbled as she stood, and I tilted my chin up, tracing her from her toes all the way up to those hazel eyes, and then I winked.

"And I'm happy to discuss all the ways I can repay you later." Her face flushed, but she did not dispute my offer, and I smiled to myself as I watched her get between her two friends.

"Selbie, why don't you and Elizabeth go fill the wineskins with some water. Barrick, you collect more wood, and I will get this fire started." Neither moved for a moment, and Skylahr placed her hands on her hips and narrowed her eyes, making it clear that she was not asking.

Deciding to avoid another argument, the three went about their duties, and she knelt on the ground and rearranged the twigs and leaves before she began to strike the rock with her dagger. Taking care to pull the meat from the fur, I hummed quietly under my breath, a soft melody my mother used to sing, and Sky stopped what she was doing to look at me.

"What is that you're singing?"

"A hymn of the Protector, my mother's favourite." Her eyes lowered back to her blade, but she nodded.

"I thought I recognized it. She used to sing it when she braided my hair while I was at Denimoore." They were painful memories for the both of us, and we remained quiet as we continued working.

But the silence went on for too long, and I immediately noticed the change in the air when everything became too still. Standing, I glanced around, my obvious change in demeanour alerting Sky that something was wrong, and she also moved to her feet.

"What is it?" she asked, her eyes roaming around the trees, but I lifted a finger, signalling her to be quiet. I could hear a faint rustling in the distance and then a voice called out.

"Skylahr!" Elizabeth screamed, her voice high and shrill with panic. We both had moved towards the sound when the guard called for her as well in the opposite direction.

Not knowing where to go, she caught my eyes and then pointed behind me. "Go find Barrick, I will meet you back here!"

"No!" I shouted, my instincts screaming at me not to let her out of my sight. "I won't leave you."

The screaming for her started again, and she ran to me, pushing at my chest roughly. "I can't choose one over the other. I need you to go to Barrick! Please! Go!"

Not knowing what else to do, I spun on my heel and let the heat consume me once more until I was running through the forest on four legs rather than two. Weaving through the trees and bushes, I hunted for the guard, focusing on any sound that caught my attention while making sure to trace his scent.

However, just as I reached where he had obviously been collecting wood, the scent had weakened, almost as if he had been carried or picked up somehow, and I looked around the area. There were no signs of an obvious struggle, but the smell of horse was strong, and there were hoof prints leading east.

I had two choices: I could turn back to Sky empty-handed, knowing that it would crush her to lose another friend, or I could go after the assailant. In the end it wasn't a difficult choice. I knew that I had to do what Sky would want me to. I had to save her guard, and then we would circle back and meet at camp.

Following the tracks, I pushed myself as hard as I could go, dodging whatever was in my path as I closed the distance between us, and through the trees, I could just make out the flanks of the grey mare as the sound of hoofbeats echoed in the air.

Lengthening my stride, I closed in, and set my sights on the riders. Barrick was in the front, but his arms were bent behind his back in an awkward angle, indicating that his hands were tied, and there was a piece of cloth wrapped around his head. It was most definitely a gag, and I wondered how long they had been watching us. It had to be a while for them to be so prepared, and the thought only fueled my rage.

Moving left, I quickly caught up to the horse before I launched myself at its jugular and took the animal to the ground. The kill was quick and painless, and when it was done, I turned to the two men who had crashed to the forest floor.

Barrick was still, his eyes clenched shut in pain, but at least he was alive. The other, however, was crawling through the mud on his hands and knees, obviously trying to gather his wits before moving to his feet. But I did not give him the chance. As soon as his eyes lifted to mine, I opened my massive jaws and clamped down on his head, tearing it from his neck with a quick jerk.

Turning from the corpse, I padded to Barrick and then took a deep breath as I forced my body to change. I fell to my knees, grabbed at his gag, and pulled it down before reaching behind him. After untying his hands, I backed up a few paces, waiting for the colour to return to his face before I spoke.

"Are you alright?" His dark eyes widened at me, almost as if he couldn't believe I would ask him that, and then he glanced at the headless man.

"I have seen a lot of death in my days, but I could have gone without seeing that," he whispered as he rubbed at his head.

"Next time I save your life, I'll be sure to ask if you have a preference on how to do it," I remarked dryly, earning me another sharp glare as he moved unsteadily to his feet, turned to the horse, and unclipped the saddle bags.

"Where is the Huntress?" he asked when he was done, his eyes searching the forest behind me.

"She's meeting us back at camp," I answered hoarsely, praying that the words were true, but the guard did not look convinced.

"Is she alright? I was certain there was more than one immortal." Panic welled inside of me, the feeling growing heavy in my chest, and I blinked at the man twice before deciding.

"Get on and stay quiet," I ordered before shifting once more, and then I lowered my front half to the ground, making it easier for him to slide on. Once certain he was stable, I darted forward, retracing my steps back to camp as quickly as I could.

Galloping across the damp earth, I prayed to the Gods that she would be there, safe and whole. But something told me that it was wishful thinking, and when we finally entered the clearing, I knew I had made the wrong choice.

Sliding from my back, Barrick began scouring the area, and I pressed my nose close to the soil, sorting through the scents until I found hers.

"Skylahr!" he called, his voice high with worry, and I snapped my jaws, ordering him to stay quiet while I searched. The last thing we needed was him alerting our visitors that we had returned.

Turning from the guard, I followed Skylahr's path towards the river, and as I approached, I noticed another smell grow heavy in the air. This time it was no horse or animal, but the hefty scent of blood, and I slid towards the water's edge as terror curled in my chest. When I heard a rustling from my right, my hackles rose, and I pulled my lips back as I slowly prowled forward.

"Protector!" Selbie's voice gasped as she limped her way from behind a tree, and I noticed the fresh wound on her thigh and the bloodied lip. Searching behind her, I held my breath as I listened for a sign of the other two, but when the space around us remained quiet, I snarled at the halfling.

"Please, it wasn't me, I had no idea they were here," she begged, falling to her knees before lifting her hands in surrender. "I promise you I had no idea. They came out of nowhere and ambushed us!"

It wasn't good enough. I wanted more than that, and I stalked forward as a growl rumbled from my chest.

"There were three of them," Selbie continued. "Two men and a woman who Elizabeth and Skylahr seemed to recognize. When they appeared, we split up. I was caught by one of the men but was able to fight him off and he fled. The other two went after Sky and Elizabeth."

"What did they look like?!" Barrick demanded as he approached.

Lifting her dark eyes to the guard, Selbie sobbed but remained on the ground. "The men were tall and thin, blond hair and light eyes, I think. But the woman had dark features like a northerner, and Skylahr knew her, I am sure she did!"

"How do you know?" Barrick snapped as he advanced.

"Skylahr and Elizabeth knew her name." Selbie hiccuped.

"Are you sure?" Barrick inquired, and my eyes slid to him.

"I'm positive."

"What was it, do you remember?" the guard asked, his body tense as he waited for her answer.

"She called her Terian."

Chapter 49

Barrick helped the halfling roll her pant leg up until the flesh above her knee was exposed, and then he poured the water from the wineskin over it, wiping away the blood while his eyes widened in wonder.

"It's nearly healed," he whispered as he inspected the now-closing wound, and Selbie nodded, though there was still a fine sheen of sweat lingering on her face.

"Still hurts though," she admitted before pressing her fingers to the skin surrounding the wound.

"It was deep," he remarked, helping her to her feet once more. "You're lucky it wasn't higher."

Pulling the fabric, Selbie lowered her eyes to the ground and nodded. She was obviously upset about being separated from the other two, but I couldn't feel anything but anger. Had she stayed with them perhaps they could have fought off their attackers. Maybe Skylahr and Elizabeth would be with us now.

"I am sorry," she said softly, as if she could read my thoughts, and I narrowed my eyes at her for a moment before turning away.

"Save your apologies, they'll do nothing for us now." Barrick sighed as I scanned the trees. "Did they say anything when they attacked? Did Terian mention anything?"

"No, Skylahr just said the name as they approached and now the rest seems like a blur." Selbie rubbed at her face. "But they had chains and hoods. They were prepared to take captives rather than kill us. They want her alive."

That had been all I needed to hear. I turned from the pair, my focus now back on following the trail the two women had left. I had yet to find a clear set of footprints, and their scents were faint due to the rain that had begun, but I desperately clung to the faint trace that was left and followed it to the river's edge.

I leapt into the water, hurried to the other side, and searched frantically once more. But whatever hint of them I had caught was now gone. Whining low in my throat, I paced back and forth, not sure which way to go but too distressed to stop moving. I heard Barrick call for me as he and Selbie crossed the water.

"If they have them, then they will most likely take them to where the rest of the immortals are—I'm guessing that temple we figured is on the mountain. But if they somehow managed to escape, then Skylahr will have hidden away until they could circle back for us. There is no way she would venture far without knowing for sure we were okay."

The guard was right, Skylahr would not have just abandoned us; she would be far too worried about her guard and the halfling.

Flattening my ears, I whined again and waited for his suggestion.

"You should go ahead. If Skylahr's with them then they have what they wanted. If she's not then she's in far more danger than we are." Barrick's face was tight with worry. "We will move farther down the coast and make another camp. Hopefully one of the other ships you sent has just been blown off course and they will appear without alerting the beast or those sea-maidens."

Selbie did not look convinced of this plan, but Barrick ignored her apprehension. "It's our best shot. We will slow you down if we go with you. Besides, I grew up in the northern wilderness, and I know how to survive."

"We aren't in the north," Selbie reminded him quietly with a frown, but then she rolled her shoulders. "But it is the best chance we have, I suppose."

Barrick's dark eyes sought mine, and then he gave me a gentle nod. "We can leave a trail for you to follow, markers or something. We will lay low and wait for you to return."

Knowing that it made the most sense, I took a step forward and pressed my head against the guard's shoulder before glancing at Selbie. The halfling still seemed intimidated by my Lupine form, so I didn't come any closer, but I held her gaze for a long moment, making sure I relayed exactly what I was thinking.

Betray my trust and I would come for her.

"It will be fine, Protector," Barrick promised, and with one quick pat to my shoulder, he sent me on my way.

Slinking through the shadows, I noticed how the trees had begun to change in a way I had never seen before. What once were evergreens and cedars turned into moss and ferns, plants that flourished only in warmer climates, and it wasn't just the vegetation that changed, but the air had as well. The farther I went, the more humid it became, and I panted in the heat as I struggled to find a way to remain hidden.

Lowering myself as much as possible, I crawled across the mud and took in the area carefully. There were no sudden movements, no noises, and had I not known better, I would have assumed I was alone. But I was certain that was not the case. I was being hunted. I could feel my instincts screaming at me that there was a predator nearby, and if it had set its sights on me, it was something to fear.

Flickering my ears, I tried to pick up any indication as to where or what it was, but there was nothing, not a single sound, and I grew more wary as the minutes passed.

Knowing that I should move to a more protected area, I stood to my full height, searching for a place that would offer me an advantage, and I noticed a wall of rock just a few hundred metres away. It would be a difficult climb, but I had little choice now.

Running towards the cliff, I leapt at the stone and managed to climb onto the first ledge, though I struggled to get my back legs under me as I stood on the narrow ridge, and then I looked at the next shelf. It was not a far distance, but the smell of rust was apparent, and I noticed the smear of red. It was not Skylahr's, but her scent was there now that the rain had finished, and fear curled in my belly.

Sitting back on my haunches, I climbed higher, ignoring the small puddle of blood beneath my paws as I scanned the area. There was no sign of them anywhere, and I prayed that Skylahr had managed to find a place to hide away while they waited for help.

Turning back to the cliff, I readied myself for the last of the climb, though the distance was nothing more than a step up, but as I rose on my hind end, there was a sharp sting radiating from my back. I snapped my jaws and then froze when four eyes peered at me. Their pupils were just narrow slits, though the irises were a deep red, and it was a stark contrast to the green scales that surrounded them.

The massive serpent tightened its jaw around my lower half and pulled me from the stone. The impact of my body hitting the earth was hard; I felt the air leave my lungs all at once, and then I was struggling to get up. But my hind end had already been nearly swallowed, and I kicked my back feet, dragging my nails against the monster's throat with as much strength as I could until it released me.

I staggered to my feet, ignoring the blood that was trickling across my fur, and went to run, but before I could muster the strength, the snake lunged forward, this time its teeth sinking into the back of my neck before it spun and then it was coiling itself around me.

Turning my head, I flailed in its hold as I tried to bite at its face, but it was no use; its grip was too strong, and as it continued to curl around me, my lungs screamed in protest. Whimpering in pain, I thrashed again, twisting, and turning in whichever way I could as I growled and barked. And then one of my paws found purchase on its side, and I dug my nails into the scales as hard as I could.

The serpent hissed in pain and pulled its teeth from me. Its body loosened for an instant, long enough for me to shuffle from its grasp, and then I dipped my head and sank my canines into its body. Shaking my head back and forth, I tore off a chunk of scaled flesh and then bit into it again.

Dropping me to the ground, the snake slithered a few feet away, and I rounded on it, lifting my lips as I snarled. It seemed to understand the challenge, and the massive body wound itself into a pile, and then it lifted its head, those four red eyes assessing me once more before its tongue flicked out. I could have sworn the irises glimmered in delight as it tasted my blood in the air before the sides of its face expanded, the shape now more comparable to a heart than the narrow rectangle it had been before.

Knowing that this was not likely a fight I would win, I took a step back, then another, moving until my hocks grazed the cliff I had just been climbing moments before while I searched for an escape. But there wasn't one, not one I could reach before it struck once more.

As though anticipating my plan, the snake slithered forward, its tongue constantly flicking, and I snapped my jaws in warning. But it paid no mind to my threat, and my heart thundered, the smell of my fear wafting in the air as it approached.

I lowered my head and growled again, though it was useless, and then the snake lifted its head, its mouth parting as those fangs gleamed. Preparing myself for what would surely be my end, I closed my eyes and prayed that Skylahr was not only alive but safe, and I hoped that she knew that I loved her. That I was sorry for all the pain I had caused, and that I had wanted nothing more than to live out the rest of my days at her side.

I could feel its breath, the rough texture of its tongue as it grazed my face, and I took in a deep breath, praying that it would be fast all while picturing her stunning hazel eyes.

Chapter 50

Being an immortal meant I had years to think about death, and I had often wondered how it would happen and why. I had never once assumed that I would truly live forever. But I had not anticipated it to be so quick that I wouldn't feel a thing. Although that wasn't quite true; I could still feel the damp earth beneath my paws, and the rock at my back. I could even feel the clotted blood in my fur, the heaviness of it pulling at my healing skin.

And I could also swear I smelled her. That I could hear her voice cursing as she gasped.

Feeling a shadow pass across my face, I opened my eyes and looked up before freezing. I hadn't imagined her, she was here, and she was currently holding the head of the serpent in the crook of her elbow as she swung her dagger at its face, using the blade to gouge out its eyes.

The serpent shrieked in pain, shifting its head back and forth as it tried to dislodge her, but Skylahr was determined, her hold remaining strong as she aimed for the final eye. Seeing the opening she had offered, I used every ounce of strength I had and lunged for the beast, tearing at the exposed belly with my teeth and claws until I was soaked with its blood. But even then I continued, and when I had dug so far into its body that I felt bone, I closed my mouth around the spine and pulled.

Now dead, the great beast began to sway, and I looked up at Skylahr in alarm, worried that the leg she had wrapped around it would be crushed when it finally fell to the ground. I shifted quickly before opening my arms, and when the serpent came crashing to the earth, I plucked her away from the scales at the last second, clutching her to my chest as we too collapsed into the dirt.

Taking in a heaving breath, I tightened my arms around her for an instant. I moved to my feet, pulling her along until she was standing before me, and then I cupped her face.

"Are you okay?" I whispered, pressing my forehead to hers. Her hands lifted to lay against my biceps before her hazel eyes peered up at me.

"I thought you were going to die," she whispered, her words coming out in a pant as she fought to catch her breath.

"I was terrified you already had," I admitted hoarsely, swallowing through the tightness of my throat.

She slid her hands down my arms and curled her fingers around my wrists, her thumbs stroking across the pulse points as if she was reassuring herself that I was alive and well. She searched my eyes, her own welling with tears before she pressed a kiss to my mouth. Curling my arms around her, I clutched at the cold metal for a second and then pulled away with a frown, hating that I couldn't feel her warmth on my skin.

"Armour?" I wondered as my eyes took in the silver, and she looked down at the breastplate she wore.

"I took it from the immortal who attacked us, he had no use for it any longer." Pride bloomed in my chest, and I laughed weakly.

"And Elizabeth?" I asked as I searched the area for the small human.

"Hidden up there." Sky pointed to the cliff. "There's a cave just a few feet from the edge. We were there when we heard growling and decided to wait until you made it to the top to be certain it was you. Though I'm not sure what I planned to do with just this." She held her dagger up.

"You did quite well with such a small weapon, if you ask me." I smiled and then indicated to the snake, and she swallowed nervously.

"We had seen it earlier after we had climbed the cliff. It had slithered out of the trees just as we reached the top." Her body trembled as she glanced at the scaled body. "We weren't sure what was happening when you were down here, but then I heard you whimper, and I knew I had to do something."

"I owe you my life," I admitted. "If you hadn't come when you did, I am sure—"

"Don't even talk about it," she snapped harshly. "This is twice now I have nearly lost you, and I don't feel like dwelling on that at the moment."

Kissing her again, I clutched her to me, and she moaned into my mouth while her hands grasped my shoulders.

"Sky?" a voice called from above, and I cursed under my breath at the interruption before lifting my eyes. Elizabeth was peering over the edge, her face pale and gaze worried, but alive, and I sighed in relief.

Glancing up at the mortal, Sky offered her a small smile and then stepped closer to me before lowering her voice. "She's wounded, not fatal, but deep and it has slowed us down."

"How? Where?" I asked before grabbing her hand and leading her to the wall of stone.

"Terian," Skylahr growled with rage. "She nicked her with her blade before we fled. It hit her just above her hip."

"That was the woman you knew from Noordeign?"

"Yes." She nodded. "She was one of my lady's maids."

My brows rose but I said nothing when Skylahr's face filled with fury. "She managed to escape with her life, but if I ever see her, I will not let that happen again."

"Do you know why she attacked you?" I inquired as I bent for her to give me her foot.

"I suppose she decided to take it upon herself to acquire the blood they needed from me. But now I consider it a debt owed. I will have hers as a replacement for what she took," she snarled and then placed her boot in my hands, and I hoisted her up.

We climbed the rest of the way without another word, and when we reached the top Elizabeth hobbled over to Skylahr and embraced her tightly before turning to me. However, just as she reached for me, her eyes lowered and then her pale face coloured, and she lifted her gaze while turning her pinkened cheeks away.

"I'm sorry, Protector, but I don't ever want to see this much of you." I glanced down, blushed, and then looked to Skylahr for a solution to my nudity.

"My cloak is in the cave; you can use that for now," she assured me and then she wrapped an arm around Elizabeth. Letting her friend lean against her, she helped the human to the shelter they had found, and I followed behind, frowning worriedly at the red stain that covered Elizabeth's side.

After settling her onto the ground, Sky tossed me her cloak, and I wrapped it around my waist quickly before falling to my knees beside Elizabeth. I waited until her eyes met mine, then inclined my head to her side, and at her nod I lifted her tunic.

Carefully peeling the damp cotton from her body, I took in the fabric that was tied around her middle and then looked to Sky.

"It was the hood of my cloak, I had nothing else to put on the wound to help stop the bleeding." It certainly wasn't ideal, and it would probably fester if it stayed on for much longer, but at least the blood had not soaked through.

"Is there anything else we can do?" Elizabeth whispered anxiously.

"If I can find the right herbs, I could make a paste to put on it. It will help with the swelling and pain and will keep the wound from getting too soiled," I said quietly while covering her torso once more. "But I think for now we should rest. We can begin our search in a few hours."

"What of Barrick and Selbie?" Sky asked, her face filled with concern, and I cupped her shoulder gently.

"They moved farther down the coast and will wait for us there," I assured her and then moved my attention back to Elizabeth. "They may end up murdering each other but otherwise are safe and well. I am sure they would want you to be looked after before we circle back."

Sighing, Elizabeth leaned back against the wall. She allowed her eyes to close as she rested her cheek against the cool stone while Skylahr watched her every move. I, however, remained silent, unsure of what comfort I could offer her.

"What do we do?" she whispered, her eyes never leaving her friend's face.

"I will go scavenge for what we need for the paste, and then we will let her catch her breath. Give her a few hours of rest and we will go," I promised.

"She will heal from this, won't she?" Skylahr whimpered.

"Sky—" I started, but she turned to face me, her brilliant hazel eyes wet with unshed tears.

"I feel like I have failed her," she cried softly.

"You haven't," I insisted while tucking a piece of hair behind her ear, and then I grabbed her chin and held her face steady in my hand. "She is still alive because of you, and she will heal."

Sniffing, she wiped at her eyes roughly, and I pressed a quick kiss to her temple before rising to my feet. Certain that Elizabeth's eyes were still closed, I lowered the cloak before stepping out of the cave and then I shifted once more.

The muscles of my hips still ached slightly from the bite of the snake, but the mild discomfort was nothing compared to how bad it could have been had my Huntress not come for me. I looked over my shoulder at her, taking her in for a long moment before descending down the cliff once more.

Elizabeth was far more stoic than I had thought she would be, and my ears would catch only the occasional whimper when she moved wrong in her sleep. Resting my head on my paws, I watched them carefully while they rested, though Sky had yet to even attempt closing her eyes, obviously too worried for her friend to even bother.

"You can rest, Kalian," she called, noticing my stare from the corner of her eye. "One of us might as well get some sleep."

I huffed loudly, shaking my head, and she sighed in frustration but said no more on the matter. Taking the small victory, I shifted onto my side, turning towards the forest below and searched the green for any sign of a threat, certain that the serpent that lay dead at the bottom of the cliff was not the only thing to be worried about.

Lost in the green that surrounded us, I took in the view, nearly missing the quiet footfalls that may have gone unnoticed had I been in my immortal form. But my Lupine body only intensified my already heightened senses, and I stood, turning towards the noise. Noticing my movement, Skylahr turned to me once more, her brows furrowing as she waited, and then she crawled forward, pausing at the entrance of the cave.

"Is someone here?" she whispered, and my head dipped just slightly while her face paled. "Close?"

My head dipped again.

"More than one?" Again, my chin lowered.

Looking at her from over my shoulder, I put together a plan and slowly slunk backwards, moving until I was nearly hidden amongst the cluster of ferns and bushes that covered the ground near the cave, and then I waited.

"Huntress?" a soft voice taunted after what felt like ages. I heard Skylahr's gasp and then she was waking Elizabeth.

"Huntress!?" the woman's voice sang out once more, and Elizabeth woke with a quiet whimper.

"Where are you, my lady?!" she called again, and my ears flattened against my head as I heard the group approach the serpent's corpse. "There is an awful lot of blood down here! Tell me, is any of it yours? Perhaps we don't need you after all."

My hackles rose at her voice, but I kept my body still, knowing that if I played this wrong it could very well end badly for the three of us. I tilted my head to listen once more.

"And how does sweet Elizabeth fare? Tell me, does she live?"

Growing impatient, the group did not bother to wait for an answer and began to climb, their quiet breathing and the sound of boots scraping across rock alerting me that there were at least seven or eight, maybe more, and given that I could hear sheaves of arrows rattling around in their quivers, I knew that they were armed.

"It's Terian, what do w—" Elizabeth's words were cut off, the rest of her question ending in a muffle that sounded like a hand had been clamped over her mouth. But it was too late, the group had heard her whisper, and a few snickers echoed from below as they closed in on us.

"She is still alive! She is stronger than I thought she would be!" Terian's voice was close now, and I swallowed.

Watching the edge, I waited as a set of fingers lifted onto the soil then another, and then they were pulling themselves up. I counted four bodies by the time they were rising to their feet, though there were most definitely more below. Keeping my eyes locked on them, I crawled forward, biding my time while I stalked my prey, and just as their attention landed on the women, I rushed forward.

The first was an easy kill; he didn't even have a chance to scream before I tore him in two. The second I rounded on, crushing him beneath my weight before closing my jaws around his face. The third I knocked off the ledge, not bothering to check to see if she was dead; I would end her life soon enough. The fourth, however, had managed to pluck an arrow from his back and the metal head sank into my shoulder with ease.

I turned on the archer, lifting my lips in a snarl, and the man looked terrified as he backed away from me hurriedly. Growling at his retreating form, I prowled across the earth and basked in the smell of his fear that wafted in the air before taking his life and then moving on.

One by one, they fell, and I did a quick count, knowing that at most there were two more. And just as I readied myself to finish this, I heard the sound of the bow string snapping and then Skylahr's horrified scream.

Terror wrapped its cold hand around my heart, and as it sank its claws into me, I spun to face her. But there she stood, tall and strong, her eyes open and bright, and I nearly collapsed in relief.

That is until I saw the wooden shaft protruding from Elizabeth's bloodied chest.

Chapter 51

After killing the one nearest to me, I then turned on the woman who still held the bow. Her dark eyes were wide as they met mine. I could see the reflection of my face in the brown irises, and then I sank my teeth into her body, ending her life far too quickly for my tastes, but Skylahr had called for me again and I would not leave her waiting when she needed me so badly.

I collapsed to my knees and crawled to her. She lifted a shaking hand to the arrow with uncertainty, her fingers splaying across the wet cotton before she blinked up at me.

"What do I do?" she sobbed as she held her friend to her chest. "What do I do?!"

"Sky—" I started weakly, not wanting to say the words out loud, and then Elizabeth coughed, red spilling from her mouth.

"Tell me what to do?! How do I save her?!" There was no saving the human; I knew that and so did she.

"I want to go home," Elizabeth cried out softly, her eyes glazing over as they searched for something. "Where is Ella? I want to go home."

Skylahr shuddered at the words, her head bowing as she pressed her temple against the mortal's.

"*Please*. I want to go home, take me home," Elizabeth begged again, though the words were harder to understand.

"We will, we're going home," I promised, shuffling closer to the human, and then I took one of her hands, doing my best not to flinch at the cold skin.

"Where's Ella?" she asked again, her eyes still seeking out the immortal.

"She's coming." I smiled, ignoring the way Skylahr groaned in agony. "She'll be here soon, and then we'll go home."

"I want to go home," Elizabeth sobbed once more, her body shaking from Skylahr's own trembling, and I held her hand tightly in mine.

And then it was quiet, the only sound being the Huntress's muffled cries as she rocked her friend's body back and forth.

Not knowing what to do, I kept my grip on the lifeless hand and I waited. I waited as Skylahr's world fell apart once more. I waited in silence while her heart shattered. I waited until her hazel eyes met mine.

"I promised nothing would happen to her," she gasped, her jaw trembling as she tried to catch her breath. "I promised to protect her."

"I'm so sorry." It was the only thing I could think to say, though it would do nothing for her.

"I failed her." Her hand was still pressed against her friend's chest, the pale fingers now soaked with the cooling blood. "I failed her and now I've lost her, *again*."

Moving to her side, I peeled one arm from the body, then the other, ignoring her feeble attempts to fight me, and once I had both of her hands in mine, I tugged her forward. Falling into my chest, Skylahr began to cry once more, and I wrapped myself around her, cradling her to me and pressing my lips to her forehead.

"I'm here," I promised, though I doubted she could hear me. And when her cries turned to screams, I tightened my hold.

Skylahr's tears had finally stopped after a long while, and now she stared blankly at me as I patted the soft soil one last time. Bowing my head, I closed my eyes. I whispered a silent prayer to the Gods, and then said goodbye.

"Rest, dear Elizabeth, you will be forever missed." Skylahr moaned but said nothing and I moved to her, my approach slow and careful as the distance closed. But she paid me no mind, her eyes didn't even lift to my face, and I peered down at her, wondering what was going through her mind. "Would you like to say goodbye?"

It was as if she didn't even hear the words, and I knelt at her feet, waiting as her lips parted. "It's a strange thing," she whispered. "I've lost her twice now. The first time I was sure my heart was bleeding beneath my skin, and it ached so terribly I knew I would never be whole again."

"Skylahr," I sighed sadly as I cupped her ruined cheek, but her gaze did not move.

"But this time…" She took a deep breath. "It's like I feel nothing now, like I have nothing left to give. Almost as if there is not enough of me to grieve the loss of her."

I stroked my thumb across her scar carefully, hating that her face was void of any emotion even when her attention finally moved to the pile of dirt that was now the resting place for her friend.

"She'll be here, alone." Her voice was soft, but matter of fact, and my chest constricted at the sound. "Her body will rot beneath this ground, and then the grass will cover her, and it will be as if she never existed. Every piece of her will be wiped clean from the world, and no one will even know where her final resting place is. She will never have visitors or flowers. She will be forgotten."

"She won't," I disagreed. "I will not forget her. Nor will you, or Ella or Barrick. She will—"

"Ella will hate me. She is going to hate me for not keeping my promise," she interrupted me. "That is if she is still alive."

"No, stop that," I demanded. "Do not turn your back on her now, do not give up. She is alive, the Healer is alive, and we will find them. But for us to do that, we have to go."

Grabbing her wrist, I tried to tug her to her feet, but her arm remained limp as she continued to stare at the grave. I bent once more, cradling her jaw between my hands. "Skylahr, we need to leave this place before more come looking."

"I can't," she admitted and then her face was crumpling. "I can't leave her here."

"I know it feels impossible, but you can. I promise you, you can, and we need to do so, now." Tucking my hands under her arms, I lifted her with me as I stood, and then I smoothed her hair before taking a step back. The pain of shifting was easy to ignore given my worry for Skylahr and my sadness for Elizabeth. The smell of death and blood, however, was not, and I pressed against her hip, urging her to climb on my back before I finally took us from this place, my heart breaking as the sobs started once more.

"What happened?!" Barrick demanded as he strode towards us, his arms immediately reaching out to Skylahr as she trembled on my back. "Whose blood is this? Are you hurt?"

Barrick pulled her from me and tried to set her on her feet, but her knees buckled, and he swooped down to catch her before she could fall to the dirt, though his eyes lifted to mine with worry.

"What is it?" Selbie asked while she hovered by the guard's shoulder, and then she gasped, her eyes widening at the state Skylahr was in. "Is she okay? Where is Elizabeth?"

Skylahr pressed her face into Barrick's neck at the mention of her friend, and he wrapped his arms around her, shushing her softly as she cried. The man's face paled the moment he understood.

"Oh, Huntress," he sighed sadly, though he said nothing else. There was nothing else to say, I supposed, and I waited for her tears to slow before changing, and then I took her from her guard. Lifting her into my arms, I turned to the man and waited for him to direct me to camp before following behind them. The air was quiet and sombre as I fell next to the fire, and I shuffled as close as I could to the flame, hoping that the warmth would stop Skylahr's shivering. Kneeling next to us, Selbie kept her eyes averted but held out a hand in our direction.

"Give me the breastplate, I will clean it." I had not even noticed the stains left on the silver metal. Sky's chin lowered as she gazed down and then her breath caught. Hurrying to undo the buckles, I all but tossed the armour at the halfling, and she moved to the other side of the fire before beginning to wipe the blood away.

"Where do we go from here?" Barrick asked, his voice low as he kept a careful eye on the woman in my arms.

"We need to find the Healer and Ella," I answered. "That hasn't changed. And then we will find the rest of her immortals, and we will stop their beast and its reign over the seas."

Both the man and halfling nodded, and then Sky shifted in my lap, glancing towards the mountain that sat in the middle of the island. Slowly the look of heartbreak melted from her face, and then her eyes narrowed, and I felt her fury burn within her.

"I will end every single immortal responsible for the deaths of our people," she said quietly, but I could hear her wrath in the words, the promise of death for those who awaited us, and I could have sworn I saw a flicker of darkness in her very soul. A shadow that had never been there before. "And then I will take that horn and summon the Siren herself before I end her too."

Chapter 52

I had planned to travel in my Lupine form for as long as I could as Skylahr led us farther and farther into the wilderness of the island. It would have been far more beneficial and safer for us all, but there was something about the way she carried herself that kept me from doing so. I knew that she had raised that wall, that armour she wore to keep herself from being hurt, and though it kept the pain out, it also locked her in. It kept her from us and the comfort she so obviously needed.

"We should not go much farther; we will run out of daylight soon," Barrick said, though he certainly sounded weary, and Selbie glanced at him before moving her attention to Skylahr. But she did not answer, and the guard looked to me, obviously seeking support.

Brushing past him, I held the waistband of the borrowed breeches he had found in the saddle bag and matched my stride to Skylahr's. She looked forward, paying me no mind, her movements stiff and jerky as she pushed her way through the weeds and brush.

"He's not wrong," I tried. "I understand that you want to find them, but we know now we are unprepared for this place, and continuing to journey at night will only pose a bigger risk for us."

"We have wasted enough time as it is," she snapped, hurrying her pace, and I sighed roughly before reaching for her.

"Skylahr, just slow down!"

Spinning on her heel, she slapped my hand away. “I can’t! I can’t slow down, I can’t wait, I need to find my friends.”

“And we will,” I promised. “But in order for us to do that, we need to have our wits about us. We need to be at our best.”

Skylahr began to shake her head, her jaw clenching as she brushed away my words, but Selbie stepped forward, interrupting us before pointing ahead.

“What is that?” Following her finger, I glanced at the view before us.

The sharp point of the mountain had looked whole before, but now that we had rounded it, I noticed a massive crack down the middle, splitting it in two and creating almost an aisleway. However, just to the left of the giant fracture was a tower, though it appeared as if it was part of the mountain itself, almost like it had been carved into the cliffside. It was an ancient building; its base was surrounded by vines and moss, and most of the arched windows were missing their glass. It had probably been built hundreds of years ago but did not look anything like the other Godly temples in Elrin.

Turning to look back at me, Skylahr lifted a brow, obviously asking if I thought that this was what we had been searching for. Eyeing the stone building once more, I shook my head.

“But it will offer us some shelter for the night at least,” Barrick called from behind us.

It was looking to be three against one, and Sky knew a loss when she saw one. Deciding to hold her tongue, she gave her guard a subtle nod and then turned back towards our new destination.

The climb was not an easy one by any means, but it was Barrick who struggled the most. We had to pause several times so he could catch his breath, though he would always growl and snarl that he was fine. Finally reaching the base of the tower, we gathered close, and then I looked at the three.

“I will go in first,” I proposed. “Once I am sure it’s safe, I will call for you.” Not waiting for them to agree, I pressed my palms against the rotting wood and pushed open the door.

The room was dark, though the walls were lined with windows, and the air was stale, though there was a lingering scent clouded by the smell of dust. Glancing around, I took in the floors that were covered in leaves and vines, the furniture left behind that looked broken and torn, having fallen victim to the animals who had nested within the building over the years, and the bookshelves lining the walls that had been damaged by the constant moisture from the island air.

Taking a moment to listen to my surroundings, I made sure that there was no threat before approaching the tables that sat in the middle of the room. They were cluttered with books and things, and I searched for a tinderbox in the drawers before gathering a pile of twigs and leaves. After starting a small fire in the fireplace, I ushered the others in.

"It will do." Barrick nodded as he scanned the space, and then he arranged the furniture around the glowing flames before falling into a chair.

Rolling her eyes, Selbie followed behind the guard and sank into one of the other seats, and I turned to Skylahr. Her eyes were still dull, her face pale, and she carefully avoided eye contact with me while she searched the room.

"What is this place?" she whispered as she crossed her arms around herself.

"A bochord, I think," I answered, turning to follow her gaze.

"A what?" she asked with a frown.

"It's what the immortals call a place like this, a place of study and research," I explained.

"Think there is anything of interest in here then? Something that might tell us where to find the temple?"

"Probably." I nodded. "I will start searching while you get some rest."

I had expected her to argue and was ready for a fight, but surprisingly she just nodded her head and then moved to the floor next to her friends. When she settled, I went to the desk and blew the dust from the surface before picking up the first book.

The text was faded from time, and the pages felt as if they would crumble from the slightest touch, so I took my time flipping through the book, growing frustrated when I realized the entire thing was a log of the moon cycles and the effects it had on the tides.

Grabbing the next, I searched the words for something important, and though this one mentioned the origins of the Forefolk, there was nothing new. On and on my search continued, my eyes growing tired as I picked up one after the other.

"The magic of the dark being was said to be used," I whispered to myself, uninterested in continuing the rest of the sentence, and I tossed it aside before lifting one more. Leaning into the back of my chair, I raised the book to rest on my chest and studied the words describing the sea-maiden's call, praying I would have something to tell Skylahr in the morning.

The quiet sound of splashing woke me from my sleep, and I jolted forward, my heart pounding as I scanned the room. Somehow, I had managed to nod off, and I frowned while I took a quick head count. Selbie was curled up on the floor, her head cushioned by her arm, and Barrick was snoring away in his chair. I was certain that the constant rumbling noise had to be the reason why I hadn't heard Skylahr sneak off. Glancing around the room, I searched for her and then spotted a door tucked in the corner. I hadn't bothered to pay it much attention when I had first entered the tower, however now it was open, and I was sure the Huntress had gone that way.

Rubbing at my eyes, I stood from my chair and crossed the floor, my hand curling around the door frame as I hesitated at the threshold. The change in temperature was immediate, and I inhaled the heavy smell. I had noted it when we had first arrived, but it had not been as strong, and I wiped at the perspiration that now blanketed my face.

Venturing down the damp stone steps, I took in the torches that hung from the wall, and then I turned to the pool of steaming water. The walls were not perfectly crafted, nor were the edges smoothed, but the natural spring was warm and welcoming.

"I couldn't sleep." Sky sighed from where she sat on the edge, her feet dangling in the water. "And I didn't want to wake you."

"You should have, I would have been happy to keep you company." I remained in place as her chin lowered while she watched the ripples spread across the surface.

"I think that's exactly why I didn't," she murmured quietly. "I'm not sure company would do me any good."

"It's better than being alone with your pain."

"I'm always alone with my pain whether you're here or not," she argued. "Your presence does not stop it from chasing me."

"No, it wouldn't." Stepping into the room, I approached her carefully and then sank to the floor next to her. "But eventually you'll find the will to face it. And when that happens it will take every ounce of strength you possess," I sighed knowingly, and then I took her hand. "But I will be here even then, waiting for you to lean on me when you tire."

Turning towards me, she pulled her hand from mine and then cupped my jaw before leaning over to kiss me. It was soft, almost unsure, and I held myself back, waiting for her to take what she needed. But whatever hesitance she had slowly disappeared, and then she was tugging at my hair while she nipped at my lower lip.

"Sky," I gasped, and she moved, carefully throwing one leg over my thighs until she was perched in my lap. She lowered her mouth, her teeth scraping against my jaw, and then she rocked her hips into my own.

"Touch me," she demanded, her hands lifting my own to cup her hips, and I was about to follow her order when I noticed the way her body was trembling. I had memorized every gasp, moan, and shiver I had ever pulled from her, and I knew exactly what to do to earn those reactions. This was not one of those times; this quivering was something entirely different.

"What is it?" I asked, but she ignored me, her hands stroking my naked shoulders.

"Skylahr," I warned again and then grabbed her fingers before leaning away from her. "What is it?"

"Please, no questions, not now," she begged, her hazel eyes glittering with unshed tears, and I frowned. "Please, Kalian, I need to feel something, anything, anything other than this sensation of drowning."

"Sky, not like this, not when you are upset," I tried, shaking my head, but she grabbed my jaw and pressed her lips to mine again.

"Please?" She sniffed, and I smoothed her hair, my thumb stroking her scar carefully before I moved her from my lap. Standing, I plucked at my laces and lowered the fabric and then stepped into the water. I turned to her and waited for her to do the same, though not with the usual eager anticipation. No, this time my heart ached at the sight of her, and when she was finally bare, I helped her into the spring and then lifted her into my arms.

"What are you doing?" she asked, confused, and I pressed my mouth to her temple while I closed my eyes.

"Holding you," I answered simply. "Nothing more and nothing less." She wrapped her arms around my shoulders and then rested her face in the crook of my neck, her breathing slow and quiet as silence settled over us.

"Kalian," she whispered after a long while, and I hummed under my breath, waiting for her to continue.

"I am sorry I have been so angry at you for so long. I now understand why you made the choice you did, and I forgive you for it." She sighed quietly, her lips so close to my cheek that the words were tattooed across the skin. "I think we might die here, and I was worried I wouldn't get the chance to say it. I want you to know in case the worst happens."

My heart stopped, the organ frozen in shock beneath my ribs as her words rang through my mind, and then it stuttered back to life, now racing as I took in her earnest expression. Her face was pale, her short bronze waves wild from the humidity. But her eyes gleamed, those greens and golds burning more vibrant than I had ever seen them, and I knew I had never witnessed something so magnificent in all my life.

"I am sorry for all the pain I have ever caused you," I sobbed, finally finding my voice though it cracked with desperation. "Please, Skylahr, know how sorry I am."

"I forgive you," she repeated as a tear rolled down her scarred cheek.

My shoulders collapsed as I fell forward, my own tears threatening to fall, and I rubbed my nose against hers as I searched her eyes again. "Promise me you mean it."

"I promise," she swore. "I promise, Kalian."

Tightening my hold, I buried my face in her hair and gasped at the warmth that was spreading through my chest. I never thought I would hear the words from her, and I had made peace with it. I had come to accept that she would never find it within her to forgive my betrayal, and now that she had, I prayed I would be able to prove to her that I would never hurt her that way again.

Chapter 53

We had slept on the stone floor after pulling ourselves from the water, me on my back with Skylahr sprawled across my body, and when my eyes fluttered open, I glanced down at her sleeping face, trying to connect the constellations of her freckles in my mind. She'd had a fitful night, and I had spent the hours soothing her every whimper, praying that she took comfort in my presence.

Inhaling deeply, Skylahr nestled further into my chest as she slowly came to, and I waited for those hazel irises to meet mine. She rested her chin on my sternum, blinking sleepily, and then offered a small smile.

"Hi," Skylahr whispered before pressing a kiss to my heart.

"Good morning," I replied while stroking a hand across her back, my fingers tracing the muscles, and I smirked when I felt her shiver as her eyes darkened. Sliding her own hand across my torso, she carefully sat up and then spread her thighs, placing them on either side of me, and I tipped my head back to gaze up at her. And as I took in every detail, I could have sworn she was not just a Chosen but she herself was the Goddess we were meant to worship for the next thousand years.

Unable to keep my hands to myself any longer, I ran them over her thighs, squeezing with just enough pressure so that I could admire the way the flesh pressed against my palms and filled the space between my fingers. Then I moved them higher, stroking her soft, rounded lower belly, loving the feel of it before my attention focused elsewhere. There was so much of her, long legs that went on for ages, her strong shoulders, thick thighs, muscled arms, but also soft, subtle rolls and heavy breasts that were tipped with perfectly pink nipples.

There was so much for me to touch, and admire, and love.

And yet somehow, not enough all at the same time.

Catching her eyes, I cupped a breast and brought my other hand to her centre, carefully angling it so that my thumb could circle her there. Watching the way her lashes fluttered, I kept my pace soft and slow, exactly the way she liked it, and when she gave that quiet little grunt that always told me she was close, I smiled to myself.

Skylahr was temptation in the flesh. Every sound, every move, every touch set me on fire, and I would gladly burn for her for all of eternity.

"Kalian," she warned, like she often did when she was close. "I'm—"

"I know, love." I smiled again, and then I stroked my index finger through the wetness, collecting it on my skin before pressing into her with a soft encouragement. "That's it, sweeting, take what you need."

Her thighs tensed, the muscles twitching, and then she was gasping my name, and I let her ride through it before pulling my hand from between her thighs. Catching her breath, she braced her palms on my chest and then lifted to her knees before reaching between us. She grasped my cock, pumped it twice, and then she was shifting so that she could drench me in her release.

"Is this okay?" she asked, her voice breathy and light, not at all matching the heat of her eyes.

"Yes." I nodded, swallowing as she carefully guided me to her entrance. Taking her time, she took me in, inch by inch, and my heart raced when she finally bottomed out. "Move, *please*."

Her gaze blazed, the mix of colours becoming an inferno, and she kept one hand on my chest while the other slid higher, not stopping until she was cupping the flesh of my throat. Skylahr did not press down, nor did she squeeze, but the message was clear: she wanted control, and I would happily give it to her.

Rolling her hips, she sank her teeth into her thick lower lip as she rode me slowly, never changing rhythm, not even when I began to pant and groan. If anything, my reaction only seemed to encourage her to slow her pace, and I grabbed her ass, my fingers sinking into the globes of flesh as I pleaded once more.

"Please, sweeting!" I moaned, my chin tilting as I clenched my jaw. "Please!"

Humming under her breath, she bent forward until her mouth was next to my ear. "Do your job and make me finish first, and then maybe I will take pity on you."

Sky had never been so forthright before, nor confident, and my cock twitched at her words. Desperate to come, I moved my thumb back to her clit, though it was nearly impossible to keep the tempo when she was taking me so well.

"Fucking hell, Skylahr!" I growled when she slowed her movements even more, and then I was sitting up, curling an arm around her before rolling us. Pressing her into the stone floor, I lifted her legs to my shoulders and bent her knees to her chest, my hands pressing against her thighs as I pounded into her.

Watching the way her mouth fell open, I changed my speed but kept my thrusts deep, and then I touched her once more, chuckling at the way the air left her lungs.

"Kalian!" she begged, and I lifted a brow.

"Who needs pity now, sweeting?" I asked, and she whimpered in response. "Ask me, Skylahr."

"Ask you what?" she cried, her brows pinching in confusion.

"You want to finish?" I questioned with a sly smile. "Ask me and use your manners."

"Please!" Her heels pressed into my back, her desperation growing, and normally I would have wanted more from her, but I was too close myself.

And so I tucked my hands under her, liftering her ass just slightly so that I hit that spot deep inside, and then her eyes were clenching shut as her walls closed in around me. Powerless to hold off any longer, I gave three more thrusts before spilling into her, and then I placed my palms on the floor next to her head. After a long moment, those bronze lashes fluttered open, and I pressed a quick kiss to her mouth before carefully rolling to my side. Settling on my back once more, I pulled her to me, re-creating the position we had woken up in, and Sky rested her ear over my heart, undisturbed by the pounding that echoed there.

"Are you alright?" I asked after the silence had gone on for some time. "I didn't hurt you, did I?"

She shook her head but did not look up at me, and I carefully rearranged her in my arms and then lifted her chin with a finger. When she met my gaze, I immediately noticed the dullness in her eyes, and I frowned.

"What happened? Where did your mind go?" I asked, rising in alarm.

"How did I forget?" she asked, her eyes misting while she quivered. "How did I just forget her?"

"Skylahr," I sighed, my guilt slamming into me. "This is my fault, I shouldn't have—"

"No!" She shook her head. "No, I wanted this, you did nothing wrong."

Wiping at her face, she seemed to gather her thoughts, and then she was crossing her arms over her breasts shyly. "But you were right to stop me last night, I see that now. I was selfish, and I was wicked for seeking a distraction, and yet I still wanted every moment of what we just did."

"You are none of those things," I argued. "Not wicked and not selfish."

"My friend is rotting in the ground as we speak, and yet I was too focused on my desire for you to even remember that just now." She sobbed, pulling away from me before grabbing at her clothes.

"Skylahr." I reached a hand out, but she turned from me and tugged her tunic on.

"Elizabeth is dead. Gaelon and Ella are still captives, and yet all I wanted this morning was to feel you love me. How is that not selfish? How is that not horrible of me?"

"It's okay," I tried to assure her, but she ignored me and then stepped into her breeches before grabbing her boots.

"It's not okay." Skylahr lowered her face, staring at her feet. "My friends deserve better than this."

And then she hurried to the stairs while the smell of her tears lingered in the air.

The room was tense when I returned with another one of those rabbit-like creatures. Skylahr had not spoken to me since leaving the spring this morning, and both Selbie and Barrick had watched us with curious eyes while we awkwardly interacted with each other. It seemed as if any of the warm moments from the night before had been forgotten, and though it hurt, I didn't blame her. She had not been in any state to say such things, and I should not have taken them to heart. People said things when they were in pain. They said sad things, and angry things, and sometimes they said things they thought others wanted to hear.

She promised me she had meant the words, but it would not be fair of me to hold her to them when I knew she was in such a state. I needed to forget those moments we shared while she grieved and healed.

Preparing our breakfast, I added more wood to the fire, very much aware of Skylahr's every move, though I had yet to actually look at her. I could feel Barrick's dark gaze burning into the side of my face.

"I don't care who you are, I won't have you taking advantage of her," he growled, and I stopped what I was doing before my eyes slowly rose to his. Selbie, who had been looking through a few books, snapped the one in her hands shut, and Sky froze, her body stiffening at her guard's words.

"What did you just say to me?" My voice was low, dangerous, and deadly as I rose to my feet. "Do you honestly think I would do anything to hurt her?"

"Haven't you already?" he retorted smugly, his arms crossing over his chest.

"Barrick," Skylahr warned, her voice stern. But the man paid her no mind, and he moved until we stood toe to toe, though I had a few inches on him.

"I have made mistakes; you are right." My eyes narrowed as I spat out the words. "But I will never repeat those. I know it and she knows it."

"Mistakes is th—" Skylahr did not waste any more time and she wedged herself between us before shoving her guard back, interrupting his next words.

Certain that he was a solid foot away, she leaned back into my chest but did nothing more, and then her chin lifted in that way that told me Barrick was about to receive a dressing down.

"I am certain you happened to overhear our conversation from earlier and that is why you have decided to intervene." Her guard's face flushed a bit, but he remained silent. "But that was not for your ears, and you have no right to interject here, Barrick. I told you once my decisions are my own, and this is one of them. Kalian did nothing wrong."

"But he—" Sky lifted a hand, silencing the man with the simple gesture.

"I appreciate your concern, and I value your protection," she said gently, though the stiffness of her body had not lessened. "But I do not need saving from him. He is my choice, and I want you to respect it."

My lips curled in a pleased smirk, and the guard huffed loudly but said nothing more.

"Are you three about finished?" Selbie interrupted, and we all turned to her as she pointed to one of the tables that was covered with a cloth, though she had flipped a corner. "Because I found something."

Stepping away from me, Skylahr crossed the room and then tugged the cloth from the table before peering down at the surface. Following behind, I knocked my shoulder into the guard's as I passed and ignored the curse he spat in my direction.

Moving behind Skylahr, I rested a hand on her lower back and then I glanced over her shoulder with a frown, examining the detailed carvings that covered the wood.

"It's a map," Skylahr whispered, looking up at me, and I nodded before tracing my fingers across the etchings.

"A map of Skohyn," I confirmed and then I rounded the table, reading the map from the right direction before pointing to a mark that sat tucked in the valley between the two peaks of the broken mountain. "The Shrine of the Sea and Tides."

"The temple?" Skylahr asked, her eyes wide with hope, and I nodded, my gaze lowering to the mark once more.

"Yes, it appears so."

Chapter 54

Looking around, I searched the room for something of use before noticing a collection of large scrolls tucked away in the corners. I grabbed one, unrolled the old paper carefully, and glanced across the portrait of the Siren before turning it over. Certain the back was blank, I moved to the firepit, grabbed at some of the black pieces left behind from last night's fire, and then returned to the desk.

Flattening the scroll over the map, I had Sky and Selbie hold the corners carefully and then took the crumbling charred wood and pressed it to the wooden surface. I smoothed the black over the entire map, taking my time so that every important detail was picked up, and then stepped back.

"We are here." I pointed to where I guessed the tower was based on the map's layout. "And now we have a set route to follow."

"How long of a journey do you think that is?" Selbie wondered.

"It depends on the weather and terrain, of course, but I'm mostly concerned about what else is out there, or rather who." Skylahr's face paled to a sickly colour, and she wrapped her arms around her torso, obviously remembering what had happened on that cliff, and I cleared my throat. "Skohyn is called the island of torment for a reason, and I have a feeling we have only seen a fraction of what lies in wait."

"What a terrifying thought," Barrick said gruffly, and Selbie nodded.

"It is, so we need to be smart about how we proceed. We know now that we should not split up, at any point in time." Skylahr flinched but said nothing. "We should only travel during daylight and give ourselves enough time to find shelter before the sun sets. I will plan to be in my wolven form at night or if anything seems amiss. Before we leave here, we should take whatever we can for supplies. Gather sticks and leaves for kindling should it rain again, grab paper from the books as well and some of the candles."

All at once the three began to move about the room, and I walked to the fireplace before grabbing the pokers. They weren't much as far as weapons went, but they could do something should the time come. I also grabbed a few of the tablecloths, laying them on the ground so that the items could be placed in the centre, and then we could tie them into packs.

I folded the map carefully, handed it to Sky to tuck into her cloak, and then gave the room a once-over. There was not much else we could use, and once I was sure we were as prepared as we could be, I waited for the others before slinging the pack over my shoulder.

"Are we ready?" We were anything but: we were outnumbered, outarmed, and not at all prepared for what could be out there, but we had no choice, we had to find the Healer and Ella. I had to find them for Skylahr and then we had to destroy the horn and whoever controlled that beast.

There was no one else who could.

The mist was heavy as we continued on our way, and Barrick frowned at the damp pack I had given him. The kindling and parchment would be too wet to use for now, but at least we had them. I glanced down at the river, watching as the women filled the wineskins. Skylahr had been silent, and both Selbie and Barrick had kept a worried eye on the Huntress. She, however, had yet to truly acknowledge us, too lost in her pain to bother, and I hated that she was suffering alone.

"I am sorry," Barrick offered gruffly, and I looked at him from the corner of my eye, doing my best to hide my surprise. I never thought the man would willingly give me an apology, but I couldn't let it be that easy for him.

Raising a brow, I crossed my arms over my chest. "You'll have to be more specific. What is it you are apologizing for?"

"For my words this morning."

"And which words are those?"

"My Gods, you are insufferable," he snapped. "How does she stand you?"

Shrugging my shoulders, I flashed him my teeth, though it was too disingenuous to really be considered a true smile. "You'll have to ask her."

Barrick scoffed, and I finally turned to really face him. "You're right, I'm insufferable, but tell me, do you still find me pretty?"

The guard's mouth fell open, his face blank for a pause, and then it pinkened and I tossed him a wink. "Everything gets back to me in my home, and you were surrounded by immortals, there are no secrets."

I expected him to storm away or maybe swing at me, but he did neither. No, instead he swallowed down his embarrassment and then focused back on his Huntress.

"She's in pain." It was a complete change of subject, but not one I was surprised by given how hard it was to ignore the way Skylahr was a shell of herself, and I nodded, all humour fading from me in an instant.

"She loved her." I swallowed. "And she had lost her once already. Now she has been through this twice, and I'm not sure how anyone could go on after that."

"She's strong," he argued.

"I never said she wasn't," I snapped. "But imagine how tiring that must be. To not only be so resilient, but to also allow yourself to love others, knowing you could lose them too."

Something flashed across Barrick's face, something that told me he knew exactly how Sky was feeling, and I waited for him to say something.

"You love her?" he questioned.

"Yes." It was immediate; I didn't even have to think about it.

"But she's the first person you've ever been in love with."

"The only," I corrected.

"Skylahr has lost family, a lot of family, and losing family is hard," he sighed. "It hurts, and it aches, but it is nothing compared to losing the person you truly love. That feels like your very soul has been ripped from your body. You feel it every moment of every day. It doesn't ease, and it never changes."

"I'm not sure I understand what you are saying." I frowned.

"Skylahr is resilient because the previous wounds have healed. The scars are there, of course, but they healed and eventually this one will too. Elizabeth's death feels all consuming to her now, but she will carry on." That was difficult to believe, but I supposed it was true. She had done it once before, and maybe she could do it again.

"But *you*." He shook his head sadly. "She's let herself fall back in love with you. I can see it even with all the hurt that she is carrying."

I wanted to tell him she hadn't, that she couldn't even say the words, but the guard turned on his heel, taking a step closer, and then his eyes held mine. "Therefore, if something happens to you, there will be no coming back from it," he warned. "So be smart and be safe, we need her whole."

My mouth quirked just slightly in the corners, and I placed a hand over my heart mockingly, surprised that he cared even to bother with the lecture. "I thought you were going to warn me about losing her."

"I didn't think I had to," Barrick admitted. "You will eventually."

The air left my lungs, and my fingernails pressed into the skin of my chest sharply, almost as if I was trying to keep my heart from shattering at the idea. "What are you talking about?"

"You're immortal and she's a halfling," he pointed out.

"Yes, but the ceremony—"

"Can only happen if the halfling is dying, and I didn't think it was guaranteed to work every time." He was right, it wasn't. There was a strong chance that she would not survive the immortal magic.

"So, you will outlive her then. Eventually she will die, and you will be left without her." Swallowing down the acid that had crept up the back of my throat, I turned my gaze to Skylahr, memorizing every detail I could, realizing I had never even taken a second to think about a future where she did not exist.

And now I had to.

Barrick's constant piss-poor mood and endless complaining about his back pain really made it difficult not to beat him with a fire poker, and I glared at the man as he rubbed at his tailbone. The only reason why I had refrained was because I knew Skylahr would never forgive me, and I didn't want her to suffer any more than she had. Though when I noticed the glare she sent in his direction, I wondered if she would be *that* upset about the idea.

"Seriously, Barrick," Selbie grumbled. "Enough."

"I am sorry if I do not have the same stamina as two halflings and an immortal," he growled back.

"What happened to being right as rain all the time?" I asked with a raised brow.

"Listen, I do—" he started, but I launched myself at him, slapping a hand over his mouth before lifting a finger to my lips. I gestured for the three to get down low to the ground. It had been quiet, no sign of anything being around, that is until the direction of the wind changed and then settled, and my instincts screamed at me that something was there.

I tugged my breeches down my legs, tossed them at the guard, and then pushed past the pain until my shadow was looming over the three. Pressing my forehead to Skylahr's shoulder, I nuzzled her for a quick moment, and then I sank away from them, only putting a few yards of distance between us while I circled our camp from the night before, though I had not detected anything while the others slept.

Searching the trees, I waited to see shining green scales or four red eyes, but there was nothing, and then I examined the ground next. The damp earth was untouched, not a single leaf out of place, but there was something there. My ears flickered, catching the sound of soft breathing and the quiet scraping of metal being unsheathed, and then a gust of wind blew again, and I smelled them.

It was odd, the heavy smell of salt water that seemed to coat the skin of her immortals, though considering how the Lupines all smelled of crisp winter winds and evergreens, I supposed I should not have been surprised.

Lowering my body, I stalked forward, taking my time as I approached, though I knew that they would hear the soft sound of my paws sinking into the mud at any moment. I would have to act fast, this time not bothering to boast in my kills. That was a mistake I learned from, and I would not make it again.

Pinpointing the group's location, I froze in my pursuit, taking a deep breath while my muscles coiled, and then I was on them.

Not prepared for my immense size or speed, the four immortals had barely readied themselves with their weapons before I had killed the first, tearing the man in two before moving on, and when the second and third met their deaths, I turned to the fourth. Pressing one massive paw on his chest, I leaned forward, my teeth just inches from his face and then I waited.

Hearing the commotion, Skylahr and her friends ran towards us, and once she had picked up a blade, I eased my weight off my captive just enough so that he would be able to answer any questions she may have. Taking the opportunity I gave her, Skylahr approached slowly, and then peered down at the blond man.

"You know who I am?" she asked, and the man nodded, his wide eyes moving frantically from me to her and then back again. "Then you know why I am here. Are my friends alive?"

"Yes," he whimpered, and I snarled in disgust at how easy it was for him to divulge the answer. He obviously was not trained in keeping secrets, and the poor choice in soldier would cost the rest of the Siren's immortals.

"Where are they being held?" The immortal shook, the smell of his fear spreading through the air.

"I'm not sure." That was a lie, though not a very good one. I snapped my jaws in his face, and the man wet himself as he quivered under my paw.

"Let's try again, where are they being held?" Skylahr asked once more, her tone growing impatient.

"The shrine! They are in the shrine's dungeons!"

"And how many of you are there?" The man clenched his eyes while his lower lip trembled, but he remained silent. "You won't tell me?"

The man made no move to answer, his bravery finally making an appearance, and I moved my eyes to Skylahr, waiting for her next direction.

"Are there more immortals hunting for us?" The man's blue eyes fluttered open, and he took in a deep breath before looking over at Skylahr.

"Not immortals, something much worse," he answered and then closed his eyes once more before praying to his Goddess. Seeming to understand that he was ready for his death, Skylahr dipped her chin just slightly but did not turn away, and I ended it quickly.

Gathering the weapons and anything else of value, we turned from the bodies, and then Barrick sighed wearily before turning to his Huntress. "What do you think he meant when he said something worse?"

But Skylahr remained silent, her attention focused elsewhere, and then Selbie spoke. "I have a feeling we will know soon enough."

Chapter 55

Light was fading quickly, and yet that wasn't my main concern. It was the way the guard continued to watch Skylahr, but in a far different manner than he had earlier. Now his eyes held something that looked similar to fear rather than concern. Not understanding the change, I hung back away from the women and matched his stride before tilting my head in confusion.

"What has you so spooked?" I whispered just loud enough for him to hear the question, and he glanced at me from the corner of his eye.

"I don't know what you're talking about," he snapped, but I did not let it deter me.

"Even if I didn't notice the fear in your eyes, I can certainly smell it," I remarked dryly, and the guard stumbled just slightly at my observation.

Realizing it was not something he could hide or lie about any longer, he swallowed roughly, and kept a careful eye on Skylahr before answering. "I just didn't expect that from her."

"Expect what?"

One massive hand ran across his face and then over his beard. "The way she just stood there and watched—"

"Watched me destroy someone who was ready to kill you, her, and the rest of us? Why would that make you so nervous?"

"The Skylahr I know does not revel in death; she finds no pleasure in it."

"Barrick, she has fought a war, she has killed many men," I reminded him with a frown.

"I know that, Protector," he growled. "But back in Noordeign, she all but begged me to keep a hostage alive, a man who had been a threat to all of us. When I killed him she was furious with me. So, considering that little detail, I have never once imagined her enjoying the death of an enemy the way she just did."

"She is angry and suffering through the loss of Elizabeth," I reasoned, but the guard seemed to almost shrug the explanation off. "She wants revenge."

"Yes, you're right, but her expression…" The words faded for a moment, his eyes examining the back of the Huntress carefully before he turned to whisper, "There was a darkness about it that I have never seen before."

I wanted to roll my eyes. I wanted to scoff at the man and tell him that he was a fool. But I too turned to look at her, watching the way she led the group towards our destination, and there was something oddly familiar about the air around her. It reminded me of the time when she had clutched her head in pain just after I had begged for her forgiveness, when she had closed her eyes and I could sense that wicked and foul power the Crimson Goddess possessed. However, the Seductress's link was said to have been closed, and the red bitch was no longer a threat.

But the closer I examined her, the more I could see what the guard was talking about. There was *something* there, something brewing just below the surface. However, I had no idea what it was or where it came from. It was not a power I recognized.

"What is that smell?" Selbie gagged as she lifted her hand to cover her nose. I exhaled through my lips as I flinched at the heavy, sickly scent of death. Whatever we were approaching had been left for days, and I worried about what we would find as the trees began to thin.

Sinking into the earth below, I reached a hand out behind me, stopping Sky from passing, and then glanced at the others from over my shoulder. "Be careful, it's rather wet up here."

But my warning had not been completely accurate. It wasn't just wet, the ground slowly began to morph into what looked to be a swamp, which was most certainly where the smell was coming from. Gazing across the tall reeds and murky waters, I searched for a way around. But the marsh was vast, spreading as far as the eye could see, and finding a route to avoid it would only add more time to our journey. More time we did not have.

Wrinkling her nose, Selbie looked at me with a hopeful expression, and I rolled my eyes before pulling off my clothes and tossing my breeches at her face. I ignored her annoyed huff, shifted, and then bent low, waiting until all three mounted, making sure to let out an over-exaggerated grunt as I stood. Certain they were settled, I took a step into the warm water.

At first the muck went only a few inches up my legs, but as I ventured farther and farther into the swamp's depths, we hit a sudden drop-off and I was belly deep. The thickness of the water made my movements sluggish and awkward, and my paws struggled to find purchase on the mud below.

"Have you ever seen anything like this?" Barrick asked as he tried to prevent his feet from getting wet.

"I've never *smelled* anything like this," Selbie groaned, and the stench grew stronger as the water became deeper and deeper.

Now unable to reach the bottom, I lifted my head, keeping my muzzle out of the swamp as I paddled the best I could, but it was difficult, and I panted as I pressed through the thick sludge. Choosing to remain quiet, the three sat still, obviously hoping that it would ease the struggle, but it truly made no difference, and I searched for the shore, trying to decide how much longer it would take to reach it.

We were still ways away, and the depths had only gotten worse;

the warm water was now covering my back. Skylahr leaned forward, stroking the fur on the back of my head as I grunted with my efforts.

"Should we drop the packs?" she whispered near my ear. "We have the weapons from the immortals now, and Barrick is holding the map over his head. Whatever other supplies we took will be ruined anyway."

At this point anything might help, so I growled out my answer. I then heard the sound of fabric untying and two splashes as the fire pokers and other things were dropped into the swamp. As suspected, it did not make a considerable difference really, and my ears flattened in annoyance as another splash sounded from behind me.

Not knowing what else they could have dropped, I waited for Skylahr to explain, but her sharp gasp of fear told me it hadn't been a pack at all.

"Oh Gods! What is that?" Barrick shouted while his body stiffened, and I hurriedly turned to see what the guard was talking about.

Two humanoid eyes blinked at us slowly, though I could see the sheen of its third eyelid from here, and I took in its round pale face as it lifted its head out of the water. The flesh was pale, nearly translucent, and its neck was long, at least two feet. The shoulders were wide, covered in little notches, and then its chest broke through the surface, and I eyed its impossibly long arms as three webbed fingers reached towards us.

It slithered, cutting through the water with ease like a reptile would, and as it approached, I realized just how big it was. This creature was unlike anything I had seen before, and it was nearly the size of my wolven form, though it was far quicker than I could ever dream to be, and I turned back to the shore, pumping my legs as fast as I could.

"Hurry, Kalian," Sky whispered, and I could feel every time she turned to glance back at the thing that stalked us. "It's close."

I didn't need the warning; I could hear it, I could feel it on my heels. Everything in me screamed that I was being hunted, and I felt one long nail catch in the wet fur at the tip of my tail as it closed in. Not knowing what to do, I tried to move to the right, hoping my change in path would somehow throw it off, but this creature lived in this place. It thrived in this swamp, and it and whatever it had been feeding on was the source of the smell we had been complaining about.

"Kalian!" she warned again, but the thing had already found its mark, those three nails sinking into my flank as it hissed in pleasure.

Using a back foot, I tried to kick it away or dislodge its hold, but nothing seemed to work. And Barrick shifted on my back, his weight sliding to one side as he grunted, and then the creature was screeching and the hand that had been lodged into my flesh loosened.

Now running on adrenaline, it was almost as if my strength had doubled. I swam as fast as I could, forcing myself to ignore the splashes behind me while I focused on the shore I could now make out ahead of us. We were still yards away, but hope bloomed in my chest that we may get out of this alive.

"Barrick!" Skylahr screamed, her voice shrill and full of panic, and the man wobbled, his body swaying unsteadily. I felt Sky move from her place and reach for her guard, the change in her position throwing my balance off, and then all three were slipping into the water.

Whirling around, I watched as Sky tugged her guard farther away from the creature, shrinking back in fear as its mouth opened wide in what looked to be a smile. Shoving him roughly towards Selbie, Skylahr tried to herd them back, creating as much space as possible while also doing her best to tread water.

But the thickness of the swamp was swallowing her down, and I lurched forward, panicked that the monster would reach her before I did.

"Get them to shore!" she screamed, not bothering to even look at me. "Get them to shore, Kalian!"

But I couldn't, not when the beast's hand was reaching for her, its fingers tangling in her hair. I whimpered in desperation as the creature tugged her head back before lifting her torso from the water. Bringing her face near its own, it flattened its tongue, swiping the long grey muscle across her face, and then it seemed to purr.

For a minute everything seemed to stand still, and even though I was hurrying towards the beast, it was as if I was making no progress at all. Growing more frantic, I watched as the thing lifted her higher. I snarled and snapped, a warning that went ignored, and then it was leaning forward. Opening its mighty jaw, the beast craned her head to the side, exposing her jugular perfectly before it began its descent.

This was it; this was her end, and I would have no way of stopping it. I could only just watch it happen.

Falling loose in its hold, Skylahr hung limply, and the monster purred once more as the distance between its jagged teeth and her pale throat closed. But as it shut its teeth around the juncture of her neck, Skylahr lifted one arm, jabbing it beneath its jaw, and it made a horrendous choking noise and its eyes widened.

She pulled her hand away, the dagger now covered in the monster's black blood, and then more of it began to coat its long neck and chest, the blood flowing rapidly, until finally it released her. Falling back into the water with a splash, Skylahr sank beneath the surface, the heavy metal of the breastplate surely making it far more difficult to keep her head above the mud.

Paddling to where she had disappeared, I dove, following her down into the dark depths until I was close enough for her to grab on to, and then I was pulling us both to the surface. Gasping for air, she wiped the mud from her eyes and mouth and then curled an arm around my neck before pressing her forehead against mine.

"Why do you never listen? You were supposed to take them to shore," she reprimanded me softly, but I ignored her as I brought us to her friends. After first helping Selbie up, she then turned to Barrick, and though he tried to fight her on it, he let her assist him as well. Reaching for her, the two pulled Skylahr to the front, and then I turned to shore once more.

Finally finding shallower waters, I dug my paws into the mud and hauled myself to land. All three of my companions let out a sigh of relief when I finally stepped onto the grass. Sliding from me, Barrick fell to his hands and knees, taking in long, shuddering breaths while the women tried to wipe as much mud from them as they could. I shook out my fur and took a minute to survey the area, and then Barrick stood, his attention focused on the swamp we had just crossed.

"What do we do now that the map is out there somewhere?" he asked irritably.

"We don't need it," Sky answered as she faced in the opposite direction, pointing to something in the distance. "We're here."

Chapter 56

The Siren's shrine was a sight to behold. Its stone walls and marble columns were covered in moss and greenery, just like everything else on this fucking island, but the mighty mountain it protruded from only made the building seem superior to the surrounding landscape. Taking in what appeared to be multiple levels, I watched and waited for any sign of guards, though I wondered if they would even bother standing outside the entrance considering all the things you would have to avoid to get to its doors.

"Have you ever seen anything like it?" Selbie whispered in awe, and I shook my head.

"It's going to be nearly impossible to find them in a place that big," Barrick muttered quietly. "What do you think the best way to go about this is?"

I truly did not know, but I was certain we needed to be on the same page before we even bothered finding a way in. Remaining low to the ground, I studied all the possible ways this could fail and realized there was no obvious answer.

"There are no guards at the doors. Why is that?" Skylahr wondered. I glanced at her from the corner of my eye before exhaling roughly.

"Usually that would tell me that they aren't concerned about visitors entering that way. It could be because they are overconfident or because they know something we don't."

"Meaning?" she clarified.

"Meaning that even if someone managed to get past the doors, they would not get far. Perhaps there is something waiting just beyond the threshold."

"So, what do we do?" she whispered, her hazel eyes narrowing at the shrine.

"We go anyway," I answered. "I can't see another option at this point, and considering both parties they sent out after us have not returned, I don't think they plan on being merciful for much longer."

Skylahr's sharp gasp echoed in my ears, and I didn't need to see her face to know how forlorn she looked. Reaching for her hand, I tangled my fingers with her own and gave it a gentle squeeze.

"What would you have us do?" I asked her. Her eyes widened as if she was surprised by my wanting to include her, and then she closed her fingers around mine tightly.

"Whatever plan we decide on, there are no guarantees that it will work. We might end up trapped, or taken hostage, or worse." She waited for me to nod before closing her eyes and letting her head fall forward in defeat. "Then I don't want to wait around any longer. I want to find them."

"And what about you two?" I looked at Barrick and Selbie.

"We have managed to come this far. If this is the end for us, let's make sure it's on our terms. I can't think of a better way than to die while trying to save the lives of the people we care for." Barrick's gruff voice was softer than I had ever heard it, and I watched as he reached an arm out to pat Sky's back gently.

"Then it's unanimous." Selbie shrugged. "I agree with the old man."

Managing to approach the imposing building without alerting anyone would have been impressive if it hadn't been for the fact that I had yet to see a single man or rather any sign of life at all. It was almost as if the shrine was empty, like it had been abandoned, and as we neared the door, I turned to look at Sky. Her hazel eyes were lifted towards the upper floor, taking in the stone and carvings with a careful gaze.

"We are sure this is it?" she whispered.

"That is what the map showed, and I don't know what else it could be." Pressing in close behind me, she rested a hand on my shoulder, and I revelled in the gentle touch for just a moment before slipping past the door.

As magnificent as the outside was, it did not compare to the interior, and I stood in the doorway while I studied every detail. It wasn't a room really, but rather an enormous winding staircase that wrapped around a great rushing waterfall, the spray from it nearly reaching me from thirty feet away. Every curved step had its own pillar, the stone smooth and shiny as they supported the stairs above, and I took a step closer, nearly slipping on the wet floor. It should have been impossibly dark within the shelter of the mountain, and yet the water that rained from above was illuminated, the colour a bright shimmering blue that filled the room with a glowing light.

"Kalian," Skylahr called quietly from behind the door, her voice filled with worry, and I pressed the wood open before ushering the three in.

"Well, this was not what I was expecting," Barrick murmured as his gaze grew wide with wonder, and I nodded.

"So which way do we go?" Selbie asked as she turned her head from the stairs leading up to the stairs leading down.

"I do not think they would keep the horn and their captives in the same place." I sighed, my attention focusing on Skylahr. "We either need to split up or we need to decide which is a priority right now."

"We stay together," she snapped. "Besides, as much as I want to destroy the horn, Ella and Gaelon come first."

"Down it is then." Barrick looked down towards the damp stairs, and then he lifted a hand, gesturing for me to move to the front of the group. Squaring my shoulders, I reached for Skylahr's hand and intertwined our fingers, waiting until she grabbed the blade she had collected from the group of immortals before taking the first step forward.

Farther and farther we descended, armed and ready for our enemy, but none came. The stairs remained empty, and I could not hear anything over the sound of rushing water. Carefully taking step after step, we hugged the solid rock wall, keeping as far away from the ledge as possible, knowing that the slickness of the stone could easily turn this attempted rescue into something else entirely.

Keeping a firm grip on Skylahr's fingers, I squinted against the mist that was now blowing in our direction. Surely by now we had to be nearing the bottom, but I could see no end in sight. As we rounded the water once more, I felt the stone beneath us shake. Pressing my hand against the wall, I tried to steady myself, but even the mountain itself was shaking, and I looked back at the halfling and guard in worry.

"What is happening?" Selbie asked, her eyes searching for the cause, and it was then that I noticed the stairs above were beginning to crack and crumble.

"Fuck!" I shouted, turning forward once more as I began to run, all but dragging Skylahr with me as I tried to find solid ground. But it was no use; the rocks beneath our own were breaking and then we were falling.

The impact of my body hitting the freezing water made my teeth rattle, and I sank down a few feet, doing my best to get out of the way of the other three as they followed, and then I kicked towards the surface. Gasping for air, I treaded water and waited for my companions to appear, ensuring that they were as well as they could be before glancing above. Thankfully the stairs we had been on were the last to disintegrate. Had they not been, surely we would have been crushed by the rubble. I thanked the Gods and then spun, trying to find a way out of the water.

There was no ledge, nothing but smooth walls and a door that sat flush against the rock. The bottom of it was about two feet above the surface of the water, and I frowned before swimming to the wood. Kicking my legs, I lifted myself out of the pool until my arm could reach the cold metal ring, and then I tugged. However, the door would not budge. I released my hold before trying again, this time using both hands while my feet pressed against the rock wall in hopes that it would give me more power.

"Fuck!" I growled through my teeth, and I tilted my head back, groaning in effort as I tried once more.

Swimming towards me, Barrick pushed me aside and then undid his belt clumsily before handing me the leather. "Loop it through and we can all pull together."

Following his instructions, I managed to slot the leather around the hoop and then grasped what little length remained. "It's not long enough for all of us to hold."

"What if I get on Barrick's shoulders?" Skylahr asked. "I might not be an immortal, but I'm strong and I'm a halfling."

"It's worth a try," her guard agreed and then lowered himself as well as he could so that she could clamber onto his shoulders. She hooked her legs over them and curled her fingers into his hair, and he growled with a wince as she tugged on the black strands while trying to find her balance.

"Easy, Huntress," he grumbled, tipping his chin back to keep himself from swallowing any water. Deciding she was situated as well as she could be, the man carefully approached the door and she grabbed onto the leather and then waited for me to take the tail end.

"On three." Nodding her head, she waited for me to count and then we heaved as hard as we could, but nothing moved, and I heard the snap of leather just before we both tumbled back into the water.

Emerging once more, I rubbed the water from my eyes, and Barrick held up the torn piece of leather. "I liked that belt."

"You don't need a belt if you're dead," Selbie snapped. "And you will be if we don't get out of this water."

Pulling her own belt from her waist, she held a hand out for Sky and waited until she did the same before passing the two pieces of leather to me. Not understanding, I looked down at the leather in my palm and then lifted my eyes to hers in question.

"It was a good idea, but we need a thicker strap and I think more power," Selbie explained.

"They won't be long enough for all of us to pull." Sky frowned and the halfling shook her head.

"We won't need to; we just need the strength of something bigger, something like an enormous beast." My eyes widened in understanding, and I glanced at the door.

"Can you do that in water?" Barrick wondered out loud and I shrugged.

"I don't see why it should be any different." I pulled off my breeches, passed the soaking wet material to Skylahr, and then I concentrated, conjuring the burning inferno I needed.

My size made it nearly impossible for the three to be anywhere but pressed against the walls, and I turned to the door where the belts hung from and carefully closed my incisors around the leather before bracing all four legs on the rock below. Digging my nails in, I heaved, and though the door groaned under the pressure, it did not open, and then suddenly the metal hook the belts had been tied to came flying off.

My companions' panic grew as they stared at the door, but I was too focused on the sounds coming from behind the wood. I glanced over my shoulder, directing them to try to squeeze behind me, and then readied myself for our visitors.

The click of the lock was my only warning before the door swung open, and I clawed my way up the wall, grabbing the first between my jaws before snapping them shut and then I launched myself out of the water. The hall was dark, the immortals hadn't even bothered to light the torches, but I didn't need to see. I could smell their fear, the salt on their skin turning sweet as their blood rushed through their veins, and I became the predator from their nightmares, a beast of terror.

Turning back to the glittering pool, I lowered my face, carefully hooking a canine onto the neckline of Barrick's tunic before lifting him from the water. I waited until he pulled the other two to the landing before shifting back into my human form.

"Thank the Gods you suggested that plan." Skylahr sighed, and then she was gazing up at my face, her eyes searching the skin before checking the rest of my body for any sign of injury. "Are you okay?"

Nodding, I grabbed at the pants that dangled in her hand and stepped into the wet fabric hurriedly before cupping her cheek and pressing a kiss to her brow. "Are you?"

"Fine," she promised.

"We better hurry," Barrick suggested from behind us, and turned to the dark hallway, searching for some light or a sign of what lay ahead.

Knowing we had no other option, I stepped over the carnage on the floor, and we began to make our way down the narrow corridor. The light from the waterfall began to fade as I ventured farther into the dark, and Skylahr's breathing changed as she grew more nervous. I felt my own heart race when I noticed the glimmer of firelight flicker from ahead.

Hurrying my strides, I all but ran towards the glow, and then when I reached the open doorway, I paused, waiting until the three had caught up before stepping into the light, and then a voice called out to me.

"Kalian?"

Chapter 57

Rushing past me, Skylahr slid to her knees and curled her long fingers around the steel bars as she sobbed. Ella, who had been too shocked to do much else other than stare at me, finally turned her attention to the woman on the floor and then moved from the cot in the corner. Crawling across the dirty ground, she stuck her arms through the bars, and I couldn't help but notice how thin and frail they appeared as she wrapped them around Skylahr's shoulders.

"Thank the Gods you're okay," Sky cried, her body shaking as her own hands lifted to cup the woman's face. They both rested their foreheads against the steel, their eyes peering into each other's for a pause.

"I thought you were dead," Ella whimpered, studying the scar on Skylahr's throat with worry. "We all thought you were dead."

"I'm fine." Skylahr offered the halfling a watery smile, and then she turned to us and beamed up at Barrick. "We are both fine."

Taking a step forward, the man knelt next to his Huntress and grabbed one of Ella's hands before pressing a quick kiss to the dark skin of her fingers. "I sure am pleased to see you, Miss Ella."

"Barrick, I never thought I'd miss your moody self." She laughed while wiping her eyes, and then those dark irises lifted to me, a slender black brow rising. "How did this all come to be?"

Noticing Selbie's hesitant approach, the immortal woman tilted her head and frowned. Selbie fidgeted under her gaze, her fingers grabbing the fabric of her shirt and wringing the water from the material, and then she cleared her throat softly. "I travelled to Denimoore when the village I was in received word from them."

"We had been trying to find you and Gaelon," Skylahr explained. "Leena had sent out hawks to all the coastal villages in the north and to some lords who she trusted in the south."

"When I heard that's where the Huntress was, I began my journey north."

"Why?" Ella asked.

"Because I knew what the Siren's immortals were planning, and I knew I had to do something to stop it." Selbie lifted her chin, peering down at the women boldly.

"You knew what they were planning?" Ella repeated, her eyes narrowing in accusation, and Skylahr cupped her shoulder reassuringly.

"She is of the Siren, El," Skylahr explained. "But she does not want to see what they're plotting come to fruition; she came to us in hopes we could stop them."

"I had come across a handful of them after I left Beilham. They had just begun to assemble before travelling to the coast. The first group I had spent some time with had never given me any inclination of what they were plotting," Selbie promised as her eyes lifted to mine. "However, when we met with the bigger group it became clear to me that their intentions were not to help the people of Elrin. I shouldn't have been surprised given their history of doing nothing to aid those who needed them, but when I realized just how wicked their plan was, I left to find you lot."

Ella looked skeptical, but Skylahr shuffled closer, her head lowering. "Ella, we can't judge her for others' choices just because they share the same God, remember what Hectoar said."

Sighing in defeat, Ella nodded but then her frown deepened, her face turning puzzled once more. "But how did you know Gaelon and I would be here? How did you know that we were still alive?"

"I had stopped in a tiny village during my travels to Denimoore.

The lord of the village was one who had been contacted by the Lupine immortal. When I had asked him to write back asking for an audience, he refused. That is until another traveller appeared, one I knew to be a close confidante to the Huntress. Apparently, she had managed to survive a voyage at sea and had returned to shore with a captain named Mira."

Ella took a second to understand what she was being told, and then her lips parted in shock and she stared up at the halfling before whispering, "Elizabeth?"

Selbie nodded. "She accompanied me to Denimoore."

"She's there then? She's well?" The room grew silent, the tension palpable while Ella's dark eyes moved from person to person and then she settled on her friend once more. However, Skylahr's chin lowered to her chest, her eyes falling to the floor just as a quiet sob broke from her.

"What?! What is it?!" Ella asked. "Where is she?"

"Miss Ella," Barrick began, but what could he possibly say to make this less painful? I saw the minute the immortal understood. Her pretty face crumpled, her dark lashes closing as her matted curls fell forward to block my view of her face. She pulled from Skylahr, shuffling back a foot or two before wrapping her arms around herself.

"Tell me," she demanded, her voice breaking while her lower lip quivered.

"She wouldn't stay behind," the guard began. "I spent hours trying to convince her, the Huntress tried as well, but she wouldn't hear it. She wanted to be here when we found you; she was desperate to help you."

Ella began to shake her head, her distraught expression slowly growing more angry as time passed.

"She was braver than any of us," the man went on. "A fierce little thing. She was determined to rescue you; she wouldn't listen to reason."

"Then you should have made her!" Ella screamed, her hands cradling her head as her wide, wild eyes focused on Skylahr. "Why didn't you make her?!"

Skylahr flinched away from her friend's fury, her shoulders curving under the weight of guilt, but Ella wasn't finished. "You brought her here, you let her go with you, and now you're telling me she's gone?! That *you* let her die?!"

"Ella," Sky whispered weakly, but the immortal wasn't having it.

"You should have done better; you should have protected her! Why didn't you protect her?!" the immortal sobbed harshly.

"Ella," I warned as I moved to the floor beside Skylahr. "This isn't her fault; you can't place the blame on her."

"She promised Elizabeth that she would always protect her, and she failed. Tell me if she isn't at fault, who is?"

It was a crushing blow, and Skylahr recoiled from the bars, her body curling in on itself.

"Ella, I know you are angry and hurt," I began softly.

"Hurt?" she spat, her head shaking. "She was safe and sound, she had made it to you and was *safe and sound*, and you brought her here to this Godsforsaken place anyway. If you hadn't let her come, she would still be alive. You brought her to her death!"

I could hear the way the air was knocked from Skylahr's lungs, and then I glared at the immortal. "Enough now, Ella."

"Who are you to—" she began but I slammed my palm against the bars in anger.

"No!" I snarled before pointing a finger at her. "You have every right to be furious and heartbroken and whatever else, but you do not get to place the blame on her shoulders. She lost her too, Ella. Sky lost her too."

The immortal's mouth snapped shut but the damage was done. I could feel the self-loathing pouring off of Skylahr, and I looked up at Barrick, seeking some sort of help or support, hoping he would be able to get Ella to see reason. But the man paid me no mind, his face troubled while he watched the immortal in the cell carefully.

"I expected better from you, Miss Ella," Barrick said as he shook his head disappointedly. "I know your tongue is sharp and you can cut down even the strongest of men with just a few words, but never in all my years did I think you would ever use that venom on someone you love in such a way."

Shame clouded the immortal's face but she said nothing, and Sky had yet to raise her head. Rubbing at his scarred face, the guard moved his attention to the empty cell next to the immortals and then to the others. Each one was as empty as the last, and his brows furrowed and then he looked to Ella once more.

"Miss Ella, we need to get you out from behind those bars and then find the Healer," Barrick explained. "Where is he?"

"I haven't seen Gaelon in days." Ella sniffed. "They sent four men down here to take him from his cell."

"Do you know why?" I asked.

"They want him to help them with something, some type of old magic that is keeping them from using the horn. Apparently their attempts at getting the blood they need have all failed."

"Do you know where they would be? How many of them there are?" The immortal didn't bother to meet my gaze, but she shook her head.

"They took him through the door over there, I am assuming to another floor above." She gestured towards the door on the other side of the room. "As for how many, it's hard to say, but I have never seen more than a few dozen at a time."

Turning to Sky, I cupped her biceps and lifted her to her feet before smoothing her wet hair gently. Then I tucked a finger under her chin, waiting until her gaze found mine before stroking a thumb across her cheek. "It's time to find your Healer."

Her stare remained blank, but her chin dipped in agreement, and then we were turning to the iron bars of Ella's cell. I studied the lock carefully and moved to the hinges. Running my fingers over the cold metal, I then searched the ground for something of use. Upon noticing a small rock no bigger than the palm of my hand, I turned to the guard.

"Did you lose your dagger in the water?" Frowning, the man shook his head and pulled the metal blade from his breeches. My brows lifted when I noticed the missing scabbard. "That was mighty brave of you."

Grunting, the guard pressed the weapon into my grasp, and I held the pommel nut to the bottom of the pin and then tapped the tip of the blade with the rock. Slowly the pin slid out of its hinge, and I repeated the process with the bottom and then grabbed the loose door before moving it aside.

Uncurling from the floor, Ella stood but made no move towards us, and Sky swallowed audibly before stepping back, giving the immortal enough space to pass through the opening. I wondered if she kept the space between them because she truly blamed the Huntress for Elizabeth, or if she knew just how badly she had wounded her friend with her words and now it was impossible to take them back.

Choosing to ignore her, I turned to the others. "The hallways will be too narrow for my Lupine form, and it may be safer if we are able to communicate with each other. What weapons do we still have?"

Both Skylahr and Selbie lifted the blades we had taken from the immortals who had tried to ambush us, and I was surprised they had managed to keep them after everything. I turned to Barrick.

"You have my only weapon." He gestured to the dagger I still held, and I gave it back to him with a frown.

"We will have to do this carefully," I advised them. "We cannot act hastily, we will need to think every decision through."

"Even if we rescue Gaelon, where will we go?" Ella asked quietly from behind me, and I looked at her from over my shoulder. "I'm assuming that you are the only ones who survived the journey, and that the beast is still out there."

"Yes," I confirmed, not knowing how I could possibly answer her question.

"Then where will we go?"

"Home." It was Skylahr who answered her now, though her voice was hoarse. "We will find every last person responsible for your capture, and we will learn how to stop their creature, and then we will return home."

Finally, the immortal lifted her shimmering eyes to the Huntress. "I don't know where home is without Elizabeth."

I could hear the whimper Skylahr tried to choke down as she blinked through her own tears. "Neither do I, but I do know it's not here." Wiping at her face, Ella tilted her chin, ignoring the way it trembled, and then she gave Skylahr curt nod.

Barrick reached for the Huntress and cupped her shoulder while his dark eyes found mine. "Excellent. Let's get off this fucking island."

Chapter 58

Using the same method, we carefully removed the door from its hinges and grabbed one of the lit torches that lined the walls. My comrades' boots squelched as we wandered through the halls carefully, though we had yet to come across another soul. However, just as I was beginning to lose hope, I could make out the sound of quiet footfalls from a distance away. I smothered out our torch and ushered us into a nearby alcove that would hide us from the men who were sauntering down the adjacent corridor, thanking the Gods that they had been too busy chatting to hear the subtle noise we made.

"I just don't understand continuing to hunt for her. Why do they think the Reide blood will work? It didn't a hundred years ago. Besides, we have the beast, why do we need to summon the Siren herself?" one of them grumbled.

"Tilair is growing tired. Apparently his claims of being the Chosen of our Goddess are proving to be false, and the Healer has no way of helping him, so it will only be a matter of days until he loses control of the beast. We need the Siren if we are to continue to rule the seas, and the only answer from the scriptures of the Second Gods is the blood of the first."

"So the Healer is reaching the end of his usefulness. I wonder how much longer he will last." One of them laughed, and I felt Skylahr stiffen next to me, her breath coming out in sharp little gasps.

"Did you see the state of him today? Tilair may not have found a way around his rapid healing, but not even the Healer's Chosen could stop himself from starving to death. He may be a bargaining tool to draw the Huntress out, but if she doesn't appear soon, her friend will meet his end."

Skylahr's hand clawed at my shoulder as she tried to move past me, but I ushered her farther back, not realizing that our scuffle would push us into Barrick, the force sending his dagger tumbling to the ground. The quiet chatter had stopped, as had their footsteps, and I glared back at Skylahr before plucking her blade from her hand despite her protests.

Waiting, I held my breath as the men turned down our hallway to investigate the noise, their gaits slow and hesitant as they searched, and when their torch began to cast shadows on the floor beneath our feet, I charged.

Covering the mouth of the first, I used the edge of my blade to cut his throat and then turned to the next. I knocked his sword from his hand, thrust the tip of my weapon into his chest, waiting until the life faded from his face, and then I carefully lowered him to the floor.

My companions approached from the shadows, and Sky cupped my face. Turning it one way, she scanned one side and then repeated the process with the other. Certain I was unhurt, she slid her fingers into my hair, and I was about to tell her now was not the time. But she did not pull me to her mouth or caress the strands softly. Instead, she curled her fingers tightly, dragging my head down harshly and then stepped close until her face was inches from mine.

"Never presume to take a blade from me again. I am no damsel, and I do not need a saviour, Kalian," she snapped, snatching the weapon back before releasing me. I inhaled roughly, unsure if the fire now spreading through my veins was from anger that she was so unappreciative for my help, or my desire to push her just a little further in hopes she would show me just how unladylike she truly was.

Ella bent to pick up the men's weapons and took one for herself before handing Barrick the other, and then it became quiet once more as our friends awkwardly waited for one of us to give them direction. Holding Skylahr's heated gaze, I lifted a hand for her to continue down the hall, an invitation she took without a second thought. I reached for the men's torch that lay burning on the stone floor, lifted it above my head, and followed behind the Huntress.

The halls were damp with moisture as we ventured farther until we reached a crossroads. Four hallways met at this point, and there was no way to say for sure which we should choose next. Moving to one, Skylahr peered down the dimly lit corridor, then moved onto the second and did the same, though by the time she reached the third, I knew for certain she had found nothing to signify which way we should go.

"This entire place is a maze," Barrick muttered under his breath. "We are better off just picking one and giving it a go rather than standing here wasting time."

Turning to Ella, Skylahr looked at the halfling with a weary expression. "Perhaps you should decide."

Selbie and Barrick eyed the Huntress with confusion, but she paid them no mind, nor did the halfling. The dark-skinned beauty pondered Skylahr's words before doing her own inspection of each entryway.

"This one." She pointed to the second, and Skylahr nodded and then moved across the floor. Not understanding why she had asked the immortal to choose, I waited for an explanation. But none came as the Huntress padded across the cobblestones, leaving us no choice but to follow. I could see no difference between this path and the last, but the guard had been right—waiting around as we tried to decide would do us no good, and so I kept my observations to myself.

However, it was not the only thing I noticed. I couldn't help but pick up on the quick glances the pair kept throwing at each other, almost as if they wanted to say something but couldn't find a way to approach it. Knowing it was not my place to interfere, I remained silent, and then the sweet scent of death hit my nose.

Gagging, Ella lifted a hand to cover her face. The scent finally found its way to the others, and we froze. I reached forward and grabbed both women by the backs of their tunics, hauling them towards me, and then I began backing up, putting as much distance between us and the helcyrbius that was now charging forward.

The creature clambered down the hall, using its front legs to pull it forward, those long blue talons dragging it across the stone faster than we had any hope in being, and readied myself for those long claws to sink into one of us.

However, it was almost as if the creature could not decide where to set its sights, and when it reached for Ella, Sky lunged forward, using her sword to cut off the arm that had lifted to strike the immortal. The limb fell to the floor with a heavy wet noise, and the skull's mouth opened as it shrieked in pain. Sky struck again, narrowly missing the other clawed hand as it swung, and then she hacked at the monster's neck. After decapitating it, she waited until its body dropped into a heap, and then she pressed a hand to her chest as she fought to catch her breath.

"Are you alright?" she asked Ella, but the immortal offered only a silent nod, and Skylahr didn't bother to press any further before turning to me.

"We should head back—" More screaming echoed around us, the shrill shrieking matching that of helcyrbius Skylahr had just killed, but this time it came from behind, and there wasn't just one this time, but multiple.

"Run!" I screamed, ushering Selbie and Barrick ahead of me and then we began to flee.

The hallway was winding, the curves hard to navigate in the flickering light of the torch I carried, and Barrick stumbled to his knees, cursing sharply as the joints crashed against the stone. I bent to help him and pressed a firm hand to his back, pushing him forward once more, but the small delay had cost us, and I could hear the scraping of the talons as the monsters closed the distance. Slowing my pace, I watched as the others continued to run, nearly making it around the bend when Skylahr froze, and then those brilliant hazel eyes were searching for me.

"Kalian! Hurry!" she shouted as she turned to come to my aid, but I lifted my gaze to her guard and gave him a gentle shake of my head. Her face paled when she realized what it meant. "No! Kalian!"

Stepping in front of her, Barrick wrapped a strong arm around her waist, ignoring her fighting and protests while he tried to haul her back. But she clawed at the wall, kicking and flailing as she tried to get to me.

"Kalian!" she called for me again, her voice growing desperate as Selbie helped her guard restrain her.

Turning away from her distressed expression, I forced myself to ignore her frantic sobs of my name and then I waited. The creatures were nearing, their screams growing louder as they hunted us down, and then when I knew there was no escape for me, I whispered a prayer.

But not to the Gods, who had always remained silent no matter how often I had called out to them, but to my mother. Skylahr's life could not be left in the hands of the ancient Deities, so I bowed my head and I called for her, knowing that she would not forsake me, not for this. Not for *her*.

"Please, Mother, please be with her. Stay with her today till the end of her days. Let her live through this, let her be safe."

One long clawed hand curled around the corner and then another, and when the massive boned face opened its jaws, I rushed forward, stuffing the torch down into its throat. The fire caught quickly, faster than I had expected, and I had to throw myself back to avoid getting caught amongst the flames when I shifted.

Landing on all fours, I watched in satisfaction as the beast threw itself to the cobblestones, thrashing and screaming as the fire consumed it, and then I waited for the rest. Soon enough they appeared, their bodies camouflaging with each other, and had it not been for their stark white skulls, they would have just looked like a massive shadow.

I clawed at the first and dragged it beneath my weight, using my front paws to pin it down while I grabbed the next by the shoulder. Tearing into it, I shook my head, waiting until the limb came loose before clamping around its jugular. However, I had been too focused on the kill that I hadn't been prepared for a third jumping on my back, its talons finding purchase in my shoulders and flank while its bone teeth reached for the side of my face.

After taking care of the one beneath me, I threw myself backwards to the floor, crushing the helcyrbius with my body before using my back legs to kick the fourth away and into the flames that were still burning. Shrieking in pain, the monster clawed itself from the blaze, frantic to rid itself of the fire that clung to its skin, and in its desperation, it collided with the fifth and final. I waited until it too slumped to the stone before lifting myself from the body I had still been lying across.

Waiting for a moment, I listened for any sign of others, and when there was none, I glanced down the hall to where my friends had disappeared. The stone walls were narrow, but not as difficult to manoeuvre as I had thought, though there was no way to remain inconspicuous in this form, and so when I knew I neared them, I shifted back into my immortal form.

There was no shouting, no crying or talking, nothing to signify that they had found anything, and as I skirted around the last bend, I noticed a soft glow at the end of the hall and hurried towards it. The door was ajar, but not fully open, and I knew what I would find beyond the wood. I could smell the rust.

Taking a deep breath, I lifted both palms and pressed the wood open, pleading that my mother had heard my prayers.

Chapter 59

The light was blinding compared to the darkness of the hall, and had it not been for my heightened senses I would have needed a minute to adjust. Thankfully, however, I could see the room clearly the minute I stepped in, but it had not been what I was expecting. Given the strong stench of blood, I was certain my friends had been killed, but had I taken a moment to really focus past the heavy smell of salt, I would have realized that it didn't belong to them.

Glancing around the room, I noticed the two corpses that were strewn across the floor and the blood-covered sword in Skylahr's hand, the blade staying strong and steady as she held it out at her side. However, she was tense, her shoulders stiff as she gazed at the stranger in front of her, and it was then that I noticed the Healer. He was not the same man I had seen at the shores; his face was sickly pale and sunken in, dark shadows hung beneath his angular eyes, his curls hung limply over his forehead, and he seemed disoriented as his attention moved about the room.

"Glad to have you join us, Protector. I see you made your way through my helcyrbi." The man smiled while he pressed the gleaming metal tip into the delicate flesh of the Healer's throat, and Sky tensed, ready to strike should he go any further.

"Now, now, Huntress," he chided. "Don't get hasty."

"Let him go," she snarled, but the immortal just rolled his eyes at her demand.

"Why would I?" he asked. "If I do that, I lose any and all power I have here, and I am not done negotiating."

"You have no power here," she snapped. "There is nothing to discuss. You can let him go and I will grant you a quick death, or you can waste more of my time and I will make you suffer. Either way you die."

The promise seemed to shake the immortal, though he hid it well, and then he glanced at the Healer in his grasp. "More of my men are coming, Huntress. They will be here at any moment, and though you are skilled, you cannot defeat a hundred of them. So, do yourself a favour and hear my demands. You can have him; I just want a small token in exchange."

"I don't think you understood me," Skylahr growled. "I am not debating the terms of your surrender."

"Is a small taste of your blood not worth your Healer's life?" he asked with a tilt of his head, his hand applying more pressure to the Healer's jugular.

"You are a fool." Skylahr laughed darkly, and the immortal's face clouded with anger, his hand lowering as he narrowed his gaze at the Huntress.

"Watch yourself, halfling," he growled.

"Halfling? Are we dropping titles already?"

The Siren's immortal seethed at her amused tone, his focus fully consumed by her, and the Healer sensed the opening.

Seeming to use all of his strength, he threw back his head, knocking his skull into the immortal's nose, and then he dropped from his hold, scurrying out of his reach just as Skylahr was pressing forward. She grabbed the Siren's immortal's wrist and pinned it to the table behind him, and then bent him back until he was sprawled across the wooden surface. Lifting her sword, she mimicked the immortal's previous position and pressed the metal to his throat.

"You should have listened to me," she warned, her face lowering to just a few inches away from his own, and he struggled against her weight. "This could have gone differently for you, but now I want to watch you suffer."

Barrick, who had been helping the Healer to his feet, froze at Skylahr's words, and I felt my own stomach fall. That lingering darkness that had been following her seemed to grow tenfold as she watched the man beneath her struggle, and then she was carefully pressing her blade into his neck.

"Skylahr," Gaelon gasped weakly, his expression horrified as she taunted the man, and she glanced over her shoulder, her expression unreadable as her eyes met the Healer's.

"You would have me show him mercy?" she asked in surprise.

"I would not have you torture him," he answered hoarsely.

"Very well." She nodded and then gazed back down at the man. "But before I send you home to the Gods, let me just enlighten you of your failure. The blood you seek does not run in my veins; I am not a true Reide and this was all for nothing." She relished his shock for just a moment and then she finished him.

No one moved, no one made a sound as we watched her clean the metal, and then she turned to us, her face vacant. Barrick had been right; something was terribly wrong, and now we could all see it.

"Skylahr," Gaelon whispered, reaching a weak hand towards her. "What has happened?"

"Elizabeth is dead," Ella said softly, though her attention never moved from the Huntress, and the Healer took in a sharp breath and then he beckoned Skylahr closer.

"I am so sorry," he murmured, his arm rising as he tried to cup her face, but when he grazed her scarred cheek, his fingers trembled. Not from exhaustion, but from something else. However, no one else appeared to notice, and I swallowed down the bile that was rising up the back of my throat, knowing he felt the coldness that had been seeping into the room up until the very moment he touched her.

Pulling from him, she glanced back at the man on the table. "Was that Tilair?"

"It was," he confirmed shakily, his careful gaze never wavering from her face.

"He was the one who controlled the beast?" Skylahr continued.

"Yes, though he was slowly losing the power to do so. The magic he had been relying on began to falter, and he did not have the Siren's power, though he continued to say otherwise."

"How did the others not notice he was not her Chosen?" I wondered, pulling the Healer's attention from Selbie, and he shrugged.

"They were desperate to believe in something, and that desperation left them blind to the truth."

"Wait," Barrick interrupted. He turned to me, though he averted his gaze from my nude form, and then he grabbed one of the curtains that hung from the window and tossed it to me. Satisfied that I was covered, he went on. "If the man who controlled the beast is dead, what does that mean? Is the beast wandering around freely now that Tilair is gone?"

"The immortals feared the opposite would happen actually." Unable to stand much longer, the Healer sank into one of the chairs. "They thought the beast would go back to where it came from without him."

"Which is where?" I inquired.

"The bottom of the sea." It should have been a relief, and to the others it was, but both the Healer and I were still too preoccupied with watching Skylahr to really feel any sense of ease, and she noticed.

Rolling her shoulders, she returned our attention with a suspicious glare but said nothing. She glanced around the room, her eyes landing on a map that hung on the wall. "Is there really a port on the other side of the island?"

"I think so." Gaelon nodded. "We were blindfolded once we reached shore, but it certainly felt like a dock, so their ships must be waiting somewhere."

"So, we could go home." Selbie sighed, but Skylahr only shook her head.

"Not yet. There's no way to say for certain that one of the others couldn't learn how to conjure their monster once more, and there's still the issue of the horn."

"But the horn is not an issue; they do not have what they need to use it," Selbie reminded her.

"There may be other Reeds in the world, men and women who have the blood they require." Skylahr rubbed a hand over her face in frustration. "We should write to your sister; tell her we are alive and what we have found. Then we find the horn and wait for more men now that the beast is no longer a threat for the time being."

"Your plan is flawed," I admitted begrudgingly. "Sending word to Leena requires a hawk, and we don't have one."

The Healer sat up straight in his seat and then he looked to me. "We might not have a hawk, but we do have a great beast of a bird. One that was caught nearly a fortnight ago. A creature from the north."

Skylahr's gaze widened in surprise and she looked to me for confirmation.

"How do you know it was from the north?" I asked.

"The immortals were talking about it; they had never seen a sightless bird before."

Selbie and Barrick looked confused.

"What kind of bird is sightless?" the guard wondered out loud, his dark eyes catching my own.

"The hafok."

Covering my mouth and nose, I squinted through the dust that was lifted into the air as the giant bird flapped his wings, racing from one side of his cell to the other. He looked no worse for wear from what I could see from the doorway, and I inhaled deeply before stepping into the room.

I always hated the damn thing, never once understanding Keyno's love for the eyeless, ugly, overgrown pigeon, and Hawk seemed to know it. Any of our interactions ended up with gashes to my back as he chased me about until I could find cover, and I wasn't so certain this would end any differently.

"Listen here, you blind chicken," I growled as I approached, my steps faltering when he turned that hideous face towards me. "Try to gouge my eyes out and we will have you for dinner."

His enormous beak opened in a scream, almost as if he was rising to the challenge, and I glared.

"I don't think those sweet words are helping your case," Sky grumbled from behind me.

"Please, this thing isn't smart enough to understand me." Hawk's head tilted to the side, and then he screamed again.

"Then stop talking to him and get on with it."

Taking her advice, I approached the cell cautiously, my movements slow and steady as he listened carefully. But when I touched the bars, he began his flapping once more, and then he launched himself towards me, talons reaching for my hands.

"Damn bloody bird!" I cursed, jumping back as he found a perch on the windowsill, his chest puffing out proudly.

"Kalian, we need him," Skylahr reminded me sternly, and I narrowed my eyes at her.

"I'm aware."

"I never thought you would be afraid of a bird." Had it been any other time, I would have been happy to see that quirk of her lip, the first hint of a smile from her in days, but I was aggravated and embarrassed.

"I'm not afraid!" I snapped, but she just rolled her eyes.

"Oh, just move aside!" Pushing past me, she reached for the cell door and unlatched the lock before stepping into the cage. Hawk's head tilted, but he did nothing more, and I waited with bated breath as she lifted a hand to stroke the feathers of his chest.

"There now, see? We mean no harm," she said softly, her fingers skimming across his body while the hafok preened under her attention. "That's a sweet bird."

Crossing my arms, I snarled at the blind creature. "Traitorous little shit."

"Ignore him," Skylahr continued, her free hand lifting the scroll carefully before tying it to Hawk's leg. Certain it was tight, she gave the hafok one last pet and then glanced over at me.

"I don't think I am strong enough to withstand his weight on my arm, so we will just have to prop open the doors and herd him out. Tell the others so that he has a straight path." Nodding, I turned to Barrick, who had remained in the hall, and passed along the message before pressing my body into the door, turning my back to them in case the thing should decide to come at me.

"Ready?" Skylahr asked from the cell.

"Ready." Closing my eyes, I waited, listening as the steel groaned under Skylahr's hands, and then a great gust of wind blew past me, the force of it strong enough for me to flinch. I kept my eyes closed, waited for another moment, and then turned to the Huntress.

"Let's pray to the Gods this works." It was just a phrase, nothing more, but her face fell, and the chill returned.

"I don't think they're listening any longer."

Chapter 60

Whatever men Tilair had warned us about had yet to appear, but we kept our guard up as we gathered whatever supplies we could while we went from room to room. The shrine was massive, its chambers rundown and picked apart, but we were able to find some things of use and had even located some fruit and bread for the Healer. The man was still weak and feeble, but he would not allow anyone to coddle him, his attention always too focused on our Huntress to even pay our worried looks any mind.

Finding a quiet room that appeared to be undisturbed by the Siren's immortals, we gathered close after laying whatever rugs, furs, and cushions we could find across the floor. It was not a feathered mattress, but it would be far better than sleeping on the stone.

I stepped into a pair of breeches and boots Ella had found. The material ended halfway down my shins, and they were far tighter than I preferred, but they were an improvement from the ragged curtain that I had been wearing.

"Now we won't have to watch you bounce all over the place." She gestured to my groin, and I flushed. There wasn't much I could do when it came to shifting, the change of my body shredded whatever I wore, but I never wanted to make anyone uncomfortable.

"I'm sorry," I apologized to the group while shoving my feet into the boots, but they all waved me off.

"I rather deal with a bit of nudity every so often and have a giant wolf at our backs than to not. Besides, the only one who is interested has seen it all before." Selbie shrugged.

My eyes drifted to Skylahr, fully expecting to see the fuchsia burning its way across her skin or maybe a shy smile, but it was as if she hadn't heard a word, too lost in her own mind to even notice we had been talking.

It was stupid of me, really, to assume something so trivial would be a focus of hers now given where we were and what all had happened. And yet, I somehow knew it wasn't just her grief and worry that kept her from paying us any attention.

"Protector," the Healer called, and I turned to face him. "I would like to check the other rooms of this corridor for more supplies. Will you help me?"

It was a poor excuse, but no one questioned it, and I moved across the floor, reaching for him so that I could help him to his feet. His injuries had healed, and he looked far better than he had a few hours ago, but he was too thin, and only rest and food could help him regain his full strength.

Closing the door behind us softly, I gestured for him to lead the way down the lengthy hall.

"We do not know each other well," he began once we were a distance away, and I lifted a brow before crossing my arms. "But we have a common interest."

"World peace?" I snapped sarcastically, and he frowned, his dark eyes lowering to the floor before he traced the length of my body, but his face remained unimpressed when he finally met my gaze.

"Skylahr," he growled, and my mouth lifted into a smirk while I took my time to do my own assessment of the man before me.

He was small, at least half a foot shorter than me and not nearly as strongly built. His hair was a dark brown, the colour only accentuating how pale his skin was. He had a pleasing face, I supposed, and I could sense the calm and warmth he carried, a true testament to his God. And a tiny part of me wondered what Sky thought when she looked at him. Did she see a whole man who had never hurt her? Did she see someone she could trust and care for without second-guessing herself? Did she think that he was the better option?

"It has never been like that for us," he whispered, almost as if he could read my mind, and my jaw clenched, my teeth grinding together in annoyance.

"No need to lie, Healer. I saw you kiss her at the shores."

"It was a moment of comfort, not passion," he explained, his face still relaxed and kind as he held my stare.

"And since?" I had no right to ask. I had no right to wonder, but I had to know. Not because it would change anything for me or my feelings, but because I needed to know if she had made a better choice and still wanted me in the end.

"She loves you." His eyes roamed across my face once more. "I don't see the appeal, but I know it to be true. Which is why I need your help."

"With what?" I asked, my hackles rising.

"With her." He glanced at the closed door and then pressed back against the wall tiredly. "Something is wrong, something is very wrong."

"She just lost her sister." His head shook at my excuse, and I knew how pitiful it sounded.

"It's more than that. You know it, and so do I." Tension flooded his face, his expression hardening as he prepared himself for my arguments. "At first I thought the Seductress had returned, using that link between them to affect her once more."

"And has she?" I questioned, terrified of the answer.

"No." My head fell forward, my chin tucked to my chest as the air left my lungs. "This is her and her alone, and now I'm starting to wonder if the link between the two of them at the shores had ever been the doing of the Crimson Goddess."

"Meaning what? That *Skylahr* is responsible for that connection somehow?"

"Maybe." The Healer shrugged.

"That's impossible. She is the *Huntress*, the Chosen of the Huntress!" Gaelon winced at my tone, his head turning away.

"I don't have any other answer for you, Kalian," he tried.

"Then shut your mouth and stop speaking on things you obviously know nothing about," I snarled, stepping forward until I towered over him. "And do not breathe a word of this to her. She carries enough guilt as it is. She doesn't need you crushing her with your best guesses and ludicrous opinions."

Turning from the man, I looked at one of the doors and kicked it open angrily. "Go look for your supplies. If we come back empty-handed then she will know it was a lie."

Ella looked up as we barged back into the room, her dark irises full of questions and accusations, and then they moved to Skylahr, who was sitting next to Barrick, watching as the man portioned out the fruit we had found earlier.

"Did you find anything?" the immortal asked, her head tilting in a way that told me she had heard every word.

"Some candles, flint, and a few cloaks," Gaelon murmured as he stepped around me. "Also, a book about the shell and its beginnings."

"A decent haul then," Barrick huffed as he tossed aside the core from the apple he had been cutting.

I crossed the room, approached the pair, and sank to the floor next to Skylahr, and when she lifted her face, I tucked a strand of hair behind her ear and stroked my thumb over the heart on her cheek. She didn't smile or blush, but there was a warmth to her eyes again, and I gladly took the small victory.

"Any chance you found some dried meat during your adventure?" Selbie asked from her chair as she watched Barrick pluck another apple from the pile, her nose wrinkling when his thumb found a particularly large bruise, the pad sinking into the fruit.

"If you don't want to eat what we have, I will happily take your portion." The guard smiled with false sincerity, and the halfling scoffed.

"You two really don't get along," Ella remarked dryly, her attention moving between them. "Probably because you are so similar."

Both turned to the immortal, their expressions ridiculously alike to each other's, and I hummed under my breath. "You're right, they are."

"I don't see it," Barrick growled, and then focused back on the task at hand.

Ella just lifted a shoulder and then turned back to the cloak she had been inspecting. The room grew quiet, with only the soft sounds of the knife cutting the fruit and the pages rustling as the Healer flipped through his book.

"Where do you think the others went?" Skylahr asked after a long moment, her hazel eyes lifting to mine once more. "Tilair said there was a hundred of them, but we haven't found any others here. Why is that?"

"Maybe he was bluffing?" Selbie guessed.

"But he had no reason to. He knew he was going to die, so warning us that there were more of them seems odd."

"Perhaps there was something else of importance they had to do," Selbie tried again.

"More important than guarding the Healer while they waited for us to come to his rescue?" The same questions had been troubling me for hours, but I hadn't come up with a better reason than the halfling.

"For now, let's focus on locating the horn. Once we have it in our possession, we can head to the shores and wait for more of my men, and then we will deal with whatever others are out there," I proposed, my hand stroking down the length of Skylahr's back.

"Do we have any idea on where it might be?" Barrick wondered, his attention moving between the Healer and Ella.

"I never saw it, only heard them talking about it occasionally." She sighed.

"It's very precious to them," the Healer said softly. "I don't think they would leave it unaccompanied."

"So you don't think it's here," I concluded.

"I thought it couldn't leave its stand." Selbie frowned.

"Leave its place of creation," Gaelon corrected, lifting the book in his hands. "And it was created on this island."

I crossed my arms while I studied the leather cover. "What else does that book say?"

"That in order to summon the Siren, it needs the blood of the first." He frowned in confusion while he read the words twice more. "The blood of the first. Who is that referring to?"

"The blood of Caedell Reide, of the Forefolk, the man who first conjured the Second Gods."

"Skylahr's ancestor?" he guessed, but Skylahr shook head.

"My *father's* ancestor, but he and I did not share blood." Her head lowered as she looked to her lap, and her body seemed to collapse in on itself at the mention of another one of her losses.

"That is why you told him you were not a true Reide" She sniffed and then cleared her throat before nodding at the Healer's words.

"So, if the horn is not here, what are our plans?" Selbie inquired quietly, and my eyes roamed the room, tracing the stone walls until they landed on the tapestry that hung above the Siren's emblem that was carved into the rock. Her features were not heavily detailed, but I still felt unnerved as her eyes seemed to watch my every move. And then, when I could not bear it any longer, I turned away and answered the halfling.

"We will leave for the shores tomorrow as planned and wait for aid. When the fleet arrives, we will search this island for the rest of the immortals and the horn. Once it is in our possession, we will destroy it."

Chapter 61

Gaelon had been the first to succumb to sleep, followed by Barrick and Selbie, and the room grew quiet. Ella, however, had yet to even close her eyes, her gaze locked on the side of Skylahr's face as the Huntress fiddled with whatever she could find. Both souls were aching under the loss of Elizabeth, and the night air was heavy with their pain. Sitting back, I observed them carefully, watching as the immortal blinked away tears, and then she cleared her throat.

"You shouldn't have brought her here." Skylahr stiffened, her quiet gasp just loud enough for me to hear, and I readied myself to interrupt.

"It was what she wanted, Ella." Skylahr sighed, her tone low and defeated.

"Then you should have followed through with your promise." Another strike that hit its mark, and Skylahr flinched as if it was a physical blow.

"I tried," Skylahr choked out. "I tried, but Terian had us cornered and—"

"I don't want your excuses." The change in the room told me that everyone was awake but had yet to move. I took in a deep breath, doing everything in my power to quell the rage that was burning through my veins.

"No, but you *do* want to make sense out of all of this, Ella." Skylahr finally turned to her friend. "I know that you think placing blame will ease your hurt, and if that's what you need to do to heal, then so be it, I will carry that weight."

Skylahr wiped her nose across the back of her hand and swallowed down a rough sob. "But know, as angry as you are with me, as responsible as you think I am for failing her…your feelings of rage and guilt could never match my own."

Standing to her feet shakily, Skylahr searched for an escape like a cornered animal and scurried from the room as quickly as she could. Not knowing what else could be in these halls, I stood to follow but paused and looked down at the immortal with a disappointed frown.

"Things said in pain are not always things we mean, but they are impossible to take back once they've been spoken. Every day she will remember those words and will always wonder if they were sincere," I warned Ella, and when her tearful gaze met mine, I glanced at the open door. "And when this anger fades and you need her, she will think back to this moment and won't know if she should let you in again."

"You don't know what you're talking about, Lupine," she scoffed.

"I do, and I know it well," I admitted. "You are hurting—"

"Hurting doesn't begin to describe the way I feel," she snapped, her eyes wet with unshed tears, and when she turned from me, I ran a hand over my face before following after Sky.

She had not made it far, just a few yards from the door, and I slowed my stride as I approached. Her arms were curled around her torso, her shoulders were hunched, and I could hear her quiet cries. Unsure of what to do, I hovered a foot away, waiting for her to face me, waiting for permission to touch her, not wanting to cross her boundaries when she was in such a state.

"She will never forgive me. I have lost them both." Her chin lifted as she peered up at me, and I held my arms open, an invitation that she immediately took. Tucking her head beneath my chin, I held her to me and waited until her breathing evened out.

"She will, Skylahr," I assured her. "This is not your doing, and Ella knows it. But when people can't make sense of a tragedy, they grasp at whatever they can hold on to and twist reality into something they can understand and accept."

She didn't respond but buried her face into my neck, and I pressed a kiss to her hair before glancing at the other doors that lined the hallway. The rooms were smaller, the things overturned after the Healer had searched them, but they would offer her privacy and quiet, a space from the others while she gathered herself once more, and I took her hand before leading her to the nearest one.

I pushed the door open, guided her into the dark room, and then grabbed the curtains that hung on either side of the arched window. Flicking the blue fabric in the air, I tried to get as much dust off as I could and then spread it across the floor. After repeating the motion with the second, I knelt on the first and waited for Skylahr to crawl to me before falling onto my back. Settling against me, she laid her head on my chest and I pulled the second piece of fabric over us.

"Sleep, love," I murmured quietly.

"What if I dream of her?" she whispered anxiously, those brilliant hazel eyes blinking up at me in worry.

"Then take the chance to tell her you love her, and you miss her, and that you will never forget her," I answered softly. "Be sure to thank her for telling your parents about everything you have achieved, because I am certain that was the first thing she did when they were reunited, and then ask her to say hello to my mother for me."

A warm tear landed on my bare chest, and I tightened my hold before closing my own eyes.

Morning came far too quickly for my liking, and I closed my eyes tightly, trying to ignore the sound of the rain pounding against the stone walls as Skylahr pressed close. She'd had a horrible night, her soft voice calling for her friend and her parents in desperation as she fought off her nightmares, and my anger at Ella grew every time she whimpered in pain. But that hadn't been the only thing to keep me awake. I had not been able to keep myself from thinking on my conversation with the Healer. He was worried, rightfully so, and although I hated what he had implied, I couldn't help but wonder if there was truth to it.

Skylahr had been different at the shores; that goodness and strength she usually carried had been blanketed with something else. In fact, I knew it had been the minute she had flinched away from me after I had saved her from the helcyrbius at the immortals' camp. I had felt the darkness even then, but surely that had been the Seductress's doing.

However, that didn't explain what was happening now, and I couldn't keep myself from noticing the similarities.

I ran my hand over her hair, listening to her breathing change, and then her eyes were fluttering open, and she was pulling from me. Loosening my hold, I watched as she swallowed down that vulnerability she had shown me last night, and then she was smoothing her hands over her thighs nervously.

"We should go back to the others," she advised but didn't bother to wait for me to respond before pulling open the door and striding down the hallway.

I followed her but remained in the doorway, watching as the group slowly organized themselves and their things, and then glanced at Ella. She looked tired, her normally radiant skin appeared dull, and her eyes had immediately moved to Skylahr and followed her every movement. I could see the internal battle, her longing for her friend and her unwillingness to reach out, and I prayed that she would give in sooner rather than later.

"So we've decided to go to the shores," Barrick began while rubbing at his lower back. "But which side of the island?"

"The men Leena sends will leave from just north of Denimoore, which means they are coming from the east," I explained. "It would make the most sense to find higher ground, somewhere that will give us a view of the ocean and the surrounding area. We don't know where the other immortals have gone, but I am certain that should our paths cross, it may end badly for us."

"I still don't understand why they would leave the shrine." Barrick frowned, his mind stuck on that detail.

"It doesn't matter," Gaelon sighed. "But if Tilair was right, and they plan to return, we should depart before that happens."

Without any further argument, the group packed their things carefully, being sure to collect the food and supplies we had found, and then we turned from the room. The halls were still dark and hard to manage, but they were quiet and empty, and we took our time, doing our best to find a way out.

Finally, after what felt like hours, I smelled the heavy scent of rain, and the air around us grew damp as we neared the face of the mountain. I motioned for the others to wait, and I rushed ahead to the door.

Pressing the wood open, I let a breath loose as I gazed across the deep green treetops and grey clouds that covered the sky above, and then I glanced at the waves. My view was slightly obstructed by the forest and rocky terrain, but the ocean seemed calm, so different from how it had been when we arrived.

"Any sign of them?" the Healer called, and I shook my head, waiting for the group to catch up before I turned for the stone stairs that would lead us down the base of the mountain, and my skin almost immediately prickled.

"Do you feel—" Gaelon had started only to lift his head towards the top of the mountain when I heard it. It was a soft rumble, barely loud enough to really notice, but it was there. Taking a step back, I squinted up at the tip of the rock, watching for a pause, and then I felt the tremors.

"Hurry! Go now!" I shouted, ushering them to the stairs in a panic. Skylahr grabbed at both Ella and Selbie, all but dragging them down the steps as she ran, and I turned to Barrick. The guard had tied the supplies to his back, and though they weren't heavy, it would be difficult to manage the Healer, and I urged him to follow the women before turning to Gaelon.

Not bothering with the awkward conversation, I bent and wrapped an arm beneath his knees before hoisting him into my arms. He was light, far lighter than I had imagined he would be, and I felt a pang of sympathy for the man, wondering how long he would have survived had we not found him when we did.

However, now was not the time to focus on such things, and once I was sure I had a secure hold on him, I hurried after the others, shouting at them to keep running even after they reached the bottom of the stairs.

The rumbling had grown louder in the little time it had taken us to step onto the wet earth, and the tremors had grown in strength, the force of them now shaking the trees that surrounded us. Taking a second to glance over my shoulder, I watched as the sharp tip of the mountain began to crumble, the boulders and dust sliding towards us in a giant wave.

"Get into the cover of the trees!" I ordered as I herded them forward, praying that the dense woods would stop the landslide from completely obliterating us.

Following my instruction, Skylahr led the women forward, her hands still clutching theirs tightly as she tugged them behind her. Barrick, who had caught up to them, continued to shout, encouraging them to move faster, and my heart pounded as we finally entered the dark forest.

But the sea of rubble and stone was closing in, its strength taking down anything in its path.

Searching the forest for an escape from what was most certainly going to be our death, I realized there was a ledge up ahead, and though I could not tell how big the overhang was, I knew it was our only option.

"There!" I gestured towards the cliff, and Skylahr turned, her eyes meeting mine for only a pause before they widened at the scene behind me, and then she pressed forward, lengthening her stride.

Sliding to a stop at the very edge, Skylahr peered down at the land below and then grabbed Ella. The immortal snatched her hands from the Huntress and took a step back, but Skylahr did not relent and then she grabbed Ella once more before bringing her to the cliff.

"Please, Ella, I'm going to lower you down," she explained in a rush. "Let me help you, *please*."

The immortal's face was unreadable, but she submitted to Skylahr's request, and Ella lowered herself to the earth. Skylahr fell to her knees, carefully lay on her belly, and then guided Ella over the edge. After a moment, Skylahr then glanced over her shoulder and beckoned Selbie to do the same.

"Your turn now, Huntress!" Barrick shouted, his voice not carrying the same panic that filled his expression, and Skylahr glanced at me.

"Go!" I encouraged her, holding my breath as her guard eased her down, and then I lowered Gaelon to the dirt. "Now him."

Barrick didn't hesitate as he manoeuvred the Healer, and I glanced down at Skylahr, watching as she waited with her arms lifted. The drop wasn't horrendous, but it was too far to jump without risking a broken limb, and when the Healer made it down safely, I looked at Barrick.

"It's your turn." The guard's dark gaze hardened as he looked up at me.

"You need to go first, Protector," he argued, his eyes glancing at the sea of rock behind me. "And we do not have time for arguments."

"Barrick," I warned, but the man shook his head.

"Our Huntress needs you, now more than ever, and you are far more important than I am in this story," he growled impatiently. "Hurry now."

I wanted to argue, I wanted to refuse, but we had no time, and so I fell to the ground. Taking hold of my forearms, the guard held me steady as he lowered me, his eyes never wavering from my own, and when he lowered me as far as he could, he finally let go. There was still a ways to go before my feet touched the ground, and I collided with Skylahr sharply when I finally reached the surface below. Grunting at the impact, Skylahr scrambled out from under me and then looked at the guard above.

Barrick had begun to turn carefully, letting his legs hang over the ledge, and I waited below, ready to catch him when he finally released his hold on the edge. The guard was not graceful with his fall, but I had been ready for it, and when my arms wrapped around him, I steadied him on his feet and gave him a rough pat to his back. However, there was no time for any other celebration; the rumbling above was growing in strength, and I pushed my comrades as far back against the wall as I could before pressing in behind Skylahr.

"Cover your faces as best you can!" I shouted over the noise, and then I closed my eyes, readying myself for the worst as the wave of rock and mud and trees swelled over the overhang above us and came crashing down.

Chapter 62

It was nearly impossible to breathe with the dust still filling the air, and we struggled under the shelter we had found, choking and coughing as we waited. And when the landslide slowed and only a bit of rubble fell from above, I stepped away from Skylahr and glanced behind me. The wreckage went on for acres, the earth now cleared of trees and covered with what was left of the mountain.

"Is that it?" Skylahr asked with a muffled voice, turning with a hand over her mouth as she took in the scene before us with wide eyes.

"We will need to hurry and find cover," I sighed, taking a step forward, pressing a foot into the sludge carefully. It wasn't deep but it was slick and would be hard to cross in a rush.

Moving out from beneath the shelter, the others followed me carefully as we began to head west towards the trees that had not been touched by the destruction of the mountain's collapse. Leading the way, I kept a watchful eye on our surroundings until we were finally protected by green once more. Turning on his heel, Barrick looked out over the debris and then towards where the mountain and its shrine once were.

"What makes an entire mountain collapse like that?" the guard wondered as he looked to Gaelon and me.

"I'm not sure," the Healer answered honestly. "But now we know why the others fled the shrine."

"Do you think they knew that was going to happen?" Selbie wondered, but I had my answer. Glancing up at the twin peak that still stood, I could just make out something blowing in the wind, something that very well could have been a cluster of blue banners.

"It seems too fortunate for the timing to be purely coincidental, though I suppose we were just as lucky," Ella muttered quietly, ignoring the way both Skylahr and Gaelon studied her.

"I believe you're right." The Healer nodded. "And we better make use of our good fortune. We should cover as much ground as we can before we lose daylight, or before the others come looking for any survivors."

Scanning the Healer from head to toe, I frowned and noticed that the guard also looked at the immortal with concern. Gaelon's skin had brightened, and he did not appear as frail, even though it had been only a night since we had found him. However, he would not be in a state to aid us should the time come to face our enemy, nor would he be as quick on his feet as he once had been. It would take time for him to gain his strength back, and I was worried it was time we did not have.

Sighing softly, I shifted beneath the weight of the three women as they curled into my fur, doing their best to absorb my warmth as the temperature continued to drop through the night. Barrick sat in front of me, his arms crossed over his chest as he kept watch, though there was nothing he would see that I wouldn't be aware of first, and I huffed under my breath.

"You can sleep, Barrick," Gaelon offered, his dark gaze moving to me. "Kalian and I will wake you should we hear anything."

The guard hesitated, his mouth opening in protest until I growled softly. Knowing he would be better off listening to the Healer, the man sank down onto the forest floor, cushioning his head with an arm before closing his eyes.

It was only a matter of minutes before the sound of the guard's snoring echoed around us, and Gaelon shook his head in amusement. "It's a wonder you made it to the shrine at all with him making that kind of racket."

"Now it's a wonder our stench won't be the reason we are caught," Skylahr grumbled as she shifted against my side.

"I never imagined you to have such complaints." Gaelon's mouth quirked up at the corners while he watched her, his relief in having some semblance of normalcy from the Huntress obvious.

Skylahr scoffed, shuffling away from me, and then she sat straight, her eyes moving to where the sound of rushing water was coming from. The hot springs were not visible through the trees, but the eggy smell was strong, and she looked at the trees in longing.

"If you go now, you can keep watch in the morning," Gaelon suggested and then his eyes caught mine. "Go ahead, take some time for yourselves while you can."

It was a gracious gift, though I knew that he had another reason for it. The Healer wanted me to talk to Skylahr, to try to piece together what it was that was clinging to her even now. I should have been angry at his scheming, but I knew he was right.

I pulled away from the other two women, waited until they settled on the ground, huddling close together, and then Skylahr draped her cloak over them carefully. Sure they were settled, I stood gazing at Gaelon once more.

"Go, you are a mere few yards away. Nothing will find us without you knowing about it." Skylahr grabbed the pack, rummaged through the supplies until she found a new tunic that would fit her, and then she ducked through the branches.

Waiting to shift until I was away from the group, I rolled my shoulders, stretching my muscles before watching Skylahr. She had toed off her mud-covered boots, unclasped her cloak, and pulled the grimy breeches from her thickly muscled legs. Swallowing at the sudden dryness in my mouth, I studied the long limbs, appreciating the way her inner thighs touched, rubbing together as she moved towards the water edge. She reached for the hem of her tunic and lifted it, exposing inch after inch of pale skin. Her back was glorious, one of my favourite parts about her, and I traced my gaze across the broad shoulders that were covered in freckles before moving my attention to the strong arms that now hung at her sides.

"Are you done with your gawking?" she asked, turning her chin to her shoulder, those brilliant hazel eyes taking my breath away once more.

"Never," I answered honestly. "I never want to be done."

Rolling her eyes, she shook her head and then faced the water once more. "There are other things you should be focused on, Kalian."

"Then it's a good thing I am an excellent multitasker," I pointed out as she stepped into the steaming springs. But she didn't respond and instead dunked beneath the surface, and I took that as my sign to follow her in.

The warmth was soothing as the water lapped at my skin, and I wandered farther in, waiting for those bronze strands to rise once more before I reached for her. Turning at my touch, Skylahr took a step forward, then another, coming close enough for me to wrap an arm around her middle before she rose onto her toes.

Pressing her mouth to mine, she kissed me softly while her arms curled over my shoulders, and then she pulled away, resting her forehead against my own. "I thought there were other things I should be focused on?"

Skylahr rolled her eyes, huffing impatiently as my lips lifted into a cocky grin, and I cupped her face, pulling her to me once more. Basking in the warmth of her affection, I chased any worries and doubts from my mind, focusing wholly on how it felt to have her in my arms again.

Running her hands over my back, she softly traced the scar that ran from shoulder to hip, and I shivered at the touch.

"Did I hurt you?" she asked, blinking up at me. "You've never reacted like that before."

"Of course not," I assured her. "It's just sensitive and your fingers are cold."

"Kalian," she started, but I interrupted her with another kiss, stopping the words on the tip of her tongue. She melted into me, her weight resting against my chest as she kissed me back.

"I've missed you," I murmured against her mouth when we finally broke apart.

"I've missed you too," she replied as she pressed her cheek against my shoulder. "We always seem to end up in this position."

"What position is that?" I wondered, resting my chin on her head while closing my eyes.

"Naked and in a pool of water of some sort." Skylahr snorted before tilting her face towards me, but I hadn't schooled my features in time, and whatever humour that had been warming her eyes dimmed as she noticed my worry. "What is it?"

"Are you alright, truly?" I asked, bracing myself for her answer.

"I forget sometimes," she sighed while her eyes closed, almost as if she was conjuring a picture in her mind. "I forget that my parents and Elizabeth cease to exist in this world, and it is a blessing. It is a gift to not remember the pain and that all-consuming darkness that just seems to wait for me around every corner."

"Is there anything else happening?" My brow furrowed as I cupped her cheek.

"Anything else?" she repeated, not understanding my meaning.

"Is it *her*?" Skylahr swallowed, her eyes lowering to the surface of the water, and then she shook her head in defeat.

"No, Kalian, whatever this shadow is, it is me and me alone." She trembled while her lower lip quivered. "The only time I feel it fade is when I'm with you; it's like your warmth chases it away. But I don't want this darkness to consume you too. I don't want to ruin you."

My thumb stroked her face, the pad smoothing over her scar carefully. "Skylahr, I will not leave you in the shadows. I will not leave you to battle this alone. So, give me your darkness and let it consume me, ruin me, and then we will journey through it until we find the light, *together*."

Those stunning hazel eyes brightened with tears as she gazed up at me, and then her mouth was on mine again while she hooked a leg over my hip. I reached down to grab her other thigh and hoisted her up, wrapping her around my waist, and then I curled my fingers into her thick bronze hair.

Her tongue was pressing into my mouth, licking at my own hotly as she rolled her centre into my hardening cock. Groaning into her mouth, I tugged her head back and pressed my lips to the scar on the throat carefully before sucking the skin that covered her collarbone.

"I want you," she whimpered, her movements growing frantic and needy, and I reached between us, stroking her softly with my fingers.

"Shh, love," I chided. "You need to be quiet."

Her thighs began to tremble against me, her sweet little whimpers quieting but coming more frequently, and I peered down at her, running my nose along hers with a smile while she panted desperately. Perhaps I was selfish, maybe it was greedy of me to want to have her again, especially when we had so many other things to be worried about.

But what if I didn't get another chance? What if we never had another opportunity to be together again and I ruined this moment only to regret it later?

"I want you, Kalian." She gasped again, softer this time.

My fingers had continued to stroke her, the warmth and slickness between her thighs growing as she neared her release, and I shifted her in my hold just slightly, opening her thighs while I lined myself up. Pausing at her entrance, I held her eyes captive, watching as they widened just slightly when I slowly pressed into her, and then she gasped, almost as if the stretch forced the air from her lungs. Grinning down at her, I nipped at her lower lip, sucking it into my mouth while I bottomed out.

"You always take me so well, sweeting," I groaned, clenching my eyes shut at the way her walls clamped down on my cock.

"Move," she demanded, her hips swivelling. "Fuck me, Kalian."

Growling under my breath, I lowered an arm and hooked her leg over my elbow before spreading her open. "Hold on to me tightly, love."

Clawing at my shoulders, Skylahr braced herself, and I buried my face into her neck before snapping my hips. My pace was ruthless as I filled her over and over again, not caring that her moans were no longer muffled. Digging my fingers into the plush globe of her ass, I held her to me tightly as I continued to move and then lowered my free hand between us before resuming my ministrations.

"Kalian," she warned as always, and I smiled, watching her face closely as she found her pleasure. Fluttering around me, her walls pulsed, and I felt that spark start at the base of my spine, and then it crashed over me like a great wave, and I spilled into her.

Sliding my arm from under her knee, I guided her leg to wrap around me once more and pressed a kiss to her hair while she caught her breath.

"Easy now, love," I whispered against her forehead, holding her tightly as she nuzzled into my chest before skimming her lips over my thundering heart.

"Thank you," she whispered, and my brows furrowed in confusion. Noticing my puzzlement, she kissed my skin again. "Thank you for not leaving me in the dark."

"Oh, Skylahr," I sighed, "you never have to thank me for that. You're everything to me, and you will never be left in the dark. You couldn't be. You are the light that guides me home. You're my starlight."

Chapter 63

After pulling on her clean tunic, Sky dropped to the water's edge and lowered the other into the springs, swirling it around until all the dust and grime lifted from the material. As she wrung it out, she looked back towards camp.

"You might as well clean yours too. Who knows when we will have another chance." Nodding, I started to head back through the leaves but stopped when Skylahr called my name. "Maybe use this to cover yourself."

I turned to the cloak Skylahr had discarded and wrapped it around myself with a sheepish grin and then continued on. Both the human and halfling were still sound asleep where we had left them. Ella and Gaelon, however, were not, and when I broke through the cover of green, they turned to look at me. Ella seemed disinterested, her face blank as her dark eyes quickly moved on. Gaelon, on the other hand, was flushed, and he averted his eyes as I approached.

"Just came for these." I bent to pick up my clothes, my face heating at the awkward silence. Shuffling my weight, I cleared my throat softly and then turned to the Healer. "She said that there is no sign of the Seductress using the link."

Gaelon sighed, running a hand over his face tiredly, apparently not pleased at the new information. "Yes, I am *aware*."

"Right." I nodded as I carded my fingers through my hair.

"But perhaps next time you could have your conversations in private," Ella snapped, though she had yet to face me. "Because some of us can't forget about our losses, and we certainly do not want to hear the way you two decide to distract yourselves from them."

"I'm sorry, Ella," I apologized, but she waved me off and kept her back to me. Gaelon, who had still been flushed and embarrassed, grew concerned as he examined the immortal woman, and I waited until his attention turned back to me.

"Why don't I take your cloak? We can give it a wash and then we will trade off," I suggested, unsure what else to say.

"Perhaps you and Skylahr should stay near the springs," he suggested, his eyes darting to the immortal, whose eyes had shut, though her breathing had yet to even out. "You are still close enough that we would be in no danger of being separated. Maybe some space would do us all some good."

Folding the clothes over my arm, I nodded in agreement and glanced at the other three once more. "When you are ready to switch places, just call for me."

Luckily the morning was warmer than the previous had been, and for the first time since stepping onto the island's shores, there was no rain or mist, though the overcast remained. Pulling the clothes from the tree branch we had used to hang them, I glanced at Skylahr from the corner of my eye as she moved towards the small fire her guard had built.

She looked better, more refreshed than before, and had slept for a few hours, though Ella's screaming for Elizabeth had woken her up, and it took ages to console her when she realized what the noise was. Thankfully Gaelon had managed to calm the immortal, his soft, steady voice soothing even to me, and then the night grew quiet once more.

"How long until your ships make it here?" Skylahr asked as she settled on the earth, ignoring the sounds that came from the springs as Selbie and Ella chatted quietly while washing.

"The hafok should reach them any day now, and once he does, Leena will send the men immediately."

"Do you think we can survive for that much longer?" she wondered, her eyes remaining downcast as she studied the flames.

"Of course we can," I promised, squatting beside her before taking one of her hands. "We are nearly done here, and then we can go home."

"And what then?" she asked, chewing at her lower lip.

"Whatever it is you want. If you want to return to Noordeign, then we will go. If you want to travel to Osallow to see the ruins of Natylity, then so be it."

"What if I want to give up my crown and live in a tiny cottage in the woods, away from lords and ladies and court? What if I want to live out the rest of my days as nothing more than a farmer?" Squeezing her fingers, I waited until her gaze met mine.

"So be it. You will need to teach me, of course. I don't have much experience with any of that. Maybe I could keep the house, waiting on you hand and foot once you come in from the fields. I could be a kept man." I smiled as she rolled her eyes.

"Spoiled brat," she scoffed, though her lips quirked, and I curled my free hand around the back of her neck, using my thumb to tilt her chin towards me.

"We will do whatever you want, Skylahr. I will follow you to the very edge of the earth and fall into the stars should you ask me to." Her cheeks flushed prettily, and I kissed her temple before turning towards the two men who were now approaching.

"Are we nearly ready to move on?" Barrick asked, and I nodded before smothering the fire, waiting until the flames were nothing more than smoking embers.

"Any luck with your foraging?" I asked the Healer as he unfolded a small cloth to reveal a handful of sprouts and weeds.

"Surprisingly so. I managed to find a number of things that could help us." Nothing in his hand looked special or interesting, but I took his word for it. "This is for Skylahr, I would suggest she brews it into a tea."

I frowned at him in confusion, and he grabbed my hand before pressing one of the roots into my palm. "Have her drink it sooner rather than later if you two plan to continue to…bond."

Flushing hotly, I turned towards the women, who were manoeuvring through the bushes, and swallowed. "We should begin to make our way to the shores. We will stay covered within the trees for as long as possible and keep an eye on the horizon. Now that the beast is gone, they will take a direct path and travel together as a fleet, and they will be prepared for the sea-maidens."

"And our plans when they reach shore?" Barrick inquired, his gaze drifting to his Huntress.

"That remains unchanged—we hunt down the rest of them," she said quietly, but the words were heavy with her rage.

Keeping a steady eye on the waves in the distance, we continued our journey to the shoreline, though our pace was slower than it had been previously, and I did not have the option to carry the entire party now that both Ella and the Healer had joined us. Cutting down the branches ahead of us, I cleared the path for the others as they followed behind and scanned the shadows for any threat that may be lurking.

"It's a shame this island is filled with swamps and creatures and mountains that collapse," Selbie muttered. "It would be beautiful if it wasn't so terrifying."

No one said anything, we all just glanced at the halfling with surprise, and she shrugged before studying the green that surrounded us. Focusing back on the task at hand, I pressed forward once more before staring up at the gloomy sky, wondering how much light we had left.

"Kalian," Gaelon called in a hushed whisper, his arms spreading wide as he stopped the guard and Ella from passing him. "Is that a fire?"

There were no murmured voices, no footfalls or any other sound of men, but the smell of burning wood was faint, and I could just make out the soft crackling. Motioning for the others to get low, I waited until they were hidden, and then I crept forward, sneaking through the branches as I neared the camp.

The fire was still going, though it had been left unattended, and I waited another moment before stepping towards the clearing. Whatever group had been here had just recently fled, the smell of the salt and roasted game now mingling with the scent of fire, and I nudged the furs they had left behind with my boot.

There hadn't been many, maybe four at most, and they were a long way from the others who I was sure I had seen on the remaining mountain when its twin peak had crumbled. Continuing my search, I found the pelt of their last meal and a scabbard from a dagger, and then as I turned towards my friends once more, I noticed it. The gold hilt was just barely visible from its hiding spot inside the hollow trunk that lay across the ground, and I bent to the earth, my fingers skimming across the cool pommel for just a moment before that sharp sting began.

Sliding my hand away, I remained in my place, keeping still as the men approached. Their breathing was shaky and nervous while their fear soiled the air, and I waited, pretending not to notice them for as long as I could. Listening for the sound of metal scraping against leather, I rolled at the last minute, and the edge of the blade cut into the log I had been sitting in front of before I turned and slammed my fist into the man's knee.

The joint did not shatter the way it would have had he been mortal, but it was enough to send him to the dirt, and I took the sword from his hand before charging at his comrades. They were armed, but not nearly as skilled as I had been expecting, and I cut the first down easily before moving on to the other two. The smaller of the pair trembled at my approach, his eyes darting to his friend nervously, but the other paid him no mind and stepped forward. He was tall and thin, but obviously had more practice with a blade, and we circled each other before he made his first move.

I blocked his onslaught of attacks and danced away from him, studying him closely as he stalked forward. But his long sword was not ideal for this type of battle, and when he lifted his arm above his head, ready to bring the steel down on me, I lowered myself to one knee and drove my weapon up into his torso in a lethal blow. Turning to the two that were left, I watched as they huddled close together, their bodies trembling in fear.

"Please, we meant no harm!" the small one cried out, raising his hands above his head, and I lifted a single brow.

"That is why you came at me armed?"

Rustling came from behind me. Skylahr was no doubt unable to wait any longer, and when she was finally visible the men gasped. "It is you."

Skylahr took in the scene before her and then turned to me with concern. Offering a subtle nod, I let her know I was fine, and then observed her carefully as she set her attention on the pair of immortals.

"They have something of yours," I muttered quietly, pointing to the tree trunk to the left, and her brow furrowed before she went to investigate. Bracing one hand on the rotting wood, she used the other to grab the hilt and then pulled it from its hiding place.

"Where did you find it?" I growled, my eyes narrowing at the men.

"It was on the ship," the first stuttered out, his hands holding his knee tightly. "The Healer's ship."

"And why do you have it?" I demanded.

"We took it when we left the shrine, we thought we could get something for it," he whimpered. "We figured we were owed."

"Owed for what?" Skylahr snarled, her hand curving around the pommel.

"We didn't want to be here; we didn't want this for our life," the smaller cried, his attention bouncing between Skylahr and me. "We didn't even want immortality, but they didn't give us a choice."

"What?" I gasped, my eyes widening in shock.

"We had reached Grimslar in the fall, finally free from the Crimsons and their hunt of the halflings, or so we thought." He sniffed. "But then the Siren's immortals gathered along the shores. At first, they were so welcoming. They spoke of unity and a community of acceptance, and we thought that we had finally found our place. But then things began to change; there were plans made to travel and gather the rest of the halflings."

Skylahr's face softened, her hazel eyes still guarded but far less fierce. "How many of you were there?"

The men's eyes met and then the blond answered. "There were a few hundred of us, but only a quarter survived their ceremonies."

"And this was done by force?" Skylahr clarified.

"Most, yes." He nodded. "Some volunteered, but most of us were not given the choice."

"What else can you tell us?" I asked, lowering my weapon and urging Skylahr to do the same.

"After a few months the rest of us had all reached the coast. We spent every last silver we had on weapons and armour, but no one had ever told us why." Turning to his comrade, the blond waited for the other man to continue.

"Tilair took the first ship, just a couple weeks before the last snow. He had been ranting and raving about the horn and the trident, that soon he would have both in his possession and the blood he needed to summon our Goddess. He and his crew came to the shrine, found the scriptures of the tide, and then he conjured that beast." The man paused, taking in a deep, shuddering breath. "We all thought he was the Chosen. We allowed him to lead us; we believed all of his false promises. But when his assassin came back empty-handed, his control over the creature began to waver."

"Wait, the horn *and* the trident?" Skylahr looked to me in confusion, but the men nodded.

"They hold the horn already," the blond whispered. "But they have not found her trident, and they need both to bring her back."

Chapter 64

"Your knee looks well on its way to being fully healed, my friend," Gaelon promised softly and then looked to the other man. "Are you sure you are uninjured?"

"I am fine, my lord," he whispered, not meeting the Healer's gaze.

"I'm pleased to hear it." Removing his hands from the stranger's leg, the Healer stood and turned to us, apparently waiting for our verdict.

I knew what I would have done with them, but it was not my decision to make, and I turned to Skylahr, keeping my face impassive while she studied our captives. Her shoulders were drawn high, her chin lifted as she peered down at the young men, all while keeping her hand on the pommel of the golden weapon now strapped to her hip.

"What were your plans before we found you?" she asked, her voice strong and unwavering.

"We had decided to head to the port and steal a ship."

Skylahr's grip tightened on the metal.

"How? There were only four of you and you said the port was now being occupied."

The men fidgeted under her stare, and she tipped her head to the side.

"You planned to wait out the immortals, hiding away from them until we were captured, or they were killed," she guessed, and they paled but did not protest. "So, what are we to do with you now that we know that you are nothing more than a pair of deserters, that you never planned to aid us?"

Gaelon inhaled sharply but remained silent as his attention lowered to the forest floor. I waited, knowing whatever choice she made I would support, though I prayed that she would show them mercy. Not because I thought they deserved it, but because I would hate to see this haunt her as well.

"We will take your swords but will leave you with your daggers," she finally announced. "We will turn the other way while you make your escape and will leave you to it."

Squatting down in front of them, she hardened her expression and lowered her voice. "But should I find that you took advantage of my kindness, you will not receive mercy from me again."

She picked up the daggers next to her, held them out for the two men to take, and then stood, waiting as they scrambled to their feet. Not sparing us another glance, they ran, throwing themselves into the shadows of the forest as they fled from the Huntress, and I exhaled roughly before turning to her.

"Do you think that was a mistake?" she asked, her face unreadable as she stared in the direction the men had gone.

"No," I answered honestly, stepping into the space next to her before reaching for her shoulder. "They were victims in this and should not have had to pay for the sins of the others."

"How can you be so sure?" Ella asked, her face lacking its usual radiance. "How can you know that they have not played a bigger part in the things that have happened to us?"

"We can't, not for certain," Gaelon said gently. "But at some point, you have to trust yourself that you made the right choice."

"Even if it means you suffer for it later?" Ella wondered, and Skylahr's frown deepened, almost as if she was wondering the same.

"Sometimes you must take that risk," Gaelon replied.

"It doesn't seem worth it," Skylahr whispered, her words barely audible over the gentle wind, but both Gaelon and I froze, and then she turned from us, keeping her hand curled over the golden blade.

Though as she walked away, I studied her long fingers carefully, noticing the deep red colour of her palm.

"We have another day at least." Gaelon sighed as he stood beside me, looking at our friends with concern.

"There is no point in hurrying. My ships have not arrived; getting to the shores before them is pointless," I reminded him. "We would be best off to take our time while we can and allow ourselves to rest."

"You mean for me to rest," he sighed while glancing at me from the corner of his eye. "I am fine. You underestimate me. I am stronger than you think, Protector."

"I'm not sure I would go that far." I lifted a brow, scanning his body from head to toe, and he scoffed.

"If you're going to try to insult me, at least be straightforward about it. This thing you're doing now does not suit you," he snapped and I nearly smiled.

"Did I make the great Healer lose that legendary patience of his?" I asked smugly.

"Good Gods, you are annoying." He rolled his eyes and then turned back to our friends. "We still have half a day of light left. Are you ready to continue?"

Skylahr nodded, but Selbie looked at Barrick with concern, and I was unable to hide my surprise at the sudden change between the two.

"We need food," the halfling murmured. "Real food, something of substance."

We had not come across any game since leaving the shrine, and the Healer had yet to find anything edible that would suffice in the meantime. Knowing our rations were running low, we had taken to skipping most meals, but now I could see that was not doing Barrick any favours. In fact, even Selbie herself was looking rather gaunt, and Skylahr's pretty skin had lost its natural rosy colour.

"I will try to hunt again," I promised.

"We should do so now so that our fire is not as obvious as it would be at night." Skylahr sighed and then looked at me. "But I do not feel right about you going on your own. I think I better accompany you."

Both Barrick and Gaelon looked ready to protest, but I lifted a hand, the motion halting whatever arguments they had.

"One of us should stay here with the rest," I advised. "They need your protection."

Barrick snorted and Ella frowned, but no one disputed the words. Skylahr observed her friends before sighing. "Promise me you'll be careful."

"Of course," I swore, leaning over to press a quick kiss to her mouth, and then I stepped behind the cover of trees and pulled my breeches off. I bundled them up in one hand and tossed them at the Healer's face, chuckling quietly when he snatched them out of the air with a growl.

Landing on all four feet, I padded my way through the forest, taking care not to move too quickly should I spook any prey. But when I searched the air for a scent, any scent that would indicate that there was something out here for us to eat, I found nothing.

I ventured farther into the trees, staying within a careful distance of the others, and then fell to the forest floor and waited.

I had no idea how much time had passed as I lay there, waiting for something to come, and just as I was about to find another location, I heard it. It was a soft flicking sound, similar to a bow string being snapped, and my ears swivelled, trying to determine which direction it was coming from.

Standing to my feet, I glanced to my left, then my right, searching for the source, but there was nothing around me. Growing frustrated, I was ready to turn back to my friends, and then that flick came again, paired with a soft slithering, and I raised my head, watching as it slid through the trees, those four eyes turning to me.

It wasn't nearly as big of a serpent as the last had been, but it was far larger than any snake I wanted to deal with, and my ears flattened as I snapped my jaws in warning. Loosening its hold on the bark, it lowered itself towards the ground, its tongue striking into the air, tasting my scent while it crept closer.

I lowered my head, my hackles rising, and took a step back, then another, never once turning away from the creature while I planned an escape.

"Kalian?" Skylahr called out anxiously, her voice capturing the snake's attention, and it swung its head, those four eyes searching for her as she darted through the forest.

"Kalian!?" she called again, cursing as she cut down some branches, and then she was there, bursting through the green, her golden sword drawn, ready to attack.

I growled out loud to draw her attention, and her hazel eyes met mine for just a pause before she looked at the snake. Sizing it up, she moved to cross the space between us, but the snake's mouth opened as the sides of its face expanded, and a deep hiss echoed through the air as it readied itself to strike.

Realizing that it planned to go after Skylahr, I waited until it turned to face her fully, and then braced my weight. The serpent was coiled tightly, and I knew I needed to do this right. It was my only chance before it struck, and when its body shifted, I launched myself at it.

Sinking my teeth into its scales, I shook my head, tearing at its throat as the snake swung to and fro. Unable to dislodge me, the great serpent began to panic, its movements quickening as it flailed, and then it was falling to the ground, crushing me into the earth.

I closed my eyes at the suffocating weight, trying to breathe through the pain. But I couldn't get enough air into my lungs, and when it realized I was struggling, it rolled across me, using more force to smother my body.

"Kalian!" Skylahr screamed, her voice barely audible over the ringing in my ears. But the quiet sound was enough, and I held on to her cries, using them to find the strength to struggle beneath the scales.

Kicking with my back feet, I scratched and clawed at the serpent, growling and whimpering as my desperation grew. However, the movement only allowed one of my back paws to get caught between the body above me and the earth, and with the serpent's next twist, the bone snapped.

Howling in pain, I tried to turn on my side in order to protect the broken limb, but I didn't have the room, and I yowled again when the snake pressed against my shattered leg.

"Kalian, hold on!" Skylahr screamed, and then she was sobbing and grunting and gasping and I could smell blood. Not just the snake's but hers as well.

"Skylahr!" Barrick called, his voice panicked as he screamed for her again. I tried once more to free myself from beneath the snake when I heard his voice crack in fear. "Skylahr!"

"Kalian is under it!" Skylahr cried hoarsely, and the serpent had fallen limp, its body no longer moving. Or least it hadn't been for a moment, but now the scales were being shoved and a pair of hands was tangling in my fur, tugging at me until I was finally free.

"Kalian?!" Skylahr sobbed as she tucked one palm beneath my massive furred head before lifting my face towards her. I blinked through the haze, sighing when I finally found those hazel eyes. "Oh, thank the Gods!"

Moving in behind her, the guard peered over her shoulder and then glanced down towards the bottom half of my body with worry. Watching his face pale, I knew it must have been a horrid sight, and I wheezed, trying to take in a deep breath before moving to my feet.

"No!" Skylahr shouted, pressing me back into the dirt. "Don't move, not until Gaelon can look at your leg." Closing my eyes, I swallowed down the bile that burned the back of my throat, and then my world spun and I fell into nothingness.

Chapter 65

Burning, blinding pain was what welcomed me back to consciousness, and I closed my eyes, biting back a scream while nimble fingers straightened my leg. At some point I had shifted back to my human form, and now my skin felt tight and sweltering hot under the Healer's gentle hands.

"Easy now," Skylahr whispered, her fingers stroking my hair from my forehead before she bent to press a kiss to my brow. "He's nearly done."

"This is the same leg he broke at the shores," Gaelon murmured, but I could hear the worry in the words, and so could Skylahr.

"Meaning what?" she asked.

"It will heal, but setting it was difficult, and it may continue to aggravate him," Gaelon replied as he wrapped a piece of fabric from my thigh to my ankle. I clenched my jaw, forcing myself to remain quiet as he finished.

"What can we do?" Skylahr asked, her fingers continuing their ministrations.

"He needs to stay off of it for now," the Healer answered. "He should rest and drink the tea I made; it will ease his pain through the night."

Sighing, Skylahr lifted my head carefully and then lowered it once more onto her lap. My eyes fluttered open so that I could look up at her. Her face was pale, and tense, her gaze watery as it roamed across my body, and there was a bloodstain on her shoulder. Noticing the tear in the cotton, I carefully lifted a hand to run my finger across frayed edges, ignoring the cool blood that soaked the spot.

"I'm fine," she promised, her own hand catching mine before she lowered my fingers from her shoulder. "Are you hungry?"

I swallowed roughly and cleared my throat. "For more bruised fruit?"

"Roasted snake actually," Barrick grumbled, and I turned to look at the guard as he bit into a spit of meat. My stomach churned at the sight, and I rolled away once more before nuzzling into the softness of Skylahr's lower belly.

"It's not as bad as I thought it would be," Selbie claimed. I squinted open one eye and stared at her in disbelief. "And now we have enough of it to last a few days, so your broken leg wasn't all for nothing."

"I'm glad I could be of some use." I rolled my eyes, ignoring the stiff pain radiating from my limb, though now I could feel the bone slowly mending and I sighed in relief.

"We will rest here until the morning, that way we can roast as much meat as we can carry, and by tomorrow, we will be ready to begin our travels once more." Everyone nodded, but Ella had yet to say anything, her dark gaze too busy lingering on Skylahr to really notice the rest of us.

"Do you still think we will reach the coastline tomorrow?" Selbie asked, interrupting my observation.

"This has been a setback," Gaelon answered honestly, "and it will depend on how quickly we can travel, but I am optimistic that we will reach the sand by nightfall."

"And what do you think we will find there?" Barrick wondered out loud.

"I don't rightly know," Gaelon sighed. "But if we have learned anything during our time here, we would be wise to prepare for the worst."

Soft murmurs roused me from my fitful sleep, but I remained still, not wanting to alert Skylahr that I had woken. Instead I just listened.

"So you've truly forgiven him." It wasn't a question but rather an observation, and Skylahr hummed under her breath.

"I have," she confirmed simply, and my heart stuttered in my chest. But her answer wasn't good enough, and Ella's tone hardened.

"Why?"

"Ella," Skylahr sighed, her fingers tracing the muscles of my back gently. It took everything in me not to react to her touch.

"I don't understand," the immortal admitted. "He betrayed you, he lied to you, he was willing to trade your life."

"For the people he loves," Skylahr whispered brokenly. "He was willing to trade my life for his family and his people, and it was long before we ever met."

"Does that excuse him then? The fact that he didn't know you yet means it's okay? You're perfectly fine with that justification?" Skylahr's fingers stopped moving, and I held my breath, waiting for her answer.

"What was Elizabeth's life worth to you?" Skylahr whispered, and the immortal gasped sharply. "What would you give to bring her back?"

"Skylahr," the immortal warned, but the Huntress wasn't having it and continued.

"Whose life would you be willing to trade just to hold her again? What lengths would you go to see her smile once more?" Ella didn't answer, so Skylahr pressed on. "Would you trade my life? Would you lead me to the enemy if they could guarantee she would come back to you?"

"How could you ask me that?" Ella snapped.

"That isn't an answer," Skylahr pointed out. "But I understand, it's an impossible choice, and it's one *he* was forced to make many years ago. Is there no small part of you that understands why he did it?"

My stomach sank as I listened to Skylahr reason with her friend, silently wondering if she still worried that I would make that choice again.

"I would not trade your life for anything," Ella finally countered.

"Even though you blame me?" Skylahr choked out, and I nearly flinched at the sadness in her voice.

Ella exhaled roughly but said nothing for a long pause, and when she finally spoke, it was so quiet I wondered if the Huntress had even heard it.

"Even then."

Skylahr sniffed, and I could feel her tremble beneath me. "I am sorry, Ella, more sorry than you will ever know."

The immortal's breath shook, and I could almost picture her distraught expression, and then she cleared her throat. "Do you love him?"

It was not what I had been expecting, and I nearly gasped at the question, wondering if the first time I would hear the words would be during a conversation I had no business listening to. But Skylahr said nothing, and there was no indication she answered other than Ella's response.

"Then I hope you never feel this pain," Ella whispered brokenly. "I hope you never lose him."

The bone in my leg had fused back together overnight, but the muscles around the break still ached as I stretched in the soft morning light, waiting for the Healer to finish his inspection with a raised brow.

"So?" I asked, growing impatient with his fiddling. "Do I have the all-knowing Healer's approval, or are you hoping this is your chance to prove just how strong you are?"

"It's a shame the serpent didn't break your jaw. A few days without having to listen to your voice may have done us all some good," he growled, and I lifted my lips in a smirk, watching in amusement while he packed his supplies and stood.

Stepping next to me, Skylahr pressed the toe of her boot into my hip and crossed her arms while peering down at me in annoyance.

"Kalian," she chided, "behave, please."

"He just makes it so easy." I shrugged as my grin grew, and she rolled her eyes.

"Centuries old and still not grown."

Reaching up, I took one of her hands and then pulled myself to my feet.

"I will apologize if it would make you happy," I offered half-heartedly.

"No need, Protector." Gaelon dismissed me with a flick of his fingers. "I enjoy watching our Huntress reprimand you. It is worth the aggravation of having to listen to all your yammering."

Scoffing, I turned from the man and looked over at the others. We had packed the roasted meat, and the embers from last night had long since gone cold. Barrick and Selbie looked brighter now that they had a full belly. However, the tension between Ella and Skylahr was heavier than it had been. Apparently, their discussion last night had not helped ease the rift and had only opened the wound once more.

"Are we ready?" the guard asked. Glancing at Skylahr, I reached for her hand once more and intertwined our fingers before gesturing for her to lead the way.

My pace was slower than normal, the slight twinge of pain keeping me from walking at my usual pace, but we still kept at it. At the head of the group, the Huntress swung her golden sword, cutting down the leaves and branches roughly, as though she too seemed to be ignoring the obvious pain she was in.

Glancing at the Healer, I wondered if he noticed the way her flesh burned under the metal, or if he saw her fingers tremble each time they reached for the pommel. However, when his dark eyes caught mine for an instant, I knew he had, and yet we both remained silent.

"It certainly sounds like we are nearing the water!" Barrick called from the back of the group, raising his voice so we could hear him over the wind that had begun to blow against us. The sound of waves crashing grew stronger as we neared our destination.

"I'm sure it's not far now!" Skylahr shouted over her shoulder, but when she cut down another group of branches, she sighed in frustration and pointed ahead.

"What is it?" Barrick inquired as he stepped forward, then his eyes moved across the horizon, his mouth falling into a frown.

We had avoided the bog on our trip back to the coastline, but the new path led us to a jagged cliff, one that was far too high above the sand for us to continue. In fact, we were nearly as high up as some of the sea stacks that stood strong against the waves, and Skylahr's shoulders slumped.

"I didn't realize there would be such a steep drop-off," she growled in frustration, and then she glanced to the right, following the ledge with her eyes. "We will have to circle back and find another way down to the sand."

"It will give my men more time to get here and will keep us from waiting for them in the open." I shrugged as I scanned the beach.

"What if they find the trident in the meantime?" she asked worriedly.

"It won't matter," I assured her. "If what those men said is true, then they not only need both horn and trident, but they also need to have the blood of a Reide."

"Let them find it," Barrick agreed. "It will save us the time, and then once the Protector's fleet arrives, we can find the immortals and destroy both the horn and trident in one fell swoop."

"Do you think that's even possible?" Ella asked doubtfully, and Skylahr frowned at her.

"What do you mean?"

"If they have the power to truly summon a God, then surely destroying them would not be so easy," Ella explained. "They must contain her magic somehow, right?"

"Maybe her Chosen could do it," Skylahr guessed, and then looked to the Healer and me. "Tilair couldn't control the creature fully because he was not her Chosen; maybe the same rules apply with her weapon and horn."

Her fingers grazed over the golden pommel strapped on her hip. "And if they truly did perform the ceremony on her halflings, then her Chosen is already immortal, which would mean they would have the power to wield her relics without issue."

Gaelon sighed and then ran a hand over his face. “Even if we managed to somehow find her true Chosen, how would we convince them to side with us?”

Skylahr’s gaze grew hard, and she turned to the waves once more. “We wouldn’t give them a choice.”

Chapter 66

We followed along the ridge best we could as we searched for a way down to the coastline, all while keeping an eye on the horizon, waiting for those sails to appear. However, as the sun began to set, we knew we would need to find another place to settle and started our search for a clearing that would suffice.

"How long have we been on this blasted island?" the guard grumbled, rubbing at his lower back. I glanced at him from the corner of my eye.

"Too long," I sighed and Barrick nodded.

"The first thing I'm doing when we get home is having a big cup of ale and a plate full of pastries, and I don't want to hear a word out of your mouths about it."

Skylahr snorted but remained tight-lipped, and I rolled my eyes.

"We will be sure to tell Leena so that she can warn the kitchens," I swore while clapping the man on the back.

"I just want a long bath, one that doesn't smell like eggs." Selbie groaned as she rubbed the back of her neck, and then she looked to the others. "What are you three the most excited for when you get home?"

Gaelon's dark eyes softened, and then he looked at Ella and Sky, watching the way they both seemed to close themselves off, and then the halfling winced.

"Sorry," she whispered while ducking her chin. "I should have thought before I spoke."

"No." Skylahr shook her head. "No apologies needed. You should hold on to the thing you are excited for."

The air around us grew tense, and the silence stretched on while we continued searching for an ideal spot to rest, though our minds were now heavy with the longing for home, and I knew tonight we would all be thinking of the comforts Elrin brought us. Or at least most of us would. Ella and Skylahr, however, looked as if returning home was the last thing they wanted to do, and I could not blame them for it. The loss of Elizabeth would be painful, and returning to a place filled with her memory would not ease that aching.

It hadn't for me when I returned to Denimoore without my mother.

"Kalian," Gaelon called, his arm reaching behind him to stop our comrades from going any farther. "Do you see that?"

He pointed ahead towards the tall trees that blew in the wind, and at first, I didn't see anything unusual. However, when another great gust rustled the leaves, I noticed the two shadows swaying high above the ground. Swallowing roughly, I looked back at the Healer and then moved my attention to Ella. Her eyes had also widened, and I knew then that she understood exactly what it was we were looking at.

"Are they…" she began roughly, and I nodded.

"Yes, they're the same men." Not understanding what we meant, Skylahr narrowed her gaze in the direction of the hanging bodies, but her senses were not strong enough to make them out from this distance.

"Who are the same men?" Skylahr demanded. However, she didn't wait for an answer before she began striding through the forest, and we had no choice but to follow her as she approached the immortals.

Standing below their feet, Skylahr peered up at the two, taking in the obvious cruelty they had faced before their deaths, and I winced at the shocking bruises and wounds that littered their faces. Barrick, who had managed to catch up to us, stood behind his Huntress, his expression unreadable as he stared at the back of her head, and then he grabbed his dagger.

"Should we cut them down?" Selbie asked in a rough voice when she noticed the guard unsheathing his weapon.

"Giving them a proper burial will take time," I murmured with a shake of my head. "And by the looks of them, they have not been dead for long. Whoever is responsible may very well still be close."

"So what, we just leave them here?" Ella snapped in outrage, and I looked to Gaelon.

"It would be the safest bet," the Healer offered gently, but Skylahr ignored us both and took Barrick's dagger before clenching it between her teeth, and then she turned to the tree trunk. Clawing at the bark, she hauled herself up the wood and then reached for the ropes before beginning to saw at them with the metal blade.

"Skylahr," Gaelon began, and she paused before glaring down at the Healer.

"You said they were victims in this, Gaelon," she reminded him. "If that's true, then they deserve some dignity. Certainly more than they were given in the last moments of their lives."

No one knew what to say, but we all knew she was right, and so they turned to me with expectant stares for just a moment and then averted their eyes. After toeing off my boots and stepping out of my breeches, I shifted and then moved a few feet away before setting to work. The earth was just as damp here as it was everywhere else on this Godsforsaken island, and I dug down deep, making sure their scent would be hidden from scavengers. Once the job was done, I waited for Barrick and Gaelon to lay the men in their graves, and then I covered them carefully before shifting once more.

"May the Gods see them home," Gaelon whispered with his head bowed, and everyone repeated the words.

Everyone but Skylahr.

The Huntress was quiet as the rest of us picked at our rations, and I lifted a piece of meat towards her, willing her to just look at me. But she shook her head, those eyes of hers searching the area around us, and I sighed in defeat.

"Why do you think they hanged them? Couldn't they have just taken them prisoner?" Selbie frowned, no longer interested in her food.

"They were deserters," Barrick explained while bracing himself against the cold gust of wind that blew across us. "They betrayed their cause, and they would have been a liability. Besides, travelling with prisoners is difficult, and they have nowhere to keep them now that their shrine is destroyed."

"But they weren't deserters, they were forced into this," Selbie murmured, her eyes lowering to her lap.

"They were." Gaelon sighed.

"They weren't given a choice; they didn't want any of this." The halfling sniffed, and the Healer reached for her shoulder, offering her what little comfort he could.

"It's not fair, but that's the consequence of war," Barrick added.

"But there was no war; there was no need for anything of this. Elrin was at peace," Selbie continued.

"Unfortunately, peace is not always what we think it is. Many see it as a waiting period before they seize their opportunity. Some thrive on chaos; they seek it out or they create it themselves."

"Why?" Selbie wondered with a furrowed brow.

"Because the only way they can gain power is to force fear into others," Gaelon explained.

"Well, wasn't that just so eloquently put, Healer," someone called, their voice carried to us by the wind, and we stood, pressing our backs together while we waited. There had been no sound of their approach, no scent on the breeze, and I wondered how they had managed to go undetected.

Listening carefully, I turned to the south and then moved my body in front of Skylahr's, shielding her from our visitors. One man appeared, his size not impressive, but the long sword he carried shone, and I lifted my gaze to his companions.

"There's at least six of them," Barrick whispered, forgetting that they could hear him, and the leader smiled at the guard.

"More than that, human." Another wave of men appeared from behind the first group, all armed and ready, and my flesh shivered as it readied itself to change.

"Don't bother," the immortal snapped, his eyes examining me closely while the man to his right lifted his bow. "The minute you move, Synd will let this arrow loose."

It was a gamble, one that I was not willing to take when I realized they were not aiming for me, but rather waiting for Skylahr to be exposed. I curled my fingers into fists while I thought of another option.

"Tell me, Huntress, are you always so weak?" the man asked, tilting his head in amusement. "To take all that time to bury those traitors, I never thought the fierce Chosen would be one to show such compassion for her enemies."

"Compassion is not a weakness," Skylahr snarled, and then group laughed.

"Is that what they taught you?" He gestured towards the Healer and me. "Surely you know better than to trust their advice; you know better than to trust *him*."

Skylahr said nothing, but I felt the way she stiffened, and my jaw clenched.

"That was quite the story," he continued. "The betrayal of the Protector made its rounds in Elrin. If I'm being honest, I almost wondered why he let you live at the shores. Surrendering you to the Crimsons would have guaranteed his mother's life. That must be a crushing blow to you, oh great Protector."

I said nothing, but I heard the quiet gasp that came from Skylahr, and so did our enemy. "Were you fond of her as well, Huntress? I heard a great many stories about the Lady Isla, but I had no idea she was so captivating."

"Keep her name out of your mouth," Skylahr growled, her body visibly shaking with a rage that nearly matched my own.

"Did she teach you her ways? Did the great Lupine lady show you how she enamoured herself to others? Is that how you convinced one of us to side with you?" His light grey eyes moved to Selbie with a raised brow, and the halfling lifted her dagger in response. "And here I thought you just wanted to belong, Selbie Warlon."

"Not with people like you," the halfling snapped.

"That was a mistake. I bet you see it now." He lifted a hand and gestured his men forward. "But don't worry, maybe we will try our hand at that compassion you are all so fond of and bury you. Though to be honest, it does seem like such a waste of time."

Brushing past me, Skylahr unsheathed her golden sword and balanced her weight. "Then I'll be sure not to offer you the same courtesy."

"Is that what you think will happen?" the leader asked with a grin. "You think you'll make it out of this alive?"

"I know we will," Skylahr answered.

"And how can you be so sure?" he wondered, almost sounding bored, but a flicker of fear moved across his face.

"You weren't at the shores," Skylahr sneered. "You didn't see the carnage I made of my enemies. You have no idea what you walked into, but you'll learn. I'll be sure to save you for last so that you can witness what little compassion I can have."

Chapter 67

The Siren's immortals moved first, the archer taking in a swift inhale before readying to release the arrow, and I launched myself at him, shifting midair before I sent him to the ground. Realizing they had misjudged just how fast I was, they swarmed, their blades and daggers thrusting at me, and I swung my head, snapping at those within reach.

Finding an opening, one of the immortals sunk their blade into my middle, the metal hitting one of my ribs, and I howled in pain and then turned on him. Yet, before I could retaliate, Skylahr was there, her great golden sword swinging at the enemy as she took his head. The body crumpled to the ground below, and then she turned, setting her sights on another while the rest of my comrades moved, each taking on their own enemy.

This was not the same as the shores. There were no banners or horns declaring the start of the battle, but it was a fight to the death, and I was determined to make us the victors. There was no other option.

Rounding on the next man, I snapped at his sword hand, removing the limb as his other came at me with a small blade, and the metal found its mark in my shoulder as he tried to fight me off. But his efforts were in vain, and I ended it quickly before moving on.

Feeling certain we were gaining the upper hand, I looked at my friends. Both Barrick and Gaelon had paired off, their backs pressed against each other's as they battled against our attackers. Following their lead, Selbie and Ella did the same, and though they were less skilled with their attacks, having immortal blood in their veins made the difference.

Now certain that they had the upper hand with their assailants, I looked for Skylahr, though I truly didn't need to. I could feel the power radiating from her even with the distance between us. She was cutting down the enemy easily, her movements fast and fierce. Those men didn't stand a chance. Seeming to come to the same realization, the leader began to back away, his hands reaching out as he felt his way through the trees. But that would not do; he needed to see just exactly what our Huntress was, what she was capable of. He needed to see her power. He needed to witness her resilience.

And her magnificence would be the last thing he ever knew.

Stalking forward, I hunted her prey, watching with careful eyes as he realized there was no escaping his fate, and when I finally reached him, I lifted my lips from my teeth in a great snarl before pressing a paw to his chest. Holding him beneath me, I waited for Skylahr, listening to her triumphs as she defeated our enemy, and when I heard her soft approach, I lifted my paw and moved aside.

She was glorious as her conquered ignite burned through her veins, and my instincts nearly screamed at me to drop to the earth before her in devotion. But she had no eyes for me. No, her entire focus was on the man who had been longing to rejoice in our deaths.

"This was a mistake. I bet you see it now," she repeated his words from earlier with a lifted brow, and the immortal trembled.

"Mercy!" he screamed frantically as his knees buckled, and I watched him sob into the dirt while Skylahr stood before him. "Mercy!"

"What would you know of mercy?" she snarled. "You mock my compassion and then beg for your life, pleading for the very thing you called weakness?"

"Please, Huntress," he cried out, but she was no longer peering down at him. Instead, she had turned to Selbie, her hand lifting in an invitation.

"Your death belongs to Selbie. There is no use wailing for me." The immortal lifted his head, his tear-soaked face paling as the halfling approached, and I waited, wondering what she would decide.

"How many others are there left?" she asked, and when the man began to shake his head, I let loose a deep warning growl.

"We split into groups," he explained hastily. "I don't know how many remain."

"How many others are left?" Selbie pressed.

"There were one hundred and fifty of us before the collapse of the shrine." He sniffed while clenching his eyes shut.

"And the horn?" Gaelon inquired as he stepped forward.

Swallowing roughly, the immortal shook and then whispered, "Syman carries it."

"And who is he?" Skylahr snapped.

"An immortal of the first age." Her hazel eyes shot to mine and then moved to the Healer in confusion.

"An immortal who was changed during the war," Gaelon explained.

"He is the oldest of us all. He knew of the prophecy, he knew of the beast, and he knew Tilair's power would not last."

"But he is not the Siren's Chosen," Skylahr guessed.

"We have no Chosen," he snapped and then his eyes met Selbie's once more.

"Where is the trident?" the halfling asked, taking a step closer.

"I do not know," he answered, his chin lifting in defiance.

"Do not lie," Selbie snapped, her patience wearing thin, and the immortal quivered.

"I do not know where the trident is! We have not been able to find it!" he swore in panic. "But take me prisoner, and I will answer whatever other questions you have."

Stepping close, the halfling held her dagger tightly and then grasped the man's hair with her free hand. "Travelling with prisoners is difficult, and you have abandoned your cause. You are a traitor now that you have told us your secrets, which means you have no honour, and so, you are a liability to both us and them."

The halfling did not bother to give the man a chance to answer before running her dagger across his throat, and then she looked to Barrick. "Thank you for teaching me that important lesson."

We didn't bother burying the bodies, but we did take whatever weapons and provisions they had, and then moved away from the scene. Our blood was thundering through our veins, the adrenaline of the fight still lingering as we moved through the dark woods, and I kept a careful eye on the surrounding area, should we find ourselves ambushed once more.

"It looks like the sun will be rising soon. We might as well continue on our way," Gaelon suggested as he pushed through the heavy green, and I glanced at the lightening sky before following behind.

"Do you think what he said is true?" Ella asked as she matched the Healer's stride, and Gaelon peered down at her with a frown.

"Which part?" the Healer asked.

"The Chosen, he said the Siren didn't have one." Gaelon's stride faltered just slightly and then his eyes caught mine over his shoulder. It wasn't for long, barely a glance, and no one else seemed to notice it.

"I'm not sure," Gaelon admitted. "But it would seem odd for the Siren to flee after the war without having the assurance that part of her magic would remain."

"Perhaps they just haven't found him yet," Skylahr proposed, and I glanced at her, noticing the way her sword hand was curled into a fist and pressed against her chest. I could smell the burning flesh from here and frowned in concern but said nothing.

"Do you think he's here though?" Ella continued, her eyes moving between the Healer and me. "Why would the Chosen not follow the Siren's people to the island and try to summon the Goddess?"

"Perhaps he doesn't agree with their desires," Barrick guessed with a shrug of his shoulders.

The subject was laid to rest after the guard's words, and we quietly continued on our way, trekking through the bushes and trees, fighting through the heavy mud as we followed the coastline. We were still too high up to climb down to the shores, but we had covered a decent distance, and I could see the forest beginning to thin just ahead. Sighing in relief, I squinted against the light drizzle that began as the night faded and then turned to the group.

"There." I pointed towards the steep slope ahead. "We can manage that climb."

The earth would be slick, the grass difficult for us to find our footing, but there was no true risk of injury, and it would not require us to climb, though we may almost be better off crawling down the hill rather than trying to walk.

"We should break our fast here perhaps and set up camp. The trees will still offer some protection while we wait," Barrick said as he took in the ocean before us.

It was a smart decision, and I nodded, pulling at our makeshift packs before turning to Skylahr. She remained off to the side, keeping some distance between herself and the rest of us, and I approached carefully, waiting until her gaze lifted to mine.

"Not hungry?" I asked with a soft smile, and she shook her head, remaining silent before she turned her focus to the sea. Exhaling, I studied her face and then took her hand, forcing her fingers open. The skin of her palm was red, the welts still visible even now, and I stroked my thumb across the heated skin. "Why didn't you say anything? Gaelon could have done something to ease the pain."

"It's nothing," Skylahr snapped, snatching her hand out of my grasp.

"It's not nothing," I argued while my brow furrowed. "The sword is causing you pain."

"As you said it might," she reminded me. "You said that it was not meant for a halfling, that this was likely to happen."

My frown deepened as I tried to reach for her hand once again. "Yes, but Sky, I don't think it should be—"

"Kalian!" Gaelon called, his voice filled with urgency, and I turned to the Healer as he indicated to the waves. "Look!"

I narrowed my gaze at the horizon and searched the dark sea. At first there was nothing but sea stacks and whitecaps, but when I took a closer look, I noticed the sails. The soft silver blended into the heavy clouds behind them, but I could just make out the Protector's seal, and my shoulders sagged in relief.

Looking at my comrades, I offered them a soft smile and then moved my attention to the Huntress. "It is nearly done now. Soon we will be home."

Chapter 68

Hurrying to the hill, we stood at the top and gazed down at the shore before stopping the others from going any farther. I scanned the area below, searching for any sign of danger, and then looked back at the approaching ship. It was still a distance away, and though the winds were heavy, the tide was not ideal, and it would take some time to reach shore. Knowing we should stay hidden for as long as possible, I herded the group back, away from the open and whatever observing eyes there may be.

"Once they near, we will make our way down to the sand to meet them," I assured my friends, but Skylahr was focused on the waters, her face paling as she studied the tide. I glanced over my shoulder, wondering what it was that caught her attention.

"The beast is no longer a risk, but they are." Glancing at the surf, I waited, watching as a flash of scales breached the surface only to disappear once more, and then their song began. Skylahr lifted her hands and covered her ears and then urged the others to do the same.

"What do we do?!" Ella called, her eyes wide with worry as the sea-maidens began to swarm.

"They were warned about them!" Barrick shouted while he clenched his eyes closed, and the Healer placed a steadying hand on his shoulder.

"Warned about their song, but how will they manage to reach shore without being attacked?!" Skylahr shouted, and then she grabbed the bow we had taken from our attackers the night before and snatched the quiver from her guard. Pulling the leather over her shoulder, she then took the hem of her tunic and tore the fabric until she had two pieces of cloth. She stuffed them into her ears, turned for the hill, and ran.

"What is she doing?!" Barrick yelled as he made to move forward, but I placed a hand on his chest, ushering him back until the Healer had a solid hold on him, and then I ran after Skylahr.

"Skylahr!" I screamed for her as I closed the distance between us, and then once I was within arm's reach, I grabbed her biceps and spun her to face me.

"We have to help them!" She pulled her arm free of my grasp, but I grabbed her once more, this time cupping the back of her neck and directing her to face me.

"And how are you going to do that?! What is it you plan to do?!" I wanted to shake her, to make her see reason, but she curled her fingers around my wrist and then tugged it away.

"I need to find higher ground. It's the only way I will have a clear shot," she explained and then looked towards the line of sea stacks. But the bottoms of the towers were smooth and damp from the constant crashing waves that slammed against them, and there was no way Skylahr could manage that climb.

Glancing back up at the hill we came from, I traced the sharp ledge until I found a place that edged closer to the sea. It was a great distance between the green of the cliff and the sea stack that sat directly in front of it, one not possible for a man to make, but a beast may be able to. Once certain that the stone pillar would be stable enough to hold my weight, I turned back to Skylahr.

"Do you trust me?" I asked, uncertain of what her answer would be, and she paused, searching my face. Unsure if she heard me over the cotton in her ears, I opened my mouth to repeat the question, but she swallowed and then lowered her chin in a subtle nod.

My shoulders sagged in relief, and I moved forward, curling my fingers into her hair before pressing a rough kiss to her mouth. Only holding the contact for a moment, I then lowered my forehead to rest against hers. "You will need to hold on tight."

Her face filled with confusion, but I chose not to waste any more time and shifted into my wolven form before bending low to the ground. Sliding a leg over my back, she tangled her hands into my fur, and then I set off, racing up the incline once more before turning for the edge of the cliff.

Setting my sights on the sea stack, I took in a deep inhale and then lowered my body, bracing myself on my haunches before taking off. The wind was sharp as it blew against us, and I felt Skylahr lower herself over my withers and then I was reaching the edge. Digging my nails into the damp earth, I pushed off, using every ounce of power I had, praying that this idea would work.

But I had misjudged the distance, and when my body collided with the solid rock, I scrambled to climb to the top, my front paws clawing at the ledge while my back legs dangled behind me. Squeezing her legs around my middle, Skylahr gasped as I struggled to get my back feet beneath me, my right far weaker after its most recent break. I growled, growing desperate as we began to slide across the grass and towards the ocean below.

"Kalian!" she cried, her voice shrill with panic, and I grunted as I lifted my back legs under me, the pads of my paws scraping against the sharp edges of the sea stack while I struggled. Digging into the pillar, I heaved myself higher and higher until I was finally splayed across the top, and I panted in exhaustion.

Skylahr crawled from my back, fell to her knees next to my head, and cupped my snout in her hands before lifting it.

"Are you alright?" she asked, her face pale and worried, and I could smell her fear as the wind grew stronger.

Sighing roughly, I blinked twice, hoping she would take the gesture as my answer, and then I stood. Peering down at the dark sea below, I scanned the surface for the long-scaled tails and translucent flesh of the creatures in its depths.

"The ship is nearing." Skylahr lifted her eyes towards the silver sails and then grabbed the bow and quiver from her shoulder. Nocking the first arrow, Skylahr took in a deep breath and then held it, waiting until there was a flash beneath the waves before letting it loose. Finding its mark, the head of the arrow sank into the flesh of one of the creatures, and a great scream echoed from below, the sound so piercing my head rang.

Skylahr reached for another arrow and armed herself once more, though now the sea-maidens had sunk deeper into the waters, avoiding the threat from above, and she growled under her breath in frustration. Fully consumed by her hunt, we peered over the pillar's edge, not realizing the danger that had found our friends until I heard the shouting, and I turned my head, looking over my shoulder towards the noise.

Running from their hiding place, our friends struggled and slid down the hill while Gaelon rushed them from the trees, and my stomach dropped when I heard the sound of armour. Noticing where my focus moved to, Skylahr stood straight, her face panicked as she watched the navy banners flutter in the breeze between the thinning trees.

"Oh Gods!" she cried, her eyes filling with tears as the severity of the situation hit her, and my stomach churned as the front line of immortals finally appeared. There were not one hundred of them, that was to be sure, but there were far more than our four friends could beat.

"What do we do?!" She moved to cross the stone, her body rigid as she watched her friends run across the sand, and then she spun on her heel. "Kalian! What do we do!?"

I searched for an answer, a way to escape the trap we had put ourselves in, and then I looked to the murky water below. The depths of the sea were unknown, not to mention the horde of sea-maidens who were surely still waiting under the surface, but the only other way was to make the jump again, this time without the space to have a running start. I doubted I could make the distance from a standstill.

"Kalian?!" Skylahr called again in desperation, and I turned to her before looking at the whitecaps once more, waiting for her to understand my meaning. "Would we survive it?"

We would survive the jump itself, but I wasn't so certain about what came after. However, we had very little choice, and the more time we spent searching for an alternative the worse the threat became for our friends. Looking to the coastline once more, I watched as the Siren's immortals headed for the slope, and then I pressed my nose to Skylahr's hip. I wanted to be able to offer her words of comfort, but I knew remaining in this form was the safest bet for both of us. I would be stronger and faster in the water and less likely to be dragged down by the sea-maidens. Running her fingers through my fur, she stroked the area behind my ears once and then nodded.

"Okay," she whispered shakily. "Okay, let's go."

Moving to the very edge of the sea stack, I looked down, searching for the best area to land, but it was no use. The waves were strong, and I could not see the bottom clearly. Praying that this wasn't a huge mistake, I closed my eyes and then threw myself towards the sea.

The impact of my body hitting the water was enough to knock the air from my lungs, and I struggled to the surface while the frigid temperature made my heart stutter in my chest. Lifting my head above the waves, I took in a deep breath and then looked up as Skylahr followed me into the sea.

Her departure from the sea stack was not graceful, and the way she crashed into the sea made my stomach drop in fear. I paddled to the spot where she had sunk below, fighting the current while I waited for her to surface. Time seemed to slow, my surroundings becoming hazy while I searched the waters, and when I finally saw her long pale fingers reach for the surface, I whimpered in relief before swimming to her.

Gasping for air, Skylahr spluttered and coughed, her eyes blinking through the sea water that fell into her lashes, and then she reached for me. I dragged herself onto my back, and she pressed in close, stiffening each time a wave rammed into us, and I struggled to right myself against the tide.

"We must hurry!" she urged, her body trembling over mine, and I turned to shore, fighting against the sea itself as it tried to drag us out.

But the water was not our only enemy. I could hear their song begin once again, the sweet melody creating a soft ache in my chest, and had I not had my magic, I surely would have followed them willingly to the bottom of the sea.

"Where are they?" Skylahr called, her fingers loosening their hold on my fur, and I swung my head, snapping at her, hoping the motion would draw her attention away from the sound long enough that I could get us safely to land.

Thrashing through the waves, I began to swim to shore, and for just a moment I had thought we would manage to escape the sea's clutches unscathed. But that had been far too optimistic of me. The very idea was foolish, and with the next great wave, we were thrown to the side, the weight of the water smothering us against the base of the sea stack we had jumped from.

I panted while Skylahr gasped for air, but the moment of reprieve did not last long. Just as soon as the first wave had retreated, another took its place, and I felt Skylahr struggle between the pillar of stone and the weight of my body.

Gasping in pain, Skylahr tried to shove me away, but it was no use, the tide continued to push forward, and each whitecap sent my giant wolven form crashing into her roughly. Choking on the salty water, I turned to face her, manoeuvring my front legs around her body, and then I braced myself against the stone, the sharp edges cutting at the pads of my paws while I tried to shield her from the sea.

"Kalian," she cried out weakly, her face pale and lips blue while her teeth chattered. "We have to try to get around to the other side of the pillar; it may block the waves enough for us to get to shore."

It wasn't a perfect plan, but it was the only one we had, and when the current began to retreat once more, I prepared myself to move. Then I heard it: the great cries of the sea-maidens. I glanced behind me as a rush of fire coated the sea's surface. Fleeing from the flames, the creatures who had been readying to attack our rescuers turned towards the shallower waters once more, and I watched as the swarm dove over the waves, spears in hand as they advanced.

"We have to go!" Skylahr cried, her eyes wide with panic, and I pressed against the sea stack, straightening my limbs as much as I could to allow Skylahr to slip out from under me.

Skylahr hurried to face the stone, her fingers clawing at the wet rock as she tried to pull herself around it. But the waves would not ease, and I watched helplessly as they knocked her into the pillar, her face smashing against the rough surface. I whimpered when the pale skin of her cheek split open.

Not giving up, she pressed on, ignoring the blood that was now running towards her jaw, and then she was gone, hidden behind the tower. Not wasting another moment, I dug my nails into the hard surface, tearing at the rock while I forced myself around it.

Reaching Skylahr once more, I held myself steady while I waited for her to swing herself onto my back. And when she had managed to crawl up my spine, I pushed off of the sea stack and began swimming to shore. I forced myself to keep my head above water, my growls of effort morphing into whimpers of desperation. Desperation to save us, to save Skylahr and her friends, to live to see another day, and when my paws finally grazed across the ocean's floor, I heaved myself from its clutches.

"We are nearly there!" she cried out, her legs tightening around my middle as she urged me faster. "We are nearly—"

There was a soft sound of something colliding with flesh, and then the rest of her words broke off in a guttural sob before she fell forward, her body slipping over my shoulder and then tumbling to the shore with a gasp. Sliding to a stop, I spun towards her in panic and as she began to crawl her way across the sand, her right arm struggling to bear any weight, and it was then that I noticed the broken spear protruding from her shoulder.

Chapter 69

Shifting, I fell onto the cold, wet sand, bracing myself on my hands and knees as I panted, fighting for air before scrambling to my feet. Running back towards her, I watched as the sea rushed up the backs of Skylahr's legs, the power of it rocking her body while she struggled to pull herself from its grasp. I fell in front of her, grabbing her roughly before tugging her to her feet. Ignoring Skylahr's cry of pain, I held her against me, my fingers seeking out the broken shaft of the spear until the tips met the warmth of her blood.

"Leave it. We must go," she demanded, shoving at my bare chest, but I tugged her closer, peering over her shoulder to get a better look at the wound. "Leave it, Kalian!"

"No!" I snarled, leaning far enough back to look down at her face, and I cupped her jaw roughly with my hand. "If I leave it in you, you will be vulnerable. You will not be able to heal."

"But Gaelon—"

"I will go to them as soon as I get this out of you," I promised, and then turned her around. Grabbing hold of the shaft, I braced my other hand against her spine and pulled as sharply as I could, praying that the quick movement would ease some of the pain.

Falling forward, Skylahr whimpered, and I caught her around her middle, pulling her into my chest for just a moment before turning her towards me once more. Cupping her face, I tilted it up towards my own and pressed a brutal kiss to her mouth.

"Stay here," I ordered.

"I will not," she snarled, and I dove my fingers into her hair, curling the wet strands around them.

"You will. You are injured and unarmed. You will be a liability, and I cannot focus on helping our friends if I am consumed with worry for your safety."

"I will not sit by—"

"You will!" I roared, and she started the noise. "My Gods, Skylahr, I know what it is I am asking of you, but I wouldn't do so unless I had no other choice! Surely you know that?"

Her lower lip trembled, and I sighed before pressing my forehead against hers. "Please, Skylahr, *please*," I begged. "Stay here, heal, and gather your strength. I will handle the Siren's immortals, and then I will come back for you. And you can curse me or kiss me, do whatever it is you want. I will gladly fall to my knees at your feet and obey your every order for the rest of my existence! Just *stay here.*"

Her eyes burned with fury, but she remained silent. I turned from her, throwing myself forward, and then I was galloping across the sand, praying that she would listen to me, just this once.

Crossing the shore, I rushed to my comrades, watching as they readied themselves for the impending battle. The Siren's immortals were near now, their swords drawn as they approached, and I lengthened my stride, setting my sights on the enemy.

At the sound of my paws pounding against the sand, the group turned to me, their eyes wide as I charged forward, and then I leapt over their heads. Landing in front of them, I lowered my head as a vicious snarl tore from me.

The immortals' approach faltered, their strides growing hesitant as they watched me with careful eyes, and I growled, baring my teeth while I counted. There were about thirty, only a quarter of their total forces, but it was enough to send fear tingling down my spine. There was no possible way we would find victory without suffering a loss, and I sent a silent prayer to my mother, begging that she would hear me once more.

And then they were there, their armour clanging as they rushed at me, and I met them head-on.

Colliding with the metal-clad bodies, I swung my paws, my nails dragging across the silver while I tore at them with my teeth. One man fell, then another, a third and a fourth followed, and the others watched as their brothers in arms perished before gathering together. Crowding around me, they began to attack, their swords slashing and stabbing, the metal cutting into my flesh, and I roared, swinging my body to knock them away.

"Kalian!" Ella called from behind, and then another mass of fur slammed into the men surrounding me, its coat a dark grey.

Crushing a man beneath his paw, Keyno caught another between his teeth, snapping the immortal in two, before moving on, and now that I had an opening, I continued my fight. One by one the immortals fell as more Lupines reached the shores, and then the air was quiet, the screaming had ceased, and now the sound of the waves was the only noise that filled the space around us.

Wincing at the pain that riddled my body, I turned to Keyno, pressing my head to his as a wave of relief fell across me, and then I embraced the heat and fell forward, collapsing into him as my skin began to stitch itself together.

"Easy now, brother." Keyno wrapped an arm around me, his hand splaying across my shoulders, the flesh of his palm slipping across the blood that covered me.

"Kalian!" Skylahr shouted, her tone filled with terror, and I glanced back, watching as the Lupines parted for their Huntress, and then she was grabbing my arms, her body shaking. "Are you alright?"

"Fine," I promised, though my smile was more of a grimace, and she sighed before pressing a kiss to my naked chest. Lifting a hand, I cupped the back of her head, clutching her to me for just a pause before she was pulling away and grabbing my face. She held my jaw steady and peered up at my face, that hazel gaze of hers searing into mine, and then she snarled.

"You insufferable, arrogant man! Don't you ever do that to me again! Don't you dare think to ever leave me behind!" Swallowing, I could do nothing but nod as a single tear rolled across the scar on her cheek, and then she sobbed.

"Careful, Hazel. You can bash him around once your Healer checks him over," Keyno advised with an amused grin. Finally realizing that he was there, Skylahr turned to him in shock and then wrapped an arm around him. He patted her back with his free hand. "I am happy to see you, Skylahr, but we must hurry, more of our enemies are coming."

"There was said to be just over a hundred on the island, which would leave only seventy or so, and your ship alone carried two hundred of you. And there are more of you coming, correct? It wouldn't even be considered a battle," Barrick advised as he approached, seeming to be no worse for wear.

"I'm not talking about the Siren's immortals that are here." Keyno shook his head, and I looked to my friends. Gaelon and Ella frowned at my brother, but his dark eyes moved to mine. "And we have no more men coming."

"What are you talking about?" I questioned, not understanding.

"The rest of our fleet was ambushed on the seas," he explained. "The men you see here are all that is left of us."

"Ambushed? By whom?" Skylahr asked, her voice hoarse as she peered up at my brother. "We thought the beast was gone."

"It wasn't the beast," Keyno clarified.

Selbie's eyes travelled over the bodies that lay across the sand. "Are there more of the Siren's immortals on the waters then?"

"No, they are not of the Siren." Keyno exhaled, his gaze hardening as it met my own. "These men carry Crimson banners."

Skylahr finished cleaning my skin free of the blood and sand with the warm wet rag she had taken from the camp, and I glanced at the tents that had been raised. The oil they had lit on fire had scared off the pod of sea-maidens, making their voyage to shore possible, and with them they brought all the items we needed to make our first decent camp since stepping foot on the island.

"I am still angry at you," she muttered. Her fingertips traced the raised scars on my flesh, the pink colour fading as they healed.

"I know," I whispered, catching her hand with one of mine before lifting her fingers to my lips. "But can you be angry with me when this is over? I would rather spend tonight with you in my arms."

"Do you think this will truly be over for us?" she asked doubtfully, and I tucked a finger under her chin.

"What is it, Skylahr?" I whispered, stroking my thumb along her jaw.

"Do I not have enough reason to be worried?" she questioned, and I sighed.

"It's just not like you. I've never known you to be so frightened of a fight."

"Kalian, we don't know what is coming," she explained, her eyes lifting to the tents. "We may not survive this."

"We will. We will survive this, Skylahr. We will survive this together."

"Do you promise?" she asked faintly.

"Yes, with everything that I am," I vowed.

"And when our duty is done, we will live on a farm in the countryside?" she asked with a small, sad smile.

"Yes, when our duty is done, and we have brought peace to Elrin, we will sow our fields and harvest our crops." I leaned forward to press a kiss to the corner of her mouth. "We will hide away from all the rest of it and live out our days as nothing more than a simple man and a woman."

Skylahr lifted to her knees and crawled into my lap, curling her arms over my shoulders before pressing her mouth to mine. The kiss was soft and slow, one that started with just a hint of a spark before it grew into a blazing inferno, and I gasped as her hips rocked into mine.

"I want you," she moaned into the kiss, and my hands grabbed a hold of her hips, guiding her movements.

"You have me," I promised, moving my lips to the length of her throat, and she tilted her head back, offering more of herself to me.

"All of you?" she asked, pulling away.

"Of course." I frowned, searching her face while her lower lip trembled.

"Swear it," she demanded. "Swear that every piece of you is mine. Promise me that it's true."

"You have me, Skylahr. You own me, body, heart, and soul. Do with them what you wish." A weak breath broke from her lips and then she swallowed roughly.

"For always?"

"For eternity," I swore to her. "Even when you and I are gone from this world, and there is nothing left of us. Even when the sun has set for the last time and this earth turns to dust, even then I will still be yours."

"Kalian," she breathed while her fingers tangled in my hair. "I I—"

Surging forward, I stopped her words with my mouth. I kissed her softly for a long moment, and then I shook my head, smoothing a hand over her hair.

"Not like this," I whispered. "I refuse to have the first time you say those words to be because you are in fear of what tomorrow will bring. Tell me when the battle is won."

Falling back onto the damp earth, I watched the way the stars glowed above and then took in her magnificence. Widening her stance, she braced her hands on my bare chest and then bent forward, skimming her nose over mine softly.

"If you won't have my words, what would you have me give you instead?" she whispered, her lips ghosting over mine.

Wrapping an arm around her back, I rolled us until I had her pinned beneath me, and then I sat back, watching the way her eyes fluttered closed when my hips pressed into the space between her thighs. I smiled down at her, my heart filling with warmth when I saw that bright flush crawl across her face.

"I will have everything and anything else you are offering to give." Those long bronze lashes flickered open, and then she was cupping my face, drawing me back down towards her own to press another kiss to my mouth.

She snagged my bottom lip with her teeth and tugged it into her mouth, and then lifted a leg, hitching her thigh to my hip before settling against the earth once more. “Then take it.”

Chapter 70

Peering down at her, I studied the way her short bronze waves covered the damp earth, and how her pale skin glowed under the night sky, the flickering flames from camp illuminating the freckles over her nose, those tiny constellations reflecting the stars above.

She was magnificent, and I could not take my eyes off her.

"What is it you're waiting for, Kalian?" she whispered, her leg dragging me to her, and I placed my palms on either side of her head, bracing myself as I resisted her request.

"As much as I enjoy having you spread before me beneath the night sky, looking like the Goddess of the earth you are, I was thinking something different for tonight."

"Oh?" A brow lifted, her interest piqued, and my lips rose into the smirk I knew she secretly adored.

"I'd much prefer you in the comfort of my tent, laid against the soft furs while I take my time memorizing every gasp." I pressed a kiss to the corner of her mouth. "Every whimper." Another to her jaw. "Every cry and every moan."

Slanting my lips over hers, I swallowed her quiet sigh while my tongue brushed hers, and she pressed the heel of her foot into my upper thigh, urging me impossibly closer. Groaning into our kiss, I trembled at the feel of her under me, and then I was pulling away, cursing myself for my lack of control.

"You are making it incredibly difficult to focus on my task." Tipping her head back into the grass, Skylahr blinked up at me.

"Am I now?" She laughed under her breath and then shoved her hands against my bare chest until I lifted myself off of her. Free of my weight, Skylahr rose to her feet, peering down her nose at me for just a moment, and then her eyes traced my skin from head to foot, her gaze leaving a burning inferno in its wake. I clenched my jaw, waiting for her to make her decision.

"Then come, Protector," she ordered. "Show me how you worship your Huntress."

She turned on her heel and strode away from me, only pausing long enough to glance at me from over her shoulder. My mouth hung open as my mind spun, and then I was scrambling to my feet and hurrying after her.

Moving past the cream-coloured canvas, Skylahr stepped into my tent, taking in the chairs and cot with little interest before spinning to face me. She waited until I tied the fabric closed behind me before lifting her fingers to the laces of her tunic. Unravelling the knot, she allowed the fabric to loosen, the sliver of pale skin growing until I could see the swells of her breasts, and then she glanced at the breeches I had tugged on at the shores.

"Well?" she asked, gesturing to the fabric that covered me, but I took a step forward instead and grabbed her fingers before lifting them to rest against my face.

"I am struggling to regain some semblance of control as it is, my love," I admitted, my face flushing hotly beneath her touch, and her lips quirked.

"I expected the Lupine alpha to have more authority over himself and his *urges*." She smiled, her hazel eyes roaming across my face, and I curled a hand into her hair.

"You shouldn't overestimate my will, not when it comes to my desire for you." I sighed, pressing a kiss to her hair while I closed my eyes, and she placed her free hand on my chest, her fingers tracing patterns across the skin.

"Skylahr," I warned, but she just laughed softly, the husky sound lighting a fire in my veins, and I growled in response, tugging her head back before crashing my mouth against hers.

Dying to feel her skin but unwilling to end our kiss, I grabbed at the neckline of her tunic and fisted the fabric in my hands before pulling, and the green material ripped right down the middle. I tugged the scraps down her arms and placed one hand along her back, my rough skin cupping the muscles of her shoulder while the other angled her head.

"Fuck, Skylahr," I panted into her mouth, smiling at the needy little gasp that broke from her. "The things you do to me."

"Tell me," she whispered as her nails raked down my torso, and my teeth gnashed together at the feeling.

"Even your softest touch lights a fire within me, and it grows until my very being is fully consumed by its blaze and its flames are ready to burn away anything in its path."

"That sounds painful," she remarked quietly, lifting her face to press her lips to my jaw. I pulled her from my skin, tangling my fingers in her bronze strands before nipping at her full lower lip.

"It is *glorious*."

I undid the knot of her breeches and loosened them, waiting for the fabric to fall to her feet before I helped her step out of the pile, and then I cupped the backs of her knees and hoisted her into my arms. Wrapping her legs around my hips, Skylahr lowered her lips to mine once more, her own hands carding through my hair as I walked us to the fur-covered cot and then I eased her down. Melting into the pelts, Skylahr hummed with happiness, her body shifting as she stroked her hands over the soft brown below her, and I watched, enraptured by the way she glowed in the flickering candlelight that surrounded us.

"What of that fire now, Kalian?" she asked, her eyes meeting my own.

"Now we let it swallow us both."

I trailed my fingertips up her thighs as she slowly let them fall open, and then I bent to press a kiss to the flesh that covered her heart, relishing its thundering as she shivered at my touch. Lowering my attention, I skimmed my mouth across the pale skin, taking time to kiss each and every freckle and mark before sucking one of her nipples into my mouth. I cupped her other breast with my hand, coaxing those delightful little whimpers from her and smiling when her hips began to lift as she grew more desperate for my touch.

"Do you feel it now?" I whispered, laving my tongue over the pink bud. "Do you feel that scorching heat under your skin?"

"Yes," she hissed, her head tipping back while her hips rocked once more, and I pinned her under my weight. Taking both wrists in one of my palms, I held them to the furs above her head.

"That is *us*, Skylahr," I whispered, running the tip of my nose over hers. "This blaze is ours, and ours alone."

"Please," she pleaded, and then her tongue darted out to wet her lips, almost as if she was parched. I moved my free hand, stroking the backs of my knuckles down the softness of her belly before cupping her.

I dipped into the wet warmth, coating my fingers with her before moving my attentions higher, and when she trembled, I stroked her softly. Leaning my weight on the hand that still held both of hers, I noticed the way her fingers curled around their captor, and then her knees were lifting, offering me more space between her thighs.

Pleased with her reaction, I carefully pressed a finger into her, giving her a chance to adjust to the feeling, and then I added a second. My strokes were slow and gentle, and I kept a careful eye on the flush that grew across her chest and the way her breathing stuttered, and then I moved my thumb, circling that spot with a practiced rhythm.

"Kalian," she cried, her thighs trembling as they closed on my wrist, and I stopped my movements, waiting until her lashes fluttered and those hazel eyes focused on mine.

"Open up for me, love." My voice was low, but the order was clear, and she let her legs fall open once more. "That's it, sweeting."

Resuming my motions, I curled my fingers until I found that spot I was searching for, and her entire body shook. I grinned down at my

Huntress, took in a steadying breath, and then when her hips tilted and her toes curled, I stopped once more.

"Kalian!" she growled, frustrated to be denied yet again, and I pulled my hand from between her legs and tugged my breeches over my hips before finding my place.

"Soon, my love," I promised as I released her hands and bent my arm, bracing my weight on my forearm before I lowered my face to hers. Capturing her mouth with my own, I poured everything I felt into the kiss and then shifted forward, pressing my length into her slowly.

Sinking to the hilt, I took in a trembling breath, resting my forehead on hers while I stared into her eyes, and then we began to move, together.

My love for her was more than I had ever imagined it could be, and the power of it left me breathless.

"Kalian," she warned again, her knees lifting to my hips, and I continued my pace, keeping my thrusts deep and even as she began to flutter around me.

"Let go now, sweeting," I urged her, knowing I could not last much longer. And after two more thrusts, her head tipped back, and she cried out for me. Following her over the edge, I groaned out her name and then collapsed into her arms, letting that heat between us simmer into a soft, everlasting warmth.

Chapter 71

"Crimson sails! Crimson sails are approaching!" Keyno shouted as he ran through the camp, alerting the rest of the men, and Skylahr lifted her head from my shoulder.

"Kalian," she whispered, turning to me in worry, and I curled my fingers in her hair, pulling her face to mine.

"We will survive this," I promised once again, and she nodded but did not look convinced.

Tightening my hold, I tilted my chin so that my mouth met hers, and I memorized the feel of her in my arms. I took my time studying the warmth of her soft lips, the weight of her against me, the way she shivered beneath my touch for what had to be the thousandth time, and then finally pulled away. "We will survive this."

"Together?" she asked breathlessly.

"Together," I swore.

Pulling from me, Skylahr left our cot and began to dress, and I immediately missed her warmth, but knew we could not prolong this any longer. I rose from the furs to help Skylahr with the chain mail Keyno had brought along with him, though it did not fit her well, and I ran my fingertips across the metal links.

"This is not nearly suitable enough for the Huntress. It's far too plain and cumbersome." I sighed, lifting the silver breastplate over her head.

"Kalian," Skylahr chided. "Now is not the time to be vain."

"I hate to correct you, my starlight, but there is always time for vanity." I grinned, hoping to pull a smile from her lips by using her new nickname. She rolled her eyes and dipped her chin while she tried to hide her amusement from me. Laughing softly, I moved to her side once more and helped her with the buckles and straps of her armour, this time with haste as I listened to the rest of the camp organize themselves.

Pulling the fabric back, we stepped out of our tent, and Keyno hurriedly steered us towards the edge of our encampment. Turning to the seas, he pointed to the ships that were still quite a distance away, and I frowned at the blowing crimson sails.

"Why would they come here?" Skylahr asked, her face now pale and her eyes worried.

"They have three Chosen isolated in one place with limited men. This is an opportunity they would not pass up."

"But how did they know we were here?" Skylahr whispered, her gaze focused on our enemy's vessels.

"I don't know, but we will have those answers," I promised, lifting a hand to her metal-clad shoulder. "But for now, we need to organize the men and formulate a plan."

Keyno and I both turned back to camp, but Skylahr remained in her place, her frown growing as she stared at the waters.

"What is it, Skylahr?" I asked, stepping behind her once more.

"Why do you think they are coming from the west?" she questioned quietly, and I lifted my eyes to the ships. "What is there?"

"Astilar."

"Is that where you think they have been hiding?" she asked.

"Perhaps, but as far as I know the island is rather desolate. There would not be much for them to survive on; the climate is hot and humid and most of the land is covered by desert."

Her brows furrowed and then a look of understanding flickered across her face. However, before I could ask her about it, shouting sounded from the north, and I spun on my heel and raced through the camp.

"What is it!?" Skylahr called as she followed behind me, but I did not turn back to face her. I couldn't. I was completely powerless to tear my eyes away from the pack of helcyrbi who led the sapphire militia that was now emerging from the cover of the forest on the cliff above.

"Holy Gods," Barrick cursed, his eyes wide with fear. The creatures were clawing to get to us but were being held back by the thick chains tied around their throats, and I looked to Skylahr as she curled her fingers around the golden pommel at her hip.

"It appears as if this will be more of a battle than you thought," Selbie whispered to the guard hoarsely as she gazed up at the cliff overhead. Ella then stepped next to her, passing the halfling a blade while the rest of the Lupines shifted into their wolven forms, ready and waiting for my signal.

"Form the lines!" Keyno ordered before taking his place next to the Healer, and I waited, watching as the long-limbed beasts pulled at their restraints, growling and screeching as they all but hung off the edge of the cliff, and then a tall red-headed man appeared. He was large in stature, his thick body covered with deep blue armour. The way the rest looked to him told me he was their leader. There was a string of pearls that crossed his chest and went under an arm, and when he turned, I saw the curve of a shell.

"Is that—" Ella gasped.

"The horn," Gaelon concluded. Looking to Keyno, I pointed to the man.

"That is the one we need." My brother nodded his head and then he shivered, his tan skin quivering before it was replaced with grey fur. Pressing in close, he backed the Huntress just as the enemy's war horns blew and her hazel eyes sought mine.

"Together," I vowed once more, tucking a strand of hair behind her ear before stroking my thumb over her mark. She took my hand, lifted it to her lips, and pressed a soft kiss to my knuckles before unsheathing her golden sword.

Releasing their hold on the shackles, the immortals sent the helcyrbi loose, watching as they clambered down the stone wall, their shrieking intensifying as they neared. I looked to my men, waiting until the last possible second before giving the order.

"Now!" I shouted, and the first wave of Lupines moved forward, running for the base of the cliff just as the creatures reached the sand, and then their fight began.

Growling and shrieking filled the air around us, the sound so loud it drowned out the waves crashing into the shore, and Skylahr stood, her head held high as we watched my men tear those beasts limb from limb. But our upper hand did not last long, and in their fight to survive, the creatures banded together, their focus changing as they fought as one.

Skylahr lifted her eyes as the immortals took their chance and moved to make their descent down the slope. I grabbed her hand and swallowed roughly, watching as the rest of our enemy charged before taking a breath, knowing that these would be our last moments together before we were forced to fight.

"It's time," I warned her, my fingers trembling beneath her steady hand. I studied her face as those brilliant hazel eyes hardened, almost as if my Skylahr was not behind them any longer. Almost as if she had shut herself away while we prepared ourselves to stare down death.

Pulling from my touch, Skylahr turned towards the men who were nearing us now and readied herself before glancing back at me. "Go, Kalian!"

Bursting from my skin, I landed on my front paws and lifted my lips to display my lethal fangs. I let out a brutal growl and then I bent, waiting until Skylahr had safely mounted before charging towards the enemy's line.

Cutting down the first men to rush us with her mighty sword, Skylahr shifted on my back, managing to sit every movement, every turn with ease, as if we were of one body and mind, and together we led the battle. Following our lead, the Healer sat astride my brother, his own weapon held high as he came down at the immortals surrounding us before his dark gaze searched the shores.

"Where is their leader? Where is Syman?" Gaelon shouted, his blade striking another immortal who had been attempting to stab at Keyno, and Skylahr turned, her weight shifting as scanned the area around us.

Crushing one of the men beneath my paws, I too spun, scanning the mass of armoured bodies and Lupines for the red-headed man, but he was not here. He was not on the shore, and I growled in frustration before sinking my teeth into another immortal.

Slowly we overpowered our enemy, my men bringing us closer to victory with every casualty, but still their leader did not come to aid them. Satisfied that we had nearly ended this, I pulled back from the chaos and death and peered up at the ridge, searching the trees for the man.

"Is he there?" Skylahr asked, her hand tightening in my fur, and I examined the forest once more, finally noticing the deep shimmering blue that remained in the shadows before I charged for the hill.

Racing up the damp grass, I weaved through the forest, following the man as he tried to escape. But it was pointless. He could not outrun me; he would not flee from his fate. And when I neared, I moved to the right slightly, slamming my shoulder into his back, forcing him to tumble to the ground before sliding to a halt.

Throwing her leg over my shoulder, Skylahr dismounted, waiting behind as I stalked towards our target, focusing on the way he whimpered in fear. However, as I neared, I realized the man's hair was not in fact the same colour of auburn it had been, and when I heard Skylahr's startled gasp, I twisted to look behind me.

"I expected more from the Protector himself," Syman chided, pressing the metal of his blade to Skylahr's throat, and I snarled, enraged that he would dare threaten her in such a way.

"Easy now, I don't want to waste it." He frowned, his hand angling the edge of the dagger just below the scar that already marked the pale skin of her neck, and then her eyes met mine.

"You do not have what you need," she growled, her chin tipping as he fisted her hair.

"You are mistaken. I have everything I need," Syman snarled.

"I see no trident." The immortal's face softened into a smile, and then he lowered his mouth near her ear.

"Don't you?" he asked, his face glowing with glee, and then his eyes moved towards the sea. "Look closer, Huntress."

Not understanding, she searched through the leaves, her hazel eyes narrowing as she tried to get a glimpse of the water, and then they widened, and a gasp escaped her.

"Luka," she whispered.

"I wondered if you knew of him," Syman said softly. "He is one of the Seductress's closest confidants after all, and he brought us a gift."

Glancing at the beach, I studied the battle that was nearing its end, and then I searched the tide and saw what had captured Skylahr's attention. Leading the group was a man, his light brown hair blowing in the wind while he stood at the front of his vessel with his arms raised above his head. I followed the length of his limbs, examining the long silver stem in his grasp before moving on to the three prongs that curved just slightly.

"He brought it all the way from the deserts of Alister," Syman explained. "Our clever Goddess hid it with her trusted Crimson sister."

"I was not aware your Goddess saw the Seductress in such a light," Skylahr snarked, wincing when the tip of the dagger nicked her skin, and I growled, shaking with rage.

Choosing to ignore me, Syman narrowed his eyes on his captive. "They share a purpose—a bond, and truces and alliances have been built on less."

"A bond?" Skylahr repeated, her eyes moving to mine in confusion.

"I don't want to spoil it all." Syman grinned at me. "I don't want to take that opportunity away from my Goddess."

"You still need Reide blood to summon her," she warned. "And that is something I cannot offer you."

"Is that what you think? That we need the blood of that mortal man?" Syman laughed, his head shaking in disbelief. "Oh, how foolish you are, Huntress."

Skylahr's brow furrowed, and I took a step closer, trying to find a way to get to her before the immortal could slit her throat. But Syman noticed my approach, and his hold tightened on Skylahr.

"Uh-uh," he chided. "I am busy educating our Huntress and I would hate to cut that short." His blue eyes narrowed at me, and I flashed my teeth in warning.

But he paid me no mind as he went on. "And I don't think I want to waste a single drop. After all, it has been so difficult to get a hold of."

"It was a fool's errand to begin with," Skylahr growled. "It won't work; I do not have what it is you require. I do not have blood of the *first* men."

Syman's bright blue eyes moved to my own, and then his hold loosened just slightly before he pointed the dagger at me. "I would have thought you understood what that meant—"

Taking her chance, Skylahr snapped her head back, slamming her skull into Syman's face. The force of the impact sent the immortal sprawling backwards, and then she threw herself over him, her hands grabbing for the dagger that was still clenched in his grasp.

But the immortal fought back, his body bucking beneath hers, and then his arm swung towards her throat, the end of the blade just missing her jugular when she bent out of his reach. Trying again, the man aimed to stab her, and I rushed forward, snapping at one of his legs and tearing the limb just below the knee.

However, my attack jostled Skylahr, and when Syman struck once more, his weapon found purchase in the flesh of her right wrist. The skin torn, her blood splattered across the ground, the deep red splashing over the man's tunic, the string of pearls, and the horn that was cast aside, and I snarled at the smell of salt.

But before I could do anything else to aid her, the armoured man I had left forgotten rose from the ground, his blade in hand and ready to slash at me, and I turned my attention to him. It was quick, not taking an ounce of true effort to end him, but it had been enough time for Syman to grab for the horn.

Pressing the blood-spattered shell to his lips, Syman blew into it, and the cold, wet air filled with a rumbling sound. Freezing, I felt my hackles rise, and I shivered at the change around us, knowing that whatever had just transpired could not be undone.

Chapter 72

Scrambling from her place, Skylahr reached across the immortal and knocked the shell from his hand before shoving the dagger into his chest. She fell back on her heels, took in a deep, shuddering breath, and then looked at the waters, searching for the man she had called Luka.

"He no longer carries the trident," she whispered, her face filled with panic, and my ears flattened as the now empty-handed man sailed closer to the shores. "What could that mean? What did he do with it?"

I had no way to answer her in this form, but even if I could I wasn't sure what I would say. I did not have time to think on it; we were needed down below. Pressing against her, I swung my head, gesturing to my back, and waited for her to take the horn and then clamber up my body before setting off once more.

The small boats were nearing, their crimson banners blowing in the wind, and I kept my attention on them as we thundered back to my men. Taking in the state of the sand, I examined the pieces of helcyrbi that were strewn across the shores and the Siren's immortals that had fallen to our forces. From what I could see we had suffered only very minor losses, though the thought of even one of my men perishing here made my stomach churn.

Sensing my distress, Skylahr stroked the fur of my shoulder. I hurried to Keyno's side as the Healer turned to us, his dark eyes widening when he noticed the horn that hung from Skylahr's shoulder. "That noise, was that—"

"The horn, yes," Skylahr answered, her fingers twisting in my fur anxiously as we faced our new enemy. I could feel her tremble as she sat astride me while we waited for the Crimson soldiers. "It appears my assumption was right after all. There is no Siren in sight; the horn was useless."

I glanced at Gaelon from the corner of my eye. His gaze found mine, and I knew he had felt it too.

"We will destroy the horn when this is done," he instructed, his attention focusing on the shell. "Keep hold of it until then." Unsheathing his sword, the Healer organized the line, and then set his sights on Luka. "We need that one alive. He will have answers to our questions and know the whereabouts of his Crimson Goddess and the rest of her faithful followers."

Lifting my lips in a snarl, I growled in agreement and then braced my weight on my front paws, preparing myself for our adversaries who were now rushing through the tide, their weapons drawn. And when the first wave of crimson reached us, the battle began once more.

These men were far more skilled than the Siren's immortals had been; years of combat while they hunted for the halflings had made them great swordsmen. However, we were not men, nor were we the prey they hunted. We were Lupines, the mighty people of the God of Protection, and we would fight with his strength.

Launching myself towards the horde of red, I snapped and clawed, grabbing at the nearest man before tearing him apart and then turning to the next. However, the men seemed to be unending, and they had turned to swarm us, their focus solely set on Skylahr and me.

"We need to separate!" Skylahr called from my back as she shoved the tip of her golden sword into one of our foes before moving to strike down another.

I wanted to argue. I wanted to keep her with me, to ensure she was safe. But she was right. We were making this too easy for them, and though we had size and strength on our side, the numbers were not in our favour.

Swiping my paw across the group, I fell back, waiting until my wolves moved to get between us and the enemy. Skylahr slid from my back and turned, ready to face the fight head-on with a pack of Lupines backing her. Compelling myself to turn away from her, I found my own opponents, their red armour an easy target, and I used every ounce of my strength against them. They would not leave this place. I would not allow her reign to begin once more, and when I felt myself start to waver, my body crying out at the gashes and wounds that now marked the skin beneath my fur, I thought of the deaths and suffering of the halflings. I thought of the deal I had made and the pain it had brought Skylahr, and I thought of my mother. I pictured the way Balor had held her head in the air as if it were a prize before tossing it to me. I forced myself to remember her striking white fur covered in blood and muck while her unseeing eyes stared into the distance. I forced myself to picture it all.

Filled with renewed fury, I continued my attack, tearing and snapping through their army until I had taken down dozens, and then I searched for my friends. Gaelon was still mounted on Keyno, the pair keeping their upper hand against the soldiers who surrounded them. Barrick, Selbie, and Ella had remained together, the trio enclosed by a handful of Lupines who had kept them safe, and then I searched for Skylahr.

She was there, her golden blade swinging as she cut down her opponents, her strength and skill unmatched as the magic of her Goddess burned through her veins. I could feel her power even from where I stood.

She spun on her heel, her hazel eyes seeking mine. The relief was evident on her face when she saw me, and then she scanned the shores. We were nearly done, the Crimson numbers were dwindling, and soon we would be victorious.

But then it came, that piercing war cry that we heard when we had arrived at Skohyn's shores, and I lifted my head, watching as the sea parted for the beast who erupted from its depths. Its massive form stood so tall its face was partially covered by the heavy clouds, and then it screamed again while it set its sights on the silver sails. The creature reached one great hand towards the vessel, raised it towards its face, and then crushed the ship, sending the crumbled pieces back into the ocean.

"The horn!" Gaelon shouted as he cut through a soldier before looking at me. "The horn must have summoned it!"

Skylahr pulled the string of pearls over her head and placed the horn on the sand, lifting her sword as she prepared to strike it, but Gaelon cried out in panic.

"Skylahr, no!" the Healer bellowed. "We don't know what that will do! We need to understand how it works before we destroy it! We need to find Luka!"

I searched the shores for the immortal who led the Crimsons here, scouring the bodies and chaos for any sign of him, but I found none. It was almost as if he had disappeared, and I would have assumed he had managed to flee had it not been for the subtle movement near the cliff.

As he crawled across the damp sand, I noticed the way he lowered to his belly, trying to hide behind his men's bodies like the coward he was, and I stalked forward, my growls growing in volume as I approached. And when he heard the deep rumbling, he froze, glancing over his shoulder with wide eyes.

"Protector," he croaked out, rolling to his side to face me, and I snarled, snapping my teeth in warning.

"Do what you will, you are too late." He lifted his hand, showing me the horrid gash across his abdomen that was bleeding at a faster rate than he could heal. However, he did not look fearful or worried. No, his lips lifted into a gleeful smile instead, and his grey eyes focused on the waters behind me. Not understanding, I stepped forward, ready to keep him in place until Gaelon could come question him. But as I neared, his bloodied hand shakily pointed to the sea.

"She is here, and she is ready to take what we need." I looked over my shoulder, and then I saw her.

Her hair was long and black, the wet strands hanging to her waist while the deep blue dress clung to her pale skin, the contrast making her flesh appear almost translucent. Moving towards us, she lifted one long arm, her webbed fingers clutching the shaft of the trident. She strode through the waves, and then those terrifying, soulless black eyes shifted. First to me, then the Healer, and then they settled on the Huntress, and her sharpened teeth gleamed as she smiled.

Coughing wetly, Luka drew in a deep breath from behind me and then laughed quietly as he said the words I knew to be true. "The Siren has been summoned."

Chapter 73

She moved with ease as the waves crashed around her, though the tide never once touched her skirts, almost as if the waters submitted to her very will, and I watched with growing fear as she neared. The beast behind her had gone quiet, its glowing eyes following its master as she stepped onto the sand, and I felt the earth quake beneath me, its surface trembling under her power.

"Huntress," she whispered, but somehow the winds carried her sweet voice, a soft melody that did not match her appearance. I shivered as the words caressed me before I turned to Skylahr.

Her sword had lowered, the gold pommel dangling from her welt-covered palm, and then those hazel eyes sought mine, the fear palpable while she clutched the horn in her other hand. Keeping my attention on the Goddess, I moved, slinking across the coast toward Skylahr, ready to do anything I needed to in order to keep the Siren from her.

But the Goddess's smile only grew as she observed me, and then her chin turned towards the Healer, her black eyes unblinking as she waited for him to do the same. Gaelon, who still sat on Keyno's back, paled while his brown curls blew in the wind, and I saw the fear clearly in his expression. He knew this was a fight we would not win.

"Come and surrender to me now, Huntress, and I will let the others live." The Siren didn't bother moving her attention to Skylahr, her focus now on Selbie. I looked at the woman who was partially hidden behind the mass of grey fur.

"Come now." She moved her trident, pointing the prongs at Selbie. "Or I will have my Chosen bring you to me with force."

Gaelon's spine straightened, but he did not look surprised that our suspicions had been confirmed. Selbie, however, froze in shock, her dark eyes widening as she looked back at the Siren.

Growling low in his chest, Keyno turned on his haunches and snarled at the halfling. Selbie took a step back in terror, her hands rising to show him she was not a threat, and Ella lifted her weapon, pointing it in the halfling's direction.

"Was this your plan all along? Did you drag the Huntress here for your Goddess?" Ella growled, her voice heavy with rage, and the halfling shook her head, her hands remaining in the air.

"No! I didn't know!" Selbie implored, her voice shaking as her eyes moved around the group frantically. "I promise you, I swear on all the halflings we have lost, I did not know."

"Ella," Gaelon called while his hand petted Keyno's shoulder in a soothing manner. "She has been nothing but loyal to us. She has proven time and time again that she is not one of them. Do not let your trust in her falter now."

Selbie turned her attention to Gaelon, her gaze filled with gratitude as he motioned for Ella to stop her threat, and the immortal watched him warily before lowering the blade just a touch.

"That's too bad," the Goddess sighed, her eyes remaining on the halfling. "I suppose you will not be useful after all. No matter, I don't need you to win this war." The Siren's smile slipped into a fierce growl as she lifted her free hand into the air.

Closing the last few feet between Skylahr and me, I moved to her shoulder, watching as the water behind the Goddess seemed to tremble, the waves lowering until the whitecaps all but disappeared, and then I saw them. At first it looked as if spools of silvers and golds covered the sea, the fine threads shimmering across the surface, and then the faces appeared, their large eyes and pale skin breaking from the ocean as they approached. But the sea-maidens were not scaled, and their fins had been replaced with long, thin limbs that carried them from the sea. Creeping closer, they entered the shallow waters, their webbed hands now visible. Each carried a spear as they set their sights on what remained of us.

"Kalian," Skylahr whispered, her voice trembling with fear as more and more of the maidens appeared. "What do we do?"

I remained quiet, watching as the Crimsons who had survived thus far moved to meet their new comrades in arms, reforming a frontline behind the sea Goddess as they awaited her instruction, and then I looked to the Healer, who was now urging Keyno towards us.

Stopping at my side, my brother pressed his shoulder into mine, a gesture that could only be interpreted as a united front, and Skylahr stepped forward, her eyes not moving from the Siren as she called out to the others.

"Barrick, take Ella and Selbie and find somewhere safe to hide," she ordered, but the guard scowled at his Huntress, and Ella was shaking her head.

"We will not leave you," the immortal snapped, her eyes narrowing at her friend.

"Ella, please, just go," Skylahr pleaded, her voice hoarse and defeated. "I couldn't save Elizabeth, but I can do this for you."

The immortal beauty's eyes glistened, but she shook her head once more. "No."

"Ella, we do not have time for this jus—"

"No!" Ella shouted, quivering. "We do not leave our family behind. Do not ask that of me now. You are my sister, and I will not leave you!"

The Huntress took in a shuddering breath, her lower lip trembling as she glanced at her friend quickly. I knew that she had thought their friendship had been lost forever, that the loss of their Elizabeth would plague them for the rest of their lives. But at this moment that didn't matter. The guilt and the blame meant nothing when we were facing our death, and I knew that Ella's words had healed something inside Skylahr. I could see it by the way her head lifted, and she held Ella's stare for a moment, her face softening before her chin lowered in a nod. It was as if the weight that had been crushing her was not as heavy, as if having Ella at her side eased the pain just enough for her to face what came next.

"That was touching." The Goddess laughed, her pointed teeth gleaming as her lips lifted into a terrifying grin. "I'll be sure to kill your sister first, Huntress. Maybe then you will give up this foolish idea of trying to win this battle and come to me willingly."

"You underestimate me, Siren," Skylahr replied. "I would rather die than surrender to you."

A sweet-sounding laugh burst from the Goddess, and her head tilted to the side. "Oh no, Huntress, we cannot have that. We have another use for you. But your friends will perish, of that I am certain. Just like how I am certain that by the time we are through with you, you will wish you had fallen with them."

"The Crimson Goddess fled from me in fear," Skylahr disputed, her weapon rising as she tipped the gold point at the Siren. "You will not be so lucky; I will be sure to run this blade through you and send you back to whatever hell you came from."

"You can try," the Siren laughed, "but I will enjoy watching you fail."

Lifting her trident, the Goddess ordered her troops forward, hanging back as they swarmed, and I stepped in front of Skylahr, keeping her hidden as my men rushed the beings. Lupines, immortals, and sea-maidens tangled together, the chaos impossible to follow, and I whimpered at the howls of pain as more of my men were slain.

"It's time now," Skylahr whispered. "It's time to end this."

Gaelon and Keyno turned to the Huntress, but she ignored them as she closed her eyes for a moment, her lips moving silently as she prayed, but to whom I wasn't sure. She had seemed to lose faith in our Gods after what had transpired here, and yet, here she was, calling on someone to give her strength, to guide her through this.

Opening her eyes, Skylahr placed one shaking hand on my shoulder and then swallowed. "Together."

"Together," Gaelon echoed, his eyes tracing her features before glancing at the other three, and then we moved.

Keyno turned left, his massive body colliding into the sea-maiden's spears, and I went straight, my eyes set on that terrifying smile of the Siren as I tried to get to her. But her creatures protected her well. Soon enough I could no longer see her as more and more of her forces crowded around me.

Snapping at the long-limbed beings, I tore into them, wincing when they screamed, and then I turned for the soldiers, using my size to knock them away while I aided the Lupines nearby. However, our attack had left Barrick, Ella, and Selbie vulnerable, and I heard the guard shout the immortal's name in worry.

Turning towards his voice, I noticed the group of maidens that were quickly approaching, their speed and agility giving them an advantage, and if they reached my friends, there would be no escape for the three. Growing panicked, I raced across the sand, but I would not get there in time to intercept the attack, and my stomach churned when I realized what was about to happen.

Gaelon spotted the danger to our friends and urged my brother forward, and then Keyno was leaping at the enemy, ready to destroy them. Landing in the space between the two groups, the great grey beast roared in warning and pushed forward. But one of the sea creatures anticipated his assault and lifted a blade just before Keyno could make contact. She slashed at his face, her weapon splitting the fur from his brow down to his snout, and blood poured from the wound that covered his entire left eye.

Yowling in pain, my brother shook his head, the movement sending his blood spraying across the others, and then Gaelon was tumbling to the sand.

"Gaelon!" Skylahr screamed, pressing her boot into the chest of the Crimson while she tugged her blade free from his red armour, and then she was racing towards the Healer.

Crossing the shore, Skylahr cut down anyone who was in her path, stabbing and slashing as she went, the gold of her blade no longer visible beneath the gore that clung to it, and then she was reaching the Healer, pulling him to his feet before they were swarmed once more.

Having been distracted by the scene, I was not prepared for my own horde of enemies, and I finally realized how near they were just as they closed in.

"You die here today, Protector!" one of the Crimson soldiers shouted as he lunged towards me with his blade, and I spun, turning to slam my hip into him before crushing him beneath my paws. But where one man fell, another took his place, and more and more came, the sea of foes endless as they filled the shores around me.

Thrashing and snapping, I killed man after man, maiden after maiden until they lay to waste at my feet, and then I set my sights on the sea Goddess once more. Her face filled with joy as she held her trident out in front of her.

"Shall this be the end of your story, Protector?" she asked, her fangs gnashing as she waited for my approach, and I braced my weight on my front half and opened my jaws wide as I released a mighty growl.

"Then so be it." She smiled. "I think it's time you are reunited with your fallen God."

Chapter 74

Charging forward, I crossed the distance between us in three long strides and then launched myself at the Goddess. However, she was fast, far faster than I had anticipated, and she braced her trident in both hands before pressing it into my body and tossing me away.

I landed onto the sand roughly and scrambled to my feet once more, lowering my head as she twirled her weapon expertly in her hand, and then I ran at her again. Dodging my attack, the Siren danced out of my path, landing on one knee before thrusting the weapon forward and striking the prongs into my hip. Growling at the sharp burn, I rounded on her with my jaws wide, and she thrust the shaft of the weapon between my teeth, pressing it on my tongue as I tried to sink my fangs into her.

"I thought you'd be stronger." She smiled as I fought against the metal in my mouth, and then she lifted a foot and slammed the heel into my gut, sending me flailing backwards. "How ashamed the Protector must be of you."

Rolling onto my belly, I examined her carefully, and she grinned, her eyes tracing the length of my body with keen interest. "You certainly look fearsome, so it's a wonder you are so weak."

Curling my lips, I bared my fangs, but the Goddess shook her head with a laugh. "Tell me, is she the reason you are so pathetic? Have you held yourself back because you fear her? Are you scared of the power that runs through her veins?"

Rising once more, I dashed towards her, anticipating her dodge this time, and when she slipped past me, I swung my head. Catching the skirt of her gown in my teeth, I hauled her onto the earth. I dove for her, ready to pin her beneath me, but she swung her trident at the last minute and the metal slashed into my shoulder.

Lurching away, I panted in pain and glanced at my blood-soaked fur, the river of red continuing to flow.

"You won't heal from my trident, Chosen." She snickered and then her eyes moved past me towards the chaos that covered the shores. "My, she is formidable. It's no wonder he wants her so badly."

I didn't bother to fall for her trap. I knew the second I moved my attention she would strike, and those black irises slid to my face, her face filled with amusement.

"Do you know his plans for her?" she asked and my teeth snapped together. "It's a shame she won't even remember who you are by the time he's through, but we all must make sacrifices, and looking at her now, I can see that untapped potential, that immense power."

Lunging forward, I aimed for her face, ready to tear the pale flesh from her skull. But it had been exactly the reaction she anticipated, and she turned her trident down, shoving the tips into the sand before using it to propel herself higher as she hurdled over me.

Whirling on the balls of her feet, she faced me once more, her weapon in hand and ready, but this had just been a game of cat and mouse. I had yet to find an advantage, and soon she would grow bored of this routine.

Not knowing what else to do, I sprang for her once more, her neck my teeth's target. But it had been pointless. Foreseeing my move, she leaned back, her shoulders nearly touching the ground, and then as my underbelly passed over her, she thrust the metal points up into my ribs.

The pain was slow to come, but all air left my lungs immediately, and then she pulled on the shaft, tugging the silver free from my flesh before she watched me collapse to the earth, now in my immortal form.

Strolling towards me, she dragged her trident across the sand, ignoring the way the bits of brown stuck to the crimson that covered it, and then she stood before me, peering down her nose as she examined my face.

"My, you are handsome, and you look so much like him," she pondered with a tilt of her head. "And you both seem to share the same weakness."

I curled my arm over my torso, clutching the wound, as if my palm would stop the bleeding, and she shook her head.

"Tell me, how did she do it? How did she make you feel for her?" I swallowed down the taste of salt as I blinked through the haze, and then my lips curled, my blood-covered teeth flashing.

"You know nothing about her," I snarled.

"I know what she is, and I know what she will be," the Siren answered, her tone almost bored as she stared down at me.

"And what is that?" I choked out, my throat now clogged.

"The end of you. The end of this world as you know it." She smiled. "And I am so disappointed to know you won't be here to see it happen."

"She will never surrender to you. She is the Huntress, she is *good*," I growled.

"Maybe," the Siren agreed. "Her Huntress side would keep her from submitting. But luckily, that's not all she is. She is so much more. She is the heir of the first."

"You are just as stupid as your men," I snapped. "She is not a true Reide; she is not his ancestor."

"Reide?" the Siren repeated. "Is that what you thought? You thought we were hunting for a Forefolk's blood?"

I frowned in confusion, not understanding what else they could mean.

"She carries the blood of the *first* God. She has the blood of Mòrbàs," the Siren explained. "She is of the Reaper."

The Reaper.

My heart stuttered in my chest, and I felt a rush of fear curl in my belly.

I had only ever heard the name whispered once in my life. It had been when I was a child travelling north with my mother. We had stopped at a small village, and I had met a group of boys who were telling tales and sharing stories they had heard of the Gods and the war that had ravaged the land.

It was alleged he was the earliest God, though by then no one continued to worship him, and the boys said it was because he was evil incarnate, that he was nothing more than death and desolation. When I went to my mother about what they had told me, she clamped a hand over my mouth and told me to never speak of him again. Her fear had been so evident, I was too shaken to ever bring it up and had long since forgotten about it.

Until now.

"Can you see it when you think of her face?" the Siren wondered. "Can you feel it when you imagine touching her skin?"

My sight continued to grow hazy, the cold seeping into my veins as my head lolled and my blood soaked the sand beneath me. But when I closed my eyes, I pictured her face. I pictured her hazel eyes and her pale skin. I imagined the blaze that burned between us, and then my lashes fluttered open once more.

"You are wrong," I whispered hoarsely, wincing as my body shuddered in pain.

"I suppose you'll never know." Lifting the trident high above her head, she aimed the tips for my face and was ready to bring it down when a voice called out for her. I turned my head weakly, glancing at the halfling who now held the horn in one hand and a dagger in the other.

"Tell me, if I shattered this horn, what happens to your creatures?" Selbie asked, her dark eyes narrowing at the Goddess, and the Siren lowered her weapon as she turned to her Chosen.

"You are bold," the Goddess whispered. "It's a shame you don't know your place. You could have done great things."

Selbie held the Siren's stare, her face tense with rage. "I still can."

Bringing the tip of metal to the shell, Selbie slammed the blade into its side. The horn cracked, and a noise came from it, the sound loud and piercing. She pulled the blade free and pierced it again, and then shoved her thumb into the hole before grabbing the horn with both hands and splitting it open.

The effects were instantaneous. The great beast in the waters shrieked, and I looked towards the waves, watching as it began to crumble until it came apart piece by piece and then fell back into the sea's depths. The maidens, who had been consumed by the battle, fell to their knees, their hands lifting to cover their ears as they cried out in pain, and the Siren's hands tightened around her trident before she lifted it to her shoulder. Realizing she meant to throw it at her Chosen, I used every ounce of strength I had and rushed to my feet before trying to tackle her. But the Siren moved at the last moment and curled a hand around my throat, her talons piercing my skin as she held me an arm's length away.

"You are nothing but a foolish boy," she growled. "And I have grown tired of playing with you."

"Then perhaps it's time for a new opponent," Gaelon called from behind me, and her black eyes looked at the Healer with interest.

"Opponent? Is that what you will be?" The Siren laughed. "Have you chosen a different path than your God?"

Her grip tightened, her palm now crushing my windpipe, but I was too weak to try to fight her hold. My injuries had still not healed, and I had lost too much blood. Running her tongue over her sharpened teeth, the Siren gave my throat one last squeeze before she dropped me and then set her sights on the Healer.

"I had little patience for his ways," the Siren muttered as she advanced on Gaelon. "Always so stoic, always so level-headed. He bored me with his constant need for virtue and kindness. He was weak, and I wish I had been the one to end him."

Gaelon did not react to her words; his face remained impassive as she prowled towards him, and then once the Goddess was close enough, he raised his sword and braced his weight.

"But you are not," she observed while eyeing his blade. "Good, I would like a little more fight before I claim your life as well."

"I do not die here on this beach today," Gaelon promised her, his dark eyes hard as he waited for her to move.

"You're wrong, Healer," she replied. "You will, and then this day will be known as the day the Chosen of the Gods of old fell to the Siren." Lunging for Gaelon, she thrust her trident at him, grinning when he fought her off, and then they circled each other.

"Perhaps you are more of a rival than I thought." Her grin grew as he blocked another one of her blows. "This will be fun."

Clutching my chest, my fingers shook as they slid across the slick skin, trying to keep my blood inside me. But it continued to flow, pressing past the space between my knuckles, and I coughed, spitting the fluid that filled my mouth before turning on my side.

Hearing my struggle, Gaelon hesitated in his pursuit, and the mistake left him open to the Goddess, who took it and slashed at him with her weapon. Shoving the prongs into his thigh, she laughed in joy and then tugged the trident free before dancing away.

"That is the problem with you," the Siren chided. "You let yourself feel for others and it leaves you vulnerable."

"Maybe," Ella called from somewhere behind me. "But it also unites us."

The Goddess spun just in time to dodge the arrow that had been aimed at her, but the attack had done its job, and Gaelon moved, swinging his sword at her armed hand.

Dropping the trident in surprise, the Siren turned on Gaelon, her talons slashing as she hissed at him. But it had been exactly what they had been waiting for, and when she lurked towards the Healer, Selbie dove for the weapon.

Curling her fingers around it, the halfling moved with more speed than I had thought possible and thrust the prongs into the Siren's back, pushing until the metal tips protruded from her chest, and then Selbie pulled the trident free.

Falling to her knees, the Siren gasped for air, her hands clutching at the wound while she peered up at the Healer before her.

"You are fools," she croaked through her teeth.

"And you are dead," Selbie snarled as she slammed the points into the back of her skull, the force of the blow folding the Goddess in half as her trident secured her to the sand, and that was the last thing I saw before my world faded to black.

Voices murmured above me, the words unclear but the sounds familiar, and I took in a shuddering breath before squinting my eyes open. Gaelon was bent over me, his skin pale and his gaze worried as his hand pressed against my jaw, and I frowned before moving my attention. Barrick was next to him, his stern face bruised and bloodied but whole, or as whole as it had been before the battle. Beside him was Ella and Selbie, the two of them huddled close as they watched me with weary eyes and then I turned my head.

Keyno was on his knees next to my shoulder, and half of his face was coated in dried blood. My heart dropped as I took in the open crevice that sat on the left side of his nose, the place where one of his warm bright brown eyes would sit, and my chin trembled as I fought my tears.

"Keyno," I choked out, lifting my hand towards his cheek, and he caught my fingers with his own before giving them a squeeze.

"Don't pity me, Kal," he demanded. "I'm still better looking than you, even with one eye."

My lips quirked in the corners, and I sniffed before allowing my stare to roam once more. But the face I sought out was nowhere to be found, and I braced my hands on the sand as I struggled to sit up.

"Where is she?" I demanded, my head lifting as I tried to search the shores, but when I still could not find her, I moved to my knees and then grabbed Keyno's bare shoulder, using his body to pull myself to my feet.

"Kalian!" Gaelon admonished as he tried to pull me back to the ground.

"Where is she!?" I roared, ignoring his cautioning while I spun in circles, my focus travelling from one end of the beach to the other.

"Skylahr!?" I screamed, stumbling away from the group. "Skylahr!?"

There were bodies littering the shore, deep red covering the sand, and when I scanned the chaos I noticed the glittering gold blade that had been left forgotten, and my heart shattered as fear curled in my belly.

"Skylahr!?" I called again, pulling away from Ella as she grabbed my arm.

"She's not here, Kalian." The immortal sobbed, her dark eyes shining as she lifted her tear-soaked face towards mine. "She's not here."

"No!" I snarled. "You're wrong. She has to be."

Turning from the immortal, I surveyed the coast, marching across the sand before picking up my pace, and then I was running, my feet pounding against the earth as I screamed for her again and again.

But that sweet, soothing voice didn't answer, and I turned for the waters before falling to my knees.

"Skylahr!"

Skylahr

EPILOGUE

My head pounded as it fell forward, and I curled my fingers until the pads traced the metal cuffs that secured my wrists to the rafters for what had to be the hundredth time while my toes grazed the dirty stone floor below me.

It was dark and it was cold; not at all what I thought hell would be like. But this had to be it. There was no other explanation, and I wondered which of my sins condemned me.

Was it my anger? My jealousy? Maybe it had been my righteousness, the very thing Gaelon had hated about me.

Or perhaps it was that darkness that lurked at the edges of my very soul. That part of me I had spent so long ignoring, pretending as if it didn't exist in hopes that it would disappear before someone would see it. Before *he* would see it.

Closing my eyes, I sank my teeth into my lower lip while a tear rolled across the cold flesh of my ruined cheek, and I sobbed, the sound echoing in the silence that surrounded me.

"Huntress, protect me," I prayed, desperate for her to hear me even though I had turned my back on her. "Please, Huntress."

Certain she would not receive my pleas, I closed my eyes tightly and choked down a whimper, and then the sound of footfalls came, their pace unhurried but sure. I sniffed before lifting my head, wondering if I wasn't forsaken after all.

Blinking in the dark, I waited with bated breath as the glow of a torch illuminated my cell, and then three figures appeared. The first seemed to be nothing more than an average man, his face stern and unreadable but ordinary. The second was taller than his friend, and though his dark curls hid his eyes from me, I could make out a handsome face and strong jaw and I noticed the way the muscles worked as his teeth clenched together. The third figure, however, towered over the pair, and its hood concealed its face from me even with the light of the torch.

"Open the door," he commanded, his voice deep and powerful, and I shuffled on my toes in an attempt to get away from my visitor.

Following his command, one of the men lifted a set of keys and then inserted it into the lock with a resounding click before pushing open the iron door. Stepping into the small space, the stranger approached, and even though I stood on the very tips of my feet, he still towered over me, and I sank away from him.

"Tell me, Skylahr Reed," he began. "Who do you pray to?"

There was something sinister about this voice, something that made my blood cool in my veins, and I shrank away from him the best I could before answering.

"My Goddess," I whispered.

The stranger said nothing but gestured for the torch that one of his men held, and then he lifted the flame towards his head while his other gloved hand pinched the fabric of his hood and pulled it down. There was no face, no features, no mouth or nose, only two bright yellow eyes that were surrounded by darkness. My chest constricted in fear as he grabbed the chain that hung from the ceiling before tugging me close to him.

My breath fogged in the freezing air that seemed to surround him, and those glowing yellow eyes searched my face before he chuckled softly.

"It is such a shame your Huntress cannot hear your prayers." He exhaled, and then his head tipped to the side, and he recited my prayer from my coronation.

"*And above all else, let me be good*," he spat out the words. "Unfortunately, being good is not the fate I had in mind for you, daughter."

ACKNOWLEDGEMENTS

I honestly don't even know where to start. I never imagined publishing a novel, much less two and yet, here we are.

First, I'd like to thank my incredible husband, the person who not only encourages me every step of the way but allows me to lean on him when I am certain I am going to fail. Matt, I would be lost without you. Thank you for everything you do. Thank you for being the golden retriever to my black cat-ness. Thank you for always giving me your warmth and never flinching at my iciness and thank you for loving me so completely.

Next, I must thank my wonderful friends. Ellen and Heather, thank you for always lending me your ear when I need it. I know I drone on and on, but you always manage to make me feel heard. Izzy, you are one of a kind. You are such an incredible friend; I would be lost without you. Thank you for always answering the phone, talking me down and for understanding my ridiculous humour. Jenn, thank you for always reading whatever it is I put down on a page- no questions asked. To my barn book club, thank you for always hyping me up any time I see you girls. You are amazing.

To my wonderful family, I adore you. Thank you for always being in my corner, I can do anything knowing I have you at my back and I hope you know just how much you mean to me.

Thank you to Beth and Nat, I could not make this series without you two and your guidance. Nat, your talent is unmatched, I am so honoured to have your art on my covers. Beth, you turn my chaos into poetry, and I cannot tell you what that means to me.

Lastly, to the readers. Thank you for your support, encouragement, and love. You have made this dream possible, and I will be forever in your debt.

ABOUT THE AUTHOR

Author K. Godin lives in beautiful Ontario Canada, with her husband and four dogs. When she isn't hiding in her office typing away, she spends her time reading, painting, or daydreaming of the fictional worlds she gets lost in.

Her passion for writing started early, and she has always had a knack for it. She excelled in her high school English classes and decided to pursue a general arts degree after graduation. However, after her first year, she knew that college just wasn't for her and found herself working for a local animal shelter. After spending nearly a decade there, she decided to change her career path and started her own business all while creating those fantastic stories in her mind once again.

PRONUNCIATION GUIDE

Characters	Gaelon: Gale-on
	Isla: Eye-la
	Kalian: Kal-ee-an
	Keyno: Key-no
	Mòrbàs: More-bas
	Reif: Reef
	Skylahr: Sky-lar
Places & Institutions	Beilham: Belly-ham
	Celinde: Cell-ee-nd
	Helreene: Hell-ree-n
	Honera: Hon-er-a
	Lynthals: Lin-thals
	Natylity: Na-ty-lity
	Noordeign: Noor-dean
	Ritari: Ri-tary

Places & Institutions cont'd	Skohyn: Sko-hin
	Suideign Shores: Sue-dean Shores
Creatures	Hafok: Ha-fock
	Helcrybi (plural): Hell-seer-bee-i
	Helcyrbius (singular): Hell-seer-bee-us
	Failinis: Fail-in-is

Made in the USA
Columbia, SC
11 November 2024

46169263R00328